Philip G. Williamson is thi
in north London with his
Under the pseudonym 'Phil
novels, *The Great Pervade*
story collection, *Paper-thin*

By the same author

The Firstworld Chronicles:

1. *Dinbig of Khimmur*
2. *The Legend of Shadd's Torment*
3. *From Enchantery*

(writing as Philip First)

The Great Pervader
Dark Night
Paper-thin and Other Stories

SCIENCE
FICTION
FANTASY

PHILIP G. WILLIAMSON

The Firstworld Chronicles

3: From Enchantery

HarperCollins*Publishers*

HarperCollins Science Fiction & Fantasy
An Imprint of HarperCollins*Publishers*
77–85 Fulham Palace Road,
Hammersmith, London W6 8JB

A Paperback Original 1993

9 8 7 6 5 4 3 2 1

A catalogue record for this book
is available from the British Library

ISBN 0 586 20907 7

Set in Linotron Trump Mediaeval by
Rowland Phototypesetting Ltd
Bury St Edmunds, Suffolk

Printed in Great Britain by
HarperCollinsManufacturing Glasgow

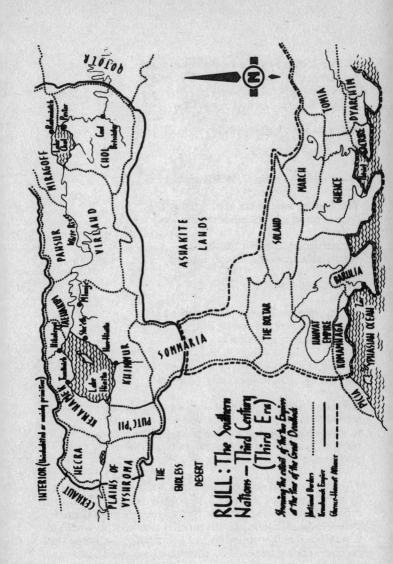

RULL: The Southern Nations—Third Century (Third Era)

Showing the extent of the two Empires at the time of the Great Destalish

National Borders ·············
Kuvahumat Empire ————
Ghoux-Humat Alliance — — —

INTERIOR (uninhabited or scantly peopled)

QOJOTA

NIRAGOFF

PANSUR

VIRLAND

CHOL

ASHAKITE LANDS

KATANARO

KHIMUR

SOMMARIA

SOLAND

MARCH

GHENCE

TOMIA

DYARCHIM

THE BOLTAR

BAKULIA

HAMYAT EMPIRE

KOMAHITAGA

PALIA

TYRNASIAN OCEAN

PUTC'PII

KEMANAREN

HECRA

PLAINS OF VYSHROMA

(EKMAUT)

THE ENDLESS DESERT

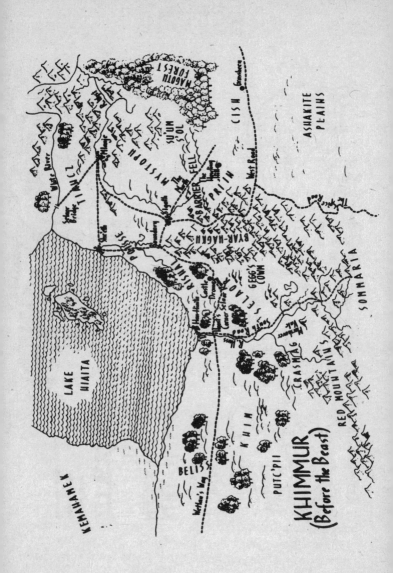

RÉSUMÉ

Hiatus: The Years of the Beast

The long-prophesied advent of that dire and mysterious creature known as the Beast of Rull has come to pass. Now its armies bestride nations. More rapidly than any could have anticipated, the lands of southern Rull have fallen under its sway.

Historically, Rull is no stranger to conflict. Wars great and small have raged since the beginning of time. Empires have risen, flourished, and diminished; some endured for centuries, others vanished more quickly than they came. But none have compared with this New Empire, Khimmur's dominion.

Kemahamek, itself one of the most potent imperial powers on the continent in more prosperous days, had been the first to fall. Lesser nations followed, toppling like dominoes. Now in the south once mighty Ghence prepares its last futile defence, desperately rallying reluctant neighbours as the hordes of Khimmur and her allies bear down.

The Beast of Rull. The Vulpasmage. Incarnate in the flesh of Khimmur's young king, Oshalan I, the monster rides south to join his warlords and oversee Ghence's fall. At his fore a contingent of dreadful creatures, vile Gneth, nether-spawn, summoned from regions where the souls of men have never dared venture. Folk flee in terror, impelled by stories of Gneth appetites; armies have retreated rather than confront these abominations.

With Ghence and her neighbours, Tomia, March, Dyarchim, in its embrace, the Beast can turn its attentions elsewhere. Perhaps to the warm southern lands beyond the wide blue ocean of Yphasia. Or yet, into the uncharted sweep of Ashakite whose fierce nomadic tribes still maintain a proud independence; or the Enchanted Land, Qotolr, where dwell five powerful and immortal beings, erstwhile foes who centuries earlier had helped vanquish the Vulpasmage from this plane, and against whom a bitter requital has long been outstanding.

But there are others who must be dealt with. Shimeril Mi' Vhuda, Arms-Master and Guardian of the Duke Shadd, Commander of the élite Mystophian Nine Hundred Paladins, who operates from temporary base-camps deep within Mystoph to disrupt and harry Khimmurian forces. And Yzwul, *dhoma*-lord of Tiancz in Mystoph, one of Khimmur's finest warriors, who has likewise chosen to oppose the creature that has possessed his king. These two, with their bands of fighters and underground network of agents, are a constant source of vexation. They command no great strength, yet they are proving themselves wily and capable adversaries, contriving nuisance and thwarting all endeavours to capture or destroy them.

Then there are the *Zan-Chassin*, the sorcerer-priests of Khimmur. Divided and greatly reduced in power, they yet work secretly to alter the Vulpasmage's design, representing a threat that cannot wisely be ignored.

And Shadd, Duke of Mystoph, King Oshalan's younger half-brother. A question mark hangs over his disappearance more than two years earlier, following the fall of Twalinieh. It is not known if he lived or died, though there has been no authenticated sighting of him since. Shadd was always enigmatic, ever unpredictable.

Now rumours fly that he has returned from self-imposed exile and aligned himself once again with the enemies of the Beast of Rull. To what extent Shadd could prove a threat is as yet undetermined; but the Beast will remain ever-vigilant as long as the chance lingers that the Duke of Mystoph roams free.

In Kemahamek and elsewhere within the burgeoning Khimmurian Empire there have been instances of resistance in the form of sudden eruptions of violence against the forces of the Beast. Swiftly and brutally suppressed, the insurgents are ultimately only driven further below ground, never wholly expunged. This is not unexpected, of course, and such factions are ragtag and of minimal concern now. But there exist certain latent circumstances, of which the Beast is not wholly ignorant, under which a small and barely significant cabal might be transformed into a powerfully disruptive force.

Specific steps have been taken to inhibit the potential for such an uprising. Yet while enemies live, the risk, however slight, remains. Action, swift and decisive, is demanded to ensure that such circumstances can never come to be.

Hitherto little was known of the Hiatus Years, other than that this was an era characterized by turmoil and bloodshed. The Beast of Rull was a clouded figure, a creature of mystery, a monstrous personage dramatized and made ever more grotesque by tavern-tale and legend. The Dinbig Manuscript has shed new light upon the period. Unearthed in the ruins of the ancient city of Rabaviatch, it comprises an invaluable record of events during this time. Its author was the eminent Khimmurian Ronbas Dinbig, who himself played a full and vital part in the unfolding of history.

This, the third volume, takes up the tale where Volume II, *The Legend of Shadd's Torment*, left off.

11

We witness, from a unique viewpoint, the continued rise of the Beast of Rull, and the valorous efforts made to stem the surging tide of its tyranny.

A word regarding this volume's predecessor. *The Legend of Shadd's Torment* was well received by our noble and discerning public. I, as its translator and editor, have benefited in no small wise as a result, receiving acclaim and promotion. Our Holy And Most Righteous Majesty, the Sage Queen-Empress Serhlin, has looked favourably upon me. Indeed, I find myself now in the enviable position of being not only a member of her privileged Inner Circle, but upon certain occasions, and in certain specific respects, her intimate, called upon to render counsel and advice, even consolation when her Most August Majesty has been beset by darker moments.

This of course is the highest honour. That she should favour me! That she should reveal in my presence her human face, her vulnerability, her womanliness. Ah, blessed am I, a mere servant, so humble and undeserving. My Queen, my Holy and Worshipful Empress, how I worship and adore her!

But I digress. Let me rather address the matter of this volume and its predecessor.

Numerous persons have remarked upon the fact of *The Legend of Shadd's Torment*, in its new context, being somewhat inconsonant with the Legend in its traditional and time-honoured form. Most specifically they refer to its ending, asserting that it lacks accord with the Legend as we have previously known it.

This is, of course, a valid observation. Indeed, as I have previously stated elsewhere, it was an issue which caused some considerable soul-searching at the time of its rewriting.

Traditionally, however, the Legend has always

known a variance of endings. The most popular version tells of Shadd's locating the lost fragments from Yshcopthe's fabled Pandect, and returning with them, after numerous adventures, to Kemahamek. There he is successful in reviving the Holy Wonasina, Seruhli. His heart's desire – that the two of them should be united – is never realized, for of course Seruhli is bound by the covenants of her exalted station. Thus Shadd leaves Kemahamek and returns to a solitary life in the wilderness.

Another version has Shadd returning to Kemahamek, only to learn that the fragments contain nothing that can aid Seruhli. She is condemned to an eternity of Non-Existence under the sorcerous agency of the Semblance of Death, applied by a treacherous Intimate within the Simbissikim. Shadd, in a paroxysm of grief, walks undefended into the Holy City of Twalinieh and is seized and torn to pieces by a howling Kemahamek mob, still convinced that he is the assassin of their revered Wonasina.

A third, less widely known variant sees Shadd's quest end with his encounter with the Enchantress Mesmia. Seduced by Mesmia's projection, the voluptuous Elore, Shadd permits Mesmia to gain possession of both the fragments and the Soul Crystal, the protective twin-stone sacred to the Gwynad race, which has been given to him by the last remaining Gwynad, Temminee. He is cast into a dungeon deep beneath Mesmia's Tower, where he languishes until his death.

The question remains, then: why, in the rewriting of *The Legend of Shadd's Torment*, did I choose to reject these endings? The answer is quite simple: it has become evident in the light of the Dinbig Manuscript that *none of these versions accords wholly with historical fact.*

13

Arguably it is history which provides the basis for the uncertainty. Undocumented as it was, The Hiatus is a period which gives itself naturally to imagination and speculative tales and commentaries. By its nature, many of these were tragic in tone, telling of dark deeds, fantastic exploits, evil beings and terrible suffering. That one of the most significant legends to emerge from that period should come with a multiplicity of endings is, then, no great surprise.

As will be seen, *The Legend of Shadd's Torment* cannot be separated from real events of The Hiatus. Shadd's story extends way beyond the boundaries set by the Legend in any of its traditional forms. Now the Legend may be seen to weave itself indelibly into the tapestry of greater myth that has been handed down to us over countless generations.

The Third Volume is again narrated for the most part by Dinbig, supplemented by the paucity of historical records available. I have once more availed myself of a certain licence in the form of minor extrapolations, based on fact, in order to enhance and authenticate Dinbig's text. Beyond this I have confined myself to nothing more than the insertion of occasional explanatory notes and comments.

Thus, the scene unfolds:

Seruhli, the Holy Wonasina of Kemahamek, lies helpless, it is said, in the Semblance of Death. The lovelorn Duke Shadd of Mystoph, making his way out of the Enchanted Land of Qotolr, believes he has, in the lost fragments from Yshcopthe's Pandect, the means to return her to life. Yet by a cruel twist of fate he is prevented from delivering the fragments to her. Her whereabouts are a secret, religiously kept, which Shadd cannot hope to be privy to, for he is deemed an enemy of Kemahamek by the Kemahamek people and those who guard the Wonasina.

He is further plagued by incertitude, for he lacks evidence that the fragments do truly contain the Formula for the Antidote to the Semblance of Death. The fragments' contents are inscribed in the Old Language of Qotol, which none but Qotol Enchanters are conversant with. The inscriptions almost certainly contain more than a single enchantment, and would thus bestow daunting power upon any knowledgeable in Qotol magical forms.

At least one of the five extant Enchanters – the Drear-hag Mesmia, known formerly as Strymnia – is aware of the existence of the fabled fragments. It is likely now that knowledge of their existence will not escape the other four.

This being so, they, like Mesmia, will stop at nothing to wrest them from Shadd.

The Beast of Rull would also seek to gain these fragments should it learn that they have been found. For the Beast is aware that in the hands of an Enchanter a single page from Yshcopthe's great Pandect could prove to be a medium of immense power.

The Beast recognizes, too, that should the Wonasina, Seruhli, be successfully revived, she would be capable of leading the Kemahamek people in an uprising against their Khimmurian overlords. Thus the Beast's agents are ceaseless in their search for knowledge of Seruhli's hidden sanctuary, so far to no avail.

And Dinbig of Khimmur, separated from Shadd by dire circumstance, has at least been reunited with his errant flesh. With his capricious spirit-ally Yo (resident now in the body of the sole surviving member of a savage vhazz pack), he, like Shadd, endeavours to leave Qotolr. Before him lie lands made perilous by enemy occupation. Beyond, in Khimmur, is his hope: his former friends, his lover, Rohse, and the infant daughter he has glimpsed but once. And the *Zan-Chassin*, whose research and dedication must somehow produce the means to overcome the Beast of Rull.

Read on . . .

Parvis Parvislopis,
Supreme Archivist, and Advisor to her Sage
and August Majesty, Serhlin, Holy Queen-
Empress and Benefactress of All Rull

Part One

1

Prior to the coming of the Beast of Rull, the most easterly province of the kingdom of Khimmur had been Mystoph, a land of rich and dramatic contrasts, peopled originally by a folk descended from settlers from a far-off land whose name, if ever it was known, has long been forgotten. Mystoph and Khimmur had become one by dint of marriage between the respective ruling families, recognizing the expedience of integration in the face of foreign encroachments.

The two cultures merged, with Khimmur and its far larger population predominating. Countless Khimmurian families and traders moved into Mystoph to establish homes, farms and businesses. To a lesser extent Mystophians took themselves west into Khimmur. Mlanje, the founding-seat of the first Mystophian settlers, had grown to become a township of some size, and was now acknowledged as the provincial capital and Khimmur's second city. Sited in majestic surrounds at an intersection of roads and river, it became home to a host of other, smaller communities, drawn from diverse lands and cultures, eager to explore its potential for commerce and trade.

Towards the end of the Third Era there came the Great Deadlock, a period of political stalemate preceded by the near-simultaneous rise of two powers, Kemahamek and the Ghence/Hanvat Alliance. Khimmur and its neighbours were occupied by Kemahamek forces. The Khimmurian hero Manshallion liberated his nation and led his troops south to significantly extend Khimmur's Mystophian frontier into the weald

19

and plains south of the Barrier Fell. Thus it had remained, despite border disputes and intermittent skirmishes with the Ashakite plains' nomads, until most recently, when King Oshalan successfully waged war by trickery upon a minor Ashakite tribe, the Seudhar, and laid claim to a further tract to the south.

No matter their merging and the shifts and vagaries of centuries, Mystophians had never wholly relinquished their cultural identity. Theirs was a culture steeped in tradition, nurturing a venerable history which extended back into mythological beginnings. They knew gods and ancient customs unshared by Khimmur, and held fast to beliefs and practices that were uniquely their own.

The Beast of Rull brought immense and sweeping changes to Khimmur. Quite suddenly the nation was at war. On the surface it was a glorious war, encompassing victory after victory, winning vast new territories with all their wealth and resources. The fighting men of Khimmur engaged their foe with a ferocity unmatched, supported by monstrous auxiliaries and spurred by successes and the cornucopia of booty. That it was a monster who led them was known only to a subsect of the Beast's closest confidants, and such knowledge, broadcast at large, would have changed nothing: bounty's tongue told a more persuasive tale.

Within Khimmur itself a network of secret police, the *Marg'dhua*, maintained a watch over the populace on the Beast's behalf. Brutal death squads appeared without warning at the homes of any who had been heard to express so much as a whisper of concern over the policies or ambitions of King Oshalan. Families disappeared or were taken into slavery; Khimmur's dungeons and torture chambers became home to unfortunates who had misguidedly voiced disapproval of the course their nation was taking; the corpses of dissenters were left to putrefy upon gibbets and frames erected on the walls of Hon-Hiaita and other towns and strongholds. Wealth there was indeed for those who sailed unhesitatingly with the stream, but a climate of terror prevailed for any of contrary opinion.

In such a climate, the mounting of organized resistance was no simple task.

Perhaps it was not surprising that the wellspring of what resistance there was lay in Mystoph where, for the Mystophian minority, ultimate loyalties lay not with the Khimmurian crown but with Mystophian tradition. Under the Beast, Mystoph became a land divided. Many of her young and able men had gone off to fight. Others remained behind, yet supported their king in word and deed, and regarded as traitorous the efforts of their kinsmen to unwork the Beast's design. But some were moved to take up arms and risk all, perceiving in the Beast of Rull an evil personified, a bringer of doom, an oppressor like none the world had ever before witnessed.

Shimeril Mi' Vhuda, scion of an ancient and noble Mystophian line, Arms-Master to the Duke Shadd, and Commander of the Nine Hundred Mystophian Paladins, had been a staunch and loyal supporter of King Oshalan. In the Holy City of Twalinieh in Kemahamek he was among the first to realize himself the dupe of the Vulpasmage's cunning. He turned at once against the King, but too late, for the Vulpasmage had foreseen the likelihood of such a development. Shimeril had been tricked into occupying a position within the Holy City where he found himself trapped, commanding only a token force and surrounded by both Kemahamek and Khimmurian military. With Duke Shadd, Shimeril eventually fought his way out of Twalinieh, losing many of his finest men. But he was powerless to prevent the fall of the city, and subsequently of Kemahamek itself.

Following these events, Duke Shadd disappeared. Shimeril led the remnants of his force, along with any other fighting men who would follow his banner, into hiding. He embarked upon an urgent diplomatic tour to inform the rulers of neighbouring nations of the threat, hoping to rally them into preparing armies capable of resisting the Khimmurian advance. But they were suspicious and slow to take heed. Meanwhile the Vulpasmage moved with swiftness and precision. Few nations were able to put up more than token resistance; most yielded quickly to Khimmurian occupation and domination.

Shimeril's force now was not strong. Many fighters, paladins among them, had died in the early days of the fighting. More took the popular view that their commander, for whatever reason, had turned traitor, and they held their allegiance to the Crown. The *dhoma*-lords of Khimmur, all save Yzwul, son of Yzwad, whose *dhoma* was Tiancz in Mystoph's north, acted likewise. Like Shimeril, Lord Yzwul carried Mystophian blood in his veins; and like Shimeril, he had lately gained renown and a price upon his head for his daring exploits against the forces of the Beast of Rull.

So it was that on a morning in spring, as the sun burned through the mists that had gathered in the chill of the night, these two warriors met in private counsel at a rendezvous known to only a few, in a location deep within Mystoph's secretive heart.

The meeting-place was carefully chosen: a simple woodcutter's hut, long abandoned, set in an overgrown clearing within the fringe of the wild Magoth Forest, at no great march from the border with Virland. This was a lonely locale which lacked human settlements. From close by, look-outs concealed in trees and upon surrounding crags were able to spy the land for some distance to give ample warning of enemy approach.

Shimeril, arriving first, stood alone inside the hut. The interior was gloomy, light entering only through holes in the wooden roof and gaps in sagging shutters and door. Etiolated docks and nettles had pushed their way up inside the walls, and the only furniture was a couple of folding stools, placed there by Shimeril's aides, and a table of mouldering, bowed grey wood. A coarse cloth had been spread upon the table's surface, and on this was a loaf of bread, a trencher of cold venison, two wooden mugs, and a bulging leather wine-sack.

Shimeril wore a simple cloth shirt and an overshirt of padded leather beneath a green cloak. Loose brown breeches were stuffed into sturdy leather boots. He had some time ago discarded his paladin's livery of gleaming breastplate, bright blue cloak and scarlet-and-blue-plumed helm for garb more suited to one accustomed to the life of an outlaw. He was tall and strongly built, a man well into middle age, yet as fit and able as one many years younger. His face, framed by a full head of curly grey hair, was prepossessing and noble without being handsome. One cheek and the forehead were scarred with the evidence of a lifetime of duels and battles. The chin was wide and firm, covered by short grey whiskers. At Shimeril's belt hung a sword and scabbard, and across his broad back was slung, sheathed, an unusual weapon, the dual-bladed *rancet*, favoured by Aphesuk tribesmen of the Endless Desert. By dint of proficiency with this weapon, Shimeril had gained a formidable reputation, and the *nom de guerre* 'The Windmill'.

He stood with his face towards the door of the hut, his expression thoughtful, his head slightly bowed. From outside, at the edge of the clearing, came the shrill whistle of a woodcock. Shimeril backed quickly into shadow, a hand moving instinctively to the haft of his *rancet*.

A soft footfall on the grass outside. The door-latch lifted; the timbers shook and the door swung open unsteadily. Into the hut stepped a paladin. His eyes peered into the dimness, settled at last upon Shimeril.

'Lord Yzwul, sir.'

The paladin stepped aside to allow Lord Yzwul entrance. He came cautiously through the door, one hand gripping the hilt of his sword. Shimeril noted that his skin and clothing were spattered with mud.

Yzwul moved so as to take himself out of the frame of the door and the daylight at his back. He stood guardedly, surveying the interior, disadvantaged by the sudden passage from brightness into gloom. He saw Shimeril, and relaxed. Shimeril came forward, a hand extended, and the two warlords greeted each other warmly as the paladin departed.

'Good, you are safe,' said Shimeril, 'though by all indications you have ridden hard. Here, be seated. Refresh yourself and give me your report.'

'My report, I fear, is of developments somewhat graver than we had believed,' stated Yzwul, as he moved to one of the stools. He was a man of young middle age, of striking appearance. His hair was long and wavy, prematurely greyed, and bound with a circlet of engraved silver. His face was weathered, with thick grey side-whiskers and flowing moustaches. He was of strong, athletic build, with broad shoulders and a deep chest. He stood some two inches shorter than Shimeril.

Taking a knife from his belt he carved a large piece of the meat and broke the loaf in two. 'Kuno's camp is a camp no more. It is a strong and well-defended fortress; but that is not the half of it.'

Shimeril poured wine and passed a mug to the

24

dhoma-lord. Yzwul drank a deep draught, expressed satisfaction, and began to eat hungrily, talking the while. 'From south or west no notable track leads there. The terrain of Oshalanesse is as harsh as the Magoth, and a man can easily become lost. My journey there was not easy. A rough trail is all that leads in from the north and is, as far as I can make out, the only means by which Kuno's wagons could gain ingress or egress. I was prevented from investigating this trail in the close proximity of the fortress. The forest is treacherous; sentries watch every approach. After I had withdrawn I skirted around towards the north, and after some searching came upon a rutted track beneath the dark shade of trees, which winds like a snake towards the vicinity of Mlanje.'

'How many sentries?'

'As many as one hundred soldiers garrison the complex, but how many might be posted in the wilderness around it was beyond my ability to determine.'

'Curious. Surely these are not H'padir? The Beast-men lack discipline for guard and look-out duties.'

Lord Yzwul shook his head, and with a napkin wiped the flowing grey moustaches that hung to below his jaw. He reached again for his mug. 'They are regular Khimmurian soldiers.'

Shimeril gave a frown. 'How so? The H'padir are wild; no soldier feels safe in their proximity.'

'The complex has been constructed with this in mind. The H'padir are housed within an inner bailey, holding-barracks, keep and little else. This is separated from the outer complex, where dwell the regular troops, by sturdy walls, deep ditches, and a system of three consecutive gate-houses. The outer bailey is itself well fortified, and the whole is built into the face of a sheer scarp, such that the fortress is accessible from only one direction.'

'And resistant to assault?'

'An approaching force would be channelled into a narrow pass within bowshot of the outer walls and main gate-house. They could be picked off with little effort. Those one hundred troops could hold off an army with ease.'

Shimeril, who had not taken a stool, rested close to the end of the table, his arms folded across his chest. He mulled in silence upon this news before asking, 'And what of the H'padir themselves? Are our concerns justified?'

'More than justified. I have witnessed something which has left me with a sense of renewed foreboding. My heart and mind endeavour to reject, out of revulsion and moral outrage, what my eyes have seen. Yet they cannot, for the evidence is irrefutable. Kuno, as you know, is absent with the King on the southern campaign. We know that he has with him more than two hundred of the Beastmen, more than we had ever believed him to command. Yet in his fortress only three days ago I have seen other H'padir warriors, to a number of perhaps one hundred.'

Shimeril's surprise was evident. His hazel-green eyes focussed piercingly on his companion, his dark brow furrowed into an expression of severity. 'How can this be? By their very nature they have always been few in number.'

'Here is the nub,' replied Yzwul with gravity. 'The fact is that the H'padir are no longer being recruited solely from among the uncontrollables and lunatics of society. Within that inner complex there are children, dozens upon dozens of them. Some are youths, many more are mere infants. I observed the most appalling and brutal treatment being meted out to them by rote. These waifs, from the earliest age, are being half starved and deprived of comfort or solace of any kind.

26

They are being trained hour after hour in deadly fighting skills; they are viciously beaten and maltreated, taught nothing but violence and hate. No doubt they feed upon mind-changing plants and powders. In short, they are being systematically driven to violent madness. Kuno no longer has to recruit his H'padir; he is creating them, there in that isolated fortress. And even this is not all, though it sickens me to have to think of it. There are females there, who suffer privations as harsh and cruel as those of the males. The only exception, the only softening of practice I observed, was towards those whose bellies are large. They, from what I was able to make out, are housed in separate dormitories and given basic care. I cannot deny what my eyes have seen. There are infants being born in that hellish stronghold; Kuno is breeding his Beast warriors.'

Shimeril made no immediate response. A hand moved with slow abstraction to his jaw and he maintained a pensive silence. Presently, in a quiet voice, he said, 'The more mature ones that you speak of – and those warriors that accompany Kuno now – where can they have come from? Are they all his unholy brood? From where have come the progenitors, the original parents of these sad creatures?'

'I have asked myself these same questions,' said Yzwul. 'The answer, it strikes me now, is simple and obvious. You will recall some years ago, the adult population of certain isolated Khimmurian hamlets and villages had been found butchered, apparently overnight, with no real clue as to who or what may have perpetrated the evil deed. It has been a sinister mystery, compounded by the simultaneous disappearance of the children of those communities, who were never seen again. I recall Dinbig, who is now gone from us, telling of one such event to which he, as a young man, was a virtual witness and almost a victim.'

Shimeril slowly nodded. 'Underfell, close upon The Murth. Dinbig spoke of an eerie procession descending at night from The Howling Hill and entering the village.'

'Most of the instances I speak of occurred in the same region.'

'It was always held to have been the work of Enchanters or their minions.' Shimeril raised his gaze to the rafters of the hut, shaking his head, a troubled expression on his face. 'This tells of years of preparation. Was Kuno long privy to the coming of the Vulpasmage?'

'It is not inconceivable. Or mayhap he acted alone, seeking simply to swell the ranks of his murderous force – by whatever means. Whatever the answer may be, the evidence is before us: the H'padir exist in far greater strength than we have ever believed or thought possible.'

'Kuno is in the south,' Shimeril said. 'Who, then, trains the H'padir now, for none but Kuno have ever been able to control them.'

'It seems he has at least one lieutenant, a man unknown to me, but as brutish and pitiless as Kuno himself. Before him those poor savages cower. They do his bidding like apes trained to dance.'

Though his hunger was unsatisfied Lord Yzwul no longer ate. With the cloth he once again wiped his lips and elegant moustaches. Shimeril bestirred himself, scowling, to cross the room to the small window in the west wall. He peered out through the gap between the shutters.

'There is other important news,' Yzwul said. 'I have received a calling.'

Shimeril turned back. 'From the *Zan-Chassin*?'

The *dhoma*-lord nodded. 'Two nights past my sleep was disturbed by a dream of Chrysdhothe. She appeared to me in a manner that I had been told to expect, and told me that we are summoned to a meeting of the Hierarchy.'

Shimeril cast him a doubtful look. 'You and your wife have been parted for many months. Is this the first time you have dreamed of her?' He quickly raised his hand. 'I apologize. I spoke without thought, and intended no sarcasm or slight. But you know my mistrust of magics, be they *Zan-Chassin* or any other form. In two years we have had barely any word from the Hierarchy. They are reduced by the influence of the Vulpasmage. Now you select a single dream out of countless dreams and, from your words, I must assume propose to act, and perhaps even stake our lives upon it. I cannot be easy in my mind with such methods.'

'I understand your misgivings. Yet I know I am not mistaken. I was long schooled for this, and the dream conformed in all its subtle details to that which I was trained to expect. In truth, it was no dream; it was Chrysdhothe communicating directly with me.'

Shimeril seemed scarcely appeased. 'It unsettles me to know that there are those who can tamper so deftly with a man's innermost thoughts. Still, I would hear more. What of this summoning, then?'

'In a week's time takes place the festival of Dis. There will be widespread celebrations; it is something the war cannot stop. Folk of many descriptions will be upon the roads, making for the main towns and villages to enjoy the fairs and pageants. It will be a relatively safe time for travelling undetected. We are to go to Sigath and there seek out the priest, Marbo, who will officiate at the ceremonies. He will guide us from there.'

'We are both called?'

'Aye.'

'This is unusual, and dangerous in the extreme.'

29

'I can only reiterate: Chrysdhothe was precise, and her codes and signals were unmistakable. She urged extreme caution, with the assurance that once we have established contact in Sigath we will have some protection.'

Shimeril grimaced and shifted his stance. 'They demand a great deal. This Marbo, what do you know of him?'

'He is a First Realm Initiate, a long-standing *Zan-Chassin*. He was quick to align himself against the Beast of Rull.' Yzwul stood. 'Shimeril, I do not question that there are dangers, but the call is genuine. We would not be summoned for anything of inconsequence.'

'Mayhap.' Shimeril stroked his grizzled jaw in sombre contemplation, then seemed to arrive at a decision within himself. 'We will go, for we can do little else. Return now to your men, inform them, and make whatever preparations you deem necessary. Return here at sunrise two mornings hence.'

2

I

The first month of the Khimmurian new year is Khulimo, named after the god who is said to rise at this time to ensure the vanquishing of winter and beckon forth the spring. Midway through Khulimo's cycle occurs the vernal equinox, and at this time festivals and ceremonies both solemn and joyful were widespread throughout Rull, where the peoples of diverse lands and societies worshipped deities or acknowledged lore which corresponded in great part with Khulimo.

Within Khimmur the succeeding month is that of Dis. A deity of lesser stature than Khulimo, Dis is nevertheless an important figure in the Khimmurian pantheon. Just as Khulimo oversees the coming of spring, Dis determines its ongoing character. He is seen as a generally benevolent god somewhat prone to temperament. Dependent upon his moods is the success or failure of the season's crops, the well-being of newborn livestock, the character of the late summer harvest. Piqued or sulking, Dis might deliver a sudden late frost, or a prolonged deluge which could sweep away the soil from the hill-terraces and turn lowlands to quagmires. He could bring winds which would destroy homes and orchards, floods from a too-rapid melt from the high peaks, or set the conditions for a subsequent drought. More typically, though, Dis shows his benign face. He presides over a month characterized in roughly equal parts by mellow sunshine and light storms, enlivened perhaps by an abrupt violent squall, usually of brief duration and not intended to do lasting damage.

Thus Dis is paid due homage and respect at his proper time. The celebrations follow a similar pattern to those of Khulimo, at the time of the full moon, when the god is perceived to be at his fullest manifestation, but they are on the whole less formalized and – prior to the Years of the Beast – tended to an easier gaiety.

True it was that the celebrations of traditions such as these, so indelibly woven into the time-steeped fabric of Khimmurian society, could not easily be suspended. Nor was it desirable that they should be. Though under the cloak of festivity subversive elements might gather more freely to plot and scheme against their overlord, the Vulpasmage was not blind to the larger function of such occasions. Common rites and customs comprised a vital part of public and private life. They contributed in no small wise to an experience of normality, of freedom. Through the exercise of their superstitious and religious beliefs, combined with the opportunity to give vent to feelings and passions, simple folk could find agreement and even contentment with their lot. To strip them of these privileges would be to offer subversion a free hand.

So the festivals proceeded, though in comparison to former times they were perhaps subdued and somewhat restrained. *Zan-Chassin* priests, vetted by the government, were allowed to officiate as custom required. After the fall of Twalinieh, when *Zan-Chassin* opposition to the Vulpasmage became evident, there had been a prohibition on all *Zan-Chassin* activities. A number of *Zan-Chassin* had been rounded up, interrogated, tortured and in many cases executed; but others had no hesitation in siding with the Crown. The *Zan-Chassin* knew grave schism. Perceiving the division, the Vulpasmage had responded with calculating providence. Hierarchy members he sought; lowlier initiates, though watched, were not believed to constitute a serious threat, and served a more useful purpose if they perceived themselves as having a degree of — strictly regulated — autonomy within the community.

The people, then, were allowed to celebrate as before, but all public gatherings were marked by the presence of soldiers in large number and, less evidently, the *Marg'dhua*, the secret police.

II

Sigath was at this time a prospering township situated in a fertile dale close beneath the foothills of the Byar-hagkh. Occupying an intersection of major roads convenient to the Selaor/Mystoph provincial border, Sigath's festivals and fetes attracted countryfolk from both provinces, and sometimes from Sommaria and lands even further afield. This year the crowds were not as dense as on previous occasions, but the inns and hostelries did not want for patrons nevertheless, and shopkeepers and stallholders assured themselves of a brisk and satisfying trade.

In meadows beside the road on the outskirts of the township, a pleasure fair had been established, and in the small central square of Sigath itself, overlooked by tall, gabled houses and administrative chambers, was a market, with areas set aside for diverse entertainments. Here too the rites honouring Dis were conducted by the *Zan-Chassin* initiate Marbo, a well-known and respected figure in the community.

The day was clement, with near-cloudless blue skies and warm sunshine, tempered by a light breeze which skittered down from the mountains, bringing just the slightest chill. Dis, it seemed, was not ill-disposed on this the most significant day of his cycle, which boded well for the coming season.

The mood of the festival was correspondingly not without cheer. In the central square the first rites had been performed with the rising of the sun; folk then lingered in the taverns, or mingled around the market-place to admire or purchase the manifold goods on display, or watch or participate in the entertainments. There were dancers and clowns, jugglers, musicians, mummers. Wealthier folk had donned festival costume, ranging from the splendid to the outrageous to the merely colourful; others of poorer stock wore what they had, embellished by perhaps a new hat or bonnet, and garlanded with bright spring flowers. Meats, fish and viands of all kinds turned upon spits or sizzled on braziers; ovens turned out pies, breads, cakes, tarts and buns, to be sold from booths or within the inns and taverns, along with a hundred different fruits, nuts, vegetables, herbs and pulses of spring. Bunting in various bright hues fluttered above the square, and the sounds of music and merry-making were carried out into the fields and woods beyond. But yet, within the crowd there were faces that did not smile or laugh, and eyes that only watched, scanning faces while ears listened to every innocent greeting, casual comment or shared banter. And about the square, at street corners, outside taverns, stood men from the local militia in twos and threes; and behind windows overhead, shadowy figures observed the comings and goings with cold and calculating intent.

At noon came a few minutes of relative hush as the second ceremony of the day was enacted. Marbo, clad in ceremonial vestments of white bordered in gold and crimson, stood atop a dais formed of the steps of the council chambers, from where he could look out upon the square. He delivered his biddings and thanksgivings with a certain cautious animation. The ritual was not of long duration, concluding with a *Zan-Chassin* chant and symbolic dance performed to drum and bells. The revelries then resumed with gusto.

Marbo descended the steps of the council chambers to join the townsfolk. He was a man somewhat gaunt, in his middle years, with a long, thin nose and chin. His eyes were large and liquid-brown, and his mouth tended to a downward droop at the corners, giving him a mournful expression. He was of average height, spare, with wisps of long grey hair surrounding a pale bald pate. He entered the crowd, exchanging greetings and embracing friends, strangers and associates, as was the custom. He worked his way gradually towards the perimeter of the square, whence he might retire to his home nearby in order to change into less formal garments.

Marbo's exchanges were brief, if not terse. He appeared somewhat tense and uneasy, though he made every endeavour to conceal it. Approaching the edge of the square he made to step around a stallholder's table on which were displayed a variety of brooches, amulets, pendants and curios of one description or another.

A man, undistinguished from the general run of the crowd, stepped forward to greet him. 'A fine ceremony, Marbo! I congratulate you!'

Marbo halted. The man carried a staff and wore a nondescript grey cloak and hood of a pilgrim or traveller. His features were partially obscured by his hood. He extended his free hand to take Marbo's, and leaned forward to press his cheek to Marbo's in the customary manner.

'Fine indeed. Dis will be pleased.' The man's voice dropped to become a whisper in Marbo's ear. 'And the day may proceed as all of true and unsullied heart would wish.'

Marbo stiffened. He drew back. What he could see of the face beneath the hood was not familiar. The stranger watched him questioningly.

Marbo forced a smile and inclined himself to return the embrace upon the other cheek. In response to the coded phrase that the stranger had uttered, he whispered, 'Go to the wagon of Dame Frema, at the fair outside the town. Announce yourself to her as one seeking relief from a bane visited upon you by the wood nymph, Wictocacta.'

The stranger released Marbo's hand and stepped back. Marbo cast his eyes nervously about him. He had turned ghostly white and a film of sweat had broken out abruptly upon his upper lip, nose and brow.

The stranger observed him curiously before saying, loudly, 'I look forward to the rites of sunset. Until then I will bid you good-day.'

He bowed his head, turned, and disappeared back into the crowd.

Marbo fumbled in his robes and drew out a square of white linen. With this he mopped his brow and moved on, taking care to depart the square via a different route to that taken by the stranger.

A man of burly build, wearing a floppy black, brimless cap, observed Marbo's departure from a first-floor balcony overlooking the square. With a nod and a gesture of one hand he signalled to another fellow positioned in the crowd, some paces from the stall beside which the stranger had greeted Marbo. This second fellow moved off in Marbo's wake.

The man on the balcony signalled once more. Another man discreetly left the square. As he moved towards the entrance of the street into which the stranger had passed, he beckoned to a pair of armed militia men stationed at the corner. They moved smartly, to fall in behind him at a distance of some yards.

III

The stranger made his way down the busy, winding street between tall houses of ancient mortar and bowed timber. He walked at a seemingly unhurried pace, pausing from time to time to peruse the wares displayed before the shops on either side. If he was conscious of being followed, he gave no indication.

A short way on the shops fell away and the crowds thinned. The stranger entered a snickelway which led via narrow steps to an area of stony waste ground and common land. Before him now were fields and open countryside, with woodland and hills beyond.

A lane, flanked by old stone walls smothered in convolvulus and blackberry, led between pastureland to the meadows where the caravans and bright pavilions of the fair were easily visible. Along this the stranger walked, in company with others making for the fair. Not once did he look back.

The fair was in full swing. Stalls and booths, trestles and platforms supplemented the tents and wagons. The entertainments here were even more diverse than in the town square. Jigs, reels or stately dances were played by groups of musicians; and actors performed masques, dramas and comedies on makeshift stages. There were sword-swallowers and fire-eaters. Children played upon see-saws, roundabouts, wooden horses, and other playground devices.

Skittles, shies, pillories and many other games drew folk of all classes. A crowd gathered inquisitively around a dancing bear; people queued with mixed expressions at the entrance to a freak-show. Vendors called out their wares; charlatans, mountebanks and miracle-workers strove to extract coin from the purses of the curious. To one side an archery range had been set up, and the straw butts thudded as competitors tested their skills.

The stranger threaded his way without hurry towards one corner of the meadow where, close to the roadside, stood a caravan painted in gay reds and blues with bright yellow wheels with red spokes. A placard suspended upon one side of the van announced, in letters of silver on red:

DAME FREMA
Healer—Thaumaturge—Sooth-sayer.
Your future revealed. A thousand ailments
relieved. Curses lifted.

A short flight of wooden steps led up to a small platform before the rear door of the van. At the foot of these sat a tow-headed lad with a sleepy-eyed look. The stranger waited a moment and observed. Curiously, though numerous persons paused to inspect the sign, few showed any inclination to tarry, and not one mounted the steps to enter Dame Frema's wagon — hence the boy's apparent boredom.

The stranger approached the boy. 'I would seek the advice of your mistress, if she is available.'

The boy squinted up at him and shifted upon the step to allow him passage. 'Go right up, sir.'

'And a fee?'

'To be agreed with Dame Frema.'

The stranger climbed the steps.

As he pushed open the light wooden door to enter the van, he sensed a tingling, scarcely perceptible, upon his skin, and a prickling of the hairs at the nape of his neck. A more percipient person might have recognized at once the presence of magic. One trained in certain specific arts would have detected an aura about this wagon, subliminal to all but the most acute of minds. Such a person would have understood then why no clients queued to avail themselves of Dame Frema's services. But this man was conscious of only the vaguest feeling of apprehension, which he shrugged off as being due to the nature of the business he was about. He stepped across the threshold, unaware that he had been observed and that the aura that enclosed the van had been altered most subtly so that he, and only he, might not be discouraged from entering.

The interior of the wagon was dim, and heady with the odours of smouldering incense and herbs. Before him hung a curtain of diaphanous blue material flecked with gold, stretching across the wagon. Through it he could make out the fuzzy glow of a candle set somewhat below the level of his waist.

A voice spoke from behind the curtain. 'Enter, sir.'

He did as he was bid, lifting the curtain aside to step through. Facing him was a woman garbed in a voluminous dark blue robe. She sat at a low, makeshift table formed of a closed wooden chest. Upon the table was set a candle of thick red wax which burned in an ornately carved iron holder. Next to this was a sphere of perfect crystal, a chart displaying zodiacal signs, and numerous oddments and curios of strange and unascertainable purpose.

In the limited light the stranger could see little of the woman's face. She appeared to be a crone of advanced years. Her eyes were deep-sunken into dark sockets, her skin was withered and sallow. A large wart grew upon one cheek, and from her head sprouted a shock of thick iron-grey hair.

'I am Dame Frema. Be seated, sir, and tell me how I may help you.'

The man sat upon a stool set before the table. He pushed back the hood of his cloak, deliberately, that Dame Frema might more easily appraise his features.

'I am advised that you are expert in the lifting of banes and curses. I seek relief from one such placed upon me by the wood nymph, Wictocacta.'

Dame Frema leaned back in her seat, and subjected him to a lengthy scrutiny.

'I know you,' said she. 'You are the paladin Duirbod, whose castle in Su'um S'ol is now abandoned. You are an outlaw.'

Duirbod tensed. One hand moved as though to slip beneath his cloak.

'Do not be alarmed,' said Dame Frema. 'I am not your enemy. You have come in the stead of two others who were called. Where are they?'

'They are close by, and will reveal themselves at an appropriate time.'

'A wise precaution.' Dame Frema raised herself. 'Good. You will remain within this van.'

She moved around the table and stepped past the paladin, through the curtain to the entrance of the wagon. She opened the door and leaned onto the platform to address the youth seated at the foot of the steps. 'Alon, make ready the horses. It is time to depart.'

The boy sprang to obey. There was a disturbance in the milling throng nearby. Six armed thugs stomped forward, fronted by a scowling, stocky fellow with florid cheeks and thick black hair and beard. He wore a jacket of studded leather and carried a sword and dagger at his belt.

He halted wide-stanced at the foot of the steps and called out, 'Dame Frema, hold!'

Dame Frema gazed down upon him without expression. 'You are, sir?'

'Logoth, constable of the guard. I will search your wagon, where you are holding a man known to me as a criminal. I am here to arrest him; you also will be taken into custody.'

With a lifting of the eyebrows Dame Frema responded. 'Logoth, you are mistaken. There is no man within this wagon. And I am simply an honest woman seeking to ply her trade.'

Logoth sneered. 'He was seen to enter but moments ago.'

He beckoned to his soldiers. 'Bring him out.'

'By all means, enter and search,' said Dame Frema. 'Though I assure you that you will find no person within. But please, there is not room for you all. Logoth, ascend and look within. With two of your men, if you fear assault from my person.'

Logoth's red cheeks reddened further and his mouth twisted in anger. 'Aye, I will look. You two, with me!'

He thrust himself up the steps. Dame Frema stepped back inside in order to allow the three to pass. As they entered she performed a small gesture with her fingers and mouthed a silent group of several syllables.

Logoth and his two henchmen peered about them at the interior.

'As you see, it is as I stated,' said Dame Frema. 'There is nothing to be seen.'

Logoth stared ahead of him, blinking stupidly. His two henchmen assumed similarly blank expressions.

'You are forgetting something, are you not?' enquired Dame Frema with a certain sardonic emphasis.

Logoth turned to her, his eyes vacant, peering with a dim and confounded expression, suddenly meek. 'There was . . . something,' he drawled. His gaze went questioningly to his henchmen. He blinked hard, screwing up his face, and scratched the back of his head.

41

Dame Frema stepped to the door of the caravan. 'Please, feel free to search as you wish,' she said loudly, so that the men outside, and any other interested party, might overhear. 'But have a care, if you will. My effectuaries are precious and not easily replaced.'

She descended the steps and peered around to the fore of the van. 'Now, Alon! Are the horses harnessed? We will be leaving as soon as the constable has completed his business.'

A moment later Logoth and his two men emerged, still slack-jawed and vague. Dame Frema awaited them as they came down the steps, rather more slowly than they had gone up. 'Well, constable, you will admit it was as I said? There was nothing to be seen.'

Logoth, shorter than she, stood before her. He gazed into her face with the confoundment of a drunkard.

'May I leave now?' asked Dame Frema.

Again Logoth scratched the back of his skull. 'Aye, begone.'

Dame Frema detached the steps and put them inside the van, then made fast the door. She walked around to the front of the caravan and climbed up onto the board-seat. When the boy Alon had finished harnessing her two horses, he climbed up beside her and took the reins.

As the caravan pulled away, Dame Frema leaned around to look to the rear where Logoth stood with his men. His face still bore the expression of a fool presented with some insoluble problem.

'Good-day, constable. May the favour of Dis fall upon you.'

The caravan rolled slowly around the back of the meadow and out onto the road.

One hundred metres or so down the road, with the fairground obscured behind woods, Dame Frema turned to push open the forward door of the van, situated behind her seat. She called softly to her passenger.

'Duirbod, the rapture was localized. Logoth and his thugs will soon recover.

'They will recall their mission and pursue us. He is in the pay of the *Marg'dhua*, the secret police. Thus I recommend, if your friends are near, that they join us now.'

'Maintain this easy pace a short while longer,' came the reply.

Duirbod moved to the back of the van, and stood upon the small platform there. He scanned the country around. Trees enclosed the road, with the sun beaming down a dappled light of bright green-gold between them. An uneven rocky gradient rose to one side. To the rear could be seen through the corridor of road and trees the picturesque roofs and gables of Sigath.

From within his cloak Duirbod took a strip of green cloth which he tied around the end of his staff. He lifted the staff and held it aloft so that its pennant fluttered in the breeze.

It took but a moment before a figure appeared on the slope. Long silver-grey hair and flowing moustaches identified him as Lord Yzwul. He scrambled swiftly down through the trees, his hair bouncing upon his shoulders. Reaching the road, he ran to the caravan. Duirbod extended a hand, and he pulled himself up onto the rear of the ambling van.

Yzwul gripped Duirbod's shoulder in greeting, then quickly entered the caravan. He cast his eyes quickly around the interior, then returned to the platform. He raised a hand, his eyes upon the woods.

Now appeared Shimeril, Commander of the Nine Hundred Mystophian Paladins. He too made directly for the caravan and climbed aboard. The three men went inside, securing the door behind them.

Duirbod moved to the fore of the van and spoke to Dame Frema. 'Your guests have arrived. We would suggest you make best speed to put us as far as possible from pursuers.'

Alon urged the horses into a trot. The van was sturdy, and obviously well sprung, for it travelled well upon the uneven surface of the road. A couple of miles further, Alon steered the horses off the road into a dense bosk of hazel, elm and flowering wild service. No way was evident from the road, but as the horses pushed through it could be seen that the brush soon thinned in the shade of the larger trees.

Alon brought the van to a halt. Dame Frema climbed to the ground and called back, 'Gentlemen, disembark, if you will. We will proceed on foot from here.'

'This is a wild and lonely place,' observed Shimeril.

'Quite so. Few would think to come here. Now, Alon will take the horses and van to a safer place.' The old woman turned and shuffled off into the wood. Lord Yzwul watched her with a curious expression, but did not make his thoughts known.

They followed a narrow pathway which wound between the trees, upwards towards the encroaching hills. Breaking out of the bosk, they entered a terrain of gentle rising grassland spotted with wild flowers, which gave way to spinneys and occasional rocky bluffs. The path that Dame Frema followed quickly petered out, and they proceeded along a trackless way. The afternoon sun was warm. Clouds of pollen and dust, thrown up by their passage, clogged eyes and noses, and they were soon bathed in sweat. In the near-distance, sometimes off to their left, sometimes

44

directly ahead, the snow-capped peaks of the Byar-hagkh stretched into the azure sky.

The terrain became markedly more difficult. They entered more woodland, denser than before, with steeper gradients and sudden outcrops of rock. At the head of a narrow ravine into which tumbled a fast-flowing stream, Dame Frema brought them to a halt.

'Await me here. From this point the way is protected by raptures. These must be altered, or your journey from hereon will be characterized by discomforts and horrors untold.'

She walked on alone, following the lip of the ravine, and was quickly lost to sight. The three moved into the cover of shrubs.

'If this should be a trap, we are isolated and without support,' muttered Shimeril.

'It is no trap,' said Yzwul.

'Are you so certain?'

'I stake my life on it. I have watched this "Dame Frema". She is a person known to me.'

'It pleases me to hear it.'

Five minutes passed and the figure of Dame Frema reappeared between the trees ahead of them. She beckoned. 'Come, it is safe now. When we are past the raptures will be recast. Pursuers will pass this point at the cost of their sanity.'

She led them down through the woods, following the course of the stream, into a glen. Here were situated a small farmhouse with outbuildings and a watermill. Though the buildings were in reasonably good repair the place seemed deserted. Dame Frema advanced to the front door of the farmhouse, which she opened and entered. The three warriors followed.

'You will be tired and soiled after your journey,' Dame Frema announced. 'Here you will find water, soap, food and refreshments. Overhead are sleeping-chambers. Avail yourself now of what you will. A meeting will convene in one hour.'

She made to leave. Lord Yzwul spoke out. 'Our thanks, Revered Lady. Our goodwill, also. And in particular, my admiration.'

Dame Frema halted halfway to the door and turned back to face him. Her old face cracked into a smile and her eyes sparkled. 'Yzwul, I had wondered whether you, of all persons, could be fooled by my appearance.'

'It is an excellent disguise,' Yzwul replied. 'And I was almost taken in. But certain things cannot be kept from the man who loves you.'

The old woman laughed, a curiously youthful sound. She reached up and grasped her shock of grey hair, yanking it from her head and shaking free a tumble of auburn locks. Her bowed stance straightened, and she seemed to shake off decades. Yet her face remained that of a hag, cragged and lined, and made strange and somehow repulsive by the long, lustrous hair that now surrounded it.

Shimeril peered closely at her. He took a step forward, then straightened in disbelief. 'Good Bagemm! Chrysdhothe! It is you, is it not?'

'It is, my lord,' replied Lord Yzwul's spouse, smiling.

'Hah! Magnificence! You had me fooled entirely!'

'And I, too,' said the paladin Duirbod. 'My lady, your disguise is most effective, but hardly becoming.'

'As is its intention.' She turned back to her husband, extending her hands. Yzwul approached, taking both hands in his.

'My husband,' said she, 'can you bear to see me like this?'

'I would prefer it otherwise, I confess. But for the nonce I have no complaint. Chrysdhothe, my cherished wife, I have missed you.'

'And I you.'

He gazed upon her wizened features for a moment with smiling bemusement, then kissed her and held her in a tender embrace. Shimeril and Duirbod cast their eyes elsewhere in self-conscious inspection of the chamber and its furnishings.

'Now, I must go,' said Chrysdhothe, drawing away. 'There will be more time, soon, Yzwul. I promise. And you will see me as I would wish, not as "Dame Frema" dictates. The disguise is partly a magical effectuation, which will require work to undo. I will be at the meeting.'

'I await with anticipation,' said Yzwul.

Chrysdhothe relinquished his hands and withdrew.

V

The meeting was convened with neither ceremony nor formality. Chrysdhothe returned after an hour, when the three had washed and refreshed themselves and eaten and drunk sufficient to satisfy their needs. Shimeril and Yzwul accompanied her from the farmhouse, leaving Duirbod alone.

Chrysdhothe led them across the yard to the millhouse beside the stream. She had changed from her former garments into a simple white blouse and grey skirt, with shoes of soft stitched leather upon her feet, and a blue wrap to ward off the chill of approaching evening. Her disguise was gone, revealing a young woman with clear skin and aristocratic visage, fair and beautiful, with resolute but compassionate blue eyes, and slender build. She walked arm-in-arm with her husband as they approached the mill, talking quietly to both him and Shimeril, and laying her head upon Yzwul's shoulder.

The sun was low, sinking towards grey cumulus over the heights to the west. Pale shafts of light slanted down between the trees, and long shadows struck out across the ground. The breeze that had earlier barely tempered the warmth of the day was now noticeably more chill.

They crossed the stream via a small stone bridge. The millpond was dammed, the race but a trickle, leaving the great wooden wheel still. They entered the mill through an arched portal of stout timber. Chrysdhothe led them past the silent mechanisms of cogged wheels and hoist, and the monolithic stones bound in a casing of wood and iron hoops, to an annexe consisting of a single room, evidently used at one time as living space.

This room, like that in the farmhouse they had just left, was austerely furnished. Dust and cobwebs clung to the sills and shelves, the stone walls and rafters. A fire blazed in a wide fireplace, and a long table stood in the centre of the floor, set with three wax candles in black iron holders. Two persons were seated at the table, conversing in low tones as the party entered. Upon setting eyes on these two, both Shimeril and Yzwul bowed.

'Revered Chariness, Sacred Mother, we are honoured,' declared Shimeril.

The Chariness rose, her eyes calm and pale grey, her smile serene. Her long auburn-grey hair, unbound, fell freely about her shoulders. She was dressed in a grey robe, belted at the waist with a leather thong. Over this was a plain woollen jacket. She wore no other adornment. Her appearance belied her status, for she was the head of the *Zan-Chassin* Hierarchy, and one of the most advanced and influential of its members. She appraised the two warriors evenly, penetratingly. Though her demeanour was one of calm benevolence, there was about her an aura, a mysteriousness, a shade

48

of detachment, commingled with a sense of fortitude and indomitable character.

'Welcome, my lords. We are pleased, more than pleased, that you have come. Be seated now. We will speak frankly, as friends and allies, without recourse to formality.'

So saying she resumed her seat. Beside her the second occupant of the room had closed her eyes. She was a strange, almost incongruous figure, small of stature, ancient and tremble-limbed, with a full head of flowing grey hair. Her features were sharp and unevenly placed. Her chin bore a wispy beard. She wore an old rust-toned robe, with a heavy shawl of striped blue-and-white wool wrapped about her thin shoulders. Under ordinary circumstances she might have been dismissed as a crone, but with fuller inspection a disarming vigour could be seen to shine in her rheumy eyes, and, as with the Chariness, she held a presence that could not be ignored. This was Crananba. She had known more years of corporeality than any could say, and her body was feeble, but not so the soul it housed. She was a Sixth Realm initiate, and arguably the most learned and powerful *Zan-Chassin* adept alive.

Crananba opened her eyes now, when the two men were seated, and spoke, in a wavering voice which lacked resonance, 'Lord Shimeril, you are discomfited.'

'My skin thrills and crawls,' replied Shimeril. 'I am ill at ease, as though something has crept into my brain and works mischief there. I cannot but say that I would prefer to be elsewhere.'

'You are sensitive to the raptures cast upon this place. They are powerful and affect certain persons so. You will understand their necessity. We are protected for as long as we remain here. I offer apology, and would urge you to try to relax. Dispel your misgivings, vanquish the tensions that you have allowed to rise within you. It is these factors which work against you, not the magic itself. Find agreement with yourself and the discomfort will pass.'

'I understand and accept what you say. Yet I cannot easily dispel my caution. My past associations with magic have not given me cause to trust or feel easy with it.'

Crananba gave a nod but said nothing more.

The Chariness, her hands laid flat upon the table, said, 'My lords, we have summoned you here for a specific purpose. Our researches over recent months have thrown up numerous facts. One in particular gives us a particular cause for concern at this time, and demands urgent response. We will discuss this in a moment. Firstly, though, let us look at the situation before us.

'We know that the Beast of Rull has ridden south to pound upon, and almost inevitably now to smash the gates of Ghence. Ghence has held out bravely for many months against both Khimmurian and Sommarian armies. Sommaria has proved a worthy ally to the Beast, but she has been discouraged from committing her fullest strength to the campaign owing to her need to guard against Ashakite incursions. But now that Chol has fallen, the entire north is under Khimmurian sway. The Beast is free to concentrate major forces, including Gneth, upon Ghence and the remaining free nations. For all we know Ghence may already have fallen.

'But can we use this fact – the Beast's being committed with so much of his strength in the south – to our advantage?'

'Aye, if we had twenty thousand men, armed and trained, we might,' said Shimeril through closed teeth. 'As it is, Khimmur is well garrisoned. Our situation is not improved. We can only harry and disrupt, but we are scarcely more of an irritant than an ant upon a

50

bull's back. As yet the bull has found no means to dislodge us with either head or tail, but soon it must discover that if it rolls its massive bulk we will be crushed in the mud.'

The Chariness considered this, her grey eyes watching Shimeril, and she nodded slowly. 'You do yourself an injustice, my lord. Your efforts in Virland have been a major success; the Beast is notably irked.'

'Irked, perhaps. But not weakened.'

Lord Yzwul interposed, 'In Virland we have had success in freeing slaves and evacuating civilians. We have hampered to some extent Khimmur's endeavours to build a road through the Magoth Forest, though the Magoth itself has proven an even greater hindrance, I think. Here in Mystoph, Shimeril's men inflicted a wounding blow upon the H'padir. But these are minor setbacks as far as the Beast is concerned. We have done no lasting damage. The garrisons are too strong to permit successful raids, and the enemy is now growing wise to our tactics and reacting accordingly. Here and over the border, Kemahamek troops augment the garrisons in great number. They fight fiercely on Khimmur's behalf. How is this, that such a proud race can be brought to so sad a state? What pact did the Beast make with Kemahamek?'

'That is a matter we have given much attention to,' replied the Chariness. 'Our agents work diligently to uncover the facts behind this grim alliance, but the task is not easy. Almost daily we learn that someone has been arrested, another been executed. The nature of the pact remains in large part a mystery. But you must remember that with the loss of both their Wonas and Wonasina, the will of the Kemahamek people to resist was effectively broken. Certainly, we are looking at betrayal within the Simbissikim ranks. We have intimations of a most dark and complex plot, which would

51

imply complicity at the very highest levels of Kemah-amek government, even among the Blessed Intimates themselves. But again, it is important to bear in mind the Kemahamek ethos and the precepts of their religious creed. The people live for and direct their lives towards a Golden Age, the time of the Ihika-Wona. The Beast of Rull took from them their living deities, the Wonas and Wonasina. Hundreds killed themselves upon the instant of receiving this news, believing all reason and purpose to have been destroyed. Yet to those who survive, the Golden Age remains real, if distant. They live on, under whatever conditions, in order that the future might yet come to be. In their distress they await the rebirth of the Twin-Wona souls; nothing else is of importance.'

'A rebirth superintended by the Vulpasmage?' said Shimeril. 'Under such a condition the Kemahamek will remain forever slaves.'

'The Beast has played brilliantly upon the Kemah-amek strings, as it did our own. From the beginning, it has manipulated all and sundry with perfect pre-cision. We do not pretend that our task is a simple one. Nonetheless, we fight on, for we must.' The Chariness lifted her hands, steepling the fingers so that the tips rested lightly against her chin, the elbows supported on the arms of her chair. She appeared to be waiting, as if for some comment from the two warriors. When none came, she spoke on. 'Brilliant though the Beast is, I do not consider him infallible. Look now at Som-maria. Two years ago King Perminias launched attacks against an Ashakite tribe, the Uljuŏk. He caught them unawares and experienced some success before they could regroup sufficiently to put a stop to his forays. Unbeknown to himself, of course, Perminias was even then being manipulated by our own king, Oshalan. At the time it was expedient. Oshalan – the Vulpasmage

– needed Sommaria. Khimmur also attacked Ashakite, though Oshalan's choice was the Seudhar, a disaffected minor tribe. By this means a powerful bond was cemented between Khimmur and Sommaria.

'But now Perminias is still distracted by the Uljuōk. Internal differences – ever the bane of the nomads, and the fortune of other nations – have prevented a sweeping attack against Sommaria. But the Uljuōk endeavour to curry favour with another tribe, the Mammubid. If they succeed, and can settle their differences elsewhere in Ashakite, a mighty force might be mustered to strike against Sommaria's flank. And if that should happen while the Beast is in the south . . . !'

Shimeril wearily shook his head. 'If, if . . . How many others have dreamed your dreams, or feared them, as is most usually the case? All Rull knows what it would mean were the Ashakites to unite in any form. But it has never happened, and I am positive it never will. The Ashakites are the Ashakites. They squabble and fight between themselves. It has always been so. They know no other way, and they will not change.'

'Perhaps so. But the Ashakites are surely aware of Khimmur's encroachment. They will see themselves being gradually encircled, and will know that their turn must surely come. It is a powerful incentive to resolve differences.'

'It is not a factor I would rely upon in devising my strategies.'

'I present it at this time only for speculation.'

'It's true that were a major strike against Sommaria to occur, the Beast would find himself sorely stretched,' Shimeril conceded. 'But coming from Ashakite, such a development might not be to our ultimate advantage.'

'Quite so. Yet my point was aimed more at exposing a flaw in the Beast's planning, regardless of what it might or might not entail for us personally. It appears that he may have laid himself open in this respect. If that is so, then we should look again, more deeply, at his strategy as a whole. It may not be as perfect or as solid as it seems.'

'Are other such flaws evident?'

The Chariness exchanged a glance with Crananba, then said only, 'We await further information.'

'In the meantime,' put in Lord Yzwul, 'I am the bearer of news that does not inspire optimism.'

Briefly he recounted the details of his recent spying mission into Oshalanesse, and his conviction regarding Kuno's terrible means of supplementing his H'pardir fighters.

The Chariness's face became grave. 'This is a disturbing development.'

'. . . which yet again underscores the Beast's capacity for advance planning,' added Shimeril, 'and begs us wonder what other surprises he still has up his sleeve.'

'In that regard, let us turn to the precise reasons for our summoning you here.' The Chariness paused, considering her words. 'Despite what some may believe, the *Zan-Chassin* have not been idle since the coming of the Beast. We have been forced into hiding and, as you know, our abilities greatly affected by the Vulpasmage's preeminence in the Spirit Realms, from where we have always drawn our power. We have become something of an invisible body. We are aware of rumours, that we have disbanded or fled, that we no longer command powers of any kind. Be assured, this is not the case. Like you, we cannot confront the Beast head-to-head, but we are far from being eliminated.

'Our researches have thrown up many valuable facts, and we have given much thought to the means by which we might attack the Beast of Rull. We have considered his assets, which range themselves before us in formidable array. And very recently a certain item of knowledge has come to light which causes us great concern, but which, with swift and decisive action, we may be able to turn to our advantage. If successful, we will preempt the Beast in a most significant wise.' Her expression took on a thoughtful cast. 'You would agree, I think, that in battle one of the Beast's greatest assets – arguably *the* greatest – is the Gneth.'

Both men nodded in solemn concurrence.

'No force will willingly stand against them,' said Yzwul. 'Armies which have withstood the onslaught of Khimmur's regular forces have collapsed almost on the instant when they have found those vile creatures in their midst.'

'Yet they are not invincible,' the Chariness said. 'With every successive engagement their numbers have diminished by a few.'

'The Beast deploys them wisely, holding them back for the most significant battles.'

'Do you have any idea how many he now commands?'

'We observed more than one hundred passing through Mystoph on their way south,' Shimeril said.

'And against Ghence he could lose as many as a third or more of those. The vital fact being, of course, that at present he lacks the means to replenish their ranks.'

'"At present"?' queried Yzwul. 'Your emphasis has an unsettling ring.'

'The Vulpasmage brought the Gneth out of Hecra, which has been their sole worldly domain for a century and a half, since The Great Deadlock,' said the Chariness. 'He is able to control them with an ability that surpasses that of any previous Gneth-masters known to us. But what he has not yet learned is the secret of their summoning.'

Shimeril fixed her with a piercing stare. 'Is it conceivable that he may do so?'

'The summoning of Gneth requires a sorcerous skill known to very few. Long ago the Hecranese king, Moshrazman III, learned that skill – from where or whom we do not know. During The Great Deadlock he brought Gneth from the Under-Realms in order to oust the invading Kemahamek from his lands. He was successful, but as we know, the Gneth then turned upon him and transformed Hecra into a wasteland. No other since has possessed the knowledge. But undoubtedly the Vulpasmage seeks to learn it, if he does not know it already.'

'Evidently he does not,' began Shimeril.

The Chariness stopped him. 'He may in fact know *how*, which is terrifying in itself. But the knowledge is not all. An effectuary is also required to open the way into the Under-Realms and bring forth the Gneth. This the Vulpasmage does not have, and our foremost task at this time is to ensure by any means possible that it does not come into his possession.'

'Do you know where it is?'

'As far as we are able to determine, the effectuary remains in Hecra still.'

'Is the Beast aware of it?'

'His presence in the south would suggest not. Were he to know of its existence it is certain he would spare no effort to procure it. But I speak guardedly, for though he is in the south, it is yet possible that his most trusted agents have been assigned to locate it. They may be in Hecra even now.'

Yzwul smoothed his moustache reflectively. 'And it is our task to locate this object first and bring it to a place of safety. Is this what you are saying?'

Crananba spoke. '*One* of you must enter Hecra and retrieve the effectuary.

56

'The other will remain here in command of your forces. In addition, for the one who remains in Mystoph, we may have another task which we will reveal presently.'

'Hecra is a wide and wild land,' said Shimeril. 'Can you not be more precise in regard to this effectuary's resting-place?'

The Chariness said, 'Our enquiries have had to be discreet. We dared not risk anyone gaining an inkling of this. But we have what we believe to be reliable information. The likelihood is that the object still rests in the place where it was last used by Moshrazman nearly two centuries ago. That is to say, within his palace, now a ruin, in the old Hecranese capital. But before I can tell you more you must decide. Which of you is to go, and which remain here in Mystoph.'

VI

Neither man hesitated.

'I will go,' declared Shimeril. 'Plainly there can be no delay.'

'That's so,' said Yzwul, 'but the matter should be weighed carefully, and decided on the basis of which of us is the better suited to the task.'

Old Crananba gave a sage nod. 'And it must be made now, before we can impart further details. You must understand, only he who is to go to Hecra can be given the name and description of the object you seek. The identities of the persons who will accompany you will also be revealed only to that one, as will the route you will take. Likewise with the mission that may be undertaken here in Mystoph. The nature of that mission must be known only to the one who embarks upon it.'

'The risks are great, and these precautions are for the sake of security,' the Chariness explained. 'Should one or the other of you ever be taken by the enemy, it is plain that you would suffer terribly at the hands of the Beast. You would quickly reveal all that you know. This is no reflection upon your courage or loyalty, it is simply a statement of fact. It is sensible, therefore, for each of you to know as little as possible.'

'Then tell us what you can,' said Yzwul. 'In Hecra, what are the dangers?'

'Gneth, in the main. The Beast took the majority when he moved upon Twalinieh, but monsters certainly remain. Brigands also, perhaps. And there are rumours of terrible mutants born out of the union between Gneth and the humans they enslaved. Possibly Khimmurian search parties also. We cannot be precise, for none have entered that accursed land for so long.'

Yzwul turned with a sober glance to his wife, Chrysdhothe, who sat unspeaking at his side, then said, 'It is plain that I am the best suited. I will go.'

'By what reasoning do you arrive at that conclusion?' growled Shimeril.

'The following: I hold in great respect your abilities and judgement. You are our leader. Should I be lost, my men will turn without hesitation to you, whom they already acknowledge as their overall commander. Were you to perish, the loss would be greater. Our men would suffer a blow to morale from which many might find it hard to recover.'

'That would be our assessment, also,' said the Chariness softly.

'Moreover, your influence extends beyond Khimmur,' Yzwul continued. 'You are known on an international stage and have contacts far and wide, some in high places. I cannot claim such eminence.'

Shimeril clenched his jaw, the muscles of his face rippling, but made no comment.

Turning to Chrysdhothe, Yzwul took her hand in his. 'I believe it has to be this way.'

Chrysdhothe squeezed his fingers and lowered her eyes with a nod.

'I sense that your argument is not entirely unsupported by other persons within this room,' muttered Shimeril with irony.

'But do you accept that I am correct?'

'There would seem to be a certain logic to it. And deference both to rank and to a fast and enduring friendship has perhaps inhibited your making mention of another factor which would weigh in your favour. I will raise it now, then, though it gives me little pleasure. The truth, it has to be said, is that you are the younger man: more nimble, more fleet and of stronger constitution than I. Such words don't come easily to me, but it is a fact of life which I cannot deny. I would that it were otherwise and that I could gainsay you. But I cannot. And in view of the urgency of this mission I will not argue further. You will go, my friend. With my blessing, though I impose upon you a single mandate.'

'What is that?'

Shimeril looked him full in the eye, and his own eyes had moistened. 'That you return.'

Yzwul's face creased into a wide grin. He reached forward and clasped his commander's hand firmly in his. 'You have my word!'

'It is settled, then,' said Crananba. 'Now, Lord Yzwul, you will pass the night here, and tomorrow leave for Hecra. Lady Chrysdhothe will advise you of all relevances and details.'

The ancient woman nodded to Chrysdhothe, who stood, followed by Yzwul and Shimeril.

59

'Go well,' said Shimeril. 'And be mindful of that condition. It is binding.'

'I intend to observe it unfailingly! Go well yourself.'

The two men embraced, not without emotion; Yzwul bowed to the Chariness and Crananba. Chrysdhothe took his hand and together they left the chamber.

'It is fitting that you have chosen this way,' said Crananba as Shimeril reseated himself. 'It is the choice we would have made, were we able, but the decision had to be your own.'

'The unevenness of the scales was not lost on me.'

The Chariness said, 'Yzwul's path is dangerous, but yours will be none the less so. And you, Lord Shimeril, by dint of your name, your past and your particular loyalties, are the man most suited to this second task.'

'Then tell me of it, please, that I might judge for myself.'

'Listen well, then. Your programme will be one of harassment and diversion, as before. You must use to advantage the fact of the Beast's being physically in the south. Physical presence is not all, of course. Though the Beast has still to command his fullest power, we witness more and more of his control within the Spirit Realms. Distracted as he is with affairs of the corporeal world, we believe he is hampered in the development of his inherent powers, which remain partially latent in the physical. Thus it is vital that he finds no opportunity for rest. Almost certainly his ultimate intention is to unleash the full power of the Realms upon the corporeal plane. His minions, entities and other Realm forces will become physically manifest in overwhelming strength. The ensuing carnage will be unimaginable. Men will be devoured, Firstworld absorbed. There will be no more room for humankind.'

Shimeril's features were set. 'And you are powerless to prevent this?'

'Our powers do not match those of the Vulpasmage. We were fortunate that he was identified, largely through the efforts of Dinbig, and forced to act before he would ideally have chosen. Had he been able to he would undoubtedly have waited, manifesting only when at, or closer to, his fullest strength. Had that happened we would not be here now.'

'Then how now do you stand?'

'You know that the *Zan-Chassin* have always depended upon our ancestral spirits within the Realms for knowledge and guidance. When the Beast deprived us of these we perceived ourselves greatly weakened. Yet we did not give in. We were forced to fall back upon individual resources, to push ourselves to limits previously unknown to us. In this wise we have gradually drawn new strength. Earlier we spoke of a possible flaw in the Beast's planning. Here, it appears, is another. Inadvertently, the Beast has provided us with the means to replenish ourselves and grow anew. The *Zan-Chassin*, weakened, are rising from their own ashes.'

Shimeril nodded, but seemed hardly moved. 'But still you are unable to combat the Beast.'

'Alone, it is true, we cannot. We need others, yourself and your forces among them – as you need us. We are one, Lord Shimeril. And we have sensed your waning confidence in us; thus I speak now to restore your belief. The *Zan-Chassin* may work sometimes unseen, and our ways may be mysterious to you, but do not doubt that we are with you. Believe in us, as we do in you.'

Shimeril massaged his grizzled jaw, his wide brow furrowed. 'I have doubted you, it is true. For two years I have fought – fought my own kind! I have seen good men die, and innocents too. Women, children, persons dear to me. At times it has seemed that I fought alone, that the *Zan-Chassin* were no more, or that they had given up and departed the field of battle.'

'We had to go underground. We were shattered; our ranks were split. It was impossible to know friend from foe. But you will be more aware in future of our presence and our contribution.'

The Chariness turned her gaze to Crananba, whose eyes were once more closed. Yet the old woman nodded, as if perceiving the look. The Chariness spoke on: 'Now, I have something to impart which I am certain will give you heart and the will to proceed. In recent weeks I have been personally in communication with Dinbig.'

'Dinbig is dead!' asserted Shimeril, his features registering disquiet.

The Chariness maintained an unwavering gaze, and Crananba, hunched upon her seat beside her, gave a muted chuckle.

'So we believed,' said the Chariness. 'When he initiated communication I doubted the veracity of what I was perceiving. I suspected a trick devised by our enemy. Yet, we have ways of discovering the truth in matters such as these.

'He lives, believe me. He has suffered many trials and known strange experiences. Conceivably he is the stronger for it.'

Shimeril shook his head in consternation, running a hand through his grey curls. 'Forgive me, Revered One, I cannot take this in. I mean no disrespect, but I will believe that Dinbig lives only when I have beheld him with my own eyes and clasped him in my own embrace.'

The Chariness smiled. 'That may soon come to pass. He is making his way back to us even as we speak.

Our communications have been infrequent and brief. The Beast believes him dead, and we cannot risk his messages being intercepted by hostile entities. Returned to us, Dinbig could be critical to our struggle. It is vital his survival remains a secret.'

'Where is he?'

'In Qotolr. He intimates that he is the bearer of information of tremendous import. Furthermore, he has had contact with Duke Shadd.'

'Shadd!' Shimeril sat back. 'Why, yes, it is possible! I received a report that Shadd may have made for Qotolr. Moban, this is news! If it be true, it is news indeed!'

'Shadd and Dinbig were together, now they are separated. Both endeavour to return to Khimmur. They may require aid.'

'Am I then to ride to Qotolr? It is a land I had hoped never to enter, but if it will help bring these two back to us I will depart now.'

'For the nonce we would ask simply that you remain vigilant, and be prepared to respond upon the instant to any new circumstance. In order that we may better fulfil our aims, you and I will henceforth be in communication.'

Shimeril gave a puzzled frown. 'How so?'

'Lord Shimeril, you are to receive initiation this night into a secret rite of the *Zan-Chassin*. To you will be assigned an entity of the Realms. She is one of my own helpers. Her name is Jogada. In moments of need you will be able to summon her and have her relay any message you wish to me. And likewise, if I have anything to impart to you, Jogada will be my agent.'

Shimeril shifted uneasily upon his seat. 'You are introducing me to things I would prefer to know nothing of.'

'You have no cause for alarm. Jogada is loyal; her role will not exceed that of message-bearer. Though she is a full and capable being in her own domain, she has no capacity for independent action in ours. I will teach you how to summon and dismiss her, and to recognize her presence when she brings a communication from me. Employ her only in times of most vital need. Minions of the Beast spy the Realms; we must be prudent in our use of our allies there. But by this means we may enhance our capacity for undermining the workings of the Beast of Rull, and facilitate the return of Shadd and Dinbig. Now, if you are agreeable, we will proceed with your initiation.'

'Hold!' came the voice of Crananba, with a sudden cutting edge. Her frail body had tensed, her eyes remained closed. 'Soldiers approach!'

Shimeril made to rise, reaching for his sword. The Chariness, unruffled, bade him be still. 'Not here. In the woods. The Sacred Mother communes with Roth, her Guardian Entity.'

Shimeril turned to the crone. 'How many come?'

'Ten, perhaps twelve. They are nearing the raptured places.'

The Chariness said, 'They are a threat only if there is a potent *Zan-Chassin* among them, able to negate the raptures.'

'Do you identify any?' Shimeril asked.

'Logoth is among them; as is Marbo,' said Crananba, her eyes still closed.

'Marbo!' Shimeril scowled. 'We observed him in Sigath. His manner did not engender confidence.'

'We have our own concerns in regard to Marbo,' the Chariness said, sadly. 'He is under duress. The authorities exert pressure upon him. They suspect him of association with the Hierarchy.'

'Can he negate your magic?'

She shook her head. 'He is low-level.'

'Hah!' Crananba smiled and nodded in satisfaction.

64

'The leading soldiers are turning away from the woods, unaware of the reason why they do so.'

A moment later: 'Logoth suspects. He is ordering them back into the woods, yet he does not venture there himself! Three soldiers are advancing.' She was silent, then the corners of her mouth turned upwards into a grin once more, and the skin around her old eyes crinkled with mirth. 'Now they retreat, at a scamper! Logoth orders them back, but they are gone, like hares before a fox. Ah, and now I see, they have Alon, bound like a dog on a leash.'

'But Marbo is not bound?' enquired Shimeril.

'He is not. Alon stands alone now. The soldiers have forgotten him. Logoth curses and screams, but his men will not enter the woods. I will instruct Roth to give Logoth a little surprise, then bring Alon and Marbo to us.'

There was another brief silence, then the crone chuckled, her bony shoulders beginning to shake. 'Heh-heh! Roth has revealed himself! Even Logoth now flees, along with his men, helter-skelter back the way he came!'

The Chariness pushed back her seat and stood. 'Good. Now, Lord Shimeril, come. We will interview Marbo outside.'

They left the room and stepped out into the yard. Evening was now descending, the great orb of the sun all but gone behind the crags and woods. Across the western sky a magnificent wash of purple, rose and gold stained the deepening blue. The light was fading, the long shadows merging into one.

Upon the path which twisted out of the nearby trees, two figures now appeared. Shimeril squinnied his eyes: behind the two loomed something strange, a tall, vague, ghostly figure, like a luminous shadow. This looming thing appeared to guide the two towards the little bridge where Shimeril and the Chariness waited.

The two sorry figures reached the bridge. The thing behind them – which Shimeril took to be the Guardian Entity, Roth – vanished. The boy, Alon, his hands now freed, came forward. His face bore swellings and livid bruises. He attempted a deep bow before the Chariness, but half stumbled and gave a stifled gasp of pain. Both Shimeril and the Chariness rushed forward to aid him.

'Forgive me, my Lady,' said Alon through gritted teeth. 'They caught up with the caravan and forced me to tell where I had left my passengers. I did not . . .'

'Alon, there is nothing to forgive. You did what was asked of you, and more. You are back safe among us, and for that we are glad. It is we who should beg your forgiveness, for you have suffered injury on our behalf. Wait here a moment upon the bridge. When my business here is done I will take you to the farmhouse and tend to your wounds.'

The Chariness turned to Marbo, her face stern. 'Come forward.'

Marbo approached hesitantly, his eyes downcast, wringing his hands. Before the Chariness he dropped to his knees, and raised his face beseechingly. 'Revered Lady, please, I had to tell them! I had to! They have long suspected me! I wished you no harm, truly! I could do nothing!'

'If you were troubled, you should have turned to us, Marbo. We would have helped you, you know that.'

Tears tumbled from Marbo's eyes. 'I dared not, my Lady. They would have known!'

'We would have removed you; taken you to a safer place. But that is what you did not want, is it not?'

Marbo shook his head. 'I am a simple man, Lady. I am not brave. I want nothing of this war.'

The Chariness flared. 'We too want nothing of it, yet we are given no choice! You, Marbo, have grown comfortable. You live a privileged life in Sigath. For you it was too much to relinquish, was it not?'

Marbo sobbed out loud. 'Lady, I believed I could be of service!'

The Chariness shook her head. 'It grieves me, Marbo. You can be of no further use to us. Return to your house in Sigath. We will not contact you again.'

Marbo climbed wretchedly to his feet. He stared imploringly into the Chariness's face, but saw no softening of resolve there. His mournful eyes went briefly to Shimeril, who looked on with a grim visage. Marbo turned, his head heavy, and shuffled away. As he left the bridge the Chariness whispered a word, the fingers of one hand shaping themselves into a curious gesture.

Marbo stopped. He turned back slowly with a woeful expression and gazed at the three upon the bridge for some time, as if uncomprehending of something. Then, shaking his head, he turned away again and resumed his journey.

'What was that?' enquired Shimeril.

The Chariness turned her grey eyes to him with a look of profound regret. 'I have placed a Distraction within Marbo's mind. It is not a serious condition, but he will never again find the concentration or will to enter full *Zan-Chassin* trance. Now, Lord Shimeril, I must attend to Alon. Be good enough to return to the mill, where I will join you presently to conduct your initiation.'

Shimeril gave a doubtful nod. 'This is an accolade I had never envisaged myself destined for.'

The Chariness smiled a small smile. Taking Alon's arm, she was about to part, then turned back to Shimeril and said, 'One other thing: how is Sar B'hut?'

'He is recovering, with notable speed. Though his injuries were grave we were fortunate and reached him in time.' Shimeril scratched his head. 'There is another mystery. I am devilled if I will ever understand.'

The Chariness's lips quivered. 'An explanation could yet be forthcoming, if all goes well. I have an intuition that Dinbig may have a revealing tale to tell in this respect.'

VII

In an unlit chamber on the upper floor of the old farmhouse, Lord Yzwul and his lady, Chrysdhothe, lay beneath a quilted coverlet upon a wooden pallet cushioned by a horsehair mattress. The chamber had been swept and cleaned, but lacked amenities or furnishings, barring a simple bowl and pitcher filled with clean water, and the few old items abandoned by former occupants. Outside the sky was cloudless. The full moon cast its mysterious luminescence upon the wild. With the motion of the breeze through the trees, a tangled latticework of shadow came to life, shifting to and fro across the floor of the nightwood, and beyond the moon's glow the milky way stretched across infinity in a ghostly haze.

'My love, it has been such a long time,' whispered Chrysdhothe languorously, her eyes half closed. Her head rested upon her husband's shoulder, one arm crooked upon his broad chest, her fingers stroking his skin.

'Too long.' Yzwul lay staring towards the darkened rafters.

'And we have but a few short hours. You must depart with the dawn.'

'Aye.' He turned his face to hers, illumined by a slim shaft of moonlight which filtered through the broken shutter of the window above their heads. 'How I long to return home to Tiancz, the two of us together. How often I ask myself whether this war will ever end, whether that day can come to be.'

Chrysdhothe touched his cheek. 'If we work together, always with that vision before us, always in the belief that it can come to be, then surely it will.'

He kissed her, then drew back. 'You have information and instructions for me. Let us deal with them now, that we may put all other thoughts aside and make the remainder of the night our own.'

'They are simple and straightforward. You are to make your way to the village of Riverway upon the White River in Putc'pii. There you will go to the inn called the Goat and Salmon Pool. Your persona will be that of a poor cloth merchant named Horsoof – we will furnish you with a horse, pack animal, and items of ware. Announce yourself as such to the landlord's wife, whose name is Lanna. She will put you in contact with certain Putc'pii fighters. To these men you will reveal yourself by means of a coded phrase. They will then guide you into Hecra, to the ruined capital and Moshrazman's palace. They are good and proven men, and will fight for you and against Khimmur. They know nothing of the real nature of your quest, which is as it should remain. Now, the code.'

She spoke a simple phrase, had Yzwul repeat it. 'Remember it well, my love; your life will depend on it!'

'This effectuary, then,' said Yzwul. 'How will I know it?'

'It is a cartouche: a rectangular tablet carved out of streaked black meteorite. Upon its surface is engraved the likeness of an open scroll, bearing glyphs and arcane characters. In its centre is the insignia of a lizard grasping between its jaws a rod, inlaid in mother-of-pearl. The head of the rod is formed of a rare blood-red diamond. Sapphires, onyx and lapis edge the tablet, which in size is no greater than a large book. Make no mistake, this is the only object you seek! In former times it was contained in a coffer of malachite and gold, lined with purple satin. The coffer bears the achievement of the royal house of Hecra. It is most likely to be found in Moshrazman's workroom in the palace, in the tower known as the Tower of Soaring Light.'

'And when I have this cartouche?'

'You bring it to us. I will give you now the name of the place which the *Zan-Chassin* have made our secret headquarters. It is to this place that you must come.'

In his ear she softly whispered a single name. He was thoughtful, then a wry twist came to his lips. 'It is fitting.'

'And now, my love, I must put into your mind a rapture,' said Chrysdhothe. 'It is an Encystment of Forgetting; a necessary precaution to ensure that, should the worst come to pass, you can never reveal your knowledge of this secret place.'

'Then how will I know where to come?'

'Return with the cartouche via Riverway and the Goat and Salmon Pool. There Lanna will speak certain words which will act as a trigger to restore the memory of the name I have just given you. Speak to no one of this. Lanna knows only that she must say certain words to you, nothing more. Later we will attend to a disguise. My love, you are a striking figure, as familiar to many of your enemies as you are to those who, like myself, hold you dear. We will effect something which will aid you in the safe accomplishment of this task.'

'Will I be as horrid and unbecoming as the hag, Dame Frema?'

Chrysdhothe pinched him and giggled. 'More so! And it will be such that not even one who loves you and knows you thoroughly will see through it.' She grew solemn. 'And lastly, I would endorse with all my heart Shimeril's mandate. Return to us, Yzwul. Return to me, for I love you, and I live for you.'

He turned his head and kissed her tenderly, seeing in the pale moonlight that her eyes were filled with tears. 'I promise you, as I promised Shimeril: I will return.'

He took her in his arms, but she held back for a moment longer. 'There is one more thing. I have to ask you about Shimeril. We are concerned. He has suffered much anguish. You, who have been closest to him, can perhaps speak most accurately as to his state of mind.'

Yzwul took his time in replying. 'This conflict – against his own countrymen and persons whom he previously served with unstinting loyalty – has done much to erode his spirit. It hurts me to say it, for I would not speak against him. But I believe he holds himself culpable for many of the deaths that our actions have inflicted upon innocents. He believes, perhaps, that he is half responsible for the entire catastrophic unfolding of events since this war began.'

Chrysdhothe interrupted with surprise. 'By what reasoning?'

'Dinbig had tried to warn him of what was about to befall Twalinieh. Shimeril – as he sees it – failed to respond quickly enough. Consequently, he also holds himself responsible for Dinbig's death. He is greatly concerned for Duke Shadd, who is of course his ward. Then there is Mercy, Shadd's mother, whom he is pledged to serve. I believe he feels he has failed her. Other imperatives laid upon him by the Aphesuk, which we can know nothing of, undoubtedly place him under further pressure. And again, he feels unease that he might yet be the dupe of the Beast of Rull, as we all have been in the past. He fears that every move he makes may yet be playing into the hands of our enemy.'

'His concerns are understandable. We have all felt such doubts, and Shimeril's task is demanding. Tell me truly, is it your opinion that his judgement is affected?'

'I *am* concerned for him. In all Rull there is no better commander than Shimeril, but while he pits his wits against the evil that has overtaken our world he also fights another struggle, perhaps as great, with himself. Placing himself under such profound scrutiny, he holds back. I worry that his very wariness and reservation may lead him to make an error, which could be the unmaking of him. No, I have not had cause to question his actions or his judgement, but I am aware of a change. Shimeril needs something: a significant success, or some other factor which can dispel the doubts from his mind and restore his fullest belief in himself once more.'

Chrysdhothe mulled over this. 'Perhaps the coming weeks can provide that.'

Yzwul observed her with interest, but knew not to enquire further.

'That would be my hope.' He raised himself onto one elbow and gazed down into her eyes. 'But now, the hours grow shorter.'

She smiled, and her hand went to the back of his head and drew him tenderly to her. 'Then let us fill them with the joy I feel at our being together once more.'

Outside an owl hooted once in the moonlight. A Wide-Faced Bear, making its way through the undergrowth of the nightwood, hesitated as it approached the farm. It rose upon its haunches, its nostrils testing the air. Sensing something of the strange, subtle force that imbued that place, it turned away and made off in another direction. The night wore on; the lovers entwined.

3

I

Ah, Qotolr! Unforgiving land, peopled by strange and unfortunate folk, ruled by tyrants of awesome stature and terrible predilections. Their ancient, forgotten magic wafts invisible upon the very air, its residue imbruing the troubled earth like a pestilence. This land was known by many as Enchantery, and I would suffer no regret for leaving it far behind.

Barely a fortnight earlier I had left Chol and climbed with my vhazz companion, Yaoww, into the Ghosting Peaks at the rim of this accursed country. Now Yaoww was dead. The entire vhazz pack, of which I had found myself a member, had perished here. I had found my great friend and former ward, Duke Shadd, and almost died upon the blade of his sword. And we had parted again. Shadd, learning by the sheer fortune of our meeting that he carried a fragment from Yshcopthe's fabled Pandect, had chosen to confront the Enchantress, Mesmia. And I had gone my own way, to intercept a fugitive, the Wanderer, whose flesh was my own.

Now I was myself again – though I could not deny that I was changed, somewhat wild and a touch addle-headed, a partial stranger to myself. I had gained a jungle of hair and facial growth, and lost a limb, and my moods were at times exceedingly queer.

I trudged westwards, towards the Chol frontier and, eventually I hoped, Khimmur. My thoughts were many; varied and vivid in nature. I communed little with my bound ally, Yo, who was, I sensed, keeping his distance. He, like me, was largely absorbed in the strangeness of his new circumstance, for he now found himself occupying the body of the vhazz, Huwoorsk. And no doubt he was wary of me, for he knew he had much to account for.

This, then, was a period of self-examination, of reflection, consideration and the tentative formulation of plans.

Perhaps irrationally my mind rested on hopes of reunion with Duke Shadd. An unlikely prospect, I knew. We shared the same destination, and our roads linked somewhere not far ahead. But Shadd had departed earlier than me, along a more direct, secret, but hazardous route which would take him to Mesmia's Tower on the edge of the Gro'd f 'ho Ib, the Mountains of the Harsh Maiden. I could only guess and hope at the outcome of his encounter with Mesmia.

Shadd had told me of the Chol fortress of Drurn March, which lay over the border, guarding the trail through the mountains into Chol. 'If I am successful at Mesmia's Tower,' he had said, 'I will make my way there – though with caution. War rages in Chol; the fortress could be occupied by Chol or Khimmurian troops. For my part, there is perhaps little difference, for I am deemed a friend of neither.'

Depending upon what he discovered at Drurn March, Shadd would decide his next move and his route and method of returning to Khimmur. To my knowledge there was within this region no other way out of Qotolr – at least, none that a limping, one-armed vagabond such as I might negotiate. So I appointed Drurn March as my first objective.

Notwithstanding my overall plight, a certain exhilaration pertained during those early days. Being Ronbas Dinbig again, after so long! I had believed my flesh to have perished and been devoured by fishes and other

74

watery denizens. Now I was filled with renewed hope and a sense of possibility and purpose. Via my Guardian Entity, Gaskh, I passed news of my survival to the *Zan-Chassin* Hierarchy. I could not journey in the Realms, for the Vulpasmage held sway there, with legion minions at his command. But what of my other former powers as a Third Realm *Zan-Chassin*? What of the raptures I had known?

I was anxious to test myself.

On that lonely, dusty trail, which was little more than a rutted cart-track above a trickling brook, I tried my first experiment. I had passed the earlier part of the morning in a gloom. The anguish of the Wanderer had descended upon me. The landscape was harsh and little-changing. Ever-encircling were the mountains of Enchantery, hazy and defiant of the focus of the eye, seeming never nearer, never further away. I found no comfort here. My eyes brimmed and I felt myself on the verge of weeping for no specific reason.

To dispel this mood I sang songs to myself. Though Yo was with me we held silence between ourselves. He came on all fours a few paces behind, his tongue lolling, his head heavy and low, rapt in his own concerns. It was now that the notion came to me to test my powers, and I pondered for a while on the nature of the rapture I would cast. Something simple and untaxing, which would evince itself in a manner which would enable me to judge my success upon the instant. Eyeing Yo, I decided he was the obvious subject. I would invoke something which would react upon his consciousness, and thereby plainly reveal its efficacy. An All-Embracing Terror? No, too potent. A lesser version, then: Motes of Unreasoning Fear? Possible, but did I really want to put such cruel frights into my companion? A Memory Haze? Not easy to gauge its effect.

I cast my mind over a few others, and Yo, discerning

my interest in him, looked up with a questioning gaze, filled with reproach. He still believed that my bestowing the vhazz body upon him was a form of punishment for his earlier misdemeanours. I gave the matter further thought, and suffered a pang of conscience. I decided against making Yo the subject of my experiment.

Presently it came to me. Long ago Yo had taught me a simple rapture which involved the conjuration of a globe of non-stuff into the air before me. I had worked on this rapture and developed it into more powerful forms. Twice it had saved my life, enabling me to slay a solitary Gneth in the garden of my villa in Twalinieh, and days later, in a much enhanced form, manifesting as a holy vision in the night sky which created sufficient diversion among Kemahamek troops to permit my escape from the barracks in which I was a prisoner. In its most basic form, which I planned to utilize now, the rapture required minimal effort or expenditure of energy.

Thus I concentrated there upon the road. Within my mind I formed a simple image which would mirror the effect I desired to create without. The image coalesced, I held it, focussing, and released it.

Something manifested in the air above my head, slightly in front of me. I was aware of it first as a sound, barely audible, a rapid fluttering, buzzing, hissing noise. It grew louder, and something in its tone made the hairs rise on the back of my neck.

Then it came, forming out of the very air. It was a misshapen ball of fiery orange-red stuff, spitting darts of liquid flame in all directions. As I watched it shifted. I had the vivid impression of strange intelligence. The manifestation rose into the air, floating backwards a little way, as if possessed of a life and volition of its own.

I stared in dismay. This thing in no part resembled

76

the gentle floating globe of delicate luminosity that I had intended to conjure. It was a fiery fury, a menacing, demonic presence. And I had the distinct sensation that it was aware of me, that it was regarding me even as I regarded it.

I had no time to consider further. Without warning the thing shot forward, straight at my head.

I leapt back with a cry, and by good fortune lost my footing in a pothole and fell. The flaming ball whizzed by me, singeing the air.

I scrambled in alarm to my knees, raising my arm to fend off a second attack. But the fireball ignored me now. Instead it threw itself at Yo.

I called out. Yo glanced up, in time to catch sight of the menace. He darted to the side. At first I thought he had been struck, so close did the fireball pass. Then it was beyond him and Yo, snarling, was turning to face it, drawing his sword.

The fireball flew again. Yo threw himself flat. This time he was not so nimble. The thing ripped across his haunches, searing his hide. Yo howled, leapt to his feet and ran. He bounded by me, smoke streaming from his rump. The fireball raced after him in hot pursuit, emitting a sound like a swarm of angry hornets. The smell of burned hair filled the air.

In panic I emptied my mind, dispelling the rapture. To my dismay the fireball did not dissolve. It gained on Yo. He glanced back, perceived it, and hurled himself down and to the side. The ball shot above his head. Yo swerved away at an angle and fled on. The thing wavered as if calculating. It shot forward on a path that would intercept him.

I watched in horror. Yo was a hundred paces distant now, haring up the slope of a stony hill. He could not outpace the menace. He ceased running and turned to confront the spitting red stuff.

I could not watch. I closed my eyes.

Silence.

It was the sudden fear that I might be the next victim of the fireball that persuaded me to look once more. I opened my eyes, expecting to see the hateful thing bearing down upon me. Instead I saw Yo, standing alone upon the slope of the hill, peering about him in perplexity. The fireball had vanished.

I was still on my knees. I crawled weakly to a nearby boulder and sat down, wiping my brow with the sleeve of my stump. Yo made his way gingerly down the slope, suspicion in his eyes, starting at every buzz of a passing bee or fly. As he drew close I observed a hairless streak across his back. His rump was part cooked, the flesh charred black and blistered red. He stood trembling before me.

'Master, what was that?'

I reasoned that the truth might prove less than expedient. I shook my head. 'My guess is that it was some bizarre and hopefully random manifestation engendered by the unnatural properties of this strange land.'

I gave attention to Yo's rear. The flesh, though tender, was toasted rather than roasted. 'I would advise sitting in yonder cool brook for a few minutes, Yo. Presently I will search for suitable plants to make a soothing medicament.'

Yo limped down to the water. I sat a while longer, mulling over what had happened. Was it the residual magic, the enchanted atmosphere of this land that had corrupted the rapture I had cast? It was a plausible explanation, and I hoped it was the right one, for I could conceive of only one other possible cause, which was that the fault lay within me. Could my knowledge and ability in the field of practical magic have been rendered imperfect by the experiences and changes I had undergone in the past two years? This was a deeply unsettling notion, but unhappily, entirely feasible.

Whatever, I resolved there and then that I would attempt no more magical experiments before I was free of Qotolr.

II

We slept a night in the wild, in the cover of a natural shelter formed beneath a tumble of rock in a copse beside the trail. The following morning dawned with ill grace, dismal, dank, and misty. The sky hung low, heavy with cloud, the ground was dark and wet with drizzle.

I ate bread and cheese from my rations; Yo went off and caught himself a scraggy old ewe on a nearby slope. He proffered me a haunch, but I had no taste for raw meat, and on this wet morn lacked the materials to make a fire.

We engaged in little conversation, though I was familiar with vhazz speech and Yo was well used to the Khimmurian tongue. I huddled over my meagre breakfast and watched as Yo tore into the sheep's corpse. I remembered how, in the very body that Yo now occupied, I had stalked and killed my prey with a cruel and savage joy.

Towards midday the drizzle blew off and we resumed our journey. As evening approached we came upon a lonely wayside inn. Here I rested for the night, while Yo remained in the wild close by, for I reasoned that folk would not take easily to the company of one such as he. I was the sole customer. The landlord, a surly, silent oaf whose nose had been eaten away by disease, gave no encouragement for conversation. He served me turnip soup with barley and bread. The turnips were fibrous, the barley hard, the bread stale. These delicacies were accompanied by a tankard of watery ale. I ate and drank without comment, observed by the landlord, who seemed relieved when I retired for the night to the cubicle he had provided in his garret.

I came upon an unnattractive little settlement called Oldmere the next day. It huddled close to a fork in the road, in a swale beside a seeping marsh. The dwellings were of timber and mortar, with roofs of old grey thatch in which grass and wild weeds grew in abundance. The place did not present a welcoming face. The few folk I passed in its central street were unsmiling and evidently poor, as was common in Qotolr. Several appeared to have halfling blood in their veins, or were perhaps congenital victims of Enchantery's bane, for they were plainly not quite human. Others lacked certain bodily parts: an eye, an ear, hand or foot. But I spied a hostelry and a shop or two, and as the afternoon was approaching its end I reasoned this would be a fair place to spend the night.

In the inn, which sported the sign of the Black Heron, I was greeted heartily, somewhat to my surprise. The landlord was a tall, spare fellow garbed in a long grey robe which gave him something of a priestly cast and brought to mind, specifically, the image of a Simbissikim novice. At my entrance he smiled broadly from behind his counter and raised his hands in a gesture of friendship.

'Sir! Welcome! Welcome to the Black Heron! You are a stranger to these parts, are you not? Then enter and be comforted. Avail yourself of our hospitality, and permit us to make your stopover a pleasant and hopefully memorable one.' He turned to address his customers, of whom there were some number. 'Friends, bid welcome to a visitor from afar!'

All immediately ceased what they were about. They

80

reached for tankards, goblets or mugs and lifted them. The common-room resounded with the sounds of welcome.

Somewhat taken aback I smiled, bowed and uttered my thanks. I stepped up to the counter. 'This is an unexpected greeting, landlord!'

The landlord smiled, showing uneven teeth. 'Oldmere is remote, and unique. We receive few visitors, but we are good and honest folk, sir. We are genuinely happy when a personage like yourself does us the honour of passing through. Our hope is that we might encourage you to linger awhile, or failing that, to depart at least with a pleasant memory of your stay and a desire to return. Now, how may I be of service to you, sir?'

'I would have a pallet for the night, if you can provide such, and a flagon of good red wine, with perhaps a modest collation.' I noticed that the landlord's eyes were yellow, with vertical green slits for pupils. His ears were of an unusual structure, seeming to emerge from his head in several sections, like small, fleshy petals. At a glance I saw that others in the room, like those I had observed outside, bore notable physical distinctions, no two being quite alike.

'Indeed, sir, it will be my pleasure,' replied the landlord. 'But a pallet, you say? Sir, why not take a comfortable bed in your own private chamber, with fresh, clean linen, soap and water, and a fire in the hearth to ward off the chill of the night?'

'Ah, would that I could. But regretfully I am not a wealthy man.'

'Nor need you be, sir, for you will find that charges in the Black Heron are exceptionally low. For example, a private chamber, as just described, will set you back but two coppers. And for food and drink, as you can see from the board here inscribed, I ask a price I believe to be incomparable.'

81

I studied the blackboard to which he referred, which hung on the wall at his back. 'It is true, your prices are exceptionally low. So low, in fact, that they all but defy belief. Is it possible to make a profit with charges as modest as these?'

The landlord beamed and clasped his hands together. 'Ah, sir, you are not of us or our country. You do not know our ways. The inn of the Black Heron is justly proud of its reputation for excellent value and service. It is true, I reap no great profit, but truth is I enjoy my business and value most greatly the opportunities it affords me to mingle with folk, like yourself, who have come from lands beyond and who oftentimes have interesting tales to tell. Suffice to say that I am able to obtain produce at very low cost to myself, and hence can mark up prices I consider cannot be matched anywhere, whilst at the same time embracing a modest but sufficient income. And I would add, I prefer the knowledge that I have satisfied my clientele far more than the accumulation of gold.'

'A noble sentiment.'

The landlord squeezed his hands further and gave a humble bow. 'And now, sir, if my tariff meets with your approval, perhaps you would like to state your choice.'

Mindful of my innards, which had not been in the best of shape these past days, I chose something simple and comparatively bland. The landlord turned to call my order through a door at his back. I observed a short, stubby tail poking through a slit in the rear of his robe. He turned back to me and leaned close upon the counter with one elbow, lowering his voice and saying with a confidential air, 'Perhaps later you might wish to enjoy the company of one of our young ladies, sir. They are discreet, most comely, and extraordinarily proficient.'

A moment's indecision, then: 'Ah, no, thank you, landlord. I think not.'

'You are sure, sir? They are expert in a variety of unusual techniques, and happily attendant to your every need. You will not quickly forget an evening passed with one of our girls.'

'You are most kind. But again, without disrespect to your ladies, whose beauty and talents I don't question, I have made a pledge of fidelity to another. She awaits me now, far from here.'

He straightened. 'I understand, sir. I accept you at your word. If you will take a seat your meal will be delivered shortly.'

Those customers who caught my eye gave friendly smiles as I seated myself alone at a vacant table. One, who bore the fleshy red crest and wattle of a rooster on throat and crown, leaned across to extend an invitation to join his company. I declined politely. 'Perhaps later, then,' said he amiably, 'when you have eaten and had a chance to rest yourself a little. We are enjoying an interesting game of dice.'

My food was delivered by a most attractive young girl with a wealth of long, glossy black hair. She was slender and shapely, dressed in a loose rust-coloured skirt and white bodice. As she bent close over me to place my plate upon the table I was afforded a tantalizing glimpse of her bounties. The warmth of her physical person, the light pressure of her flesh on mine, and the intoxicating swathe of her perfume of meadow-flowers and musk, set my blood instantly astir. For the first time since returning to my own flesh I was aware of the One-Eye, who came vigorously to life and set me to questioning my prior rejection of the landlord's kind offer.

The girl introduced herself as Alele. 'I hope you will enjoy your meal, sir. If there is anything else I can bring you, don't hesitate to ask.'

83

She parted her lips in a smile, tossing back her hair, and flounced away. I watched, mesmerized. Her skirt, though loose, fell close over the twin globes of her buttocks and swung about her well-formed calves. She looked to be in robust good health – unusual for a Qotol – and devoid of the strange features of her folk. She was an enticing prospect; it had been a long time.

My thoughts went to Rohse, so far away in Khimmur, and that little girl, Eroniss, whom I had seen but once. I forced my mind off Alele and gave my attention to my food.

Thoughts of my family brought me to consideration of the journey ahead. By my calculations I was within a few days' walk now of the Qotol/Chol border. I carried sufficient coin in my purse to support myself for some weeks under ordinary circumstances. Certainly, it could provide for my basic needs during my journey back to Khimmur. Once there, I suspected I would be dependent upon others, for my wealth was gone, seized by the Crown. It remained to be discovered what measure of support I might find among my former business associates.

My meal, there in the Black Heron, proved adequate: a plate of thinly sliced braised pork with a plump sausage stuffed with herbs, and potatoes in a light almond and fennel sauce, with beans and bread. The pork, cut into tiny round slices, had a slightly unusual flavour and texture, as did the sausage, which was somewhat tough, particularly its skin; I put this down to a quirk of the region. But the wine was exceptional! It was an elegant, tawny young thing which revealed unexpected character, full, fruity, vivacious, a touch playful, yet admirably balanced. I was most pleasantly surprised, and warmed instantly to its company, relishing its glow in my veins.

Alele wafted forth and removed my plate, and the

wattled fellow at the neighbouring table, seeing that my meal was done, again invited me to join his game. I was of a mellow disposition by this time and found the prospect of company not disagreeable. So I called for another flagon of that distinguished vintage and took my place at the table with him and his three companions.

They proved to be a friendly enough bunch. Besides he of the wattles, who introduced himself as Dek, there was one who I believe was female, named Bispere, who was covered from head to toe in sleek grey fur. The third had a tail, clawed fingers, high, pointed ears and extraordinarily large, round brown eyes, and called himself Redfane; and the last, Akatave, swathed in robes and cowl, seemed, from what glimpses I gained, to lack all but the most rudimentary of facial features.

We played for an hour or so. My companions were not great conversationalists; they seemed intent almost exclusively upon their pastime. I won a few coppers, lost a few, won a few back, then lost more. Alele sauntered across to watch. After a few moments she sat down beside me. She whispered encouragement in my ear as I played, filling my goblet as its contents diminished. I was very aware of her proximity. Her arm came to rest lightly upon my shoulder, and from time to time her hand fell to brush against my thigh. Her perfume lingered in my nostrils; her thigh pressed gently against mine. I could not but take account of her, and when I turned to her, as I frequently did, my gaze fell to her neck, her shoulders, her generous cleavage and the large, dark nipples which impressed themselves against the thin cloth of her bodice. Her eyes, meeting mine, were warm and inviting; the wine suffused my brain with an unusual languorousness.

The game came to its end. I had lost an amount equal to a little over two silver pieces in value. More than I could afford. Yet I had no reason to believe that the play had been unfair. I prepared to leave, but to my surprise my companions pushed back across the table to me an amount equal to the silver that they had won from me.

'What is this, my good friends?' enquired I, slurred and comfortable. 'This money is yours. You won it from me fairly and squarely.'

'Ah no,' replied she of the sleek grey fur, smiling. 'This coin we return to you. We would not have you leaving us out of pocket.'

'This is most generous, but I must protest. The money is yours. Had I felt that I had been cheated, I would not hesitate to say. But that is not the case. I have enjoyed your company and this game immensely, and feel no resentment at the loss. Indeed, I am the richer for the experience.'

The wattled fellow, Dek, shook his head, smiling. 'You are not of us,' he said. 'You do not know our ways. It is not our custom to deprive a guest of his wherewithal.'

The swathed one added: 'We of Oldmere are good and honest folk. We take pride in our ways. Were you a wealthy fellow perhaps we would think differently, but – with respect – your dress and bearing make it evident that you are not. Thus, we will take nothing from you. That is our custom. We too have enjoyed your company, and we would wish you to depart our little village with only pleasant memories, hopefully with the desire to return.'

It was evident that to demur further would be ungracious. Unsteadily, I gathered up the loose coins, and Alele helped me drop them into my purse. 'Then I thank you, and hope indeed that we may meet again.'

'Oh, I'm sure we will, sir,' said the landlord, who had come over to stand close by my shoulder.

'Then I will bid you all goodnight,' I said.

I moved away. The room dipped swimmingly before

my eyes. The delicious Alele was at my side. I understood that my arm was around her slender waist, that she was to some extent supporting my weight. We were singing, she and I, some nonsense or doggerel that I do not recall. She was laughing, her laughter seductive music in my ears. I know that deep within me a voice was warning of danger, but I was intoxicated by that venerable Qotol wine or something in it, and incapable of taking heed.

With Alele I rolled from the common-room. A twisting flight of wooden stairs led to the sleeping-chambers. Before we had ascended halfway our mouths had collided in a sweet and delirious kiss. I pulled her willing body to mine.

Ordinarily I would have enhanced our loving at this point with minor raptures. Mindful of my experience of the previous day, however, I held magic carefully under wraps. And it would have perhaps been superfluous. Alele's innate talents and natural charms and adornments were hardly in need of embellishment.

With sighs and moans she led me to the chamber. Inside I pulled aside her bodice and fastened my hand, then my lips, upon those magnificent breasts and their splendid dark, swollen nipples. She struggled to tear my clothes away. We fell upon the bed; Alele's slender fingers freed the exultant One-Eye. I should have known; I was lost before I had even begun.

III

I awoke with a pounding head, my mouth horribly parched and coated with a sour, disgusting rime. My tortured eyes made out the faintest seep of grey light through the window, indicating that dawn was still on its way. Alele had gone.

My first thought was for my purse. I sat up. My head reeled and thudded. I was lifted on a fearful wave of nausea. I grasped the side of the bed, and when the pain and sickness had subsided sufficiently, searched out my belongings.

Nothing had been removed. With a shaking hand I poured cold water from a jug beside the bed, drank a draught and splashed my face. I lay back again.

Now the guilt and the remorse. *Rohse! How could I have done it! Oh, odious fellow! Pernicious dog! Faithless snake! So often and so recently I had sworn fidelity to you. And now, scarcely days had passed, and already I had fallen back into my ways.*

A clamour of lame excuses arrayed themselves before me. I was not myself. Something else had taken control. I had been through so much. I didn't know what I was doing. It had been so long. I was lonely and so far from home.

And that wine – surely it was a concoction not normally served to innocent patrons of country inns!

Rohse, I swear it will not happen again!

Bah! It was pathetic and wholly inadequate! The facts were plain. I had given way to the first beautiful woman to come my way. I had needed no coaxing. I had taken my pleasure, and that was that. No manner of excuse could suffice. What consequence the numberless vows, the anguished prayers and entreaties when, as the vhazz Huwoorsk, I'd promised the earth if I could but be human once more?

And what if the wine was drugged? I was no innocent. I ought to have suspected. The Ronbas Dinbig of old would have been on his guard from the moment he entered the village. He would not have allowed himself to be tricked.

Tricked? Where was the trickery?

I considered this. I had enjoyed a night of fine entertainment, decent – if somewhat oddly flavoured – food, and interesting company; and the most splendid erotic pleasures. And it had cost me scarcely a copper! I found no trickery – but treachery, yes. *I* had forsaken my promises. *I* had betrayed the woman I had sworn to love.

I lay there berating myself until interrupted by a peremptory knock upon the door of my chamber, unreasonably loud and resounding to my delicate ears. With difficulty I rose and lurched to the door. The landlord blocked the passage outside, grasping a nightlight. Behind him were two others.

Squinting and bleary, I endeavoured to smile. The landlord, however, wore a stern countenance. His yellow and green eyes showed none of the warmth and welcome of before. His kindly smile was nowhere in evidence.

'Would you mind stepping down to the common-room,' he said. 'There is a matter we must discuss.'

I requested a moment to dress. The landlord nodded and departed.

I closed the door, quickly washed and donned my garb. My curiosity was aroused. What manner of business could necessitate the rousing of a guest from his slumber at such an unsocial hour?

In the hallway outside I found the landlord's two companions stationed beside my door. Both had stony expressions. I noted, with a twinge of apprehension, that they carried short, heavy sticks at their sides. Unspeaking, they accompanied me down the stairs.

The common-room had been rearranged. Tables and benches had been shifted to form a semi-circle facing an area left empty but for a solitary bench. A fire blazed in the hearth, and candles upon the tables and a pair of torches set in brackets on the walls further relieved the gloom. About a dozen or so persons were assembled, among them my four dice-playing companions of the previous evening. All had donned grey robes. None greeted me. Their faces were uniformly sombre. I had the distinct impression that I was no longer considered a welcome guest.

To one side sat Alele, who refused to meet my gaze. A small table had been set beside her. On this lay a gleaming, wide-bladed kitchen knife and a shallow metal pan. A buzz of hushed conversation fell silent at my entrance. The landlord stepped forward from behind Alele and indicated the solitary bench.

'Be seated.'

I did as I was bid. At the same time those persons standing moved to take seats before me. The landlord stood with his feet apart, arms folded on his chest. His gaze was forbidding. In contrast to yesterday, he now struck a somewhat ominous figure in his priestly robes.

'You have offended against our ways,' announced he with terse accusation.

I was taken aback. 'Good landlord, to my knowledge I have done no such thing.'

'To your knowledge?' The landlord glanced loftily aside to Alele. 'Do you claim, then, to recall no detail of your conduct during this night that has just passed?'

I shifted a little upon my seat. Alele kept her eyes downcast. 'I believe I recall with pleasure everything that occurred prior to my falling asleep,' I said innocently. 'Thus I am unaware of having in any way stepped beyond the normal bounds of hospitality, or of having infringed against any common code.'

The landlord's yellow eyes narrowed. 'Not aware that you have infringed? Are you denying the fact?'

'Which fact?'

'That you availed yourself of the talents and comforts of this young lady of our community, whose name is Alele and who sits here before you?'

'I cannot deny this, no.'

There were murmurings from those assembled.

'Then, by your own admission, you are guilty!' declared the landlord.

'Guilty of what? Alele was my willing partner. You yourself made an offer of her services when I first arrived in your inn.'

'Just so! Precisely! And you declined my generous offer, did you not?'

'Indeed I did. But with the passing of time, the imbibing of your rare wine and, I will say, the encouragement of Alele herself, I was induced to change my mind.'

Another murmur from the assembly. The landlord stood back, eyes wide, hands ingenuously open at his side. 'Sir, we of Oldmere are good and honest folk. We ask little of visitors to our happy community. But our word is our bond, and we expect the same of every man.'

'I'm afraid I still fail to understand.'

'Sir, Alele was offered to you. You turned her down. Twice, as I recall. More, you asserted fidelity to another. Such was your bond, and we accepted it. But then, to our shock and abhorrence, we find that you have broken it, advantaging yourself of that which you professed to have no interest in.'

'But this is preposterous!' I cried. 'Are you saying that a man has no right to change his mind?'

The landlord half smiled. There was a calmly triumphant air about him, and I felt my apprehension grow. Slowly shaking his head, he said with unctuous complacency, 'You are not of us. You do not know our ways. We are simple and honest folk. We have nothing to hide. We speak always what is in our hearts, that there might be no misunderstanding between us. A declaration made is irrevocable. That is the one way of it, in each and every concern.'

I stammered in disbelief. 'But what — what of errors,

unforeseen circumstances, words spoken in the heat of a moment? Surely one cannot be bound to every minor statement of intent, no matter what? We are fallible creatures, every one. We cannot foresee the future. We may desire to be honest, but the very nature of our lives decrees that we must from time to time reconsider our plans and intentions.'

'By our custom, which we consider to be fair and just, we are bound to give profound contemplation to every aspect of our lives,' said the landlord. 'But it is true that we are not infallible. Thus a person from time to time may find, even after full and sincere consideration, that through no fault of his own the way of his stated intent turns out to hold no advantage. Under such a circumstance – thankfully rare – he may desire to reconsider. That being so he can request a meeting of the community council, whose members are ranged here before you, and plead his case. If all agree that the plaintiff has acted correctly in every respect, that the fault is not his own, and that there is no other favourable recourse, then they may rule in his favour. He will be asked to make an appropriate tribute, and his name, title, and the full nature of his case will be entered upon the community record, for the edification of future generations. His statement is then publicly repealed.'

'It surely makes life unduly complex,' I said.

'It is our law,' stated the landlord coldly.

I could see that I was caught, for I had already confessed my guilt. I said, 'Then I accept that I have inadvertently transgressed. For this I can only apologize. But – as you have correctly pointed out – I am a stranger here, and unaccustomed to your ways. I would plead innocence and ignorance in respect of your unusual laws.'

The landlord gave this scarcely a moment's consideration. 'Within our small community we have established a system of adjudication which we consider meet. Punishments are intended in the main to serve as deterrents. However, they are such as to ensure that the malefactor will be reminded of his offence for the remainder of his life.'

A sudden clutch of unease in the pit of my stomach. I glanced at the faces before me. All were grim and intent, their eyes seeming to shine with an unwholesome rapture. Alele continued to gaze at the floor, her face hidden by her veil of glossy black hair.

'I will gladly pay whatever fine is considered appropriate, and then depart,' said I hurriedly. 'Though bear in mind that I am not wealthy.'

The landlord ignored me.

'If a man steals,' he intoned, 'be it a single potato, a herd of goats, or a hoard of treasure, he can expect, upon being found guilty, to lose his offending hand. If he commits murder, then of course, he will be killed. If he unlawfully spies upon another, he must expect to lose either the eyes with which he has seen, or the ears with which he has heard. If he speaks untruths he may expect to lose his tongue. And so on, sir. That is our way.'

'It is a harsh system,' I said, my mouth going dry.

'Perhaps not as harsh as it at first appears,' the landlord replied. 'Oldmere is a sacred place. The hollow in which it resides is blessed with an unusual property.'

Murmurings of agreement from those assembled – murmurings coloured with an unmistakable quality of awe, quite eerie and disturbing to my mind.

The landlord was not yet done. 'Those who for whatever reason are relieved of bodily parts find that others eventually grow in their place.'

Again I glanced at the strange faces and unnatural bodies before me. This revelation was scarcely comforting. 'It would appear that the replacement has a

93

tendency to differ somewhat from the original,' I remarked.

'That we have found to be the case. But we are blessed, and are grateful for the blessing. You see, many of us – innocent of any offence – have been given new or altered limbs, features, physical adornments. We do not complain – quite the contrary. This is the miracle of Oldmere, our sacred and happy home. We are the unique ones, privileged to receive the gift of our wondrous land.'

Only now did it strike me that I had entered a community of religious lunatics. My mind raced. Was there any way out of this predicament?

'Now,' said the landlord, 'to return to the matter at hand. I put it to you that you have committed a compound transgression against us. Namely, you have broken your bond to myself, and have then taken pleasure of a female of our community when she had been led to believe you wished no association with her.'

'But Alele was willing! Nay, she was a leading partner in the affray!'

'What? Are you saying that a transaction of business took place between you? Did the aforementioned lady of our community accept coin or other form of payment from you?'

'No, but . . .'

'Then your appeal cannot be upheld. Now, you are accused. How do you plead?'

'Not guilty!'

'Yet you have already confessed to the crimes. Are you now adding yet another to the list? Hah! No matter!' He wheeled to face the assembly. His little stubby tail was erect and wagging. 'You have heard the prisoner's plea, and the case against him. He has broken his parole, made to myself in the hearing of others, and taken advantage of this innocent female after leading

94

her to believe herself safe in his company. Furthermore, having confessed to the crimes, he now pleads otherwise. How do you find him?'

'Guilty!' came the unanimous cry. 'Guilty on all counts!'

The landlord turned back to me with a gleaming eye. 'Then I will pronounce sentence.'

He stepped over to the counter and took up a cloth hat with high, floppy blue crown and wide, drooping brim from which two white laces hung. He placed the hat upon his head, securing the laces beneath his chin so that the wide brim formed an irregularly shaped wimple. He turned and fixed me with an implacable gaze.

'Sir, you have been found guilty of the crimes heretofore described. I thus pass sentence upon you. For the first crime, that of breaking your bond unto me, you will pay with the loss of your offending organ – namely, the tongue which resides within your head. For the second, that of unfairly advantaging yourself of an innocent female of our community, you will pay in like form – namely, the loss of those physical parts most readily associated with the act.'

My mouth gaped. I jerked back in my seat, hardly believing what I was hearing. My head banged hard against the wall behind.

'I would add that it is our custom, whenever feasible, for the offender to be punished by that person or persons against whom he has offended,' continued the landlord. 'Thus, the tongue is mine. Alele, however, will perform the first separation.'

I looked across to Alele. Suddenly I understood the purpose of the kitchen knife and metal pan. She had turned to take them both from the table. Now she rose and faced me.

Somebody else moved to the fire and pulled out a cauterizing iron, glowing white hot. I leapt to my feet, crying, 'Again, I plead mitigating circumstances!'

The two thugs flanking me secured me by my arms. Two others rushed forward, cudgels at the ready.

'Am I correct in thinking that you refer to your unfamiliarity with our customs?' enquired the landlord.

'Indeed, you are! Is it fair or just to pass judgement upon one who is a stranger to your ways?'

'The matter was discussed prior to waking you. Ordinarily such a plea would be given consideration. However, we have not failed to take note of your physical character. Plainly you have erred before, and received meet punishment. And evidently you failed to learn from the experience. Your appeal has thus been dismissed.'

I shook free the bandaged stump of my left arm and waved it. 'This was no punishment, it is a legacy of battle!'

'Battle!' A gasp went up. 'Then you have fought with men, and killed, no doubt!'

The landlord eyed me with deep concern. 'Consider yourself lucky. Were it within our jurisdiction we would judge you for that crime also. You reveal yourself to be a vile, unprincipled, violent felon. Be thankful that you leave here with your life. Now, no more delay!'

I was dragged to a table and laid across it. The landlord loomed above me, fervour in his eyes. Alongside him stood Alele, beautiful Alele, knife in hand. I was held firm as my trousers were wrenched to my knees. Alele leaned over me. I was aware of the heat of the iron in close proximity to the flesh of my thigh. My legs were forced apart, the cold metal dish thrust between my thighs.

No doubt I whimpered and pleaded. No doubt I trembled. Alele's eyes met mine, but there was no compassion there. She was one with her weird mutant folk.

She lifted the knife; its blade glinted in the dreadful light. I could not move. I cried out again, but someone silenced me with a hand clasped roughly over my mouth. In utter desperation I reached into my mind. Heedless of what might come, I summoned a rapture.

There was a buzzing, a horrible susurrating, then a sudden bright flash of light.

Then shrieks and yells.

The hands that held me released their grip. I rolled instinctively, fell heavily from the table-top onto the hard floor. I scrambled beneath the table like a frightened beetle.

The common-room was in pandemonium. The air was suddenly laced with the smell of burning hair, clothing and flesh. Acrid smoke was beginning to fill the room.

Folk hurled themselves back and forth in panic. I watched legs from my vantage-point upon the sawdust-strewn floor. There was a violent thumping which caused the ground to vibrate. An unearthly sound, a profound, billowing roar, interspersed with a blood-curdling whining hum. Something monstrous had manifested in that room.

The smoke thickened rapidly. Low down, I was beneath its pall. Coughs and splutters, groans and wheezings were added to the terrified shrieks. I hauled my trousers up to my waist, calculating the position of the entrance. On hand and knees I came from beneath the table and scurried across the floor.

A figure ran at me, blind, screaming, clothes ablaze. In the chaos we collided. The fleeing body fell headlong over my back. I rushed on, unheeding.

Coming erect, I shouldered my way through panic-stricken bodies. I reached the door with several others. We clawed and kicked. I had dissolved the rapture as I went, that I might not become a victim of my own creation. The heat within that room had grown intense. Glancing over my shoulder I glimpsed a large moving shape, grotesque and frightening, all molten flame and writhing tentacles of dripping fire, half obscured by smoke. The press at the door gave way suddenly. I tumbled through, scrambled to my feet and fled for my life.

I ran for the countryside beyond the village, oblivious to the pain of my gouty toe. Behind me I heard shouts. Looking back I saw in the early half-light a group of persons emerging from the Black Heron. Smoke poured from windows and doorway. Shouts still came from inside but the panic seemed to have subsided. Evidently the elemental thing had vanished.

The landlord appeared, his robes blackened, his wimple skew-whiff and smoking on his head. He was brandishing a cudgel. Others held knives or axes. The landlord pointed my way. With yells and whoops they gave chase.

I ran on. I dared not attempt to protect myself with more magic, but the furious folk were fleeter than I, and were gaining on me.

I passed the last of the village dwellings, my pursuers only fifteen paces behind. Something moved in the bushes to one side. I swerved to avoid it. A bulky shape leapt out into my path. With sudden relief I recognized Yo.

'Yo! I have need of you!'

'I am your servant, Master.'

'Put yourself among these folk, for they will kill me if they catch me.'

Yo turned to stare down the road. Already, at the sight of him, the strange village-folk had halted. One or two edged forward. Yo growled. They came no closer.

'There are more of them than of me,' said Yo.

'But you are savage vhazz. They are afraid.'

'I hope that is the case, for I do not regard myself as brave.'

The landlord hailed me breathlessly. 'Sir, return now and accept your punishment. Your suffering will be greater if you fail to atone for your misdeeds.'

'Then I will suffer, gladly,' cried I. I could no longer ignore the throbbing of my foot, and hobbled on, unable to run.

A couple of fellows had moved to the side, endeavouring to circle around Yo. He put himself among them with a sudden lunge. His sharp fangs ripped the hand of one. The men leapt back. Pleased with himself, Yo seemed to grow in stature.

'Sir,' the landlord called again. 'What you do is wrong! Can you not see? We wish you no harm. When the punishment is done, you will be a welcome guest among us once more, free to enjoy our hospitality, yet with the benefit of a fuller understanding of our ways.'

It struck me that the fellow was quite mad, or perverse, or both.

'Your offer is a generous one, though from where I stand, hardly persuasive,' I called back. 'I prefer to go my own way, intact.'

'New parts will grow,' cried the landlord. 'The blessing of Oldmere will be yours.'

'I have grown attached to those I have. Ordinary though they may be, I prefer to retain them. Apply your blessings elsewhere.'

I had put a goodly distance between us now. Yo began to back along the trail, snarling the while. The villagers did not pursue. The landlord hailed me again. But none now heard him, save his own weird companions and perhaps any birds that perched in nearby trees, or beasts that waited in the woods. For I, thank Moban, was gone.

4

I

In the shortest possible time I put the maximum possible distance between Oldmere and myself.

Fearing the worst, I sent Yo on regular scouting missions in my wake. He assured me that the mad villagers did not pursue, yet I hobbled on, refusing to pause. In my mind's eye the glint of sharp steel still hovered with unambiguous menace, and my sensitive flesh still recoiled with a shudder from the touch of the cold metallic rim of that empty dish.

Eventually I could walk no further. My toe throbbed incessantly, and the act of walking upon the heel had caused strains and cramps all up my legs and back. I flopped down upon a fallen log beside the road. Noon had come and gone, and the afternoon was well advanced. The air was mild and almost still, the sky obscured by a bright overcast. The day had scarcely begun when I fled Oldmere; I was truly exhausted.

I removed my boot and examined the offending toe. In any land but this my agony could have been much reduced with a healing rapture. My feet were blistered and bruised. I raised my fist and vented obscenities at the ever-present mountains of the Gro'd f'ho Ib, the Harsh Maiden. The Maiden, her heights lost in cloud, remained indifferent to my plight.

Rough hills and crags rose about me. Like the mountains they were ill defined and disconcerting to the eye and brain. On the other side of the road was a small grassy meadow. Green willows sheltered a glade at one end, and between their fronds I spied the soft glimmer of water.

I heaved myself erect, my weight upon the staff that Yo had cut for me from an ash sapling. 'Come, Yo, I will rest up in yonder spot and soak my aching feet.'

The cold water was bliss. I sat upon the bank, gazed at dancing reflections, and let my feet grow numb. For the moment my troubles were forgotten.

Yo, however, was not content with silence. After a few moments of snuffling and scratching, he interrupted my meditations with a statement.

'It is fortunate this morning that I was to hand.'

This was not his first reference to the incident with those lunatic folk who had hoped to separate me and my parts. His manoeuvring was quite transparent, though he endeavoured to disguise it.

'That's true, Yo. And as I have said already, I am indebted to you for your assistance.'

'On the whole I have proven indispensable to you since we were so happily reunited. Isn't that so?'

'It is. Yes.'

He paused to consider his next words. 'Then do you not yet feel that you might exercise a little leniency in regard to my suffering?'

I gave a sigh. Despite all efforts I had been unable to disabuse Yo of the conviction that he was currently undergoing punishment for his earlier mischiefs.

'Yo, I have told you before, your occupancy of the body of a vhazz is not a punishment. It was all that was to hand.'

'Mmmh. But, Master, how much longer must I undergo this pu– I mean, inhabit this form?'

'That is impossible to predict. As you know, the usual procedure for bestowing a life-form upon a bound entity is long and complicated. It requires planning and forethought, and much arcane ritual. The form has to be chosen at a prenatal stage, and both entity and Master must be present – in non-corporeal form – prior to and during birth. You will recall when you were first bound to my service: was that not the way of your being born into this corporeal existence?'

'As a Wide-Faced Bear cub, yes. But . . .'

'But nothing, Yo. I understand that you are confused by the process through which I reclaimed my own form and bestowed the vhazz upon you. But it is not the same thing. This was and is *my* body. My leaving the vhazz to reclaim it left the vhazz vacant. There was no time for me to seek out an unborn beast. Nor would I trust myself to conduct the ritual here in Qotolr. Bagemm knows what might result!'

'But it is an unhappy existence, Master. The vhazz is bewildered and filled with dreadful sorrow. It knows an existential angst which leaves it very much ill at ease with itself. Its skin is plagued with parasites; its innards likewise. Its joints ache, even more than did yours. It . . .'

'Yo, I am aware of these things. I was that vhazz, have you forgotten? But recall, you found fault with the Wide-Faced Bear. Also with my own flesh. Perfection does not manifest in physical form, it is as simple as that. Now, I will hear no more. Other matters are pressing.'

With my good hand I reached behind me for my bag, for I had a ferocious hunger. Only now did I remember that I had left the bag in my room at the inn of the Black Heron. I had coin secure in my purse at my belt, but coin was valueless just now. My rations for the journey were in the bag.

Again I was moved to curse and curse again my misfortune.

'Yo, can you catch me something to eat? I took my

last meal more than eighteen hours ago. It was basic and somewhat bland, and . . .'

I hesitated, recollecting that last meal. The meat, with its unusual flavour and unfamiliar texture. The charge so low as to barely permit profit under the laws of normal transaction. A most horrible thought rose to the fore of my brain. Reflexively my hand went to my mouth, then down, as I went over the details of my sham trial that morning.

What in all Firstworld had I eaten last night?

My stomach turned over. I pulled myself away from the water's edge, retching painfully on an empty belly. As my innards grew more calm I dragged myself to a willow and rested with my back against the bole. 'On second thoughts, Yo, I will wait awhile. Quite suddenly my appetite has deserted me.'

The nausea abated. I closed my eyes. My thoughts drifted onto a less troubled plane.

It was pleasant here beside the pool. The sun had emerged to send warm rays slanting gently down through the foliage. Dragonflies darted to and fro across the water; finches chattered in the trees. The air bore the perfume of helleborine and lily, watermint, cow parsley, yarrow and a host of other scents. I was extraordinarily tired.

'Yo, the atmosphere here is congenial. I will take a short nap. Will you keep watch for me?'

'Yes, Master. Though the congeniality of an open cemetery is something that escapes the grasp of my comprehension.'

I was already slipping into a blissful dreaminess. Yo's voice was woolly and far away. But his sentiment somehow hooked my attention. With great effort I opened one eye. 'What was that, Yo?'

'Men are strange. What pleasure can be gained from lying down in a copse full of rotting corpses?'

I could barely keep my eyelids apart, but I looked around me, and saw nothing of what he described. 'Yo, to what are you referring? This is a tranquil dell, pleasing to the eye and restful to the spirit.'

'Very well, Master.'

His attitude was condescending enough to irk me to further response. 'Please clarify yourself, Yo. To what do you refer?'

'Can I be any clearer, Master? I have told you what I see. What else can I say?'

I sat up. 'We obviously don't share the same vision.'

'Obviously. Do you recall the last time you were here?'

'I have never been here before.'

'Ah.' Yo nodded sagely. 'Well, I remember it well. While I was Custodian of your Wandering flesh I passed this way several times. Each time I seemed to be drawn to this spot for a reason I could not quite fathom. And on each occasion I found myself – that is, yourself – most grossly offended by the presence of all these cadavers.'

'*What* cadavers?'

'You are not even aware of the stench?'

'I smell only wild flowers and herbs.'

Yo pulled an odd face. I stared at him with growing unease, peered again at my surrounds, again saw nothing of what he described.

My thoughts were foggy, my head heavy. Truly, I wanted only to rest awhile. I fought the desire and forced myself to shake off the fugginess of my brain. Something distant was clawing at my memory.

There – I had it! The account given to me by Shadd and his companion, the hylozote. They'd spoken of an enchanted glade in which Shadd had nearly succumbed to terminal sleep. The hylozote had also witnessed the presence there of my Wandering flesh. Apparently I had then been impervious to the glade's enchantments.

I screwed up my eyes and rubbed them, stared hard. Still I saw only a tranquil grassy glade, partly shaded from the sun. At its centre was a placid pool fringed by willows. It looked such a pretty place.

Under normal conditions a rapture of All-Seeing would have revealed the truth, but conditions were far from normal. I therefore had no choice but to take Yo at his word. I thrust myself to standing.

'Yo, what precisely do you see when you cast your eyes about this place?'

'As I have said, Master, corpses, and the remains of corpses.'

'Are they human?'

'In the main. They are in varying states of putrefaction. One, just here, has hardly begun to stiffen. Others are skeletons, picked clean by birds and beasts. Some wear clothing, others only dried ribbons of flesh. Some are half sunk into the earth, or overgrown by grass and vegetation; others lie here as if they have quite recently arrived. It is a place of death, Master, and plainly it has been so for many years.'

I picked up my boots and staff. 'Yo, let us begone from this place without further ado.'

At least I was on the right road. This in itself was some comfort, for I had begun to wonder.

There were many tales told about the strange nature of Qotolr. Among them was the proposition that its landscape was ever-altering form; that it was never the same twice around. A wayfarer might make a map, then return to find his efforts wasted, the map being irrelevant to the terrain he now traversed, even though by his own calculations he followed his former path.

More than one eminent philosopher had theorized that the nature of Enchantery was such that it formed itself anew every time one crossed its borders, magically interacting with the conscious and unconscious expectations of those who walked its roads. Its horizons were blurred, it was said, for they had not yet been ideated into an acceptable reality.

Of course, one could raise manifold objections to the notion. What happens, for instance, when two or more persons enter Enchantery together and gaze upon the same landscape? Do they perceive the same things? Is the land formed in accordance with the mentation of an individual beholder, or does it take elements from the consciousness of each and coalesce them into something jointly representative?

What of its inhabitants? In what manner do they contribute, if any? And what happens to them if the land is under continual remorphism?

And who or what directs the elemental force that imbrues the place? The Enchanters, though mighty, were no longer the gods they had been. In many respects they had become victims of their own former power. Did there exist a force greater than they?

Was the land itself sentient?

There were no answers. Qotolr was an enigma, and really that was all that could be said. But it was impossible to resist speculation.

Anyway, my experience now appeared to render the above hypothesis invalid. The land was as it had been over at least a number of weeks, perceived so by myself and others at varying times.

But I could not rid myself of a fear that it might yet change. Or that, while my route appeared to remain true, it could still have been transplanted. Was I genuinely walking in the direction of the Chol border and Drurn March, or had I and my surrounds been removed to some remote quarter of this unknown land, plodding haplessly towards further unknowns?

I had little option but to continue hopefully along my

preplanned way, in the direction I perceived as west.

I will not linger here on an account of the following days. Suffice to say that after certain hardships and adventures I emerged, to my relief, from an extraordinary and exotic belt of thick forest which I recognized from Shadd's description as forming the border of Enchantery's western reach. My perceptions had not deceived me, nor had I fallen foul of the vagaries of that strange land. Confronting me now was a landscape of menacing stones formed into myriad unearthly forms. Beyond this, I knew, stretched an empty plain, giving onto the wildlands of Drurn March.

II

I made my way between the looming stones. They crowded in intimidating postures, close upon me, like monstrous, once-living things now fixed and immobile. Eldritch creatures, with limbs, claws, wings, tentacles, mouths . . . or so my imagination would have me believe.

In this unsettling domain I was prey to tricks of the mind. My nerves were on edge. Frequently I jumped at an imagined sound close by. A contorted boulder seemed to shift position, come momentarily to life. I almost sensed a deathlike touch upon my shoulder, or something cold and slithering wrap itself about my ankle. I felt myself watched, menaced, stalked. I glanced frequently to left, right and rear. Yo kept close beside me, his hackles high, tail to belly. From time to time he whimpered and, like me, leapt aside as if to dodge some illusionary menace.

What were these things? They were too strange to be natural formations, yet they were unreal. Had they once had life? Had they walked upon this land? I had

witnessed nothing like them in my experience, except
. . . I could not hold back the thought: except Gneth.

And here they were massed across this wilderness in
their thousands.

Presently their dreadful ranks began to thin, then
dropped away entirely. I entered a stretch of sparse
woodland, and stopped to rest. In easy sight now, away
across a rocky waste, were the heights of eastern Chol,
reassuringly harsh and firm to my gaze. Somewhere
there was Drurn March fortress, and my only conceivable route back.

I waited for dusk, for in daylight a traveller would be
exposed upon that barren plain. According to Shadd's
directions I would find a rough trail on the far edge of
the plain. The fortress of Drurn March bestrode this
way two or three miles further on.

With the fading light I struck out from the trees.
Night was upon me long before I had crossed the plain.
Reaching the foot of the Chol heights I sent Yo to
search out a suitable spot to make camp. He quickly
returned and guided me to a covert nearby, where
numerous rills spilled down from the highlands to
spread a network of trickling water across the earth.
We ate a reasonable meal of bread, cheese, dried meat
and fruit from a stock of rations I had replenished three
days earlier in a Qotol village. I washed this down with
fresh water, then gathered grass and leaves to make a
rude litter, lay down and slept until morning.

III

The fortress crouched low upon a rocky hill, overlooking a deep, sheer-sided defile. Its contours were to
a large extent moulded to that of the hillside, and made
inspired use of the natural protection of the land. Its

thick stone walls, hewn from the hill itself, spoke of strength and durability, and helped convey an impression that the fortress had actually grown up out of the mountainous slopes.

The stronghold's gate-house, set below the main keep and compound, actually straddled the road which passed above the defile. A pair of squat stone towers, fused on one side with the cliff and the overhanging rock above, and flush with the lip of the drop on the other, faced east and west. At the base of each was a massive double-rung timber door bound with black iron straps. To pass Drurn March fortress entailed entering the gate-house through one of these doors and exiting via the other.

Upon the summit a pole on the roof of the keep flew the Chol flag. Khimmur had yet to take possession of this place, then. Even so I was hardly encouraged by the knowledge, for beyond the pass, beyond the fortress, I spied tents and wooden huts dotted across the valley floor. I could not count them, for the distance was too great and the fortress and the crag on which it sat obscured much of my view. But a wooden palisade had been erected to protect the huts and tents, and the encampment was rife with movement. Soldiery in great number.

Khimmur was here.

Drurn March was under investment.

Was the Prince Regent still within the fortress walls? His options would have been few. He might have fled south prior to the arrival of the Khimmurian force. Failing that there were only two possibilities: either he remained within, or he had gone east, into Qotolr.

There was but the one route eastwards, and along that way I had seen no indication of the passage of a force of any size. Fhir Oube would hardly have gone alone. Thus my guess was that he remained, and probably gazed down even now from the battlements at the army arrayed against him.

And I had somehow to pass through that fortress, and evade the enemy on the other side.

It was true that when I had entered Qotolr it had been by another way, further to the north. But then I had been with Yaoww. I had occupied the body of a fleet and nimble vhazz – the same body in which Yo now resided. So even were I to find that other route again – and I doubted that I could – it would not serve me, a lame, one-handed human.

Shadd had spoken of a third alternative through the Chol heights, but his description made it evident that the same conditions applied. No, there was but one route, and that was the one before me.

I had been pondering this impasse for more than an hour while observing the fortress from a tumble of rocks hidden in dense scrub some way above the road. At my back the sun had risen above the far Qotol mountains into a sky of pale gold and deepening azure. The day was clear, bright and already warm.

I climbed to my feet, discouraged, and began to make my way back down the steep slope to the roadside, keeping the rise of the slope between myself and Drurn March. I intended to return to the site where I had rested overnight, and eat a little whilst looking further at my quandary.

Quite suddenly I realized I was being watched. I looked up and saw, less than ten paces away, two persons blocking my path. They seemed quite literally to have risen out of the earth, for the ground immediately around them offered little scope for concealment, and they had not been there seconds earlier when I had begun my descent.

I halted. Yo, with a low growl, unsheathed his sword. They were not soldiers. At least, not Chol or

Khimmurian. Both carried weapons, however, but neither had a blade drawn. They were a man and a woman. He was young, bearded, dark-haired, his skin brown and weathered. He was of short, lithe build, yet gave the impression of sinewy strength. She was younger, seeming scarcely more than a girl. Her build was slight, yet again conveyed an impression of vigour and stamina. Her hair was almost black, cut short to frame an alert, attentive, resourceful face. Both of them wore loose, nondescript clothing. They seemed strangely familiar, yet I could not place them.

After moments of mutual scrutiny the girl spoke. 'Dinbig, it is you. We are pleased. It has been a long time.'

The man raised his hands to his mouth, tilted his head back, and made a sound like the cry of a hawk. He repeated this three times.

From behind rocks, higher to my left, another figure rose. He came bounding down the slope towards me, a tall, slender young man, clean-shaven, hollow-cheeked, long white hair bouncing behind his shoulders.

Yo gave another growl and came forward into a defensive crouch. The newcomer skidded to a halt five paces from us. I stayed Yo with my hand. 'Hold, Yo. It is all right.'

I grinned wide, throwing open my arms. With a whoop Duke Shadd leapt forward and clasped me in a fierce embrace.

'Dinbig! Dinbig! You made it!'

I thumped his back. 'I made it, but I will make it no further if you continue to crush the life from me!'

He released me and drew back, elation in his strange features. We laughed. I noticed a movement at his shoulder, saw a tiny form hovering there, and recognized the Gwynad, Temminee.

111

'Many times I thought about you,' said Shadd, and I saw the concern in his huge, pale, otherworldly eyes. 'I rebuked myself for having left you. I feared that you had perished.'

'You could have done nothing other. We both knew and accepted that, no matter what we wished. I cannot tell you how much joy it brings me to see you now.'

'But you have changed! I would scarcely have recognized you!'

'Indeed, I have changed in many ways, I believe. Not all of them are yet apparent.'

'And who is this?' enquired Shadd, turning to Yo.

'It is my Custodian, Yo. You will have divined that he now occupies the vhazz body that was previously mine.'

'It was not a fitting guise for you, Dinbig.' Shadd performed a courteous bow and extended a hand to grip Yo's paw. 'I am pleased and honoured to make your acquaintance.'

Yo, bedraggled and bemused, perked up visibly at being so addressed.

'And now, my companions,' Shadd said. 'Kekhi, greet my great friend and warden, Ronbas Dinbig, and his stalwart Custodian, Yo.'

The girl came forward, making a sign with one hand. '*Jhoso*, Dinbig. *Jhoso*, Yo.'

Jhoso! I knew the greeting. She was Aphesuk!

'And Rin,' said Shadd. Kekhi's bearded companion stepped forward with the same greeting.

I studied them with renewed interest. Of course they were familiar! They were Shadd's bodyguards, and would have been assigned to him when he came from the Endless Desert. They were, moreover, spies, both for Shadd and for the Aphesuk tribe. And they were potentially his executioners. I wondered now how many of these roles they were here to perform.

Kekhi seemed amused. No doubt she deduced something of my thoughts. For my part I remained puzzled. I had always known that such bodyguards were secretly present in Shadd's entourage. Many times I had looked among the Nine Hundred Paladins, assuming that it would be among warriors that the Aphesuk would take their place. Yet these two had not been paladins, I was certain of it. Doubly certain in Kekhi's case, for the Nine Hundred numbered no women in their ranks.

Yet they were familiar. Where had I seen them?

Kekhi's lips spread into a most attractive smile and her deep brown eyes shone brightly.

'You are but a hair's breadth from it, Dinbig. I can tell!'

And then I had it.

'Bagemm, yes! Palace Moonshade! You were an under-maid!'

She laughed delightedly. 'Your memory serves you well!'

It was perfect, of course. No one would have thought to look among the lowly domestic staff. She was inconspicuous, yet had access at all times to the young Duke. I turned my attention to Rin, whom I had still to place.

'I will save you the trouble,' said Shadd. 'Rin was a stable-hand. And an exceptional one, at that, for someone who has had little experience with horses.'

Rin chuckled. I scratched my head, smiling. 'But how are you here? Is it coincidence that brings us together now?'

Shadd shook his head. 'These two are here because they came to find me. Had they not done so I would certainly have died at Mesmia's hands. And we are here because I knew that you, if you survived, would pass this way.'

'The fragment from the Pandect . . .' I said, suddenly anxious.

113

Shadd nodded and patted the waistband of his tunic. 'Come, there is much to discuss. But before anything else we should move. We are exposed and vulnerable here beside the road. We will take you to a safer place.'

IV

We moved to higher ground, a hollow hidden in trees, from which we could look out and survey the fortress on its crag.

'They are the men of Rishal,' said Shadd in response to my enquiry, 'supplemented by a contingent of Poisse axe and bow. In all they number some seven thousand. Lord Marsinenicon is their commander. There is also, curiously, a small detachment of Sommarians.'

'And inside the fortress?'

'The last of Fhir Oube's loyal Chol – and a few others beside.'

I noted with curiosity the bitter inflection in his voice. He went on, 'Fhir Oube is severely outnumbered. His troops are demoralized after numerous defeats, most recently in a terrible battle upon the Coul Road to the west of here. Count Vess, Fhir Oube's cousin, was killed there. Although the stronghold can withstand any assault by Marsinenicon's force, the Prince Regent is nevertheless holed up. Supplies are short and his only possible retreat is into Qotolr. Even that may be cut off if Marsinenicon can succeed in getting sufficient men over the heights to this side.'

'You evidently know a great deal about the situation.'

'More than I have so far revealed. We have been into both the fortress and the Khimmurian camp and ...'

'You have entered fort and camp?' I exclaimed. 'How?'

It was of course a foolish question. I sat among Aphesuk, and Shadd himself was quite adept at their techniques. Shadd chose to answer nonetheless.

'Not I, but Kekhi and Rin. It was essential to discover the lie of the land. And as luck would have it, we learned something more. There is treachery afoot and we are pondering how best to deal with it.'

'Tell me more.'

Kekhi spoke. 'Two nights ago I went to enter the fort while Rin took the Khimmurian camp. Shadd remained here, for he, like you, cannot risk being discovered. The cost would be too great. I had entered the lower compound and was making my way up when I heard the rattle of stones falling from somewhere over the wall on the western side. Curious, I avoided the guard and climbed to the parapet. I could see nothing, but from the faint sounds that reached me it was evident that somebody was on the cliff below me, climbing down to the road. I decided to investigate, and left the fortress again to descend onto the cliff.

'A man was there, clambering down with the aid of a rope. Evidently he had emerged from some secret place, for I could not conceive that he had scaled the fortress wall. On the road he made his way rapidly down towards the valley floor. I followed for some distance, which was not difficult, for he was slow and as noisy as an ox. It became obvious that his objective was the Khimmurian camp. I called a coded warning to Rin, who I knew was somewhere close to the camp. Upon hearing his reply I returned to spy the fort.'

Rin took up the tale. 'I was about to enter the camp when I heard Kekhi's cry. I moved to the roadside and waited. Within seconds the man passed by me. He made straight for the camp gate, then loudly announced his presence to the sentries. Called to approach, he named himself as one Dade, a lieutenant

115

of the Drurn March garrison, and demanded an audience with the Khimmurian commander on a matter of utmost urgency. He was held under guard for some moments, then escorted into the camp.

'I followed. Out of caution my entrance was slowed, for the place is efficiently patrolled. I took a gamble that this Dade had been taken to Lord Marsinenicon's headquarters, which we had spied out earlier. I could not get into the headquarters, but waited hidden outside. After two minutes Dade emerged, flanked by guards. With him was Lord Marsinenicon.

'"Tell Commander Odus that should he fail I will personally attend to his fate, and yours," said he. "You will endure unspeakable agonies, begging for a death that will be long in coming."

'"We will not fail," replied Dade, who seemed excessively nervous. He was then marched off back to the perimeter and released.

'I swiftly left the camp,' Rin continued, 'and climbed to the fortress to find Kekhi. I calculated that Dade would take some time to return. I told Kekhi what had transpired below.'

Now Kekhi resumed once more. I listened, enthralled. How casually they spoke of their exploits, as though they had done nothing more than taken a walk through the forest.

'Rin's assumption was that Dade would be returning to report to his commander,' Kekhi said, 'so I made my way to Odus's private chamber, where he paced up and down in a state of heightened agitation. I positioned myself at a window where I might overhear anything said within. At length Dade arrived, breathless and sweating, to make his report. In short, these two have arranged to betray their Prince Regent by secretly leaving unbarred the west door, which will permit the Khimmurians entry to Drurn March.'

116

'What treachery!' I cried, appalled.

Shadd scowled. 'It scarcely surprises me. I know this Odus. Dade also. The former is something of a lout and an opportunist, little better than a bandit, though oddly not altogether dislikeable. His loyalties lie wherever his most immediate interests would seem to be served. Thus the assurance of safe passage for himself and his accomplices, plus, I would guess, the promise of a little gold, speaks more persuasively under current circumstances than does allegiance to his Prince Regent and country.'

'And when is this treacherous deed to take place?' I asked.

'Tonight. Dade commands the gate-house guard. The Khimmurians will come up the trail under the cover of darkness and enter unopposed. There will be much bloodshed, and Fhir Oube will die or be made prisoner.'

'We must act!'

'As we have proposed to do. But it is not so simple. I am known to the Prince Regent. Were I to enter Drurn March to warn him it is likely I would be disbelieved. What is almost certain is that I would be arrested, as would Kekhi or Rin. Fhir Oube considers me untrustworthy. He might see a way out of his dilemma by offering me to Marsinenicon.'

'I have more than a passing acquaintance with Fhir Oube,' I said. 'He may be persuaded to listen to me.'

Shadd shook his head. 'No doubt he would listen to any one of us – to the extent of taking steps to avert tonight's treachery. But you, Dinbig, would be considered almost as great a prize as me. You cannot reveal yourself. Your survival must at all costs be kept secret.'

I smiled, without particular humour. 'Yes, I am of greater value "dead" than living. But what, then? Are we to simply sit by and watch while Khimmur gains another bloody victory?'

117

'We have given it much thought. We are confronted simultaneously with another problem: that of getting past both the fortress and the Khimmurian camp beyond.'

I passed my eyes over the three of them. 'I don't think that is a great problem for you. It is I who am really the problem, is it not?'

'You know *Zan-Chassin* magic,' said Kekhi. 'Have you a spell of concealment?'

'I could conjure a veil upon myself which will partially obscure my form from any who gaze at it. But I have had strange experiences with magic these last few days in that godforsaken land. Is it safe here?'

Shadd glanced back in the direction of Qotolr. 'My abilities also were adversely affected, though I was scarcely aware of it at the time. Enchantery strikes me as being a place without true life. Here I find the land, the trees, the breeze are like old friends whose passage tells me much. I can attune myself to them. There, nothing spoke. It is a relief, too, to look upon a landscape that does not try to avoid the focus of my gaze. I feel that I have emerged from a dream into the land of the waking. So, yes, Dinbig, I believe your magic will be uncorrupted here.'

'Good. Then I will start by applying myself immediately to my swollen toe. I will be happier if I know that I can at least run.' A new thought struck me, and my spirits fell. 'Marsinenicon . . . he is *Zan-Chassin* too.'

'Is that significant?' asked Kekhi.

'We are both of Third Realm, and therefore of comparable abilities. Doubtless he also has others with him, both human and entities. They will be alert. My rapture could thus have precisely the contrary effect to that which is intended. If I pass close to another *Zan-Chassin* who is focused to detect magic, my veil

118

will draw attention to me rather than diverting it away.'

Shadd screwed up his face. 'Then you must not use it.'

'What choice do I have?'

He shook his head and cast a weighted glance to his two companions. 'I don't know. We will consider. But I fear that much blood will be spilled this night.'

V

Night came, deep and oddly silent. Nocturnal creatures of wood and mountain seemed not to stir, as though they sensed that something was afoot, that this night would bring events which men would recall for many years.

All seemed still in the fastness of Drum March. The keep was an opaque blotch upon the summit of the hill, solid against the inky blue-blackness of the sky. The walls were invisible, merged into the blankness of the steep slopes. No lamps burned upon the battlements.

In contrast, hundreds of small flickering flares were the campfires of the invaders in the valley below. The palisade showed a brazen face, lit at regular spaces with lanterns, scornful of the beleaguered Chol upon whose land the army mustered.

I crouched in darkness, the gate-house of Drum March fortress bulking above me. Only yards away the east-facing door, which would allow access into the outer compound of the stronghold and to the west gate and the road to Khimmur beyond, was closed fast and barred. My companions – all but Yo – had gone.

I shivered, more from tenseness than the night's chill, and wondered for the thousandth time what the next hour would bring. I waited for a sign, not knowing whether it would ever come, and my mind worked in a fever of guesswork, hope and apprehension. All around me the silence was unnerving. And I could do nothing but remain unmoving, where I was.

The gate-house guard was changed. I heard the stomp of heavy feet as the traitors came down from the main compound to replace those whose duty was done. Muffled commands, then the footsteps of the relieved guard making their way back up, to a welcome meal, a pallet and, if Odus and the Khimmurians had their way, death.

Silence once more. I considered those who now manned the gate-house. Could they truly be blamed for simply trying to salvage their own lives? Is it not natural to resort to any means to save one's self? But what of conscience, knowing that one's actions will bring about the deaths of others who have placed their trust in you? Ah, such an intricate web! Such matters transcended the laws of men. I was not prepared to judge the right and wrong of it.

An hour passed, then another. I was stiff and cramped, and my gut had knotted. But within the fortress walls the action had begun.

The gate-house night-watch, commanded by Dade and Odus, consisted of thirty Chol soldiers. Another thirty were barracked inside the lower compound, to be quickly roused from sleep in the event of an emergency. How many of the watch were accomplices in Odus's plan will probably never be known. Certainly at least half.

The first task had been to lock the sleeping reserves inside their barracks, and remove their weapons. This done, three men entered the room above the west door and set to upon the windlass to haul up the portcullis.

A fourth soldier was with them. Seeing what they were doing he questioned their action. He was told to hold silence. He turned to leave, intending to report directly to his commander, only to find Odus standing before him, blocking the doorway.

'Sir . . .' he began, and got no further. Odus's sword stabbed silently into the loyal soldier's soft gut. He staggered back, was stabbed again from behind, and fell dead to the floor.

Odus wiped his blade clean as the portcullis reached its full height.

'Good. Now the door.'

The three troopers descended to draw back the bar on the inside of the double door. The way was now free to allow entrance from outside.

Odus returned to the gate-house. His men made to go back to their posts. Something slipped from the shadows. Two men died silently. The third, hearing a sound, turned to investigate. A silent blade slipped across his throat, and he too was sent in ignorance from this world.

Two figures moved quickly to the double door and replaced the bar, then darted soundlessly across the court to the east door. They slipped inside the tower. The bodies of two Chol soldiers were already stretched upon the floor. The assassins moved up to the first level. Another Chol corpse was spreadeagled there, and a third figure, tall and gaunt, stepped out of the shadows to join them.

Shadd and Rin took the windlass and began to turn. Kekhi crept back downstairs, anticipating intervention as the chains rattled and the windlass creaked under the weight of the portcullis.

This was my signal. With Yo beside me I crept from hiding and ran crouching up to the door. If things went awry now I knew I was dead.

Voices inside. A sudden sharp cry, then silence. The windlass also had ceased to turn.

Now a dull thump against the inside of the door. I gripped the hilt of the shortsword given me earlier by Shadd. Yo held his vhazz blade ready. I heard the bar lift on the inside. There were muffled cries.

Suddenly the gate swung inwards. Shadd stood there. He reached out, grabbed me and literally half dragged me through the opening. Yo slunk in swiftly behind. Shadd put his weight to the door and pushed it shut, replacing the bar.

Out of the darkness came a running form. Something moved in front of me. The man fell. A hand took my arm. I glimpsed Kekhi's face.

'Quickly!' she hissed. 'The Khimmurians are already on the road. You must be gone before they reach the west door.'

Together we ran back across the court, hugging the wall. From behind us came the sounds of a scuffle. In the dark nothing was clear. Shadd seemed to have vanished, and I had seen nothing of Rin.

Suddenly we were under attack. Kekhi, a blur of movement, stabbed, slashed, lunged. Shouts. A shape came at me, weapon raised. More swiftly than me, Yo leapt. He bore the man to the ground, tearing at his throat. The soldier struggled, then lay still.

Kekhi was with me again. I stumbled on the body of the man she had just slain. Another man came from the dark. Kekhi ducked, kicked out. I heard the sickening snap as her assailant's head jerked back under the force of the kick. Her blade slid up into his chest.

She took my arm again, even as he fell, and led me on.

We were at the west door. Kekhi slipped forward, pulled it open a crack. She put her head outside.

'Go!'

With Yo I pushed through. The great door closed behind me.

I gripped the strap of Yo's body armour. He, with his superior night vision, was my guide along the road beneath the rearing cliff.

We had covered no more than twenty paces when he halted.

'What is the matter, Yo? What do you see?'

'It is not what I see, Master, it is what I smell. There are soldiers. Ahead. In great number. Do you not hear them?'

I heard nothing. 'These are Marsinenicon's men. If they find us we are dead.'

Yo crept on with greater caution. Not far away, by Shadd's account, the road twisted in a sharp loop. There was a deep cleft in the cliff, where it was possible to clamber up to a rocky shelf above the road. Here I was to hide until Shadd or one of the Aphesuk came for me.

'If we fail to join you within an hour you must consider that you are on your own,' he had said, clasping my shoulder and adding: 'Make wise decisions.'

It seemed now that I was not going to reach that safe harbour. Timing had been crucial, and it looked as though the Khimmurians were closer than we had intended. There was no way back; the doors were barred.

Suddenly behind us a tocsin rang, splitting the silence of the night. Shadd's agreed signal, alerting the fortress to the danger. I heard shouts on the road below us, close.

'They are running towards us now,' said Yo.

'Go on, Yo! We are almost there! Do you see no crevice?'

'Not yet. Here they come!'

I could not see them, but the Khimmurians were

123

rushing up towards the gate, confused by the sound of the bell. I heard their feet, the clatter of their armour, their hushed, excited voices. They were almost upon us.

Footsteps ran past us, so close I felt I could have reached out and touched a man. I smelt their sweat. I pressed myself hard into the rock. We edged on down. The tocsin continued to peal. Shouts came from the fortress.

More soldiers came by us. And more. One actually stumbled and fell against me, then regained his footing and ran on uphill, not realizing what had happened. Now I saw torches below, illuminating running figures crowding the trail. Faces dimly lit beneath helmets, weapons held before them. They rushed on by, but at any moment I knew we would be seen.

Then Yo pulled me violently in towards the cliff. My shoulder scraped painfully against harsh rock.

'This is it!' rasped Yo. 'Quickly, up!'

In the dark, half terrified, I tried to climb. Blind, one-handed, not knowing where I went. I slipped; Yo grabbed me. I hauled myself higher as the army swept by beneath my feet. My hand found the lip of a ledge. The muscles of my arm trembled with the effort. Yo reached down, took me beneath the arm. He dragged me higher. The cliff gave way; I was groping in empty space. I slumped forward and lay panting in exhaustion upon level rock and earth.

The din from the gate-house now was horrendous. A cacophony of shouts, crashes, screams, almost drowning the sound of the tocsin which, as I listened, ceased abruptly to toll.

'Can you see anything, Yo?'

'Nothing of the fortress, Master. The cliff blocks my view. But evidently the Khimmurians have reached the entrance and found it closed. I would guess that the defenders are now alerted and are pouring fire upon their heads.'

Still more soldiers continued to press upwards below us. I guessed that as yet their commanders had not divined the situation. Chaos and panic. Slaughter in the night. Drurn March echoed with the cries of dying men.

VI

The fighting endured for another ten minutes or so, then it became obvious to all concerned that things were not going to the Khimmurian plan. Lord Marsinenicon's men were taking heavy losses, and the order was given to retreat. The Khimmurians fell back in disarray, returning down the trail into the valley and camp.

We remained as we were, lying flat in scrub above the road. Presently Yo hissed, 'Someone approaches!'

I neither heard nor saw a thing, but I knew enough to trust his superior senses. Hardly had he spoken when there was a light touch upon my shoulder. Kekhi's voice spoke softly in my ear. 'We must go.'

'Where are Shadd and Rin?' I enquired.

'Below, checking the road for sentries. We must be quick and silent.'

'We should send Yo down to help them. In darkness he can see where even Aphesuk cannot.'

'Temminee performs that function, as does the hylozote, though without mobility. Yo, if he will, can serve us better as we descend.'

We climbed from the shelf of rock to the road. Behind in the darkness, from the vicinity of Drurn March fortress, came groans and occasional shouts. Yo led the way downwards, with me, holding onto Kekhi's belt, just behind.

We descended for some minutes. Twice we came upon the garroted corpses of Khimmurian soldiers beside the trail. From them I took a sword, daggers and a lamellar vest.

Presently Yo halted, whispering, 'Duke Shadd is nearby. I have his scent. Shall I take you to him?'

'Wait.' Kekhi put her hands about her mouth and gave a call, as Rin had done the previous day – a sound indistinguishable from the cry of a hawk. A moment later there came an answering cry from off to our right.

'Now you may lead us to him,' Kekhi said.

Shadd was crouched in bushes upon a steep slope overlooking the Khimmurian camp. He gripped my arm firmly as I settled myself beside him. 'Our task now is to get past that.'

'Correction,' I replied. 'As I have already pointed out, *you* will have little difficulty in avoiding Marsinenicon's forces. It is I who am the task.'

Shadd gazed sombrely at the camp below. 'It's true, we could have sneaked by the camp, or climbed higher to join the road further on, though the climbing will not be easy even for us.'

'Thus it will be impossible for me. My friend, you should go on. It is vital that you return to Khimmur with the pages from the Pandect. That is all that really counts. Leave me. I will make my own way. By one means or another I will succeed.'

Shadd was quiet for a while, then said, 'You are trapped here, unable to go forward or back. I cannot permit you to fall into Marsinenicon's hands. Rin is further down, reconnoitring. We will wait here until we have heard what he has to say.'

126

5

I

It was an opportunity for discussion while Kekhi, Temminee and Yo kept watch. Below us lights moved to and fro on the valley floor and the muted hubbub of voices was borne up to us on the air. Confusion and anger in the Khimmurian camp, cries of pain, and no doubt plans for retribution. Shadd told me briefly of what had befallen him after we had parted in Qotolr.

'Then again, I can only emphasize how vital it is that you do not allow me to delay you,' I said when he had done. 'You are Seruhli's only hope; and Moban knows what else may be inscribed upon that Fragment.'

'What hope, when we have no means of translating its contents?'

'At least get the Fragment away from here. With Mesmia searching for it – and likely the other Enchanters too – you must remove it as far from Qotolr as possible.'

'And then?' said Shadd, with chagrin. 'How do I know that it is not all a lie? How do I know that there is a hope of reviving her?'

I stared at the pale oval of his face in the darkness. I could not make out his expression, but knew the hopelessness in his voice. I said, 'Shadd, I have other evidence to support the theory that she is alive. That is, she may truly be held in the Semblance of Death, but she is not gone from this world.'

He looked up. 'Do you say this purely to give me heart? What is your evidence?'

127

I told him Yo's tale: how in a secret passage beneath the city of Twalinieh in Kemahamek, Yo, in my body, had been dragged half drowned and near bloodless from the waters of Death's Deep. His saviours – *my* saviours – he described as a group of Simbissikim and other influential Kemahamek. They were spiriting away from the capital a mysterious cargo, a shrouded bundle borne upon a litter, which they carried with immense care and respect, as if it were something precious beyond telling.

'Yo was taken with them, Shadd, and left to recover in the care of a priest deep within the forest somewhere to the north-east of Twalinieh. The party travelled on with its precious cargo. By all descriptions it was without doubt a body they carried – the body of a person greatly loved and accorded much respect. It was Seruhli, Shadd. It can only have been! They took her away to some unknown place, to safeguard her in the hope of finding the means to bring her back to life.'

'It may have been only her corpse,' muttered Shadd, though his cynicism lacked total conviction.

'And you are prepared to leave it at that? Never knowing?'

He sighed deeply. 'I think you know that I cannot.'

'You *are* her only hope. You cannot allow anything to stand in your way. Seruhli could bring the people of Kemahamek back to life. She could stand against the Beast of Rull.'

'*If* I can find her. *If* the formula for the antidote is written here. *If* a way can be found to translate the old language.' He stared broodingly into the night. 'And even then, what? I love her so deeply, Dinbig. The very knowledge that she has lived upon this world racks my soul with anguish. Yet what is she? A goddess, proud and aloof, untouched by the ways of men. I know so little of her, but she holds such a power over me. I love

128

her unquestioningly, even knowing that, should she live, I am in her eyes beneath contempt.'

I noticed Kekhi had joined us, materializing behind Shadd as if out of the very air. She was perched upon a rock, her arms wrapped around her shins, her slight form a vague silhouette against the night sky. I sensed that she listened intently to our words, and her eyes seemed to be on Shadd. And I thought: Shadd, there is something here that you do not see. Or do you see it and are indifferent? Would it change anything?

Shadd said, 'I saw her, Dinbig. At the Lake of Clouds, close beneath Mesmia's Tower. She appeared to me, like a ghost at the water's edge. She beseeched me to help her. But I do not know if she was a ghost, or a genuine projection from Seruhli's trapped soul, or an apparition of Mesmia's devised to ensnare me further into her design.' He shook his head in a welter of unspoken feelings.

'Since then, after finding the Fragment, I have pledged that I will not rest until I know the truth and have done all in my power to aid her.'

'Well spoken.'

I looked up. A shadow moved. Kekhi had gone, returning silently to the watch. Another voice spoke with quiet authority.

'Duke Shadd, remember Temminee's gift. The Soul Crystal will surely tell you what is true, if you allow it.'

'Perhaps.' Shadd reached into his pouch and brought forth the hylozote. 'Look at this, Dinbig, will you. A conscious rock, possessed of all the normal senses of a man. What are you, hylozote? A good friend, yes. An advisor, yes. Wise and ancient, yet ever an enigma.'

'I am what I am,' replied the hylozote flatly. 'Like you, I had no say in my making.'

'It has struck me that I should find a name for you,'

129

said Shadd. 'Hylozote is a description only, and is insufficient. I would prefer something else, but only now has it come to me what that should be.'

'All names are descriptions, or become them, even in the abstract. Still, I am intrigued. What name would you have me bear?'

'Antinomy, for that is just what you are: a contradiction, a paradox. You should not exist, yet no one can deny that you do.'

'That might equally be said of you and your kind,' said the hylozote. 'You are but flesh and bone and liquid stuff, made up of the elements of world. Yet you are stuff that thinks and moves and expresses its thoughts. I likewise. Remember, all things are of one mind and one soul, which is everywhere. Not all express themselves in ways that you find perceptible. And not all have self-awareness. It is a mistake to hold yourself superior because of that.'

'Point taken,' said Shadd. 'But what of your new name? Is it acceptable to you?'

'Antinomy . . . Antinomy the Hylozote. Yes, it has a certain ring, and is not without irony. I like it. Henceforth that is how I shall be known.'

Shadd turned back to me. 'When gloom threatens to overwhelm me this rocky fellow has the ability to steer my thoughts onto lighter planes, or fascinate me with his notions of the nature of existence. I would not be without him.'

'Then I thank you also, Antinomy,' I said. 'Duke Shadd is dear to me, as he is to many others. I welcome anyone, rock or other, who shares that affection.'

There was a distant shout, from way back up the roadway at Drurn March.

'I gather you were successful,' I said. 'The Khimmurians were driven back.'

130

'With only moments to spare. Many men were killed, both Khimmurian and Chol.'

'And the conspirators?'

'We had to slay most of those we came upon in the gate-house. Some may have been innocents insofar as the conspiracy went, yet they considered us their enemies. Hopefully their deaths will at least not have been in vain, for Drurn March is still in the hands of the Prince Regent. How long he can hold it is another question.'

'What of Commander Odus and his lieutenant, Dade?'

'Odus we trussed up with a notice hung around his neck, telling of his treachery. His fate is now for Fhir Oube to decide. Of Dade I cannot say.'

Kekhi reappeared beside us. 'Rin is back,' she said, and a moment later I glimpsed a dark movement against the sky, and Rin was among us.

'There is a possible way,' he said, crouching beside us. 'We can follow the road down a little further, avoiding the guards, then take to the wild. It will involve some climbing, but nothing too difficult. We will pass close to the camp, but the darkness will hide us and the Khimmurians are presently in uproar due to the events of this night. With care we can avoid them. A deep ravine presents an obstacle. Dinbig will not be able to manage it. But let us get there and then consider the options, for the only alternative is to go through the camp itself, which will involve the risk of Dinbig casting his Veil of Invisibility. We must at all costs be away from here before daylight.'

Blackness, and a sickening lurching as I swung in emptiness, not knowing which way was up, which down. My limbs were locked tight, my jaws clenched in terror. Cold sweat drenched my clothing.

Beneath me my feet dangled in a void, a hundred feet or more above unseen rocks. And somewhere above and behind, in the eastern sky, the first feeble wash of grey was signalling the approach of dawn.

Rin swung again. I closed my eyes as his movement threw me forward, back, tossed me like a cocoon in the wind. I fought down the whimper that rose into my throat. For the one hundredth time – or was it the one thousandth – my stomach threatened to eject its contents.

Rin's voice, strained, in my ear: 'Relax, Dinbig! Relax! Don't look down!'

'Which way is down?' I croaked. My head spun and I had lost all sense of orientation. I groaned. I couldn't help it, this was all so ghastly.

'Loosen your grip! You're choking me,' gasped Rin. 'You need do nothing. Don't even hold on. Just hang there and let me do the work!'

It was true. It was Rin's hands, linked by a short length of rope strapped around each wrist, that gripped the line stretched above our heads. It was he who carried both our weights, who slid and swung inch by tiny inch across that black chasm. How did he do it? Later I would marvel. For now, bound as I was like an oversized knapsack upon his back, I was too ill, too afraid. My life was literally in his hands. I was helpless, caught in a losing battle with my own terror.

It seemed a lifetime that he had been working his way along this taut rope. For hours we had clambered along the steep rocky slope, descending so close to the

Khimmurian camp that I was sure we would be heard if not seen. And all that time it had been me who had to be helped, me who was the burden, the crippled child in the midst of capable grown-ups.

Kekhi had held my arm, telling me of every rut, every stone, every hazard. Yo was immediately before me, while I gripped the strap of his spine-guard. A rope looped beneath my armpits had kept me attached to both Shadd and Rin. Our progress was slow, so slow. The night wore on, moving inexorably towards the dawn.

At last we had veered away from the road and the Khimmurian camp. We ascended higher into the wild crags of the March. And as Rin had forecast we came at length to a deep ravine, a blackness opening at our feet, a nothingness that even I could make out as contrasting with the vague shapes and solids of the land upon which we stood.

We sat down and waited, all but Kekhi and Yo. Shadd wanted to descend into the ravine, but was vetoed by the two Aphesuk. Speed was of the essence, they argued, and his climbing skills could not compare with Kekhi's. It was she who had to go, taking a rope with her over the lip of the sheer face.

And Yo went his own way, for the climb was too severe even for him. His plan was to return by the route we had come until he reached the Khimmurian camp. He would then sneak along beside the road, and once clear ascend to the far side of the chasm and pick up our scent there. We were not to wait for him; he would find us.

An interminable, gut-knotting wait. Rin sat silently, cross-legged, working with a length of fine rope in his lap. Shadd watched, while I sat upon a rock, engrossed in my own dread.

At length Kekhi's rope, one end of which was secured

around a tree beside us, was pulled taut. She had reached the other side.

Rin rose to his feet. With both hands he held out a strange rope contraption that he had made. 'It is time to go, Dinbig. Put this on.'

For a moment I was nonplussed.

'Put your arms through here, your legs here,' explained Rin, and at last I understood. It was a harness!

Shadd showed me where to put my legs, which loops went over my shoulders, which over my back. Rin knelt upon the ground for a few moments in silence, his buttocks resting between his heels. His eyes were closed in an attitude of deep concentration. Then he rose, turned his back and stepped backwards against me. He put his arms through two loose loops of the harness, secured a third across his belly. Following his instructions, Shadd made adjustments, and bound certain parts of the harness with cloth to pad them. Rin bent forward; my feet left the ground. He took a few steps, carrying me upon his back. He reached up and grasped the branch of a tree, then hoisted himself off the ground so that we both swung above the earth.

He lowered himself. 'Good.'

Shadd took wads of cloth and bound them around Rin's hands.

'You need do nothing, Dinbig. It is Rin who has the work. You are just a passenger.'

Only now did I realize what was expected of me. Even more, what was expected of Rin!

Trussed like a gigantic babe upon Rin's back I began to stutter incoherent words of shock and dissent.

'Walk with me!' said Rin, with an air of command.

Together we edged to the lip of the abyss. Kekhi's line extended at waist height, disappearing into the dark. Shadd now fastened rope around Rin's wrists, looping it over the line. This, I understood, was to prevent us falling should Rin's strength give out.

'Bend your knees!' said Rin.

Simultaneously we lowered our bodies at the edge of the abyss. With both hands Rin grasped the taut line. Shadd slapped my back. 'Go well, friend!'

Rin leaned forward and stepped out into space.

We lurched. We seemed to pitch and plunge all at once. Then we were jerked violently back, swinging and tossing helplessly. My stomach came up into my mouth. I almost passed out. A dreadful, involuntary sound issued from between my clamped teeth. I gripped Rin with the fierceness of a rabid hound.

I became aware of Rin, shaking his head and making a throttled noise. I understood that I was strangling him, but my muscles had locked tight. I could not let go. He twisted his head, somehow wedged his chin beneath my forearm, and bit me hard. Slowly the pain got through; I jerked my arm away.

'Do nothing, Dinbig!' urged Rin when he had found his voice. 'Do nothing. You are quite safe.'

I hung there on his back in the blackness, and he commenced, hand over hand, the terrible, endless crossing of that deep abyss.

How long were we in space? I will never know. It seemed like hours. Certainly the light changed. I could make out the vague face of the cliff before us, still such a distance away. Trees were silhouetted against the sky, or emerged as black shapes against the lighter rock. The heights beyond started to emerge out of the gloom. Rin's hoarse breath rasped in my ears. There was no other sound, but for the disconcerting creak of the rope and the fluttering whistle of wind chasing down through the chasm.

A landscape was forming far below. Tumbles of boulders, trees and scrub, an almost sheer slope descending

135

to the valley. And there, far away beneath us, the palisade and the tiny huts and tents clustered within.

Would we be seen? Minute by minute the dawn was gaining strength. We were so far from the Khimmurian camp, yet to an alert sentry scanning the ravine we would surely be visible. I closed my eyes as Rin lurched forward again. And again.

I had not been told by my companions, but it was impossible to gain the far side of the ravine by this method. We were more than halfway across, but now our combined weight had taken us to a level much lower than our objective. I could see Kekhi kneeling at the cliff's edge, anxiously observing our progress. The rope stretched taut away from us at a steeply ascending angle. Rin struggled forward another inch, and another, but with each movement the angle deepened further. I saw that he was beginning to slip back. Only now did it dawn on me that we could go no further.

What now? We seemed doomed, hanging like flightless bats, unable to move forward or back.

'Brace yourself, Dinbig!' warned Rin. And suddenly we were falling, plummeting through empty space.

I shrieked. It was the end.

Yet we were not falling earthwards. Rin still clung to the rope; the far cliff rushed towards us with sickening velocity. We would be smashed upon the rock!

Rin flew, his feet held before him. A sudden, shattering, jarring jolt! I slammed against Rin's body as he collided with the cliff face. He juddered, rolled, spun. I crashed against the rock.

'Reach out, Dinbig! Find a handhold!'

I groped frantically. My fingers closed around a lip of rock. I held fast. Rin did likewise. We clung there like flies.

Seconds later there was a soft slithering sound overhead. I looked around, to see a second rope quivering alongside us. Rin, regaining his breath, reached out and took it.

'Are you all right?'

I nodded, uncertain of my sensations. 'Are you?'

'Yes.'

'What happened? Did the rope break?'

'Shadd released it from the other side. It was the only way. Now we must climb from here.' He passed back the new rope. 'Put this around yourself. I am going to release the harness. Find a foothold on the rock and allow the rope to bear most of your weight.'

He slipped himself free of the harness, then lay back against the rock, his legs stretched wide upon the sheer face. At length he looked at me and grinned.

'I am going up now to join Kekhi. We will then take your weight on the rope and bring you up. You must do some climbing, but it will not be too hard. Take it slowly, and remember, we have your weight. Shadd is climbing down the other side. He will come up here presently to help you. You will soon be on level ground again!'

I was still in no fit state to respond. Rin quickly checked that the rope that held me was secure. Then he winked and was gone, using the original rope to climb upwards with the nimbleness of a monkey.

I clung there for long minutes. In due course I grew aware of a gentle tugging upon my rope. It was my signal to commence climbing. Laboriously, terrified, I began my ascent. In contrast to my companions, I was a happy as a lump-ox on a barn roof.

Again it seemed that hours passed. I felt I had made scarcely any progress. The top of the cliff was beyond my sight. I slipped and scrambled frequently, scraping my skin raw, buffeting and bruising myself. But each time I was saved from certain death by the two Aphesuk, unseen overhead, holding the rope. And then,

quite suddenly, Shadd was at my side. He gave me a
wide grin and gripped my shoulder.

'Well met, Dinbig, old friend. Come, I'll help you the
rest of the way.'

'Even Oldmere was preferable to this!' I muttered,
but I was greatly reassured by his presence. He guided
me from there on, moving my hand or a foot to ledges
and grips that I could not see. We edged our way painfully up that infernal bluff, and at last there were Kekhi
and Rin looking down at us. Rin scrambled down to
grab me; Shadd put his shoulder beneath and pushed
me up. I scrabbled and heaved, and at length was
sprawled at Kekhi's feet upon the grass.

III

We rested only briefly before making our way onwards
into the wilds of Chol. Rin astounded me further. After
the exertions he had put himself through, he merely
knelt in trance for perhaps five minutes, then rose and
declared himself revitalized and ready to travel on.

There was no sign of Yo, but I was not overly concerned. Now that it was light I guessed that he would
take the opportunity to sleep, for the vhazz was by
habit a nocturnal beast. I was fairly confident that in
the darkness he would have encountered minimal
difficulty in slipping by Lord Marsinenicon's camp, and
had little doubt that he would then pick up our trail
with ease. Should that prove not to be, I could always
resort to a summoning to discover his whereabouts.

We moved on, traversing a steep slope into a rugged
valley, back and forth beneath firs and pine. Rin strode
before me, his gait loose and easy, and I watched him
with admiration. His build was not massive, and belied
the sheer strength required to make the crossing of that

chasm with me upon his back. The feat was unmatched by anything in my experience, yet he seemed barely tested by it. Lacking first-hand experience, I had always been intrigued by the many tales related of Aphesuk abilities. I knew them to be an exceptional people, but felt that their larger-than-life reputation might have been exaggerated somewhat by ignorance and imagination. Now any scepticism I had harboured was dispelled. From this day on I would think of these people with a respect that fell little short of awe.

In stark contrast were my feelings towards myself. Rin's feat, and indeed those of Kekhi and Shadd, simply promoted an ever more dismal awareness of my own shortcomings. I could walk ably now, having applied a healing rapture to my swollen toe, yet I was still far and away the slowest and most cumbersome of our party. The others would not leave me, though the importance of their mission demanded that they make the swiftest possible passage. My presence significantly increased the risk of discovery and capture, and I could not see that any useful purpose was gained by their holding back on my behalf. The brutal fact was that I was an unnecessary burden, yet they remained of one voice: they would not go on without me.

Avoiding Khimmurian patrols, occupied townships, outposts and depots, we moved on across Chol. It became depressingly evident that nothing of significance had escaped the Khimmurian yoke. Perhaps a few isolated loyalist bands fought on further to the south, but in the central lands the story was one of consolidation by an invader who knew himself to have full and uncontested control. The others did not voice their thoughts, but I am certain that, like me, they wondered many times about the fortress of Drum March that we had left behind, and the Prince Regent, Fhir Oube, and the impossible choices he faced.

The days were warm, sometimes hot, as spring merged into summer. The land was cloaked in green, rugged and dangerous. As far as possible we kept away from the roads. Kekhi and Rin generally acted as scouts, going ahead of Shadd and me to provide fore-warning of enemy presence and search out possible alternative routes. It struck me one morning that I had not seen Temminee for some days.

'Temminee has left us,' said Shadd. He put his hand into his shirt and brought forth the brilliant twin-stone, the sacred Soul Crystal of the Gwynad. He lifted its chain over his head and held the crystal between his fingers, turning it so that its many facets flashed and sparkled in the sunlight, displaying its brilliant lustre, colour and fire. 'For reasons of her own she has gone back to Enchantery.'

'But why? What is there for her there?'

He smiled a hollow smile. 'What is there anywhere for someone who is the last of her race?'

'Could you not have dissuaded her?'

'She expressed an idea of which I did not wholly approve. Yet I could tell that her mind was already made up. We argued, but she is a free agent and I would not prevent her from choosing her own course. I regret that we parted on a note of discord.'

Shadd turned and looked me directly in the eye. His lips were compressed, and in those mysterious wide eyes I discerned an unfathomable expression which left me mystified and – after his next words – deeply disturbed: 'From what she has said, it is now my belief that she intends to betray me.'

'In what manner?'

He continued to stare at me. His face was haggard, but now I thought there was a look of worldworn amusement. 'Temminee believes in Destiny,' he said in a melancholic voice.

140

'I don't understand.'

'Do any of us?'

With that he grew silent. No matter my urgings, he would say nothing more on the subject. We marched on as the sun passed its zenith and began its descent into the long afternoon.

IV

Two days later disaster struck.

Kekhi appeared with disconcerting suddenness on the trail immediately before us. She told us that the way ahead was blocked, and we moved with her cautiously up through the woods to a low ridge. Here Rin lay prone in the grass, observing the road some distance away across a flat valley floor.

For as far as I could see to left and right the road was clogged with a long column of troops moving baggage and supplies south. Their passage was hampered by hundreds and hundreds of people trudging slowly in the opposite direction. These citizens, under the guidance of Khimmurian soldiers, pushed heavily laden carts or drove pack-animals and livestock, or simply carried loads upon their backs. Sentries were posted in pairs along the sides of the road at frequent intervals. Some kind of way-station had been set up, and it appeared that every person who wished to pass along that road was being checked by Khimmurian guards before being allowed to move on. It was plain that we would not be able to cross the road without waiting both for nightfall and for the two columns to pass.

It was still early morning. We moved back into the woods and established a bivouac. My companions were anxious to gain intelligence concerning this major movement of troops and citizens, and to discover if it

141

was possible to cross the road further to the north or south. I was left alone, having been cautioned not to move from our campsite, which was well concealed in a damp gully overgrown with ferns, bushes and small trees, and not easily approached.

I prepared some food for a meal later on, but soon grew restive and decided to climb back up to the edge of the woods to observe again the train on the road. Still well hidden in the trees, I was able to view the troop movements from a safe distance. But I was too far away to discern much detail, and watching thousands of folk pass slowly along a road a long way off soon proved to be less than diverting. I wandered back into the woods, explored a little way while keeping at all times within easy reach of the gully and our campsite.

I came upon a wide, shallow stream beneath the trees, and sat down to rest and soak my feet. My thoughts were on many things, but eventually came to dwell upon Yo. The days had passed and he should by now have caught up with us. I was somewhat concerned, and it seemed the most advisable course to summon him now in order to discover the reason for his delay.

I withdrew my feet from the water and made myself comfortable upon the grass. Concentrating my inner faculties I familiarized myself with my surroundings, then dissolved the world. I entered trance, rose out of my corporeal form and summoned Yo.

At first there was no response. I felt a weight of misgiving. Tardy arrivals had characterized his appearances before, had been the precursor of mischiefs and egregious transgressions, culminating in my bloody encounter with the Orl Kilroth on Holdikor's Bridge in Twalinieh. After all that we had been through, was the cycle to begin over again?

142

I had no time for further thought. Yo manifested.

'Master, I am here.'

'Yo, I was concerned. You have not caught up with our party, though you have had ample time. And now I can't help but note that you are laggardly in your response to my summons.'

'Master, I will explain. The fault is not mine on either count. It is the vhazz. After I left you upon the precipice and made my way back down towards the soldiers' camp I found myself quite suddenly beset by sore and debilitating bewilderment. I crept most unhappily by the camp, possessed by a most dreadful longing and an irrepressible urge to return, back the other way, into Enchantery. I wept, without being fully able to divine the reason why. I felt that an abyss had opened within me, a most terrible, desolate void. And I felt too that I was being called. With every step that I took to be reunited with you, the urge grew stronger to turn around and go back. It became so overpowering that I could not fight it. I turned and went back. Then greater conflict, for I knew that this could not be right. I turned again, back to the west in order to follow you. Yet I was further beset by a turmoil of indecision. And so have my days been characterized. I go first one way, then turn and retrace my steps, then grow ever more anguished and turn back again. Suffice to say that I get nowhere in either direction, and my confusion and bewilderment grow. Master, I can only conclude that this is the nature of the vhazz, whose head hangs low and whose tail clings hard to its belly. For it is not I who propel myself backward and forward so unprofitably. Indeed, I wish for nothing more than to be back at your side, but I can exert little control over this distraught beast.'

I silenced a curse. I had never thought to explain. 'Forgive me, Yo; it should have occurred to me. The

143

vhazz is by nature an animal of the pack. It knows a powerful sense of community and identity with its family-group, and has an innate dread of solitary existence. The body that you occupy was formerly a male vhazz who went by the name of Huwoorsk. He came from a large pack which had been hunted incessantly by men. In the hope of finding a safer abode the pack moved east into Qotolr. There a terrible massacre took place. Every member of the pack, all excepting Huwoorsk and a handful of others, was killed. Hours later the others died in combat, leaving Huwoorsk alone. The vhazz, even more than humans, does not know how to be alone. Its very being rebels against the condition. Thus you experience great anguish. I can offer little solace, other than to say that the calling you perceive from Enchantery is insidious. Huwoorsk's pack is no more. None survived. I know, for, you will recall, I was Huwoorsk. Thus, you must resist it. There is nothing for you in Enchantery.'

'It explains much,' said Yo disconsolately. 'But something else confuses me. A day ago I became convinced that there existed another vhazz pack not too far distant. I could not ignore this feeling. It grew and grew within me and eventually I diverted myself to go in search of them. I came close to them, I sensed it. Then suddenly I was confronted by three male vhazz. Though I tried to talk to them, they were quite hostile. It seems I am an outcast. They set upon me with unambiguous ferocity and drove me off. Now I'm alone again, and even more bewildered.'

'You were not of their pack, Yo. You are an outsider. They will not accept you.'

There was a small untruth here. Yo might have been accepted had he managed to explain his pitiful circumstances to the elder sisters of the pack. But what purpose could that serve? He was, after all, an entity of the Realms, not a true vhazz. He would be no happier among vhazz than was I. His chances were far better if he stuck with me.

'I am distressed,' said Yo plaintively.

'Where are you now, Yo?'

'I don't know, Master. I seem to have travelled many miles in as many directions. I could be anywhere.'

I gave a sigh. 'Yo, somehow you must pick up my trail and find your way back to me. Can you do that?'

'I will try.'

'Remember what I have said, and permit yourself no diversion. Fight the vhazz nature. It is tyrannical, but you must learn to better it. You are Yo, an entity of the Realms. You are not vhazz. Recite that to yourself at all times.'

'Yes, Master. You referred also to my lateness in responding to your summons. Again, it is the vhazz that is to blame. The creature fights to prevent me leaving its body.'

'Yes, I recall that that is so.'

'I will be glad when . . .'

He spoke no more. He uttered a sudden shriek and cried out, 'Master, help! What is happening?'

At the same time I felt something shift dangerously in the ethereal flux of reality in which we rested between the corporeal and the Realms. I glimpsed movement about me, things almost indiscernible, and felt myself under the influence of some potent, intangible force. Instantly I adopted a defensive posture.

'We are attacked! Yo, return to the body immediately!'

I sensed the drag as I was pulled against my will, away from the corporeal into First Realm. I fought back, but my assailants were strong, and there seemed to be many of them. I reached inwards and in desperation sent forth a summons to my Guardian Entity, Gaskh.

145

He was there upon the moment, and needed no instruction. With the fury of a vengeful demon he was among the entities that assailed me. Lashing, howling, roaring, Gaskh scattered them and drove them back. Though he was unable to manifest fully in the between-world in which we hovered, the same was also true of the entities. I felt their power over me diminish and was able to draw back towards my flesh.

'Gaskh, have a care for yourself! I am returning to my form!'

'I am not at risk,' Gaskh called. 'These things are puny. But more are summoned. Begone, Master, before it is too late.'

I withdrew. I entered my empty body and opened my eyes. The air seemed almost to sizzle around me, but I was no longer menaced. I quickly donned my boots and made to leave.

I was profoundly disconcerted by the attack. It implied an extraordinary vigilance. I had not rent the fabric to pass into First Realm, and my summons to Yo had been brief. That the minions of the Vulpasmage should have responded so swiftly and accurately to so insignificant a ripple outside the normal pale of their domain was a cause for immense concern. How far had the Vulpasmage's influence in the Realms extended?

I had only gone a few paces from the stream back towards the camp when I became aware that I was no longer alone. A voice called from somewhere in the trees. Then another. I heard the drumming of hooves and the chink of harness. I glimpsed shapes moving. Men on horseback galloped through the dappled shadows.

'He is here somewhere!' came a hoarse shout from my left.

I dropped to one knee, then turned and made a dash back the way I had come.

'There!'

Riders broke out of the brush on the other side of the stream. They put heels to flanks and galloped towards me. There was nowhere to run. In moments I was surrounded.

They were Khimmurian and numbered about a dozen in all. Their captain was a tall, bearded Sulerinan with veined purple cheeks, a crooked nose and mean black eyes. He leaned back in his saddle and surveyed me. 'Well, what have we here?'

I considered a rapture of All-Embracing Terror. Normally it was too localized and of insufficient power to affect more than four or five persons at the most, but it struck me that it might well throw a panic into the horses and provide me with an opportunity to escape in the subsequent disarray.

As my thoughts raced, my eyes fell upon a civilian wearing dark robes who sat among the soldiers. My heart fell. I recognized him; he was *Zan-Chassin*.

His name was Egil – Molpaton Egil – and he hailed from Hissik in the province of Selaor. Some four years earlier I had officiated at his First Realm initiation.

Though he stared at me with evident curiosity, Egil appeared not to have recognized me. I recalled that at the time of his initiation I had been dressed in full ceremonial garb, with my face adorned in the customary manner. Moreover, I took some comfort in the knowledge that my appearance had changed quite markedly since then. But I little doubted from the swiftness with which these soldiers had located me that it was this fellow who had pinpointed my position.

How strong was he? Man to man I was confident that I could best him in a duel of *Zan-Chassin* abilities. But in this situation I would inevitably be cut down by the soldiers as I concentrated upon Egil. I could not win. It seemed at that moment preferable to play innocent and keep my magic to myself.

I was disconcerted by Egil's presence here. Coincidence seemed improbable. More likely that the Vulpasmage was deploying *Zan-Chassin* collaborators among his troops. It would be a canny strategy. They would be trained specifically in nullification or repulsion techniques, diminishing the effects of magic unleashed against them or the soldiers they accompanied. Furthermore, they would be spying the Realms, alert for summonings or journeyings. Hence, by the sheer fact of being in proximity to Molpaton Egil, I had given myself away when I summoned Yo. Egil's eyes, showing traces of trance-blear, supported this.

Two men dropped from their horses and seized me. They quickly stripped me of weapons and belongings. My arms were bound with rope, I was gagged, slung over the back of a mount and lashed fast.

'Bring him,' ordered the Sulerinan, twisting his horse around. 'The rest of you search the area. He may not be alone.'

With the Sulerinan, Egil and three other troopers, I was taken back through the woods and down towards the road and the Khimmurian way-station.

V

The soldiers drove their horses through the press of people queueing to pass the sentry-post, lashing out indiscriminately with horse-whips to clear a way. Beside the road was a wooden stockade where a number of huts had been erected. We entered and halted outside one of these. I was untied, taken down from the horse, and marched into the hut to be brought before the officer-in-command.

148

He, summoned from a meal, came into the room in a foul humour and appraised me as he would a cur. He was a short, stocky man, sallow of skin, with thick, dark eyebrows and a harsh, wild look in his eye. He was accompanied by an adjutant who strode to a make-shift desk in the centre of the room and took up a ledger lying there.

'Name?' snapped the officer.

'Valno,' I replied. The adjutant wrote it down.

'Nationality?'

I hesitated. 'Chol.'

The officer eyed me keenly and his voice took on a more purposeful tone. 'Place of birth?'

'I don't know.'

'Why were you spying upon us?'

'Sir, I was not spying. I am a traveller, nothing more. Please, I have done nothing wrong. Let me go. I can offer you no harm.'

'Pah!' He gave a snort of derision. 'You were watching us, and by all accounts used magic.'

'I am no magician,' I said. 'Someone has made a mistake.'

Molpaton Egil, who had accompanied us into the hut, spoke up. 'He lies. He reeks of magic. There is no mistake. He was responsible for the summoning.'

I protested. 'I assure you it is not so. I came across others skulking in the woods. Doubtless they are the ones you seek. For my part, I am simply a poor man making my way north in the hope of finding work.'

'A poor man who avoids roads, and who carries Khimmurian arms and wears Khimmurian armour,' said the officer, his voice rising in pitch.

'I took these from the bodies of soldiers I found dead beside the road.'

He gave me a look of disgust and turned to the Suleri-nan who stood beside me. 'Put him with the others,

149

but make a special note of the circumstances under which he arrived here. At East Camp Five they can decide what to do with him.' He looked back to me. 'I fear it is the worst for you, my one-handed spy. A cripple is of little use in a slave-gang. If the work doesn't kill you, your workmates will. Your handicap will prevent them achieving their quota, so they will not eat as long as you are among them. But that is by the by, for my real opinion is that you will not survive interrogation. There is far more to you than you are admitting, but it is not my job to squeeze it out of you. At East Camp Five they will have you squawking the truth in no time, mark my words. Take him away.'

I was marched outside and deeper into the stockade to the rear of a row of huts where a party of sorry-looking individuals sat upon the ground, guarded by a pair of slouching sentries. There were about twenty in all, and they looked to be Chol in the main. Each had an iron collar around his neck, from which ran a light chain which linked him to the next man. Around their ankles were iron shackles on short chains.

At our approach a short, bald, muscle-packed fellow in a brown leather tunic rose from where he was squatting beside the group.

'One more for you, Telm,' declared one of my guards. 'This one's a special.'.

Telm, who was hardly taller than a dwarf, looked up at me, cocking his wide, square head and stretching his lips across broken, discoloured teeth in an unpleasant leer.

'Sit,' he commanded, pointing to a spot beside the other captives.

He produced an iron collar, chain and shackles and clamped them around my neck and ankles. 'Say nothing, do nothing, except follow orders, and you will suffer no harm from me. Cause trouble and I will cut off your balls.'

Telm made off on bowed legs. My guards departed. I looked around me hopelessly. The fellow next to me had his head hung towards the floor and did not look my way. Others briefly caught my eye, but quickly averted their gaze. I sensed that this was not the time to try and gain information. I observed the sentries who guarded us. They did not appear to be particularly watchful, but they hardly needed to be. We could move only *en masse*, and with the greatest difficulty, and there were soldiers by the dozen around the stockade. A short distance away Telm squatted on a low hummock of earth, watching me with a cynical grin. And beyond was Molpaton Egil, leaning in an attitude of nonchalance against the side of a hut. He too was observing me, and made no attempt to disguise his interest. I looked away, fighting back my despair. Soon, I knew, by one means or another, I must be found out.

Half an hour passed and we were split into groups and loaded into wagons. The tarpaulin of the wagon in which I found myself along with nine others was drawn closed and tied. Outside there was much activity. I gathered a troop of soldiers was being assembled to escort us. Presently, with a lurch, the wagon drew away.

We travelled for several hours. I had no means of assessing direction or whereabouts. Slowly the daylight that filtered through the tarpaulin faded. Night was descending. The interior of the wagon, cramped and stuffy and reeking of the bodily odours of my companions, gradually became dark.

I had attempted conversation with the others. My nearest neighbour, I discovered, was named Aladron. He was a Chol, a labourer who had been taken forcibly from his village, along with most other able-bodied males, when the Khimmurians rode in. Opposite was a burly fellow called Chavun, likewise Chol. He spoke with a tremor in his voice, relating how he had been forced to witness the rape and murder of his wife and young daughter by a group of soldiers. His two youngest children had been carried off, he knew not where, and he had been brutally beaten and roped into the slave-gang. The others told similar stories. Most had already spent weeks, if not months, labouring under Khimmurian domination on some work project or other. Now it seemed that they, along with many others, were being moved to a new location.

East Camp Five, I gathered, was one of many Khimmurian slave-camps, generally set up in the vicinity of a fortified village or township. None knew its precise location, nor what manner of labour we might expect to find ourselves engaged in once we arrived. For my part, I remembered the words of the Khimmurian officer that morning. I did not expect to find myself working with any of these fellows.

None of my companions seemed inclined to speak further. All were weary, their spirits broken. They sat in gloomy silence, absorbed in their miseries, as the wagon rattled and jarred along its unseen way.

At last we stopped. After a pause of some minutes the tarpaulin was untied and drawn back. A soldier barked an order to unload.

We clambered out, stiff and sore. It was pitch dark and we could see virtually nothing of our surroundings. Nearby a group of soldiers stood around a blazing fire.

'Sit!' ordered our guard.

We waited as the wagon-driver cooked meat and vegetables in a thick broth which bubbled inside a huge round pot on the fire. Another ten captives from the second wagon were brought and made to sit alongside us. Tired and hungry, we were forced to watch in silence as our guards then ate their fill and swigged ale from wooden tankards. At last they had done, and as they made to depart one of them called to us, 'There is food here. Eat your fill!'

Nervously we climbed to our feet and shuffled towards the dying fire. There was scarcely anything left in the pot bar a few scraps and leaves floating in a watery mess. Certainly it would not feed twenty of us. Yet it was all we had. Some scraps of bread had been left on the earth near the fire, and some carrot tops and discarded lettuce leaves. These vegetables we threw into the pot, and using the bread to scoop, made what we could of the meagre meal.

Done, we were permitted to relieve ourselves in the bushes, then loaded back into the wagons where we were to spend the night. As I made to climb aboard, I felt the pressure of a hand upon my shoulder, and turned to see Molpaton Egil beside me, smiling like a fox, his dark eyes reflecting the fire.

'I am watching you closely,' said he. 'Be warned, I will not permit you to make trouble, so forget your magical mischiefs. You interest me, and I have an intuition that my reward for delivering you will be substantial.'

With that he gave a nod to someone standing behind me. I made to turn my head, to see who this person was. I felt a sudden, resounding pain at the back of my skull. There was a violent flashing, and a fuzzy roar. My legs gave way; the world rushed away from me.

A sensation of falling.

Then nothing.

VI

I was slumped upon the floor of the wagon, an excruciating pain stabbing across the back of my skull and down my neck. My spine was twisted awkwardly, my iron collar bit into my shoulder and jaw. I was half smothered by the body of one of my travelling companions, who was sprawled sleeping across me. We were moving, the wagon bumping and shaking along a hard road.

With difficulty I managed to squirm free and sit up.

The movement of the wagon made me feel sick. Light was visible through the tarpaulin. Beyond that I could tell nothing.

Chavun's eyes were on me. He leaned forward to pass me something. 'I saved it for you. They gave us these and some water at dawn.'

I took the object he held. It was a large, round biscuit, baked hard. I thanked him and put the biscuit into my shirt. 'I will save it. For now I would prefer the water.'

Chavun shook his head. 'There was nothing to keep it in. I'm sorry.'

'How long have we been travelling?'

'About two hours. Maybe more.'

And so the day wore on. We stopped once, for another inadequate meal and a few minutes to stretch our limbs. Molpaton Egil lurked always somewhere within my line of vision. I felt that he was daring me to try something, and I held back. Something about this fellow troubled me deeply. Though he was of a lower level than me, my experience in summoning Yo had made me very cautious. Could Egil summon forth entities that were not his own – the allies or minions of others? The implications were alarming.

We travelled on. Dusk drew in and the routine was repeated. As we shuffled back to the wagon after gulping down our pathetic provisions, Egil sidled up to me once more.

I raised my hand. 'If you intend to disable me again, do so by some less painful means.'

He grinned a mirthless grin. 'What would you suggest?'

'Surely you can render me senseless with magic?'

'Ho! And surely you have defences to negate it? No, Valno, or whatever you choose to call yourself. Don't take me for a fool. I know your value, and I am alert to your wiles.'

He nodded to a soldier beside him. I glimpsed a movement as the soldier raised the pommel of his sword. Again the searing pain, the flash of bright lights, the lurching descent into oblivion.

At some point during the afternoon of the following day the painful monotony of our journey was interrupted. I heard shouts from outside. The wagon-driver called out. The wagon lurched to a halt, then jerked roughly forward and back. Horses whinnied in fear, and the shouting was multiplied. I heard our driver striving to control his horses, then he gave a strange grunt. A moment later he toppled back against the tarpaulin. A dark stain formed on the outside of the thick material. Moments later blood began to run inside onto the floor of the wagon.

The driver's thrashings and struggling at length caused the tarpaulin to rip free of its moorings. The man tumbled inside to land writhing at our feet. He clawed at an arrow protruding from his chest, his face contorted with pain, his eyes imploring.

We stared stupefied, and outside the sounds of battle raged. At last I snapped out of my shock and clambered to my feet. I roused the others with shouts and slaps, for I could not move without them. I bent and took the knife that the dying driver had at his belt. Stepping to the back of the wagon I cut the ties on the tarpaulin and peered out.

Khimmurian soldiers knelt behind rocks and bushes some yards off. They discharged arrows at assailants I could not see. Ignoring the driver I climbed out of the wagon. The others followed.

Now I saw the raiders. There were thirty at least. Archers were concealed among trees on both sides of the road. Mounted fighters and others on foot bearing swords and axes charged down upon our Khimmurian escort. Several Khimmurians lay dead or wounded. The rest were pinned down by the raiders.

A horseman galloped towards us. He brought his mount to a halt, pointing, 'Quickly, into the woods!'

A Khimmurian rushed at him, sword raised. The horseman wheeled, warding off the blow, and brought his own sword down from above. The blade bit through the man's helmet and clove his skull in two. But a second soldier appeared from around the side of the wagon. He stabbed up at the horseman. The rider deflected the blow, but the Khimmurian's sword glanced off the man's thigh-guard and penetrated his horse's neck. The horse reared with a scream, throwing its rider from the saddle.

The man fell, and lay for a moment winded upon the ground. The Khimmurian raised his sword and rushed forward to finish him off. Without thinking, I stepped in and lunged with the wagon-driver's knife, stabbing deep into the Khimmurian's back. The man yelled and arched his spine. He spun around, clutching at his back. I slid the knife free and sank it into his belly. He gurgled, bubbles of blood foaming upon his lips, and toppled.

The horseman was on his feet. He acknowledged my action with an appreciative nod, then pointed again. 'That way!'

Hampered by our chains we made for the woods. Further along the road I glimpsed similar actions as captives fled from the second wagon. The raiders were doing all they could to aid them, and others now rushed to cover us as we struggled to flee.

The Khimmurians had withdrawn into a knot beside the road. Well disciplined, they were able to hold their attackers at bay, but were incapable of preventing our escape. We reached the cover of the trees. The horseman rode up beside us again. 'That way!'

Two men, weapons drawn, came running with urgent gestures to us to move in the same direction. They flanked us as we shuffled frantically onward, deeper into the woods and away from the carnage beside the road.

Presently the two bade us halt. We could no longer hear the battle behind us. We huddled, bewildered and out of breath. Another man appeared. He carried a heavy iron hammer and a chisel.

'Over here,' he said, indicating a large flat boulder. We lined up and one by one he struck through the chains that hobbled us, then those that linked us together. The other prisoners were arriving, accompanied by the fighting-men who had raided the wagons. Some were bloody; one or two were quite badly wounded. All were freed of their chains. Though the iron collars and shackles on our ankles remained, we were at least able to walk freely.

'Don't worry, lads,' one of the Chol assured us. 'It will all come off in time. But for now, let's get away from here. Stay with us.'

Following our liberators we moved off deeper into the shade of the forest.

It turned out that our rescuers were Chol, remnants of the nation's Third Army which, under the Prince Regent Fhir Oube, had been defeated more than two months earlier when Khimmurian forces first poured across their borders from north and west. These regular soldiers were supplemented by men, plus women and children, who had fled their homes to avoid the Khimmurians. A dozen or so Miragoffian soldiers, whose nation had fallen much earlier, also made up their number.

We were taken to their camp and our irons struck off. We were given food and drink, and when we had eaten, were addressed by their leader. He was a captain of the Chol army who went by the name of Dagril. He was a tall, laconic fellow, aged perhaps thirty-five, with wide shoulders, deep chest and narrow waist. His hair was long and black, his skin pale, with eyes of piercing blue. He carried himself with loose, confident movements, and conveyed a natural air of command. I could well see that he was a capable and inspiring leader.

'It is my pleasure to tell each of you that you are now free men,' said Dagril, standing before us with his feet set firmly apart, his hands upon his hips. 'Join with me and my loyal fighters if you will, to bear arms against these bastard dogs of Khimmur, or go your own way. The choice is yours. Be warned, neither way is easy. Khimmur has might, which we lack. But we fight, day by day, with the knowledge that every Khimmurian heart that is pierced by a Chol sword is a step towards freedom. Chol crawls with the filth of Khimmur and her base allies. You know already that it is a dangerous place. If you choose to leave, it will be with my blessing, but you will go alone. We cannot protect you.'

Most opted to remain with Dagril. They were Chol, after all, and their homes had been destroyed, their families were gone. They had nowhere else to go. For my part, I could only go onwards.

158

When an opportunity presented itself I spoke to Dagril, and told him of my choice.

'Which way do you go, then, my friend?' he enquired.

'West.'

'Into the Magoth?'

'If it must be.'

He looked at me curiously, but said nothing.

'It is possible that I may have information that will be of interest to you,' I said. 'Do you know anything of the fate of your Prince Regent, Fhir Oube?'

Dagril averted his gaze into the middle distance and spoke in a toneless voice. 'He may have died in the first battle, though some say he survived and rode south to join the Second Army. It is impossible to say. Do you know something?'

'Fhir Oube is in Drurn March fortress, by the Qotol border. He is under siege by a large Khimmurian force led by Lord Marsinenicon of Rishal.'

Dagril's eyebrows lifted and he directed a penetrating look at me. 'How do you know this?'

'I was coming from Drurn March when I was captured.'

'How long ago?'

'A week or so. The Prince Regent was betrayed by his garrison commander, one Odus. He almost suffered defeat. Fortunately, through the agency of friends of mine, Fhir Oube was alerted and the conspiracy foiled. To my knowledge he remains in the fortress, but his resources are low. His cousin, Count Vess, has been killed, along with many of his men in a battle on the Coul Road.'

Dagril pursed his lips. 'I can do nothing. West, south and north the Khimmurians hold all roads. I have hardly more than one hundred fighting-men, and we are limited to operating within this small region.'

'Where precisely are we?' I asked.

'This is the fringe of the Magoth. Go that way and you enter Virland. South, beyond the bastards' outposts, are the plains of Ashakite.'

Then inadvertently my captors had brought me further along my way. My journey had scarcely been delayed by their intervention.

'You speak of friends,' said Dagril. 'Where are they?'

'We were separated when I was captured. They will be following, of that I am sure. Should you meet them, though I doubt that you will, be good enough to tell them that I am safe and have continued on my way.'

'What are their names?'

'I cannot tell you that.'

He nodded solemnly. 'Can I not persuade you to remain with us?'

'Of what use is a one-armed man?'

Dagril gave a half-grin. 'Every hand is one more that can wield a weapon against our foe.'

'I wish I could remain, but I am on a journey of great importance. I cannot delay.'

'The Magoth is not your destination, then, Valno?'

(Even with these, my rescuers, I had deemed it prudent to keep my identity secret.)

'I am seeking the freedom-fighters of Mystoph and Khimmur. Have you any news of Lord Shimeril Mi' Vhuda, or Yzwul, the former Lord of Tiancz?'

Dagril regarded me intently. I sensed he was giving careful consideration to his words. 'Their efforts are known to us, though we have had no direct contact. Quite recently they were operating within Virland, though in the west, close to Khimmur's border. Beyond that I cannot say.'

'Nor would you if you could.'

'Quite so. You are Khimmurian, then, Valno?'

I took my heart in my hand. 'I am.'

160

He nodded shrewdly. 'Yet you kill Khimmurians in defence of Chol.'

'Would that I did not have to, yet that is the way of it. I am a bitter enemy of the Beast of Rull.' Silently I thanked Moban that I had killed that soldier earlier. His death was my passport out of here. 'I will be forever indebted to you for liberating me from my captors, Dagril. Had you not intervened I would have been found out eventually. I do not pretend great bravery, nor a resistance to prolonged torture.'

'Found out?'

Again I entrusted my fate to this man. 'There are things I may not speak of, other than to Shimeril or Yzwul. I hope you will not ask me more.'

Dagril pursed his lips, his eyes upon me, then looked away into the trees. 'The Magoth is formidable, inhabited by strange peoples and other denizens we know nothing of. Not even Khimmur was successful in forging a way through. If it is your choice to go that way I will not prevent you. I wish you well, Valno. Your journey will not be an easy one.'

6

I

I left the Chol camp the following morning. I was led blindfold deep into the forest by two of Dagril's men. They guided me for more than an hour, then at last halted and removed the blindfold.

We stood in a small clearing surrounded by huge twisted oaks and towering elms. One of my guides handed me a belt which held a light sword in a scabbard and a dagger and hunting-knife in a sheath. 'From Dagril,' he said. 'This also.'

He passed me a knapsack and a small leather pouch. Inside the knapsack I found basic provisions sufficient to sustain me for some days; in the pouch were a few copper and silver coins.

'Tell Dagril I am once more indebted to him.'

The fellow raised an arm and pointed into the dimness beneath the trees. A vague trail could just be made out, twisting around a thicket of blackthorn. 'That way is west. The trail peters out after a mile or so. I can say nothing more, other than to wish you good luck.'

We shook hands, and I will confess I was tempted to change my mind and return to Dagril's camp. Instead I turned and walked slowly into the forest.

Almost immediately I was in near-darkness: the canopy was so dense that the sunlight could not penetrate to the forest floor. I hesitated a moment, allowing my eyes to adjust, and cursed providence for delivering me here alone. I moved on.

The trail, as my escort had said, remained true for a

distance of about a mile, then it ended abruptly at the base of a moss-covered outcrop of rock. I detoured around the rock, pushed on through a thicket of alders, struggled through dense creepers, waded across a stream. My progress was slow and I quickly worked up a sweat. I wondered again about the wisdom of my choice.

My plan, vague though it was, was to head in a southerly direction. I knew from Dagril that approximately thirty miles in that direction the great shroud of the Magoth would begin to thin as it gave on to the northernmost limit of the Plains of Ashakite. There, keeping to the edge of the forest, I ought to be able to move with greater ease. There was risk of running into far-roaming bands of Ashakite tribesmen, though they didn't generally come so far north. Khimmur was perhaps a greater threat, but I hazarded a guess that she was not making extensive use of the plains, at least not this far from her own border. According to Dagril, a Khimmurian force had clashed with Ashakite tribesmen some months earlier, and had not fared well. Whatever the risk, I knew that I could go no other way. The Magoth was vast, its heart impenetrable. I would become hopelessly lost and wander blindly until exhaustion, infirmity, or some roving beast or wood-spirit claimed me. I had to find a more navigable way.

I came upon a dry stream-bed which had formed a channel between the great boles of the trees. It cut towards the south and I was able to walk along it for some distance, finding it easier than struggling through dense thickets, up steep banks and rocky shoulders. Eventually the bed curved away towards the east and I was obliged to take to the trackless forest way again. So difficult was my passage, and so often did I have to twist and turn to avoid obstacles of one kind or another, that I soon lost all sense of direction. But from time to time I stumbled into a glade or natural clearing – once even emerging into an area in which several trees had been felled by axe and removed – and in these I was able to gaze up to the sky and gauge my bearings from the position of the sun.

I spied wild animals and birds from time to time. None were large enough to menace me. Once I heard the thrashing of something huge lumbering through the undergrowth some way ahead. I halted and waited, listening tensely. The noise receded into the distance and was superseded by a quite eerie silence.

I glanced often behind me, for I was haunted by a sensation of being followed. I had only a vague presentiment to support this, and put it down to an overactive imagination prompted by gloomy solitude and the direful Magoth. Yet I could not rid myself of it and at times had to struggle with myself to fight down an almost paralysing fear.

At around midday I paused in a small clearing formed around a toppled oak furnished with ornate shelves of fungus. Seated in sunlight upon the fallen bole, my back resting against roots that were thicker than my torso, I ate from the provisions in my knapsack. I drank clear water from a fast-running stream, rested a few more minutes, then carried on.

I was fortunate in some respects, inasmuch as the terrain here was comparatively easy. Though I came upon steep rocky slopes, and vegetation-choked gullies or ravines, all of which had to be negotiated one way or another, they were not of the character of the landscape further west. There, in Virland's heart, sheer, forest-clad peaks and crags soared, and sudden plummeting ravines gaped, while raging torrents, tributaries of the great White River to the north, swept through them.

When eventually the light became too dim to see by I slumped exhausted to the ground at the base of a tall, leaning, moss-clad slab of granite which loomed out of a cluster of foxgloves. Beneath the rock was a rude shelter, and into this I crawled. I ate quickly, then gathered dry moss and lay down and was soon asleep.

I was awoken in the middle of the night by a terrible shriek. It came from somewhere close by, and as I sat up, frozen with fear, I seemed to still hear it reverberating into the distance. My hand clutched the hilt of my sword. Not twenty paces away there was a loud crashing and violent snapping of undergrowth. The darkness was intense and I could see nothing, not even my hand in front of me. But something was approaching, lumbering through the thick wood towards where I sat.

The ground shook as massive feet thumped up close to the rock under which I hid. The creature, whatever it was, halted. It was mere feet away, beyond the foxgloves. Its stentorian breathing came from overhead, a sound like colossal bellows. At times I thought I felt the hot vapour of its breath upon my skin, and smelt the stink of meat digesting in its belly. I waited, not breathing, expecting at any moment a looming shadow, something I would never know, a long, clawed arm that would reach in and pluck me from my nook. But the thing moved on again, bending and crushing bushes and small trees as it went. An aeon passed. I lay down again, but slept hardly a wink for the remainder of that night.

With the first glimmer of light I was up and on my way once more. Outside my den I came upon the gruesome remains of a meal: the head, claws and a few discarded bones of a black bear. The beast had been torn to pieces. I shuddered, and wondered once again what manner of creature had visited me last night.

I climbed a low rise and gained a sense of the hidden sun's ascent, then pushed on in the direction I calculated to be south. My passage was much as the previous day, but I was more tired and an oppression was beginning to grow within me. The Magoth, so interminably dim, resistant and unending. The rank, pungent odours of rotting vegetation and muck. Damp tendrils of moss and vine, cloying, clutching at my face and limbs. Roots, brambles and fallen branches tripping me. I had covered only a few miles since entering the forest. It would take days to reach Ashakite, and then what? On foot it was a long and by no means easy journey to Khimmur's frontier.

I was uneasy in my mind, wondering ceaselessly about Yo, about Shadd and his two Aphesuk companions, about the *Zan-Chassin*. And often the image of my faithful Rohse formed before me, and beside her my little copper-curled daughter, Eroniss. It was the thought of that child, whose face I had seen but once, that kept me going through my darkest moments. For many times, entangled in briars, slipping or rolling down some crumbling earth-bank, stumbling over some stray root, many times I lay down and wept and longed to give up. But prostrate there in the depths of my despair, it was the vision of that little girl that pulled me up, that forced my feet into motion again, that kept me fighting. Eroniss, more than anything else, was the reason this fight had to be fought. She was the future. Her innocent green eyes had gazed just once into my own, but I had seen there everything that could be. I knew I had a purpose. It was my daughter's world, a child's world, that I was fighting to preserve. It had been permeated and debased by the stench of evil, but it could not be permitted to die. Not as long as men still had the power to dream.

Soon after midday the conviction that I was being watched began to grow again. This time it was stronger. Once, glancing up into the trees, I saw something leap from a branch and slip out of sight. I had caught only a glimpse and could not be sure of anything, but I believed it was vaguely human. Apes lived in the forest; many other things too. I waited, alert, but saw nothing more.

I had entered a particularly dense area. Huge grey tree trunks towered close all about me. They stretched straight upwards like monumental stone columns in some great temple. Their first leaves appeared only a long way overhead, and the ground beneath was relatively clear, for little could grow in this shade. The gloom cast a weight upon my spirit.

I sat down to eat. As I reached into my knapsack something touched my head.

A light weight fell over me. I leapt instantly to my feet, reaching to draw my sword. I found myself caught in a fine net. Like a fool I struggled. Something came from behind and pushed me hard, knocking me to the floor again. There was a strange gibbering sound from overhead. I felt myself lifted from the ground. Suspended in the net, I was hauled up into the trees.

I thrashed wildly but could not break free. Now I was too far from the ground for any hope of escape. As I broke through the foliage I caught a glimpse of faces overhead, hideous, inquisitive, vaguely man-like. Nimble, semi-naked bodies ran or swung among the branches. I was hauled up towards a massive bough. Then something sharp dug painfully into my thigh. I cried out. Dexterous fingers worked to secure the net beneath the bough. I dangled there in mid-air, watched by half a dozen curious faces. I felt drowsy. Warm and comfortable. Heavy. Why struggle? My limbs no longer wanted to move. My eyes closed, retaining the vision of a row of inquisitive faces staring down at me.

I was no longer concerned. I floated away into a deep, dreamless sleep.

From a far distance: a muted murmuring, drawing closer, accompanied by the frenetic rhythms of a hand-drum.

Now lights, flickering and dancing, relieving a solid blackness.

I became aware that I was lying on a hard floor. I couldn't move; my arms and legs were bound. I was in the centre of a wide circular chamber or hall. The floor was rough wooden planking laid with rushes. Overhead was a conical roof of light thatch, supported by wooden beams and posts. The flickering lights were torches set around a wall which seemed to be constructed from branches and mud. The torch flames threw a shadowy, smoky orange luminescence across the hall. Encircling me all around were faces.

They were the faces of wild and primitive folk, pale-skinned and flat-cheeked, with beetling brows, heavy jaws and long, uniformly black hair which had been left to grow more or less as it would. In the dim light I could see that some of the faces were painted or stained, or had been etched with strange designs. Lips, ears and nostrils were in some cases run through or misshapen with adornments of bone, ivory, wood or metal, causing deformities that were to my eyes quite grotesque. Their bodies were stocky and powerfully muscled, short in neck and torso, but long in the limb. Again, many were decorated in various colours. They wore little other than loincloths or rough tunics of cloth or hide, and decorations in the form of necklaces, bracelets, ornamental breastplates and the like.

All were seated or squatted around the edge of the circular room, leaving a space at the hub of which I lay. I estimated as many as eighty or a hundred in all. Men, women and children, from infancy to dotage, staring intently, with me the object of their attention.

Seeing that my eyes were open they nudged one another, pointed and nodded, and quickly grew silent. A man, naked but for a bearskin loincloth and some strange leafy adornments covering elbows and knees, rose from among them and stepped forward. He approached me tentatively. His skin in the fiery light gleamed with the lustre of oil. Tattoos in abstract patterns covered much of his pale flesh. He held in one hand a short thrusting spear, and in the other a hollow instrument made of wood and stretched hide from which two pairs of beads hung on short leather thongs.

At a distance of a few feet from me he halted. He bent forward, his head cocked to one side, peering. The whites of his eyes glistened. He extended an arm to prod me with the spear.

'I'm awake!' I said loudly.

My utterance caused a sensation. The crowd gave a gasp. The man leapt back, jabbering in a rapid guttural speech that made no sense to me. He twisted his wrist vigorously back and forth so that the instrument he held rattled loudly. He thrust it towards me as though warding me off. His people came to life, chattering, their voices rising to become a hubbub. They shook bells and rattles of their own, banged hand-gongs, and struck up wild, erratic rhythms on hand-drums.

After a minute or so of this the fellow with the spear and rattle threw his arms in the air and gave forth a series of great whoops. He stamped his feet hard so that the floor vibrated, and banged the haft of his spear on the wooden planks. Slowly the noise abated. He signalled. Two men came out of the crowd and approached me. Taking me by the upper arms they lifted me into a sitting position. A wooden block was shoved behind me that I might sit unaided. Then the two withdrew and the primitive with the spear and rattle addressed me.

'Mgig? Vum folo d'oob?'

I shook my head. I was still dazed from the effects of the drug that had put me to sleep, but I was certain that the tongue was none that I had ever heard.

'I don't understand.'

'Mgig?' he said, knitting his brow. 'Mgig? Vum folo, Nbu!'

The last word brought our audience to life once more. Quietly they began to intone: 'Nbu. Nbu. Nbu.'

My interlocutor turned and gestured them to silence. He spoke to me once more, with animation. 'Nbu! Har soloolum gas. Nbu! Nbu!'

He was becoming quite agitated. I shook my head once more. 'I don't know. I don't understand. What is Nbu?'

He nodded his head eagerly. 'Nbu! Hi, Nbu! Nbu!'

And the word was repeated over and over by the others, accompanied by excited babbling.

I sat with growing unease, unable to make head or tail of what was being said.

An entranceway in the wall opened and a young woman entered the hall. She was bare-breasted, with long black hair that fell almost to her waist. Wound around her middle was a loose skirt in pale cloth. The seated figures parted to allow her to step through to the edge of the circle. My interlocutor moved to join her. They conferred briefly in low tones, then the young woman withdrew and seated herself among the others.

My fellow leapt back into the arena. He thrust his arms high, shaking his head wildly and stamping his feet. 'Nbu modone!' he shrieked. 'Nbu! Nbu! Nbu!'

And the crowd took up the chant again. More vigorously now. 'Nbu!' they called. 'Nbu! Nbu! Nbu! Nbu!'

The drums went wild, pummelling a frenetic rhythm. The rattles, bells and gongs were shaken and beaten in a crazed cacophony. The people began leaping to their feet. They swayed and danced, shaking their limbs, whooping and ululating and chanting over and over and over: 'NBU! NBU! NBU! NBU! NBU!'

Then abruptly all ceased. The silence was a shock, disorienting in its suddenness. As one, faces were turned to the entrance. The door flew back and into the room leapt a monstrous and terrifying figure.

It had the head of a gigantic beast, with huge, round owl eyes, long snout and wide, gaping jaws. Hair of many colours sprang in all directions, and fire came from its eyes, ears and nostrils and mouth. A headdress of feathers and leaves sat upon its head, with a long train flowing in its wake. The creature's body was that of a man, but clad in the scaly skin of a huge reptile. It was markedly taller than the natives seated all around. Its limbs were covered in long black fur. It clasped a pair of ceremonial rattles in its hands, and streamers and tatters of brightly coloured cloth and hide hung from its body.

Without pause it advanced in great leaps into the clear area at the centre of the circular chamber. It shrieked and howled, kicking and twirling, beating its chest and advancing towards me. It thrust out its arms at me and shook its rattles. It stamped hard, then leapt again, to perform another crazed, screaming dance around me.

I gaped, mesmerized, terrified, and eventually this strange apparition ceased its wild motions and stood before me. The chamber was silent.

I had realized part-way through its dance that it was a man, or at least a man-*thing*. The headpiece was an ornate mask which sat upon the wearer's shoulders. When he had turned I had glimpsed the back of his head inside a framework of wooden struts and leather straps. The flames issued from small brands, presumably steeped in pitch or some other combustible material. Considering the nature of his costume, in particular the mask and headdress, it was a marvel that he had not set himself ablaze. But the knowledge that I was faced with a being that was as human as me in at least most major respects scarcely alleviated my fears, or reduced my peril. I sat bathed in sweat, unable to move, and wondered what would happen next.

The man-thing stood close over me, leaning forward, its hands held out to its sides, vibrating its rattles. Between narrow slits at the centres of the eyes of the mask I saw two eyes glittering. One hand came around, arm extended, to shake the rattle at me. Then a resonant voice issued from within: 'Y'mer kamda. Obada Nbu!'

It thumped its chest and stamped one foot. The crowd softly intoned, 'Nbu, Nbu.'

I gave my head a shake. The figure stood erect, then spoke again. This time it employed the quasi-Kemahamek dialect that served as the common tongue throughout much of the region. 'I am Nbu, God of the Mask. Understand?'

Now I nodded, but I was hardly comforted. 'I am Valno, a traveller.'

'You are the Trespasser!' declared Nbu. 'You have entered the domain of the Eovir, trampling their sacred Life-giving ground.'

'I'm sorry,' I began. 'I was unaware . . .'

'Silence!' roared Nbu, shaking his rattles aggressively. He turned to the assembled audience and spoke rapid words to them.

'N'mda! N'mda!' came a yell, and was taken up by another, then another.

Suddenly all were shouting, 'N'mda! N'mda!', and the noise of their voices grew deafening.

Nbu raised his hands to calm them, and as they grew quiet turned back to me.

'They demand your life,' he said. 'You will be taken outside and executed.'

Before I could even begin to protest four men rushed forward and picked me up. They ran with me between the ranks of their folk and out through the entrance. I remember a moment of surprise amidst my panic as I was half dazzled by near-daylight; I had presumed nighttime from the darkness and torches within. Further, I discovered that we were not on the ground, but a long way above, in the brighter, dizzying heights of the trees. I gaped about me as my bearers ran along the bough of a vast oak. Huts, large and small, linked by a system of wooden catwalks and bridges, had been built among the branches of the trees. Far below, through a dense tapestry of varying greens, I glimpsed the forest floor.

All of this came in a numbing blur of sensation. All around me the strange tree-dwellers swarmed, pouring from the hut out of which we had come, which I took to be the village meeting-hall. They rushed by us, jabbering excitedly, racing along branches and walkways with simian surefootedness. Nbu was nowhere in evidence. My bearers suddenly stopped running and set me down on my feet. A new rope was thrown around me and bound tight. Then, without warning, I was thrust from the bough into space.

The ground rushed at me. I shrieked; then was swinging wildly just feet beneath the bough. Looking up I saw my captors, faces set in concentration. They lowered me down swiftly through the leaves until I bumped heavily against the earth, and lay there, helpless. Now other Eovir ran forward, picked me up, and

173

rushed with me to a small clearing nearby. I quailed in fear. At the centre of the clearing a huge bonfire had been built. But I was carried past this to the side of the clearing, where a tall wooden stake had been sunk vertically into the earth. I was tied to this stake, while once again the entire village assembled around me.

Half demented with shock I blurted out hysterical protests. Useless of course, for we spoke different tongues. But now Nbu, the God of the Mask, reappeared. He came between his people with a strange loping strut, and stood before me, hairy arms folded.

'Look, this is absurd!' I cried.

'It is the way,' said Nbu gravely. 'But take heart, my friend. Death is perhaps not as terrible as you might fear.'

In the better light of the glade he seemed to be studying me intently from behind the mask. Now he stepped up close and leaned his face towards me. I saw two eyes in the shadow of the mask, lustrous brown, bright, twinkling. They were the eyes of a man of intelligence, of no great age. His voice too, though deadened somewhat by the mask, was that of a cultured person. He was surely no primitive. I thought, just for a moment . . . but no.

Yet Nbu was scrutinizing me with interest as great if not greater than my own. And presently, from behind that bizarre mask, I heard his voice, low and muffled, and filled with wonder. 'By the Unity!'

He straightened suddenly, swivelled on his heels and spoke quickly to his people. Then he leaned close to me again and murmured, 'Trust me, Dinbig. Whatever you may believe, you are safe.'

Dinbig? *Dinbig?* I scarcely believed what I heard. The fellow knew me!

There was no opportunity to say more. Nbu strode away and placed himself before his people, facing me.

He raised an arm, held it for long moments, then let it fall. A wild-faced man, naked but for a loincloth, leapt agilely forward. In his hand he carried a strange implement, or weapon. It resembled a set of shears, with two broad, short metal blades crossed one upon the other.

Uttering intimidating noises this fellow jumped at me as all around bells and horns rang out and drums beat wildly. He brandished the weapon before me, snapping the blades open and closed with a horrible slicing sound. He writhed and bent, brought the blades up from my feet to my head, unnervingly close.

I cringed there, unable to move a muscle. My eyes went from this, my executioner, to Nbu, and back again. Was it a joke Nbu was playing? How could I possibly trust him? Yet, what choice did I have?

With an ear-splitting howl the executioner lunged at me and grabbed a great hank of my hair. I shrank. The shears flew up in a blur of movement. A metallic scything sound alongside my ear. Then another great howl.

The executioner leapt away. In his left hand was the hank of hair which he had liberated from my head. Immediately everyone was on their feet, dancing, singing, ululating like creatures possessed. Two warriors dashed forward and untied the rope that bound me to the post. Freed, I found that my legs would not support me. I slid to the floor and sat there, stunned.

I was left alone. The entire crowd was moving off, surrounding the fellow who had my hair. Nbu strode forward and crouched beside me. 'I am sorry, my friend. I could do nothing to prevent the ceremony. But it's done now.'

I stared in stupefaction at that weird mask, and with difficulty found my tongue. 'In Moban's name, what is happening here? Who *are* you?'

Nbu put his hands to the base of the heavy mask. He lifted it carefully, raising it above his head. 'Ah, Sir

175

Dinbig, it brings me inexpressible pleasure to see you again!'

And I gaped, slack-jawed and speechless with astonishment. For I was looking into the urbanely smiling, unruffled features of my old friend, confederate and trading-partner, a man of many talents and almost as many faces, best known perhaps as one of the Kemahamek High Council of Five Marshals, Count Inbuel m' Anakastii.

III

'First thing: you must get away from here immediately,' said Inbuel. He took my arm and helped me to my feet.

'You mean I am free?'

'Providing you don't linger.' He glanced back over his shoulder. The Eovir villagers had put a torch to the bonfire. They were dancing frenziedly around it, making the most awful din. I glimpsed the 'executioner', who still flourished my hair on high. He, or perhaps the hank, was quite evidently the centre of attention.

'It's vital that you go immediately,' resumed Inbuel. 'I will explain everything later.'

He had lowered the mask back down over his head, seeming reluctant to be observed without it.

'But my execution?' I said stupidly, still in shock.

'I'll explain later!' He pushed me towards the edge of the clearing, away from the dancing Eovir. As we entered the trees he said, 'Go south along this path. Ten minutes' walking will bring you to a cave outside which three carved posts stand. Wait there for me. I will join you presently ... certainly before nightfall.

Whatever you do, do not under any circumstance return here.'

With that he turned and walked back into the clearing. As he approached the celebrating Eovir he assumed the walk of a deity and raised his hands high. I made off into the forest, the chant of 'Nbu! Nbu! Nbu!' receding at my back.

In short order I came to the cave that Inbuel had described, and sat down outside to await him. I was still in a daze and hopelessly disoriented. Yet again I was without provisions or weapons. But an hour passed and I heard the sound of someone whistling a Kemahamek folk-tune. I hid in the undergrowth as the sound grew closer. Count Inbuel came into view, strolling jauntily along the forest path. He had changed from his ceremonial garb and mask and now wore a green cloth shirt and light leathers, with a slim sword at his waist and a shortbow and quiver of arrows across his back. Furthermore, he carried my knapsack and weapons.

I stepped out to greet him. He halted before me, grinning waggishly. 'That was a lucky break for you, Sir Dinbig!'

'Why didn't you reveal yourself earlier?'

'The truth is I hadn't recognized you earlier. You look quite different. And besides, the Eovir demanded your life. There was no other way.'

'I fail to understand. This was an execution? I'm confused, for I live, unless I am dead and dreaming.'

'It is no dream, Sir Dinbig. Neither was it a sham . . . at least, not in the eyes of the Eovir. You see, they are a primitive and simple tree-dwelling folk. They practise a magic based on the supposed sympathy existing between a man and any severed portion of his person, such as fingernails or hair. Their belief is that anything done to the one must affect the other in like manner. Thus, they have your hair and may work their will upon it, confident in the knowledge that whatever is done to it will also be done to you. It is remarkably ineffective, but to their minds it works, and is also tidy and convenient. No corpses littering the place, you see, nor are they burdened with any sense of guilt at having themselves slain a man. They simply wait a short while to permit you to get well away from the village, then destroy your hair, confident in the knowledge that you have been likewise destroyed.'

'And that has been done?'

'Indeed so. I presided over your execution myself. Your hair was cast with due ceremony into the flames. It burned quite exceptionally well.'

'And now I am dead.'

'Oh, and a most cruel and agonizing death it was too, I think you will agree. The Eovir know no mercy when it comes to Trespassers.'

I was not entirely comfortable with the explanation. Not that I disbelieved; it was more that I knew of certain forms of magic based upon similar precepts of sympathy and contagion which, properly conducted, could wreak marvellous and terrible effects over great distances. But I examined myself once more, ascertained that I breathed and thought, and that I was not in the least bit overwarm, and from this concluded that the Eovir were no experts in their chosen form.

'What if I were to return?' I asked Inbuel.

'Ah, that I would advise against. They would consider you to be a ghost returned to haunt them. To appease you they would accord you godly status. You would become the God of the Mask.'

'Indeed? And what of the present God of the Mask?'

'Your return would reveal me to be an impostor. I would be cut, unsympathetically, into a thousand pieces, which would be distributed at random to a thousand locations around the Magoth. Therefore I

178

implore you, Sir Dinbig, should you ever consider passing this way again, be a good fellow and give me ample warning!'

'I'm in no hurry to return.'

'I am glad to hear it.'

'But I am fascinated to learn how your apotheosis came about.'

'All in good time. For now, we should put distance between ourselves and the Eovir, just in case.'

'You are accompanying me?'

'Indeed I am. Believe me, Godhead is not all pampering and pleasure. Far from it, in my experience. Tedium and frustration have predominated throughout my days here. It is time for a change. But what of you? By all accounts today is not the first time you have survived death. I will confess, I am overjoyed at meeting you here, for the story is that you died in Twalinieh, slain by Orl Kilroth. Yet here you are, somewhat altered, and lacking a hand, yet demonstrably living!'

'It is a long story.'

'As is mine. Come, we will talk on the march.'

IV

I managed to avoid telling my tale for the moment, and listened entranced as Inbuel revealed his. By his account elevation from mere Kemahamek Marshal to Eovir deity had come about some five months earlier. It seemed that he had blundered into the Eovir in similar manner to myself, though in his case he was fleeing north into the Magoth from the Ashakite plains to escape a nomad raiding-party. Since Khimmur's rise he had been running a profitable business dealing in contraband, and had additionally smuggled several desperate persons to safety. The job had its risks, and in avoiding Khimmur he had on this occasion come to the notice of the nomads.

'The nomads took the caravan. There was nothing to be done about that. Several of my men were killed. A few others fled with me, but we became separated. I have tried to locate them since, but have had no luck.

'Like you, I suffered the horrors of execution by the Eovir. When the ceremony was done and my coif disarranged, my predecessor led me from the clearing into the forest on the pretext of taking me to safety. He was a low and disagreeable fellow . . . I never did discover his origins. But I was suspicious, and was therefore not taken entirely unawares when he tried to stab me from behind. We fought, though I was unarmed, and he was an expert knifeman. But by a happy circumstance he lost his footing on a wet rock and knocked his head as he fell. I was able to overpower him, and left him for dead beside the path.

'By sheer haphazard I then got lost and somehow blundered back into the village. Thus, having returned from the dead, I became to my surprise Nbu, God of the Mask. A party of warriors went in search of my predecessor and found him still alive where I had left him. He was grievously wounded, but they cared for him most tenderly over a couple of weeks in order that they might inflict upon him the Death of A Thousand Pieces.

'It is a grisly ceremony, Dinbig. I still hear his screams, even now. They cut small slices of flesh from the body, piece by tiny piece, while the victim is still fully conscious. The skin and outer flesh are entirely removed, yet still he lives. The slivers are taken and distributed all across the forest. It is hours, many hours, before death comes.'

Inbuel closed his eyes and shuddered. 'I would not wish such suffering upon anyone.'

We walked a few paces in silence before he resumed. 'As Nbu I was housed in the most luxurious tree-hut, which is to say a bare hovel one hundred feet above ground which is swept countless times each day by a trio of near-naked wenches. Aha, I hear you say, pleasures untold to while away the hours. But it is not so. Women I am not permitted to touch. Or, more accurately, they are not permitted to touch me, for I am divine. Nor may I eat and drink my fill. It is deemed ungodly to quaff ale or wine, or to eat flesh of any kind. Thus I have survived these past months on a diet of little more than water and nuts. Look at me! I have all but faded away.'

I smiled. 'And duties? What of those?'

'I am required to preside at ceremonies, bless their food and newborn infants, and ... torment of torments! ... be present as observer when a virgin gives herself to a man. Imagine! I sit and pretend beatific indifference while before me, scarcely an arm's length away, a tender beauty is rogered by some galloping young oaf. And when it is done I sprinkle powdered porcupine claws upon their two sated bodies. Then the entire village partakes of wild revelling and love-making throughout the night, while Nbu sits quietly in their midst upon a wooden platform and from time to time gives an approving shake of his rattle.'

'Curious,' I said.

'And at all times, except when alone in my hovel, I am expected to wear the mask,' Inbuel went on. 'It is a heavy and cumbersome thing, but the Eovir do not take kindly to the sight of a god's naked face. In ceremonies, such as the one you have just witnessed, I must dance and gyrate in the most energetic manner, or my blessings may be rendered ineffective. It is not easy.'

'You seem free to wander as you will.'

'I took to taking long walks, for distraction. They put it down to a godly quirk and after the first couple of times paid me no attention. Little by little I discovered my whereabouts, and have been contemplating taking my leave for good these last few days. With your arrival, the decision was made. Hence, here we are!'

'You have evidently grown fluent in their tongue in a relatively short time.'

'I have a certain facility with language, as you know. And Eovir is a simple tongue, closely related to Vir, with which I was already familiar. Do you know that in Eovir the word "Magoth" means life? That is what the forest is to them; that is why they hold it sacred.'

'That also perhaps accounts for so many folk becoming lost along its winding, trackless paths,' I said.

Inbuel chuckled. 'Quite so. But enough of my adventures. I would hear your story now, Sir Dinbig, if you will.'

So I told him my tale . . . at least, those elements of it that I deemed of direct relevance. Certain aspects I preferred for the present to keep to myself.

Dusk was closing in before I had done, and we stopped to make camp for the night. Inbuel had brought with him some portions of fresh meat wrapped in leaves. These we cut up into cubes, which we spitted and toasted over a fire. As we worked Inbuel produced a leather sack of rich red wine, murmuring words of appreciation and anticipation. Thus we drank and feasted merrily there in the great primordial wood, and entertained one another further with tales of our exploits over the past couple of years.

Now I learned from Inbuel that he had escaped Twalinieh via a secret way when the city was stormed by Khimmur. He was a little vague on this, and I did not immediately press him for particulars, though I was eager to do so. His report, if lacking in fine details, validated in large part the picture I had composed out of the information that had come my way since my rebirth.

I sensed that he was feeling me out, just as I was him. We had been confederates, Inbuel and I. We had shared many adventures and worked profitably together over many years. But now, such was the turmoil across this land and so extraordinary the broad circumstances which had brought us together, we were a little wary of one another.

'And your family?' I enquired. Inbuel was married to a quite strikingly beautiful and gracious Kemahamek lady named Puhlre. They had an equally becoming teenaged daughter, Miona.

'They are well, thank you. I personally supervised their evacuation. Now they are in the country, in somewhat reduced circumstances, but safe and comfortable nevertheless. I return as often as is feasible to see them.'

'What of your own fortunes? The war must have altered your situation drastically.'

'I have not fared badly, Sir Dinbig, all things considered. Commerce, as you know, survives the rigours of war, though of course it has been advisable to modify my arrangements somewhat. I have maintained a legitimate business in certain respects, but there is a thriving black market which I have to some degree underwritten. Under the circumstances it would have been a demonstration of unusual foolishness to ignore it.'

'Then you still have many contacts?'

'Far and wide.'

'For my own network, as for my business, I fear the worst. Everything was seized by the Crown, and everyone believes me dead.'

'Indeed,' said Inbuel. He stared at me across the

flames, his eyes twinkling, a quizzical smile upon his lips. 'Yet a tale reached my ears, well substantiated too, that by a miracle or a quirk of fate you had survived but that your mind was irreparably damaged.'

My heart gave a thump. None but the Intimates of Princess Seruhli could have known this. Inbuel was giving me his confidence, inviting me to enquire further. I gave careful thought to my words. 'And I was made aware of another rumour, to the effect that the ritual suicide of the Holy Wonasina was a charade acted out for the benefit of Khimmur. That despite this, she was the victim of the most heinous betrayal by one or more of her Intimates acting in league with the Vulpasmage. That she did not die but nor could she truly be said to have lived; rather that she is held in a state called Semblance of Death, for which no antidote is known to exist. I heard also that her lifeless form was smuggled by loyal followers from Twalinieh via a secret way.'

Count Inbuel, leaning upon one elbow on the grass, permitted an eyebrow to lift. 'It seems you absorbed much for a man whose mind was gone. And now, though your condition was diagnosed as hopeless, you sit before me in good and robust mental health. At least, so it appears. I am pleased, Sir Dinbig, and intrigued. And, I must add, just a little uneasy.'

Now I knew I had to confess all. I explained how Yo had usurped my flesh and brought about my downfall in Twalinieh. I told him how my insanity was quite genuine, for my flesh was unwitting host to an entity who not only knew nothing of events, but was unable to control my corporeal form and thus reduced me to the condition of a loon. I told him again how, as the vhazz Huwoorsk, I had eventually located and confronted my Wandering flesh. I revealed the existence of the Fragment from Yshcopthe's Pandect, but

184

said only that it had been found by a loyal and trusted friend. In my fervour, as I spoke, I reached out and grasped Inbuel's arm tightly. 'Inbuel, Inbuel, my friend, do you see what this means? We may have the means to revive her! Ah, we are well met here in this great dark wood. We are well met indeed!'

Inbuel, unexcitable as always, sat up and began to stoke the fire with a charred stick, nodding pensively to himself. 'This is extraordinary news.'

I pushed him further. 'Were you there, Inbuel, when they took the body from Twalinieh? Were you among those who hauled me from the water? Was it you who argued for my life?'

'Indeed it was,' he said with a nonchalant gesture. 'It was largely my words that prevented you from being murdered and thrown back into Death's Deep, for most still believed you to be acting for the Vulpasmage, or King Oshalan as we knew him then. And it was I who, from a distance, supervised your convalescence. Through my authority you were eventually allowed your liberty, after it had been ascertained that you were wholly addled and beyond recovery. I will confess I was greatly saddened at the sight of you.'

I hardly listened now. 'Then it was her? It was Seruhli?'

After a pause he nodded. 'It was.'

'Ah, Moban! It has not all been in vain!'

Inbuel looked up. 'What of this Fragment? Where is it now?'

'It is on its way to Khimmur, being taken there by Duke Shadd.'

'Shadd?'

'It is he who, at considerable peril to himself, searched out and found the Fragment. I was with him just days ago. We were parted in Chol through adverse circumstances.'

185

'Then he could be anywhere. Or indeed, he could be dead.'

'I know only that he has pledged himself to Seruhli. He will not rest until he has discovered the secret of the Pandect, and delivered it to her. Do you know where she is kept hidden?'

He hesitated, then said, 'I do not.'

'But have you a means to locate those who do?'

'As I have said, I have many connections. Under certain circumstances a way might be found to get word to someone who knows of the whereabouts of our Beloved Lady. But of course there is immense danger. The Beast of Rull was the mastermind behind the plot that brought her to this state. His agents scour Kemahamek and beyond in search of her. Many still believe Duke Shadd to be in league with the Beast. And any who seek to locate Seruhli will be considered an enemy.'

'But not you, Inbuel.'

He gave me a rueful look. 'Our Beloved Lady was betrayed by a Blessed Intimate. Hence no one can be above suspicion.'

'You must come with me,' I said. 'To Khimmur. We will contact the *Zan-Chassin* and the Khimmurian resistance. Somehow, we will find a way. Ah, after all we have endured, it seems that Fate or Moban, or perhaps both, may yet be on our side.'

7

I

My brain was a fever of excitement that night. I did not sleep, and though Count Inbuel gave little outward sign, I believe he was equally affected. We broke camp the following morning and continued on south through the dark entangled Magoth. I asked Inbuel whether he knew anything of conditions in the south, where the Beast had marshalled forces against Ghence. He replied that he had been in receipt of few reports in recent weeks, having been wholly cut off from his intelligence network during his time among the Eovir. What he did say more or less confirmed what I already knew, that the Beast was endeavouring to breach the Great Wall of Ghence, using armies of Khimmurian and Sommarian troops, and auxiliaries from Kemahamek, Anxau, Cexhaut and other far-flung loci. And, of course, Gneth.

'There is a rumour that March has given way,' Inbuel added. 'Unsubstantiated, but not unfeasible. The story is that the Beast merely dispatched three hundred light cavalry across the border, and the entire nation threw down its arms rather than face what would surely follow. If it is true then it is dire news for Ghence. There is a possibility, not too far-fetched, that Tomia and Dyarchim may follow suit. Such is the terror that your former king now inspires. I have heard many tales of atrocities – indeed, I have witnessed the terrible brutalities committed in his name. Of course, they discourage resistance, but more often than not it is not those who resist who suffer the most. It is innocents, men, women and children who are simply caught in

187

the invaders' path. I will not revolt you with details, nor with the stories I have heard concerning your former king's appetite. Suffice to say that the Beast has demonstrated a capacity for the most horrible cruelties. His war is one of perverse gratification. I am sickened by what I have heard.'

I recalled words spoken to me more than two years earlier, in a squalid old house in the Gell, the poorest district of Hon-Hiaita: *'This is no ordinary war. We are entering a time of blood and turmoil, of faithlessness, incertitude and hollow mockery. Only the eaters of gore, the seekers of carrion and the diggers of graves will have cause to rejoice.'*

Thus had spoken the crone, Hisdra, mother of Crananba, and Sacred Mother of the *Zan-Chassin*. Soon after uttering this warning she had made her last journey into the Realms. Her soul was now believed trapped there, suffering endless torment at the hands of the minions of the Beast. And not for the first time I wondered, What had she known? For certainly she had given clues which implied a prescience of the manner in which events would unfold. If this were so, why could she not have revealed more? Why could she not have endeavoured to forestall it?

Speculation now was pointless. Things were as they were. I forced myself to concentrate upon the present.

'What of Ashakite?' I asked Inbuel. 'Do you still have a source emplaced there?'

'I do – at least as far as I know. We have hardly had contact since I left Twalinieh, for her coded messages were always delivered to me there. Two of the contacts she used to convey them to me have disappeared, and the Ashakite network has largely disintegrated. For what it's worth it seems that things continue as they always have. There is no indication of a unity in the face of Khimmur's threat. The one item of possible

188

significance is that the Uljuōk have ingratiated themselves with the Mammubid, thus attaining an uneasy peace. But the only observable result of this appears to be that it has allowed the Mammubid to concentrate more fully on their conflict with the Itain, who themselves have thrown in their lot with the Olish.' Inbuel threw up his hands. 'It is useless to speak of these people.'

I considered carefully before putting my next question, for I was aware that I might be stepping on very sensitive ground. As it happened, I was about to be given the most startling and perhaps most troubling piece of information that I had yet heard.

'And in Kemahamek?' I asked. 'Information that has come my way has implied complicity with the enemy at a very high level.'

'Complicity! Bah!' snapped Inbuel heatedly. 'Apathy also. I am ashamed of what my people have done.'

'The Sacred Citadel was given up without a fight, so I understand.'

'Dinbig, you do not know the half of it. The impossible, the inconceivable, came to be. We were betrayed from within, by a faction operating at the very highest level, even within the Blessed Intimates themselves!'

I kept my voice even. 'How is this?'

'Listen and I will tell you. The movements of our Wonas, Homek, were given to Khimmur so that he might be ambushed and murdered. Information pertaining to his trip to the Hulminilli Mountains was known only by a very few within the topmost stratum of government. That is to say, certain arch-priests of the Simbissikim, members of Homek's Blessed Intimates, certain highly placed warlords, the Council of Five Marshals, and a handful of others. Seruhli was betrayed by one of her Intimates. We know who: her name was Migik-Prahn, but she died conveniently almost immediately after the deed was done. Certain

Simbissikim then conceded defeat and struck a bond with the Beast. In order that the carnage might cease they gave up the Sacred Citadel. That appears to imply their complicity in the plot, but it is not conclusive. And it came close to blowing back in their faces, for other elements loyal to Kemahamek had pronounced Duke Shadd the Assassin of the Wonasina, thus turning the fury of the people against Khimmur. But Khimmur won through the streets of the capital anyway, and was at the gates of the Sacred Citadel. So certainly, by surrendering the Citadel, much bloodshed was averted.'

'And your people enslaved.'

'Remember, we live for the future, the time of the Ihika-Wona. To that end we adapt quickly to change of circumstances. The Kemahamek dream was destroyed, for the people believed both our sacred rulers dead. But then Khimmur played an ace. The Beast, King Oshalan, announced its plan to maintain the sacred conditions of Kemahamek rule. Homek was gone, but his soul awaited rebirth. King Oshalan declared that the usual procedure would be followed. There is a select body of Simbissikim called the Telik, whose task it is to locate the newborn infant whose destiny it is to rule our land. These were ostensibly sent forth to find the new child and bring him to Twalinieh. Within weeks Oshalan produced a babe, and that babe now resides within the Palace of the Wona, and is being schooled for future rule.'

'So the people believe their Wonas has been reborn. And in fourteen or perhaps fifteen years he will be eligible to sit upon the throne. Thus your people have been given something to live for. But the babe is of course not the true Wonas.'

Inbuel made a sound of anger. 'Aye, but you still do not know the half of it, Dinbig. The babe is not the Wonas, of course it's not. *There has not been a true Wonas for generations.*'

190

This brought me up short. 'What do you mean?'

Inbuel's face was now pale with emotion. 'There have been suspicions for some time – at least, intimations – that all was not as it should be. But only now has the truth come to light. The male line has been corrupted. For generations my country has had impostors upon the throne. While the female line has remained true, the male, and thus the nation, has been manipulated by an enemy unknown.'

This revelation was of such moment that I could not at first take it in. 'How many generations?'

Inbuel shrugged. 'Go back two centuries, to the time of Hermat XIII and his abortive crusade which resulted in The Great Deadlock. There, possibly, you have the origin of this plot. Certainly, Kemahamek has seen a succession of feckless males on the throne since then.'

I shook my head incredulously. 'And the Vulpasmage is behind it all, from the beginning?'

Again a fretful shrug. 'It is impossible to say. The one certainty is that Kemahamek, through its male ruling line, has strayed far from its golden path for a very long time.'

'So, then, what of the true Wonas – the babe who all those generations ago should have been installed upon the throne?'

Inbuel shook his head with a bleak expression. 'He never knew. He would have grown up displaying great intelligence and unusual talents. But un-nurtured they would have gradually diminished. He would probably have been considered a freak, and lived a life of near-isolation. With successive reincarnations he would, as far as we can tell, have reverted more and more towards the human norm.'

'Then he is lost. Somewhere in the world there exists a child, or man, who is potentially a virtual god, yet who knows nothing of his power or his destiny.'

'His destiny, Dinbig, is to be what he is, never knowing. He has been cheated of all else, as have we, the Kemahamek race.'

'And what of the female line?'

'As I said, it remains true. Seruhli was the paragon, the highest possible expression in human form of the evolving female Principle. She was truly what she should have been. Those who went before her, likewise. Think back again to The Great Deadlock. Empress Chryphte wanted nothing of Hermat's war, nor his gains. She tried to dismantle the empire, and was poisoned. But, mercifully, no untrue babe was substituted in her successor's place. This we know.'

'So the Beast of Rull now raises a puppet in Kemahamek. And Seruhli lies in the Semblance of Death, unable to be reborn. It would follow, then, that a female babe is to be substituted now, to take her place in due course. The Beast then controls the destiny of Kemahamek.'

Count Inbuel was impassioned, almost distraught. I had never seen him so upset, and I realized just how deeply this must have affected him. 'The Beast prevents the unfolding of our future, our rightful heritage.' He clenched his fists in anger. 'We are beset by a demon! I ask myself, where can it have come from? And I receive no answer, other than: It is here, and it defiles everything that men and women hold sacred!'

And I recalled that Inbuel knew nothing of the origins of the Vulpasmage, as had been revealed to me by Shadd. I said, 'I have learned that the Vulpasmage was one of the original Qotol Enchanters of yore. Long before the Great Pooling, in which Yshcopthe played her fabled Ruse and brought about the eventual end of the Enchanter Wars – long before that, four of the original Enchanters were beaten, deprived of physical form and forced to depart the world of matter, space and time. One of these was a creature of unsurpassed evil, who even then showed signs of having gained access to forces unmastered by any other. Certain of the others, apprehending the threat this creature posed, banded together in order to defeat it. It was banished into limbo, where for aeons it has waited, biding its time. Now it has returned. Having escaped the consequences of Yshcopthe's Ruse, it is potentially as strong now as it was then. Certainly it has the power of the other surviving Enchanters combined.'

Inbuel was still, a deepening frown forming on his brow.

I continued. 'Moreover, it appears that he has been brought now to this plane by dint of our own ignorance. He was one of the Four Sovereign Entities acknowledged and revered by the *Zan-Chassin*. It was through our agency, quite unwitting, that he was able to gain access to the physical plane. Through ignorance and self-delusion we have unleashed a monster that is far greater than we. Our one hope now lies in the knowledge that he has not yet been able to bring his full power to bear in the physical, nor yet wholly in the Realms. But he is growing. Day by day, week by week, I am made aware that he is growing.'

II

I thought of the Eovir, who worshipped a man, believing him to be a god. Now Kemahamek likewise. And we of the *Zan-Chassin*, who also believed ourselves wise. Such carnage out of faith. Myriad were the guises of ignorance, and bitter the consequences. Yet how *could* we have known? What else could we have done?

I walked on behind Inbuel beneath the shadows of the great trees. I realized that I had now to get a message through to the Chariness and the *Zan-Chassin*

193

Hierarchy. Our last communication had been weeks ago, and I would need help if I was to return safely to Khimmur. There was a risk of detection, but here, deep within the vast, lonely mantle of the Magoth, was surely as safe a place as any to chance a summoning. I did not know what had become of Molpaton Egil since my rescue by Dagril's raiders, but I was certain he could not have followed me this far. And it was highly unlikely that the Vulpasmage would have others close by. Inbuel assured me that there were no Khimmurian outposts within a day's march of our position.

I had Inbuel map out for me his intended route back to Khimmur. He knew of villages and caravanserai along the way where we might gain shelter and aid, and I felt it preferable to rely on his guidance as my own knowledge of the land was now outdated. With an approximate route in my head, then, I seated myself upon the forest floor and entered trance.

I summoned Yo.

He arrived upon the instant, much to my relief.

'Yo, I must be brief. Where are you, and what is your state of health?'

'I have your trail, Master. Your scent is faint but growing stronger.'

'Good, then you are on the right path.'

'And a straight course. I have to some extent over-come the nature of the vhazz. I am still beset by its anguish, fear and anxieties, but with the exertion of my own considerable personality I am able to put these aside. Thus I no longer run wildly hither and thither.'

'Take care as you come, Yo. I am in the forest of Magoth, moving south with a companion. Our desti-nation is Khimmur. Remember, your way is dangerous. Avoid men at all times. They will kill you on sight.'

'I am accustomed to the ways of men, Master.'

I gave Yo further details, laying emphasis on the facts

of my captivity, for there would be no scent to follow during my time of captivity in the Khimmurian wagon. As best I could I described Dagril's camp, and my journey from there into the Magoth. 'I will summon you again in a couple of days, to check on your progress. Now, I must journey briefly. Will you guard my body?'

'I am your servant, Master.'

I rose from the corporeal me and allowed my Custodian to enter. I lifted myself high above the world. With utmost caution I probed the between-world fabric. I sensed no immediate danger. I rent the fabric and entered First Realm, sending forth a single word, *'Gaskh.'*

'I am here, Master.'

'Gaskh, you are unharmed after our last encounter?'

'I am, though I was forced to remove myself quickly. Other entities were summoned.'

'And now, are we watched?'

'I think not. It was an isolated incident. You were unfortunate in that there was a vigilance within your vicinity.'

'As I thought.'

'Still, we should not linger, Master. The Realms are never wholly free of watchers.'

'Can you convey a communication to the Chariness, Gaskh?'

'I believe so, though I must time it carefully. Many hostile entities are assigned to locate her whereabouts. I have contact with her Guardian Entity. I will pass the communication to him, that he may deliver it at an appropriate moment.'

'Good, then convey this: I am returning along the southern Magoth, with a new companion. I have been parted from Shadd but believe him safe. I have more vital information. We will be at Khimmur's border within ten days, and will come via Grassheen or the township of Murdren. I will require assistance from there on.'

195

'Is that all, Master?'

'It is.' I thanked Gaskh and dismissed him, then returned to my corporeal form. 'Yo, make every effort to catch me. I wish you good speed.'

My Custodian departed and I re-entered my flesh.

We passed another night in the forest depths. The following afternoon we began to ascend a long, steep slope. I noted a gradual thinning of the canopy overhead. Sharp beams of sunlight stabbed down with startling brightness. As we neared the head of the slope, Inbuel led me along a traverse to where a sudden jut of limestone rose above the trees. This he climbed, reaching down frequently to help me. When we stood upon the top he pointed. 'Look.'

I followed his gaze. Below us the Magoth stretched away in a rich, undulating carpet of varying greens, swaying under a warm breeze blowing down from our backs. The sun was hot, and for a few seconds I was half dazzled. Overhead the sky was pale blue, carrying fleecy white clouds which cast swiftly moving shadows across the landscape.

At a distance of perhaps three or four miles from where we stood the trees ended abruptly. Beyond could be seen open grassland, stretching to the horizon.

It was a welcome sight, yet I greeted it with some foreboding. Our journey was far from over. And if we reached Khimmur, what then? The task before us was immense, and our foe growing stronger by the day.

We seated ourselves upon the rock and Inbuel produced his wine-flask, now filled only with water. 'Drink, Sir Dinbig. We have come this far. We have farther yet to go. Let us drink to safe journeys and successful endeavours.'

I took the flask. 'Aye, and to wisdom,' I said. 'The wisdom to know how to distinguish what is from what appears to be.'

Part Two

8

I

The Great Wall of Ghence had stood intact for almost a century and a half. Built mainly of sandstone brought from local quarries and standing eighty feet high, the Wall was on average thirty feet thick at the base, supporting a protected walkway wide enough to accommodate six men marching abreast. It presented a redoubtable obstacle. In its original form it had stretched some one hundred and twenty miles, north from the coast of the Blue Gulf along the Ghence/Hanvat border as far as Soland, utilizing to best advantage the contours of the land. Later augmentations had extended the Wall east for another sixty miles along Ghence's frontier with Soland.

By a curious set of circumstances the Wall became the property of Ghence only after its completion. It was originally constructed by the member states of the Hanvat Confederacy as a defence against Ghence, Hanvat's former ally. Hanvat and Ghence had united when, two centuries earlier, Ghence had begun to flex her military muscles.

Several lesser nations had already fallen to Ghence when Hanvat, after consultation with its neighbour Komamnaga, had opted to support Ghence rather than oppose her. The Ghence/Hanvat Alliance was established, creating an indomitable political and military force which had rapidly taken control of the south.

Ghence's programme of expansion was halted only when her army in southern Sommaria found itself confronted by the forces of Kemahamek which, under Hermat XIII, had risen almost simultaneously to overwhelm the north. Then came The Great Deadlock, a well-documented period of stalemate which lasted for more than half a century. The armies of Ghence and Kemahamek eyeballed each other across Sommaria, engaging in occasional skirmishes, but never came seriously to blows.

Gradually internal problems began to erode the strengths and confidence of the two empires. In time both were forced out of Sommaria.

Later, internal dissension began to undermine the alliance between Ghence and Hanvat. Both nations suffered massive military setbacks, and were further divided by ideological and political differences. As their empire shrank they bickered over possessions and policy. The alliance was formally dissolved.

A grave misunderstanding led to a Ghentine force stumbling at night upon a Hanvatian military encampment close to the border. Believing, as they subsequently claimed, that it was an enemy force striking down from the north, the Ghentines attacked. They routed the surprised Hanvat troops, slaughtering as many as half their number before the error was realized.

Hanvat responded with heated rhetoric and demands for compensation. An agreement was reached between the two governments, but the terms were never met by Ghence.

Suspicion and resentment grew between the two former allies. A hot-headed Hanvatian warlord determined, without official sanction, to avenge the deaths of those soldiers killed in the Ghentine attack. He led a strike-force over the Ghentine border to loot and pillage a couple of remote Ghentine towns. Ghence responded by marching eight thousand troops into

Hanvat, then appeared to change its mind, and withdrew.

A week later Hanvat commenced the construction of the Great Wall.

Ghence observed with apparent bemusement but made no attempt to intervene. For three and a half years Hanvat laboured, and at last the edifice was complete. Then Ghence struck. Before Hanvat had had time to fully garrison its new defence, the Ghentine army swarmed onto the Wall in twenty-three separate locations.

The defenders were taken by surprise, and dislodged almost without effort. The greater part of the Wall was overrun in a day. Sections in the south, which had been completed earlier and were thus fully garrisoned, held on for some weeks, but eventually the entire Wall was in Ghentine hands. Hanvat withdrew, smouldering in humiliation and dismay. Ghence celebrated.

Numerous modifications were required now. Towers had to be redesigned so that their main fortifications faced into Hanvat rather than Ghence. Existing gatehouses, of which there were only four at this time, were largely taken apart and rebuilt to incorporate massive barbicans, and the battlements were augmented on the Hanvat side.

Then came the Soland extension: a precaution against a Hanvat incursion out of Soland. Ghence laboured for another two years to lengthen the Great Wall along the Soland frontier, adding two new gatehouses.

Three years passed. Hanvat launched a massive strike, endeavouring to storm the Wall, and learned to its cost the effectiveness of the mighty edifice it had constructed. Its army was repulsed with heavy casualties, and minimal loss to Ghence.

Domestic strife brought Hanvat further troubles and

she made no more attempts to retake the Wall. Thus the Great Wall of Hanvat became the Great Wall of Ghence, and so it had remained. But now the Wall was being put to the test once more as Khimmur and her allies, under the Beast of Rull, pounded at Ghence's borders, determined to breach the defence and march on into the heartland.

Fighting had been under way for some months. Khimmur's initial expeditionary force, linked with that of Sommaria, had taken Hanvat with relative ease and subsequently laid siege to the Great Wall along much of its length. The invaders had made no concerted attempt to breach the Wall. The warlords of both Khimmur and Sommaria had calculated the likely cost of such a venture, and it had been early disposed of as a viable option.

Instead a war of nerves had ensued. Batteries of artillery relentlessly bombarded the Wall, backed up by large companies of infantry and bowmen. Flying columns of horse-troops, light and heavy, were established in fortresses built or commandeered close in the rear. These could move swiftly to any point where Ghence might essay an attack.

Under the pounding of the siege-engines the Wall began to crack in places; battlements were seen to crumple and shear. Tunnels were begun, as if to bore beneath the Wall and undermine its foundations. The defenders were kept ever occupied attempting to thwart the enemy's endeavours and repair the damage. Yet it seemed that this was Khimmur's sole aim, for though the bombardment continued without surcease the besieging army did not commit itself to an all-out assault.

As the weeks went by, Ghentine morale suffered. Khimmur had resorted to inhuman measures to break her foe's spirit. Helpless civilians were herded to the front line, loaded into the great trebuchets, and hurled into the Ghentine ranks. Rotting corpses and the carcasses of dead animals were likewise used as ammunition in an attempt to spread pestilence among the defending troops.

Sommaria led an assault force into Soland, and quickly took control there, thus applying pressure to the northern extension of the Great Wall. The Ghentine defenders were being stretched to their limit.

Under pressure to boost her forces' morale, the Ghentine government launched a seaborne strike from Barulia, designed to take the enemy in the rear. The plan almost succeeded, but Khimmur was prepared. The Ghentines were driven back with terrible losses; Khimmur seized control of the Blue Gulf. Ghence's navy, historically her great pride, was suddenly hard pressed to retain control of her coast.

Now came the news that the last of the northern nations had fallen. The Khimmurian armies in the north were free to march south. This they did, almost doubling the strength of the forces arrayed before the Great Wall of Ghence.

Among the Ghentine defenders the rumour quickly spread that supplementing this new force were the most feared of Khimmur's weapons, the monstrous legions which the Beast of Rull had deployed with such devastating effect in Kemahamek and elsewhere: the Gneth.

II

For operational headquarters the Beast of Rull had taken over the fortified country manor of a defeated Hanvatian noble, set deep in picturesque countryside among dry, pine-forested hills close upon the Soland border, a few miles west of the Great Wall. Thirty miles to the south-west, in Hanvat's second city, Encopt, the former presidential summer palace had been made ready, for it was expected that this would become the temporary residence of the conquering king. The capital, Urde, lay a hundred miles to the west, too far away for practical purposes. But a move to Encopt would have been been seen as a declaration of majesty and dominion, as well as furnishing the Beast with an estate of far greater amenity than this isolated rural demesne.

But the Beast displayed no interest in sumptuousness and splendour, and as he saw it there were several advantages to the site. He was close upon the Wall, and so might oversee operations there. Additionally he was anxious to keep his soldiers from the taverns, pleasure-houses and diverse entertainments of the city, where undoubtedly quarrels and violence would erupt with the townsfolk. He required that his troops be at all times alert and ready for battle. Here in the country they trained and exercised constantly. There were whores and entertainments aplenty, as always accompanied an army on the move, but the risks were significantly reduced.

Roads close to the manor led to Barulia and Ghence, deeper into Hanvat, and through Soland and the Boltar to link with the Spice Road, the trade route which wound down from Sommaria and the north. And the manor was a field base, nothing more. The Beast had been in residence here for less than two weeks, and his intention was to remain only a few days longer.

Khimmur's king had become a remote, brooding, mysterious figure. He kept largely to himself within a suite of chambers in the west wing of the manor. Other than in battle or on troop inspections he was rarely seen. He held company only with his closest confidants, and even this was restricted to matters of necessity rather than pleasure. Gone were the royal feasts and banquets, the grand collations and fetes that had been loved by the former King Oshalan. His officers and men enjoyed good food and ale in moderation, according to availability. But the King ate alone in his rooms. His appetite had grown prodigious. He had commanded that large portions of fresh meat be delivered to him several times each day. The food was neither cooked nor garnished. It was placed upon a dining-table by a single servant, who collected the empty dishes from a previous meal and then departed, usually without setting eyes on his sovereign.

On this particular day the domestic staff hurried to and fro in preparation for the arrival of an important guest. Upon the road a mile or so away a carriage approached, drawn by four fine strong white horses, its wheels throwing up a plume of yellow dust from the parched surface. A cavalcade of twenty knights in light armour and tabards of tan and red rode escort, with men-at-arms behind. Within the carriage sat Perminias, King of Sommaria, gazing out upon the landscape with an expression of mild irritation.

The day was hot and sultry, with summer storm-clouds lowering on the western horizon. Fields of vines and corn stretched away into the distance. All around soldiers trained in the shimmering heat, their bodies streaked with sweat and dirt. King Perminias mopped his moist brow with a linen kerchief. The carriage entered the cypress-lined driveway which led up to the manor. King Perminias perceived the first hint of a cloying taint held upon the torrid air. He wrinkled his nostrils, but gave the matter no great thought.

The odour grew stronger as the carriage rolled towards the manor gate. King Perminias leaned to the window to see the way ahead, and perceived the source of the stench. Lining the drive, and arrayed before the outer wall of the manor, were bodies stretched upon crude wooden frames standing erect upon the ground. Some were in advanced state of decay, others had been affixed to the frames quite recently.

The carriage drew up to the main gate. There was the briefest halt as formalities were conducted with the guard. The stench here was overwhelming. King Perminias, no stranger to death and the brutalities of war, nevertheless found himself reaching into his tunic to draw forth another kerchief, this one scented with oil of geranium, which he pressed to his nostrils.

The gate opened and the carriage pulled away. Perminias heard the faintest groan. He glanced to the nearest of the frames, to see that life still clung to the victim stretched there. The man's head rolled, revealing bloody, cavernous sockets, the eyes having been taken by crows. The spine arched in agony. The mouth was twisted into a contorted grimace, a swollen tongue visible between parched, cracked lips.

The carriage entered the forecourt; the sight was obscured.

At the head of a short flight of steps leading up to the main entrance to the house a reception committee awaited. The carriage came to a halt, a servant opened the door and King Perminias stepped down. He was a man of middle years, with short black hair and beard. His features were regular, if a little sharp, and a dark, strong brow centred with a permanent crease told of a man ruled by impulse and a love of action.

Down the steps came the huge bulk of the Orl Kilroth of Selaor, dressed in light leather armour. Alongside him was Count Genelb Phan, cousin to King Oshalan, and commander of the élite White Blade Guard. The two performed curt, polite bows before the Sommarian king.

'Sir, welcome. We are honoured by your visit. King

Oshalan awaits you in his chambers. If you will accompany us, he would speak with you immediately.'

King Perminias nodded his head. No doubt the exigencies of the day imposed greatly upon his host; nevertheless Perminias was tired after his journey, and would have appreciated an hour or so to wash and refresh himself before the meeting with his esteemed ally.

He was conducted through the reception hall to the west wing of the manor, up two flights of winding stairs to the second level. Here he entered a large dining-room, the two Khimmurian nobles accompanying him. From this room, through a wide arched window, a view extended over the fields and low hills of northern Hanvat.

A modest collation of meats and seafood, salad, rice, bread, fruit and a selection of cordials, ales and wines had been set upon an oval dining-table which occupied the centre of the chamber. Upon his arrival King Perminias had been both hungry and thirsty; but a hint of carrion still hung in the air here, and he found that his appetite was no longer an issue.

Orl Kilroth, enquiring as to the Sommarian king's preference, poured sweet amber wine into a golden goblet. 'King Oshalan will arrive in a moment.'

Hardly had he spoken when a portal opened in the western wall, and into the chamber stepped Oshalan, the Beast of Rull, the Vulpasmage incarnate.

'Sir, I am delighted.' Khimmur's king strode forward, arms extended, to clasp Perminias in formal embrace. 'Forgive me, I have prepared neither banquet nor festivities, and I regret that our meeting must be brief. Time makes unreasonable demands upon me, and we are on the verge of the most important stage of our campaign. Impending events will be decisive, as you know, and there is much to be done.'

For his part, King Perminias was taken aback by the

appearance of the young man who now faced him. More than a year had passed since they'd last met, and though he had received reports from others who had been briefly in King Oshalan's presence, he was yet unprepared for the sight that met his eyes.

Oshalan was hardly recognizable. He had lost weight, but his tall, well-proportioned body seemed somehow to have gained rather than diminished in physical power. But it was a power manifestly unlike that which he had possessed before; not the loose, confident, natural energy of the trained warrior and athlete, more an extraordinary energy, nervous, wild, barely controlled, held in check as though on a spring.

Oshalan's face was gaunt, strained and abnormally pale, yet the sallow flesh held a vital, if unwholesome, lustre. The pale blue eyes were bloodshot, bulging from within dark sockets, and blazing with a ferocious intensity. His dark hair hung lank and uncombed over his shoulders; his beard likewise was unkempt. He seemed hunched in upon himself. His mouth, though he smiled, was contorted into a grimace. The veins stood out on his forehead and neck. It seemed that he was racked by some inner force of unspeakable strength, which conveyed via his flesh an impression of demonic wrath. As he had entered the room the ambience had undergone a change, as if his presence brought with it an influence, insidious, life-eroding, setting nerves instantly on edge and causing muscles to tense. Indeed, as Oshalan strode towards Perminias, the Sommarian king found himself stepping back apace involuntarily, as though driven by the force radiating from his ally.

The two embraced and Perminias's muscles stiffened where Oshalan's hands gripped him. His flesh recoiled, without his being able to say precisely why. He found himself fighting to suppress a shudder.

'Apologies are entirely unnecessary,' he replied,

thoroughly unsettled. 'Indeed, I am also pressed and must return to my troops as soon as possible.'

'Then let us sit, informally, and review the matter at hand. You will note the absence of servants. I prefer that we speak alone, with only the good Orl and Count Phan to hear us. Eat if you will, but take no offence if I do not join you.'

Perminias took a seat at the table, but accepted no food. The Beast of Rull seated himself opposite him. Orl Kilroth and Genelb Phan likewise took their places.

'There is much to discuss, but I will endeavour to be brief,' said the Beast.

His eyes, lighting on Perminias, were maniacal. His hands gripped the edge of the table so that the knuckles whitened. Perminias noted the nails, long, broken and blackened with grime. The Beast's pallid lips quivered; he stretched his jaw. He seemed almost to vibrate with tension.

Perminias gave his attention to his wine, but his eyes were drawn irresistibly back to that face, tormented and depraved, and the eyes that bored into him with a glare of what could only be described as blank hatred.

King Perminias found himself shifting uncomfortably in his seat. The Beast of Rull closed his eyes, though it seemed it took a colossal effort. He remained still for several seconds, breathing hard. Then his eyes opened again. His hands loosened their grip on the table. His body was still and his expression, if dark, was no longer malign.

'First, my thanks,' he said, 'for your most generous gift, dispatched to me in Postor.'

'The lions? Ah, think nothing of it. They were a small but sincere token of my gratitude and esteem for you. I hear that you utilized them to great effect.'

'Their deployment turned the tide of an important battle in our favour. Indeed, it was the last great battle in Chol. The day was won by us in no small wise. Such beasts are worth their weight in gold. Have you others?'

'Alas, too few! My menagerie is my pride and joy, as you know. But to train war-beasts to the standard of those magnificent creatures is a long and arduous task – and a vain labour more often than not. Even harder is it to come by trainers of the calibre of Fland. He controls his great cats like no man I have known before. Without him directing them they would almost certainly have run amok. I am delighted that they served you well, but I regret it may be a long time before I am able to furnish you with others.'

'Ah, well, no matter,' spoke the Beast in a suddenly distant tone, and his fingernails rapped on the table. 'I have my own pets.'

Perminias nodded, but offered no comment. He, like many others, was far from easy with the knowledge that his forces would be fighting on the same battlefield as Gneth. It had to be admitted that Oshalan deployed them with tremendous skill, resulting in major victories. Perminias was not so unwise as to openly criticize his great ally. Sommaria had profited immensely from Khimmur's rise, and Perminias was astute enough to perceive in which directions his best fortunes lay. Nevertheless, Gneth . . . The very name brought a chill to his blood. And observing Oshalan now, he could only wonder what it cost him to control these hideous creatures.

A waft of air carried in the sudden overpowering stench of putrefying flesh. Perminias, who had been about to speak, choked upon his words and reached quickly for his perfumed kerchief.

'Ah, the stink offends you. I am sorry,' said the Beast. He nodded to Genelb Phan. 'If you will.'

Phan rose and crossed the chamber to draw shut the windows.

'It may become a little stuffy,' said the Beast. 'However, the heat here is such that it seems to make little difference whether windows are open or closed. At least now you should be less bothered by the odour.'

'Who were they?' enquired Perminias.

The Beast gave a gesture of indifference. 'I don't know. Hanvatians . . .'

'Then they have committed no crime?'

'It is not possible to say. They are dead and cannot speak.'

'Not all are yet dead.'

'Then I will dispatch a servant to ask them, before they die, whether they are guilty of any crime.'

'Please, not on my account.'

'But you are interested, my friend, are you not?'

'Only insofar as I wondered to what extent their punishment fitted their crime.'

'Ah well, I must reproach you for a mild presumption. It is not a punishment that they suffer, at least not to my knowledge. It is merely a state of being.'

The Beast's mood seemed to change abruptly. He pushed himself suddenly to standing and strode quickly to the end of the room, then back again. His breath came in deep, seething blasts between clenched jaws, and his face was lined and drawn, as if in extreme pain. Perminias watched him uncertainly. At length he ceased walking. He spoke hurriedly. 'Let us deal with the matter at hand. Two nights hence I will breach this "Great" Wall which has held us at bay for so long. Your troops are prepared?'

'Indeed they are. And I received a dispatch from my son, Prince Eperminid, only yesterday. His force has now entered March.'

'Good. What is its strength?'

'One thousand light horse, supplemented by two

hundred elephant cavalry, and five thousand infantry.'

The Beast nodded. 'I have seen to it that the enemy is aware of Prince Eperminid's movements.'

King Perminias's eyes went wide. He thrust himself erect. 'You have done *what*?'

The Beast of Rull gave a twisted smile. 'Calm yourself, my friend. It was entirely necessary. Your son is in no peril, as long as he obeys orders and attempts no rash forays. His force is at present a decoy, nothing more. Its presence is designed to persuade Ghence that we intend a major thrust over the border out of March. And it has worked. Already the Ghentines are rushing four thousand troops northwards to reinforce their border garrisons. Thus their resources are stretched even further.'

'He could be overwhelmed, especially if the March capitulation was a ploy.'

The Beast shook his head. 'There will be no attack by the men of March. Their king, Ambath, gave me his utmost assurance.'

'And you trust him?'

'I hold his children hostage. A young princeling, seven years of age, and a princess. Gwothen, I believe her name is. A quite beautiful maiden on the verge of womanhood. Most becoming. King Ambath will do nothing to incur my displeasure.'

King Perminias resumed his seat, his cheeks flushed. 'Then you do not intend an attack out of March?'

'Not immediately. I simply wish the enemy to believe that I do. There is no wall there, so it stands to reason that that is where our main thrust will come from. Still, I am sending a small force to supplement Prince Eperminid, for the moment will soon come when they will be needed.'

'Then two nights hence, where will our attack be concentrated?'

'Upon the barbican and gate-house eleven miles south of here.'

'But that is massively fortified.'

'That is of no consequence. My pets do not recognize walls and towers. They will lead the assault, and once over the Wall will cause such terror and disarray among the Ghentines as to permit one thousand men with towers and scaling ladders to move up to the Wall relatively unopposed.'

The Beast of Rull wheeled away again suddenly. A strange, agonized sound came from deep within his chest. His back to King Perminias, he said, in a hoarse, clipped voice, 'Kilroth and Phan are apprised of all details. They will discuss these with you now, and make all final arrangements.'

He turned and came quickly around the table and grabbed Perminias's hand before the Sommarian king had had time to rise from his seat. 'Forgive me, my friend, I must leave. But be assured, the Great Wall is no longer an obstacle. Ghence is almost ours.'

With no further word he turned and strode swiftly from the chamber.

III

In the passageway beyond the chamber the Beast reeled. He pressed himself hard up against the wall, his fingers clawing at the cold stone. His face was deathly pale, his eyes aflame, rolling back in his head. He breathed hard. From his lips came a sound of garbled, strangled words. His mouth stretched across his teeth, and out of the corners issued a flood of sticky, yellowish substance which dripped from his chin and ran to the floor.

The Beast wiped his mouth and beard with the sleeve

213

of his shirt. He pushed himself away erect and stood in the centre of the passage. Calming himself, he seemed to take stock of his surroundings, then strode on at a determined pace.

He passed downstairs to the ground floor and was crossing the main hall to enter the corridor leading to the dungeons below when a figure emerged from a doorway to his left. It was Croman, the Chief Chamberlain, whom the Beast had appointed head of his travelling household.

Absorbed in the fury of his inner world, the Beast failed to notice Croman. Croman nervously cleared his throat as his master swept by. 'Sire. Your Majesty.'

The Beast of Rull wheeled, advancing upon Croman, and snapped, 'What is it? I am hungry. I must eat.'

Stuttering, Croman backed into the doorway, dismayed by the unnatural force that emanated from his king.

'Sire, a messenger. From Hon-Hiaita. He says he brings important news.'

The Beast of Rull struck at the air with a savage gesture. 'Gah! Where is he?'

'He waits in the adjoining chamber, Sire.'

The Beast pushed past Croman into the room. Croman, with relief, turned and made off to busy himself with other duties.

As his liege entered the chamber where he waited, the messenger stiffened, then bowed. He was a short, portly fellow, with sagging jowls, balding head and a face that now gleamed under a film of sweat. The Beast looked him up and down.

'You are?'

'Vesrhim, Sire.'

'Ah yes. I recall. You are *Zan-Chassin*, are you not?'

'I am, Sire. I have come from your esteemed deputy in Khimmur, Lord Mostin, with news of developments

214

in regard to certain research he is engaged in on your behalf.'

'What news?'

'Lord Mostin declares that his researches have now cast light upon a particular area of his research which has previously been elusive to his probing. Specifically, he has identified a certain artifact used long ago by the Hecran king Moshrazman.'

The Beast of Rull, who had been glaring at the messenger with a wrathful intensity, let out a long breath. His features suddenly changed, to assume an expression of dreadful rapture. 'Does he have the artifact?'

'Not at present, Sire. But he believes he may now know where it lies. Armed search parties have been sent out to locate it and bring it to Hon-Hiaita. In view of the importance of this matter, Lord Mostin urges that you return to Hon-Hiaita at your earliest convenience.'

The Beast stretched his lips, exhaling bitter words under his breath. 'I cannot; not yet. You will inform Mostin that I endeavour to wind things up here with great dispatch. Within weeks, I hope, I will be able to return. What of Kemahamek? Is there news of the Wonasina?'

'Lord Mostin stated that the search continues. There is still no indication of where she may be hidden.'

'He must not let up! Reiterate this. She is to be found, at all costs.'

'I will relay that message, Sire.'

'Is there anything else?'

Vesrhim opened a leather satchel which hung at his side. From within he took a letter, bound and sealed. This he held out to the Beast of Rull, bowing his head. 'Explicit details, for your eyes alone, Sire, are contained herein.'

The Beast snatched the letter from him. 'Good. Apply to my stewards. They will provide you with refreshment.'

'Thank you, Sire.'

The Beast strode from the chamber. As he passed again through the main hall he muttered to himself, a murderous smile taut upon his lips, 'Ah, my pets, my pets. Soon you will have brothers and sisters beside you. The way to your domain is almost open.'

He passed into a dank corridor, down winding stone steps into a crypt-like area with low roof supported by stout, arched stone columns. Through another portal he went down a second flight of narrow steps, and was now in the dungeon of the manor. Evidently the former owner's life had not been entirely blameless. The dungeon was furnished with a number of tiny cells, and a torture chamber, amply if not particularly imaginatively equipped.

The Beast came to a heavy wooden door with black iron hinges and straps. Beside the door stood a sentry, who snapped to attention at the sight of his king.

'Open,' snapped the Beast. The soldier fumbled with a set of keys at his belt. He unlocked the door. The Beast strode through, along a narrow torchlit corridor between two rows of cells set into the walls. Within the cells, behind bars of iron, prisoners sat in filth and gloom. Some looked up as he passed, others stared dully into space, unmoved.

Glancing to neither right nor left, the Beast entered a larger area, better lit by torches and the orange-red glow of a brazier. Beside the brazier sat Irlo, the Chief Executioner, whetting the twin hooked prongs of a gouging instrument. He stood as his king entered, and bowed.

The Beast stopped before him, sweeping his eyes briefly around the chamber. Here were situated the apparatus of torture: rack and wheel, hanging-frames, presses, griddles. Upon racks on the wall were pincers, hooks, hammers, crushers, whips and a host of other instruments.

'I hunger,' said the Beast. 'Bring three.'

Irlo signalled to a pair of guards, who marched immediately to the cells. The Beast seated himself in a wooden chair at the side of the room, set before a horizontal wooden frame from one end of which two steel chains ran over a beam in the ceiling, and down to connect with a winch.

The guards reappeared, bringing three prisoners in chains, whom they pushed into the centre of the chamber.

The Beast appraised the prisoners with burning eyes. All three were naked and stood in attitudes of pathetic helplessness. The first was a man of advanced years, thin, with bowed back and emaciated white flesh, grey hair and beard. Next to him stood a younger man with short stubby legs, wide, round shoulders and a flabby belly. He shook with fear, his hands held self-consciously over his manhood. The third prisoner was little more than a boy, aged perhaps fifteen. He was of average height, slim but well formed, with a thin face, long chin and wavy blond hair.

The Beast of Rull rose from his chair and approached them.

The old man spoke imploringly, 'If you please, Sir, we are innocents. We have committed no crime. We do not understand . . .'

In a swift, brutal movement the Beast raised an arm and brought it backhanded across the old man's face. The force of the blow was such that it lifted its victim off his feet, propelling him backwards across the chamber. The frail body smashed into the wall and crumpled to the floor. Blood trickled from the mouth, the neck was twisted at an unnatural angle. The scrawny limbs twitched spasmodically.

The Beast continued his appraisal of the other two, who now stood stiffly, wide-eyed and quaking. He passed behind them; his eyes ran up and down over their flesh. He slid his hands over their shoulders, down their backs, pinching, rolling the flesh. At length he nodded to Irlo. 'This one.'

The two soldiers ran forward and dragged the second prisoner back to his cell. The boy stood alone in the centre of the chamber, his jaw trembling so violently that the teeth chattered, his breathing rapid, shallow, staccato. The Beast resumed his seat. Irlo came forward and almost gently took the boy's arm and led him to the horizontal frame.

The soldiers returned. The Beast watched as they helped Irlo lie the terrified youth upon the frame, spreadeagled, and secured his wrists and ankles with clamps at the corners. When they had done they stepped away to man the winch set behind the frame.

As they turned the handles of the winch, the frame, borne on its chains, lifted at one end. They continued to wind until it stood erect, resting a foot or so above the stone floor. Straps then secured it to a pair of iron posts, rendering it immobile.

Now the Beast left his seat and came forward again. He lifted his gaze to study the face of his victim.

The boy whimpered and rolled his eyes in terror. His entire body shook uncontrollably. The Beast reached out with both hands and ran them tenderly over the boy's flank. He leaned forward and pressed a cheek to the white flesh.

He listened for a moment to the hammering of the poor wretch's heart. Then he stepped back. One hand reached out, open-palmed. Irlo pressed the haft of a short-bladed knife into the hand.

With a single swift motion the Beast of Rull slit the prisoner's abdomen from sternum to groin. The boy let forth a dismal moan. The Beast gazed at the long, red gash before his eyes. Blood issued forth, streaming over the pale thighs and dripping to the floor. Pressing outwards against the flesh, the glisten of pulsing innards could just be seen.

With his hands the Beast of Rull gently parted the opening. He stared at the living organs. Then he slipped his hands inside and slowly brought forward the quivering, liquid guts.

The boy let forth the most anguished cry, 'Mama! Mama!'

The Beast gazed again into the tortured face. Then he bent his head and lifting the hot, slippery stuff, pressed his face forward. He opened his mouth wide in rapture, and began to eat.

IV

In accordance with the plan, the assault upon the Great Wall of Ghence was launched two nights later. The Khimmurian forces adhered to a strategy similar to that which had been employed with notable success more than two years earlier at Twalinieh, and with variations at other locations across Rull since.

During the previous day, a Khimmurian contingent led by the *dhoma*-lord Alakis of Pri'in, supplemented by Anxau auxiliaries, passed into March through Soland and linked with Prince Eperminid's Sommarians there. *En route* they were joined by a band of mercenary tribesmen out of Soland.

They moved cautiously up to the Ghentine border, and sent forward groups of skirmishers to harry the defenders and probe their strengths. The Ghentines responded accordingly, precisely as the Beast of Rull had predicted: within twenty-four hours Ghentine reinforcements some four thousand strong marched up from inland. Khimmur and Sommaria dug in to await developments.

Meanwhile at the Hanvat border the attack upon the northernmost barbican and gate-house began. Soon after dark the first wave of Gneth emerged from the woods a mile or so to the west of the Wall. Creeping, hopping, slithering, crawling, flying, they advanced unseen across the open ground before the great edifice. For these creatures the Wall was no obstacle. They came seemingly out of nowhere, at a position about half a mile north of the barbican.

The Wall was well garrisoned. Ghence was aware of the recent concentration of troops in the region, and the likelihood that Gneth were among them. Nevertheless, the first the defenders knew of the attack was when they found monsters suddenly in their midst.

With suckered limbs or needle-hook claws the Gneth scaled the Wall with the ease of ants. Out of the air on gigantic wings they came, and fell upon the Ghentine troops.

Within minutes of this assault, which was a diversion aimed at concentrating Ghentine energies on a particular section of the Wall, the second wave of Gneth came out of the woods. Huge mardols, vigrits, aj-ghouls and gobes advanced upon the gates of the barbican. Simultaneously the trebuchets and mangonels ranged upon the plain resumed their bombardment. More than fifty of the great engines unleashed a barrage of massive boulders and barrels of wildfire over the Wall into the gate-house and the passage and compound behind. In the darkness they fired almost blind, but the desired effect – to create havoc and confusion, hindering and imperilling the defenders who rushed to combat the attacking monsters – was achieved.

And now the bulk of the Beast's forces came forward.

For a week Ghentine observers had been watching their enemies levelling an area of the rough open ground before the Wall. The earth had been packed hard, wide causeways formed which ran almost to the foot of the Wall itself. Working beneath movable shelters with roofs of metal or water-soaked hide, the Khimmurians had been subjected to constant fire from the defenders, while their own archers and crossbowmen had moved up behind pavises to provide counter-fire.

Now the fruits of that dangerous labour were to be born. In the darkness a dozen siege-towers, built in sections, had been brought forward out of the woods. Still well beyond bowshot, and as yet invisible to the defenders, the sections were fitted together. After the Gneth advance the towers began to lumber towards the Wall, each one pulled by dozens of soldiers, while more pushed from behind. Missile troops again moved up in support, unleashing sighing clouds of arrows and bolts against their opponents on the ramparts.

Side by side, the six towers rolled up to the Wall just south of the barbican. Men dropped, pierced by arrows and spears, but others ran forward to take their places. Slowly, inexorably, the leviathan-like towers continued on.

Fire arrows trailed through the night, pouring into the towers. But the most vulnerable parts of the towers were protected with dampened hides or fine metal mesh. Platforms were extended from their upper levels, hooking onto the battlements of the Wall. Storm troops poured across these narrow ways to engage the enemy, and simultaneously more troops rushed out of the night, bearing scaling ladders and ropes and grapple-hooks.

The fighting was hard and bloody. The Ghentine defenders put their all into repelling the invaders. Hundreds of Khimmurians and their allies died; the Ghentine losses were numerically fewer, but in practical terms they were of far greater significance, for such was the nature of the assault that it prevented them from replenishing their fallen troops with sufficient reinforcements.

Little by little the soldiers of the Beast gained vital ground. The first wave of Gneth, breaching the Wall, had quickly slaughtered the initial defenders there. They then veered south, marauding in a frenzy among the Ghentine reinforcements rushing to beat them back. Behind the Gneth came a force of two thousand of King Perminias's Sommarians, with ladders and grappling-ropes, to take advantage of the gap in the defence.

Meanwhile hundreds more Ghentines were forced to man the gate-house and barbican. They poured flaming oil and boiling water, and dropped great boulders onto the monsters storming the gate. But to their dismay the tactic had little effect. The Gneth were largely impervious to their efforts, and pounded on regardless, while the Khimmurian siege-engines maintained their relentless bombardment of their foe.

A sense of dismay and panic began to spread among the Ghentine troops as they found themselves forced to give up more and more ground. Due to the multi-pronged nature of the attack, the Khimmurian assault troops beside the barbican met with less resistance than would otherwise have been the case. Though the ramparts were quickly drenched with blood, and Khimmurians in their dozens were cut down by sword, arrow and axe, or sent pitching from the battlements and towers to die on the earth below, the survivors managed nevertheless to battle their way slowly forward.

222

In time a desperate force, spurred by two years of victories, was able to force a gap large enough in the defenders' ranks to permit free access onto the Wall from the siege-towers. Twenty won through, then twenty more. They began to press towards the gate-house.

Now the defenders there perceived their full plight. They were assailed on three sides: by monstrous creatures at the gate and rampaging down from the northern ramparts, and by soldiers winning through from the south. The choice was to seal themselves inside the gate-house and put up a last-ditch defence, or retreat.

It was apparent now that with the presence of the Gneth the barbican and gate-house were no longer the unassailable stronghold they had been. So the Ghentines chose the latter course, while the opportunity still remained to do so, for it was quite evident that that option would soon be denied them.

Disorganized now, a terrified rabble, they abandoned the gate-house and the Wall around, and fled.

From within, the victorious Khimmurians raised the portcullises at barbican and gate-house. The Gneth smashed through the gates in a howling, roaring, nightmare hoard. Incensed and insensate, they stormed on into the wild backlands of Ghence in pursuit of the fleeing troops.

The Great Wall was breached. That which could not be achieved over months of siege and bombardment had come about in a single, death-ridden night. Yet again the Vulpasmage had demonstrated his brilliance and cunning to full effect. The doorway into Ghence was open. Now the road led inwards, via the nation's lesser organs straight to its now vulnerable heart: the great capital of Trore.

V

The following day Orl Kilroth rode east through northern Ghence at the head of a force of three thousand
Khimmurian infantry and five hundred horse. Supplementing these was a hired mercenary group, five
hundred strong, led by a former Pansurian brigand
named Barqualio. Also with the force was a train of
black wagons containing more than two hundred and
fifty of Kuno's H'padir warriors.

Kilroth's orders were to drive quickly to the March
border. A courier had already been dispatched through
Soland to inform Lord Alakis and the Sommarian
Prince Eperminid of the successful breaching of the
Wall. With the arrival of Kilroth's force an all-out
assault was to be launched upon the Ghentine
defenders at the border with March. Attacked by three
armies they would be trapped with no avenue of escape.
When the killing was done Kilroth was to leave a sufficient garrison in the border strongholds, and continue
on south to join the main army making for Trore.

Meanwhile, after a day's rest, the victorious army
rode south, the Beast of Rull at its fore, mounted on
his black stallion Roaig. Clad in gleaming armour of
gold-and-black lamellar, the Vulpasmage helm upon
his head, he was a fearsome and imposing figure. Five
hundred mounted White Blade knights formed his personal guard, a wave of glinting light armour and pale
blue uniforms, pennants fluttering aloft in a hot, dry
breeze, their kite-shields emblazoned with the emblem
of the radiant white sword on a field of azure.

A strong force was left behind to garrison the gate-
house and barbican on the Ghence Wall. No attempt
was made to dislodge the defenders from elsewhere
in their strongholds along the Wall. Such a move was
unnecessary, it being important only to ensure that

the way remained open and in Khimmurian hands. To retake the gate-house and reseal the breach, Ghence would need to attack with a force far greater than it could spare.

At the Beast's side rode Genelb Phan, the White Blade commander. To his other side was a man named Thiontillo, a former member of the *Zan-Chassin* Hierarchy, who had thrown his lot in favour of Crown and Empire. Behind came the soldiers of Khimmur, Sommaria, Kemahamek, Cexhaut and elsewhere: horse-soldiers, infantry and archers, siege-weapons and engineers, and all the baggage, followers, pack-animals, whores and other appurtenances of war.

Some distance to the west, following a parallel course away from the roads, came the Gneth. They had taken huge losses in the assault upon the Wall. In particular, the first wave of monsters, so vital as shock troops capable of surmounting almost any fortifications, had been reduced by almost half. This was disturbing news for the Beast, though he had anticipated heavy losses. During the northern campaign the Gneth had been depleted little by little, and he had thus held them in reserve for the most difficult tasks. After the fall of Postor in Chol, he had ridden immediately south in order to deploy them against Ghence.

Now the mighty walls of Trore awaited him. Without doubt Ghence's ruling Oligarchal Council would be pulling back all available troops to hold the capital. Ghence's heart might be vulnerable, but it was beating hard and far from being pierced. Trore could conceivably hold out for a long time, and taking it would be no simple task. Gneth were vital, but had he sufficient numbers left to storm its walls?

The alternative was a prolonged siege, something he hoped to avoid at all costs. Men far from home quickly succumbed to boredom and grew disaffected under such conditions. The spectre of relief lingered ever close by: until he had taken Trore he could not safely move on into Tomia, Dyarchim and the lands beyond. Ghence might yet summon aid from any of these nations, or others further south across the Yphasian Ocean. He would needs surround the city on land and sea, and Ghence still maintained a formidable navy and had control of the bay of Trore. Thus supplies could be brought in from the east, via Ibisiel, the capital of the old Ghentine dominion of Acrire. The siege would test his troops to the limit. It would be costly in men and materiel, and held no guarantee of success.

He reflected upon the message brought to him by Vesrhim from Mostin in Hon-Hiaita. There lay the answer – the magical artifact employed by the Hecranese king Moshrazman III during The Great Deadlock. Its existence had long been posited by researchers into the arcane arts, but none knew what it was, from where Moshrazman might have brought it, or where it now lay. The Beast had made its acquisition a priority, with Mostin being appointed to lead the research in the quest for knowledge of the artifact. Until now Mostin's endeavours had been without positive result. But at last, according to his message, there had been a breakthrough.

A thrill of excitement surged through the Beast's tortured frame. He sucked in air through clenched teeth. With such a weapon in his hands he would be truly invincible. Somehow he had to return quickly to Khimmur.

The great army forged a bloody road south, razing towns and villages, looting, pillaging and murdering at will. Six days after taking the Wall the Beast of Rull stood upon a low knoll gazing at the roofs and towers of mighty Trore half a mile distant. Beyond it was the sea, blue and glittering, lit with a million dazzling, shimmering diamonds reflected in the scorching heat of the sun. Before him his great army was drawn up in battle formation, ready at a signal to move forward, siege-engines at the fore, and begin its relentless pounding of the city walls.

The Beast had been in good humour. An hour earlier a courier had arrived from the north, bearing news from Orl Kilroth. The operation had been successful, the Ghentine defenders overwhelmed. Kilroth and his troops were within two days' march of the capital.

But now the Beast considered the high, sturdy walls and their many towers and turrets. Undoubtedly well-trained and disciplined troops waited within. And a conscript army of untold numbers of terrified, desperate citizens could also be expected. The Beast's mood grew darker.

Gneth. Gneth. They were the key.

For the first time since setting out from Hon-Hiaita on his campaign of conquest, the Beast of Rull was experiencing the hollow, nagging sensations of self-doubt. His Gneth force was hardly sufficient to meet his needs here today, this he was coming increasingly to accept. The first wave lacked the numbers to create the desired havoc and diversion within the city walls. Trore was comparable in strength to Twalinieh in Kemahamek. But Twalinieh had not been taken by pure, Gneth-backed military force. It had required months – years! – of careful planning to bring about Twalinieh's downfall. In the end it had come about through cunning, guile and intrigue, as much as military manoeuvre. The Gneth had been at their strongest, and no one had known of their coming. But additionally the Beast had infiltrated forces into the city in advance of the assault. His secret assassins in the Simbissikim had done their work too. Twalinieh's people had been destroyed by the knowledge that their Twin

227

Wona-Souls had been taken from them, and their soldiery had been taken completely by surprise. Here, in Trore, he had no such advantages.

He stood wide-stanced, his arms folded across his deep chest, in brooding contemplation of the problem before him.

Beside him Genelb Phan pointed a finger towards the city. 'A gate has opened. Riders approach.'

The main gate of the city had swung wide, to emit a column of horsemen from within. They could be seen emerging in stately procession, their armour glinting distantly in the sun as they filed down the straight road. The gate swung to at their backs. Without hurry they came towards the waiting army, thirty in all, riding three abreast.

As they came closer it could be seen that they wore only light or partial armour, and were otherwise garbed in richly coloured robes and cloaks. They held erect lances from which blue pennants fluttered. Their horses, stepping proudly, were caparisoned in many bright colours. At their fore rode a herald, holding aloft a standard which bore the arms of the Union of the Presiding Houses of Ghence: five golden globes on a field of white.

'It would appear to be a delegation from the Oligarchal Council,' Phan observed with a cold smile. 'Evidently they have a desire to talk.'

The company of Ghence knights came to a halt at a point equidistant between the city walls and the front ranks of the invading Khimmurian army.

The Beast of Rull cocked his head. 'Send forth a herald to enquire as to their business.'

Genelb Phan turned, summoned his herald, Gorod, who stood ten yards away, and issued a curt order. The herald saluted and quickly made off. Moments later a company of six Hon-Hiaitan knights, preceded by

Gorod bearing the White Blade standard, rode out to meet the Ghence contingent. They halted upon the road, forty yards distant from the Ghentine knights. There was a pause of half a minute or so, then the Ghentine herald urged his horse forward alone.

The two heralds conferred, then Gorod wheeled his horse around and galloped back towards the waiting army, accompanied by the Khimmurian knights. The Ghentine herald turned his horse and walked slowly back to his men.

In due course Gorod arrived at the run before Genelb Phan and the Beast of Rull.

'Sire, it is a deputation representing the most noble houses of Ghence. Their herald, speaking with the voice of all of them, states the following: the Ruling Oligarchal Council of Ghence is no more. Its members have fled, unseen and undeclared, abusing the privilege and responsibilities of their station, and abandoning their nation to its fate. We, the senior members of the great houses, now constitute an emergency parliament, with full and complete powers of rule and government. On behalf of ourselves and our nation we request a meeting with Oshalan I, King of Khimmur. At such a time we will formally declare ourselves willing to surrender our arms and throw open the gates of Trore, on the condition that no acts of harm or molestation, vengeance or violence are inflicted upon us or our citizens. A document detailing Terms of Capitulation will be presented to King Oshalan in person, at which time, once it has been agreed and signed by both parties, we will acknowledge King Oshalan to be our just and rightful overlord and undisputed ruler of Ghence.'

For some moments the Beast stared at the herald, Gorod, his face immobile. The herald grew uneasy under his stare, blanched and began to fidget. Then slowly the Beast's maddened eyes softened and his pallid lips twisted into a semblance of a smile. Suddenly he threw back his head and guffawed out loud. Hands upon his hips he stood there, racked with near-hysterical laughter.

The herald observed blank-faced. Genelb Phan stood by, gazing out with an expressionless visage at the thirty Ghentines on the road below. The Beast calmed himself sufficiently to speak. He reached out and slapped Genelb Phan's shoulder. 'Ha-ha! What irony! What perfect, fateful irony! Yes! Yes!'

Genelb Phan permitted a small smile to touch his lips.

'It is divine providence!' laughed the Beast. 'It is Destiny! Yes, Herald, call them here. We will have our meeting and agree our terms. Yes, bring ale, bring wine and meat, the finest we can provide. Do not stint. Let these defeated nobles of Ghence sit at table with us and enjoy the full measure of our generosity. And we will listen well as they define the conditions of their capitulation. Ha-ha! Yes indeed, this is a day for celebration! Trore upon a golden platter! Make ready, my friends. The gates are about to be opened; we will enter unopposed. And the terms? Ah, if they suit us we will abide by them; if not, well, there will be plenty of time to reconsider, eh? We have won, my friends. We have won. Ghence is mine. At last, Ghence is mine!'

9

I

The township of Murdren is a small market town within the *dhoma* of Su'um S'ol in eastern Mystoph. It is situated some way above the Barrier Fell, nestling between the gentle Gladwillow Hills upon whose chalky, south-facing slopes the famous Maut grape grows in abundance, producing an elegant, distinct, captivating white wine which is unrivalled in the region. In better days I had been the owner of two quite splendid estates here. Now I had returned, an outcast and desperado, presumed dead. My properties, I assumed, and their respective revenues, were in the hands of men not likely to throw open their arms in joy at the sight of me.

Our journey here, along the southern fringe of the Magoth, had not been without incident. For the first few days we had seen not a soul. We kept to the shelter of the thinning forest, the wide grassland of the Ashakite steppe never far away, glimpsed between the trees as a belt of shifting sunlit green. Here at the edge of the forest the way was not particularly difficult, and we made good speed.

On day four Count Inbuel turned north-west, heading back into the forest. When I queried this he replied that he was making for a remote Vir village set a few miles within the Magoth. There he hoped to gain intelligence and an up-to-date picture of the situation locally.

Three hours later we arrived at the outskirts of the

village. It was a small cluster of wooden huts protected by a palisade of sharpened stakes. It was occupied by Khimmurian troops.

'I suppose I should not be surprised,' whispered Inbuel as we crouched in the undergrowth, forty yards from the palisade. 'Yet I had hoped that this one might have remained free.'

My eyes were on the guard-tower constructed beside the gate. Two soldiers stood listlessly in its upper level. I scratched distractedly at the stump of my severed arm, which had been causing me some mild irritation these past few days.

'By my estimation we are still at least four days from the border,' I said.

Inbuel nodded, rotating his stubbled chin against the fingers of one hand. 'They have infiltrated further than this, but generally their encroachments have been more northerly. This does not bode well for the remaining villages I had hoped to visit between here and Khimmur.'

We made to withdraw, but had gone only a few yards when we heard the sound of a distressed cry from the woods nearby. Close upon this came harsh male laughter, and another cry. We drew our swords and made off, crouching, towards the source of the disturbance.

In a small clearing beside a pond of deep black water covered with water lilies we came upon a group of six soldiers making sport with a young Vir woman. Evidently she was from the village we had just left, and they, it could be reasonably assumed, made up part of its garrison.

The men stood in an unformed circle, laughing and making lewd comments. They thrust the woman back and forth between themselves, pawing and groping at her, planting brutal, slobbering kisses on her mouth and neck. The young woman sobbed and cried out in her distress, trying hopelessly to resist. She clutched her peasant's smock, which was badly ripped, to her bosom. Close to the pond a small child, hardly more than a baby, sat beneath a dewberry bush, wailing pitifully.

My ire rose at the sight. Into my mind came an image of my daughter, Eroniss, and her young mother Rohse. Gripping my sword I made to rise. 'I cannot stand by and watch this!'

Count Inbuel gripped my arm. 'Nor I, but if we march in like buffoons we will be hacked to pieces. Like you, I am no weapons master.' He was unslinging his bow and notching an arrow to the string. 'How are your knife-throwing skills these days, Dinbig?'

'I am out of practice, but would consider myself as good as the next man. But I've only two blades, and neither is balanced for flight.'

'Here is a third,' said Inbuel, handing me his dagger. 'For the want of any better, they'll have to do. I'll circle around a short way. Do not cast a blade until you see the first man pierced by my arrow.'

He crept silently away. The soldiers maintained their brutish game, impervious to the woman's pleas or the bruises and abrasions appearing on her face and limbs. I sensed that their excitement was rising, and with it their impatience. As if in confirmation of this, one of the group, who though he bore no evident rank was older than the others and seemed to have pronounced himself leader, suddenly took the young woman and crushed her to him. He kissed her hard upon the mouth, then released her and threw her to the ground.

He stood over her, leering.

'Enough foolery!' he growled. He unbuckled his sword-belt and let it fall, then began to untie his trousers.

The woman tried to crawl away towards her infant.

The ruffian leaned down and dragged her back. He struck her harshly across the mouth. 'Lie still, wench!'

One of the other soldiers came forward and took the woman's hands, stretching her arms over her head. Two more forced her thighs apart. The leader thrust down his trousers and positioned himself between her legs. The other three gathered around, smirking and joking.

Still the girl struggled, writhing and twisting her body. As the leader extended himself over her, groping with his genital member, she spat defiantly in his eye. 'Khimmurian filth!'

He drew back, wiping his face with the back of his hand. He issued an angry command. 'Dabar, the brat!'

A young soldier ran to grab the screaming child. He held it up by its ankle and waded knee-deep into the pond. There he dangled the infant over the dark water, looking back at the helpless Vir woman, grinning.

Craning her neck, the woman cried out, 'No! My baby! My baby!'

'Be still, then!' ordered the leader. 'Make it easy for yourself. Give us our fun and the brat won't suffer.'

The woman went limp, her eyes still on the child. The soldier leaned over her again and ripped away her clothing. He groped once more at his crotch, his heavy white buttocks presented to me. I hefted my first dagger, but despite my rage I knew that he could not be the initial target, for he was the least well disposed to retaliate.

Silently I urged Inbuel to make haste, for the terrible deed was almost done.

There was a faint hissing sound. A soldier cried out, staggered forward, the shaft of an arrow sticking from his back. Instantly I hurled my first knife. My target was the back of the man nearest to me, but with the unbalanced weapon my aim was untrue. The blade

234

buried itself in the back of his thigh, just below the buttock. He reeled with a howl.

A second arrow struck another man in the chest as he wheeled to investigate. I threw another knife, but missed. All was pandemonium as the soldiers scattered for cover, drawing weapons and yelling in alarm.

We had still not been spotted. Inbuel released another shaft. It grazed the shoulder of the leading soldier, who was lurching away, wrenching up his trousers with one hand. He sprawled headlong across the grass, then scrambled on again, barely touched.

The woman was on her feet, running for her child which the soldier, Dabar, had dropped into the shallow water as he raced for cover. She put herself in the path of our fire, preventing us from firing again.

At that moment the leading soldier seemed to have a second thought. He lunged for the water and grabbed the struggling infant.

The woman shrieked and threw herself upon him, clawing and beating, but he thrust her off with a savage blow. She fell into the muddy shallows. The soldier, clutching the child, threw himself behind a tree.

Dabar now stepped from bushes at the water's edge and grabbed the woman as she righted herself. He pinioned her hard against him so that her body shielded his. Sword at her throat he peered with wild defiance into the underbrush, edging back towards cover.

The leader's harsh voice came from behind the tree. 'Throw down your weapons, or woman and brat die!'

My heart fell. Dabar, his back to a tree trunk, now brazenly faced us, his arm around the woman's neck. I could see one of the other soldiers, the one I had wounded, pressed to the ground behind a rotting log. Another lay dead on the ground, while another, with Inbuel's arrow in his back, was trying to crawl with agonized slowness across the clearing. The last man was hidden somewhere out of sight.

The leading soldier emerged, kneeling, from behind his tree. He held the child to his chest, the point of a knife against its neck.

'Come out,' he called again.

I hesitated in a welter of indecision. There was nothing for it. Slowly I rose. Out of the corner of my eye I saw that Inbuel had done the same. The Khimmurians eyed us suspiciously. 'Only two?'

The leader peered further into the shadows of the forest, then gestured with his knife. 'Come forward. Drop your weapons.'

We did as we were told. The soldier with the thigh wound rose from behind his log, limped forward and sat down, clutching his leg. The last man came out of hiding and stood at the edge of the clearing, sword drawn.

'Lie down, face down on the floor,' ordered the leader.

I lowered myself wretchedly. My attention was caught by the sudden change of expression on the Khimmurian's face. His triumphal leer was transformed into a grimace of pain. He spun around on his knees, letting the infant drop. One hand clawed frantically at a spot high up on his back. I saw the red flights of a small dart protruding from his spine.

In the same moment a shape, swift, dusty-brown and big as a man, flew out of the undergrowth. It hurled itself at the leading soldier, stabbing with a short-bladed sword. He fell back with a gargled scream as savage jaws closed around his windpipe.

Yo!

I jumped to my feet, running to regain my dropped sword. Inbuel, who had not yet relinquished his, leapt forward, blade flashing. The soldier at the edge of the clearing had spun in alarm at Yo's sudden appearance.

236

Inbuel's blade slid hard between his ribs. He tottered forward with a groan, groping at the wound. Inbuel struck again, and he fell dead.

Dabar tried to back away, still holding the child's mother, blade pressed to her throat.

'I'll kill her!' he screamed. But Yo had slipped around behind him, rising on to hind legs. Wild-eyed, Dabar tried to turn, flinging up his arm to protect himself.

The woman twisted free of his grip. She dashed without a moment's thought to her screaming babe. I lunged forward and buried my blade in Dabar's undefended flank. He cried out, spinning around, and Yo's vhazz sword finished him off.

Now only the soldier whom I had wounded in the thigh remained standing. He stood alone, clearly terrified. He cast his weapon to the ground.

I stepped back. Count Inbuel still stood in a defensive stance, blade before him, pointed towards Yo.

'It is all right,' I breathed. 'It is Yo, my ally.'

Warily, Inbuel lowered his blade.

'Yo, a timely entrance! My thanks. You are forgiven for your misdeeds.'

'All of them, Master?'

I realized what I had said, but nodded. 'We will have recourse to discussion later on. It is important that you understand completely the folly of your earlier actions. But you are forgiven, yes. There will be no castigation.'

I looked around me. Two Khimmurians still lived. He with the arrow in his back was barely conscious; the other was ashen-faced, clutching his bloodstained leg. Out of fear and weakness through loss of blood he had sunk to the ground, where he sat gaping up at us.

'They have to die,' muttered Inbuel. 'We cannot be identified.'

I nodded grimly. The soldier with the thigh wound stared at me, pleading, tears streaming down his face.

He was aged about twenty; I was not sure I could murder him in cold blood.

'Please, sir, I don't want to die. Let me go, please. I won't tell no one.'

I stared at him irresolutely, aware that Inbuel was dealing with his companion. There was a movement beside me. The young Vir woman had rushed forward, holding a sword taken from one of the dead. She glared venomously at the wounded Khimmurian.

'It is better than you deserve!' she said. She curled her lip and spat hard into his face, then stabbed down with the sword with both hands, sinking the blade deep into his breast.

He sat there, impaled upon the blade, staring upwards with a ghastly, sorrowful expression. I had a sudden shattering sense of what could have been, then the young head flopped forward.

The woman released the weapon. She stepped backwards, then let forth a great sob and began to shake uncontrollably. I drew her away and lowered her to the ground, for she seemed about to faint. Inbuel brought the baby and placed it in her arms. He looked up at me with a drawn countenance.

I put my foot upon the young soldier's shoulder and pulled free the blade. The body collapsed limply, its life-blood spilling into the earth.

We dragged the six corpses deep into cover beneath dense bushes, concealing them further with fallen branches, loose earth and leaves.

'It will not be wise for you to return to the village,' Inbuel said to the young woman, whose name, we learned, was Haidi. 'These men may already have been missed. The others will be looking for them.'

'And when they find them,' said Haidi, 'they will bring out three of our women or children for each of these dead soldiers, and hang them before the

238

assembled village. The men they will save, for they perform Khimmur's labour.'

I exchanged a weighted glance with Inbuel. 'How many soldiers occupy your village?' I asked Haidi.

'Twenty.'

'So there are now fourteen?'

She nodded.

Inbuel looked at me gravely. 'And we are but three.'

'Four,' said Haidi resolutely, having recovered from her earlier shock.

I looked at her bruised face. 'Are all fourteen presently inside the village?'

Haidi shook her head. 'Four guard the work-gang.'

'Which will return when?'

'At dusk.'

'Approximately two hours. Tell me, Haidi, with these soldiers, are there any others? Khimmurians, probably, but who wear no uniform?'

She shook her head.

'You are sure? Not even one?'

'No. There are only the soldiers.'

'And since they have been there, have you or any of your folk witnessed magic in any form being used by any of them? Think carefully now. It is very important.'

She looked at me with widening eyes. The very idea of magic unsettled her. 'No, I am sure of it. There's been no magic.'

I looked across at Inbuel. His eyes were twinkling, and a glimmer of a smile hovered on his lips. 'Can you do it, Sir Dinbig?'

'I will not know without trying. It will be dangerous.'

'You will be jeopardizing your mission.'

'Would you leave these people to suffer the atrocities that will surely follow our actions here?'

239

'Not if I believed there was a slender hope that my intervention might help avert such repercussions.'

'Then I take it you are with me.'

'Do you truly need to ask such a question?'

'Good. Then let us put our skills to the test now, before the work-gang returns.'

II

The Veil of Invisibility is a far from simple rapture to invoke effectively. It demands a deal of energy in its casting, and even greater concentration in maintaining its effect for the desired period of time.

Skilfully and properly cast, it can obscure the caster from the sight of others. In effect, one blends into one's surroundings; yet it is not the Blending skill utilized with such consummate artistry by the Aphesuk. Their techniques are almost certainly based on different principles and the development of innate talents. They can be used at will by an expert practitioner, seemingly with little effort. The Veil of Invisibility, on the other hand, can be used only infrequently, and for limited periods, due to the energy expended in its casting and the effort of concentration required.

The Veil is effected through the mental disruption of light immediately surrounding one's physical person. An aura is formed through which light cannot pass. This aura, perceived by another, deceives their vision to the extent that they see nothing before them, or at most a vague mist.

For this reason the rapture cannot be cast upon another person, for it is the caster's own mental energy that is all-important in creating and maintaining the aura.

We quickly devised a plan, as detailed as we could

240

make it under the circumstances. Speed was of the essence, for I doubted my ability to maintain the Veil for more than a few minutes, particularly as I would be simultaneously performing other tasks. Moreover, I lacked the proficiency to render myself totally invisible. Thus, in order to get through the village gate and past the sentries, I would need some kind of diversion to hold their attention.

I sat in profound concentration for some minutes, slowly building up the rapture. I grew aware of a dim aura manifesting about my corporeal form.

'How do I look?' I asked, for I could not tell the effect as it appeared to others.

'I don't know. I can't see you,' replied Inbuel with a grin, then more seriously: 'What I see is difficult to describe. You are a faint blur, which my eyes seem naturally to slide away from. It is not true to say that I can see what is immediately behind you; instead I see a kind of semblance of things, an aggregate of what I would expect to see. Were I not deliberately looking at you now, I am certain I would not be aware of you.'

I walked away a few paces. 'And now?'

'Motion declares the presence of something, but it is impossible to say what. And again, my eyes seem unwilling to notice you.'

I glanced at Haidi, whose hand was raised to her open mouth. The other clutched her child, and her fearful expression told me all I needed to know.

'Good,' I said. 'I'll go.'

I moved up slowly through the undergrowth, to within feet of the gate. Ordinarily I would have been in full view of the two sentries. I could hear them talking in bored tones as they leaned against the parapet of their wooden tower. A few seconds passed, and Haidi came running out of the forest, along the path to the gate. Clutching her child, she called out as she ran, 'Help! Quickly! A man has been hurt!'

Two helmeted heads peered down at her. She thumped her hand repeatedly against the gate.

'Quickly! One of your comrades is lying wounded on the path!'

'Where are the others?' demanded a male voice.

Haidi effected a look of blank distress. 'I don't know. I've seen no others. Let me in.'

The guard who had spoken reached for the tocsin rope that hung within the tower, and set the bell to clanging. The other lowered himself through the trap-door in the floor of the tower, climbed down the ladder below and raised the bar on the gate.

Haidi pushed in, stumbling so that she both fell against the guard and knocked the gate wider. I darted forward, unnoticed, slipped through the gate and beneath the guard-tower.

Alerted by the tocsin, soldiers were running towards the gate. I counted eight, which included a fat Suleri-nan with bloated cheeks and a drooping black moustache: the full complement – if Haidi was not mistaken in her figures.

'What's the fuss?' demanded the Sulerinan, scowling at Haidi and the sentry.

'This woman says one of our men is injured on the path out there.'

'Injured? How?'

'I don't know,' cried Haidi. 'I found him and came straightway for help.'

'How far?'

'A hundred yards, no more.'

The Sulerinan gestured irritably at his men. 'You four, go and see.'

Four troopers quickly filed through the gate and made off at a brisk trot into the trees.

So far so good. These four would be dealt with by Yo and Inbuel, who were hidden beside the path in the forest. Six now remained inside the village.

Haidi's child had begun to howl again. The Sulerinan frowned. 'Keep me informed.'

He turned and stomped away. The other three soldiers followed him. Haidi trailed a little way behind. The sentry pushed the gate shut and replaced the bar, then climbed back up the ladder to rejoin his companion in the tower.

I took careful note of where the others went. The Sulerinan entered a wooden hut a little way off. One of the soldiers accompanied him. A second soldier went around the back and disappeared into a rickety shelter. The last man went on further into the village.

I came out from under the tower and slipped up to the gate. Overhead the two sentries leaned on the parapet, their eyes on the forest path along which their four companions had just departed. With immense care I took the weight of the bar on the gate and lifted it free of its rest.

Now I stole into the village, going first to the outhouse into which the lone soldier had gone.

It was a latrine, as I had supposed. I wrenched open the door. The soldier, his breeches around his ankles, sat across a raised board suspended above a wide, stinking pit. He looked up, blinking, at the open door with no one in it. He never knew what happened. I stepped in and ran my sword through his heart, then pushed him back off the board. With a little manoeuvring I was able to tip his body into the pit, where his weapons and light armour quickly dragged him down beneath the ooze.

I slipped back outside and closed the latrine door. The tocsin had started ringing again. Something had alerted the sentries in the tower. I ran quickly around to the front of the hut occupied by the Sulerinan and the other soldier.

As I arrived the door flew open. The Sulerinan came out, cursing. I stabbed into his soft gut. His face creased in pain, his cheeks blew out, his eyes bulged. He gave a long moan and a spume of bloody foam sprayed from between his lips.

I withdrew the blade and stabbed again. He toppled, face down. Behind him the soldier had drawn his sword. He was staring right at me, and I realized I was at least part-visible.

The soldier vented a fierce yell and leapt straight at me, lunging with his sword. Shocked by the vigour of his attack, I moved back. The soldier was over the body of his Sulerinan and through the door. He advanced upon me, unafraid, slashing and striking. This was no green recruit. I was outmatched in strength and swordsmanship.

Our blades clashed, with a shock that sent a tremor from hand to shoulder. I backed away further, my arm almost numb. The soldier came on, triumph in his eyes, lunging, swinging. Metal clanged on metal, again and again. I recalled that there was another soldier still at large, and was suddenly seized with concern that I might be trapped between the two.

I parried another blow, then slipped upon a loose stone. I fell onto one knee. The Khimmurian raised his blade high. There was a strange keening sound behind me. The soldier looked over my head, and his face fell. He suddenly backed off, lowering his sword, then turned and began to run across the compound towards the gate-tower.

I looked behind me. Just yards away, from between two huts, came a group of women. Haidi at their fore, they rushed forward shrieking, brandishing reap-hooks, knives, hatchets. They ran by me, intent on the fleeing trooper.

In the tower the two sentries had bows drawn. The gate was part-open. I glimpsed a brown shape streaking towards me. The running soldier saw it at the same time and tried to veer away. An arrow thudded into the ground just behind the vhazz. It darted aside, raced on, leapt upon the soldier, knocking him to the ground. Without pausing the vhazz ran on towards me.

The soldier tried to scramble to his feet, but the Vir women had reached him now. He disappeared beneath a hail of blows.

I saw Inbuel slip in through the gate, glancing briefly around. Bow drawn, he ran beneath the tower, his arrow notched and pointed at the trapdoor overhead.

The two sentries in the tower ceased firing. Perceiving the gravity of their situation they stared white-faced, unsure of what to do. Yo came to a halt beside me.

'There is one other soldier hidden hereabouts,' I said. 'Can you find him?'

The vhazz nodded.

'Take care,' I said as he slipped away between the huts.

I walked towards the tower. The Vir women had completed their gruesome work. They stood back, to reveal the butchered Khimmurian body spreadeagled upon the soil of the compound, blood glistening in the sunlight. The women began to taunt the two men in the tower, heedless of their bows. The two soldiers stared down with stricken faces.

Inbuel called to them. 'You are trapped. Throw down your arms and surrender. Your lives will be spared.'

The two men made no response. Haidi detached herself from the group of women and walked over to me.

'Your friend says they will be spared, but they will not. Their crimes have been too great.'

I sighed and scratched the butt of my severed arm. 'They must be persuaded down from that tower before their comrades return with the work-gang.'

'I'll speak to the women.'

'There is still one more soldier at large,' I added.

Haidi returned to the group of women. She spoke in a hushed voice, and with reluctance they gradually ceased their taunts. Haidi called to the guards. 'Come down now. We will not kill you. Stay and we will set the tower ablaze and dance as you roast.'

One of the Khimmurians leaned over the parapet and spoke to Inbuel. 'You won't permit them to harm us?'

'As long as I am here you will suffer no harm.'

The two soldiers conferred in muted tones, then they put aside their bows and swords and climbed down from the tower. At once the Vir women surrounded them, jeering, jabbing, pulling their hair. Both Inbuel and I stepped between them.

'We have given these men our word!'

'They are dogs!' came the reply. 'They have shown us no compassion, they deserve none in return.'

'At least wait until your men return. Allow them a fair hearing.'

The women spoke among themselves, then came to an agreement. 'They will wait in the gaol, where they have left so many of us to rot. When the men come, we will decide.'

They took the two Khimmurians away.

'Here is a third,' I said, for coming from around the side of a hut was Yo, the last Khimmurian weaponless before him, blood pouring from a wound on his arm. The women hesitated, uncertain of Yo. He pushed his prisoner towards them and came on to where I stood with Inbuel.

246

I spoke to Inbuel. 'I would not like to wager on their survival.'

'Nor I. But my word was that they would not die while I am here. I can do no more than honour that.'

'What of the four in the woods?' I asked.

'They are dead.'

An hour passed. Dusk gathered in the forest, and gradually cloaked the Vir village where we waited. Inbuel and I donned the helmets and leather jerkins of the sentries and took our place in the guard-tower. In due course the faint chink of metal was heard along the forest path. It grew a little louder, then we glimpsed the first glimmer of a torch through the trees.

Out of the twilight traipsed the men of the village, heads bowed, linked one to the other on light chains. Four guards accompanied them, one on each side, one at the rear, and one carrying the torch in front.

'Open the gate!' came the cry.

I climbed from the tower to the gate and raised the bar, then backed into the shadows to hide my face.

The troop began to file through, suspecting nothing. As the last man entered I came forward, sword in hand, and took his life. Inbuel, who had also descended, took the flank guard, almost decapitating him as he struck savagely from behind.

There was a commotion up front. Yo had come from hiding and tackled the torch-bearer. The last soldier wheeled in sudden bewilderment. He drew his sword, but was confronted by Inbuel and me, our weapons at his throat. Behind us were half a dozen Vir women, holding captured swords.

We would have spared this man, leaving him to whatever fate the Vir had in store for him. But the Vir men, suddenly understanding what was happening, came to life. A chain flew over the soldier's head and was wound tightly around his neck. He was dragged struggling to the floor and strangled, and such was the affray that we could do nothing to save him.

Later, with night fully upon the forest, we sat in the central hall of the village and ate with the Vir. They related news of recent events in the region, which added hardly anything to what we already knew. Some two months earlier a number of villages further to the north had been liberated from the Khimmurian yoke – liberated by bands of valiant fighters led by Lord Yzwul of Tiancz. The Beast of Rull had essayed brutal retaliation. In the main his endeavours had been without consequence, for most of the villages had been swiftly and secretly evacuated, the villagers moving deep into the relative safety of the Magoth. But here to the south the Vir had not received adequate warning. With woeful faces our hosts recounted the treatment that Khimmur had meted out.

Twenty of their number had been taken at random, horribly tortured, then hanged from trees just beyond the palisade.

'Their bodies were left for weeks in full view of all of us,' stuttered one frail old fellow. 'It was only when it got . . . the smell, you know. The soldiers couldn't stand it any more. They made us cut them down and burn them.'

His voice trailed away.

'You cannot stay here now,' I said after a respectful silence. 'None of you.'

'We will do what the others did,' said one. 'We will go into the Magoth. She will protect us.'

We probed them for news of events further afield, but the Vir are by nature a shy and private folk. They bother themselves little with what goes on outside their immediate community, and so could furnish us with no worthwhile intelligence.

At length the talking was done. The villagers bade

us goodnight, and left us to return to their own huts. Inbuel and I spread blankets upon the wooden floor, Yo stretched out upon the bare boards, and we slept till morning.

III

As the first glimmer of grey light filtered through the massive trees of the Magoth, we took our leave of the village and continued on our way, making once again for the edge of the Ashakite Plains. I wondered about Shadd and the two Aphesuk. If Yo had found me, why had not they? The Aphesuk possessed tracking skills as great if not greater than the vhazz. Were they still on my trail, or had they gone on directly for Khimmur, intent on the greater mission? I had asked Yo whether he had found any sign of them, but his report was in the negative.

After a day of walking we came upon a caravanserai situated in rough, hilly grassland just beyond the fringe of the forest. These little islands of dubious hospitality dotted the Great Trade Routes all over Rull. They had survived with little change for decades, or probably centuries, unmolested by warring nations, bandits, or the nomads of the steppe. All, even the nomads, recognized their worth, and knew what the real cost would be were the caravanserais to fall directly under the wing of any single regional power. For these were stateless locations. Within their walls one could mingle with traders, travellers, and persons of less honourable station, and gain a wealth of information, purchase supplies, exchange or barter for all manner of goods, hire labour or, alternatively, find a job. Beyond the walls anything was fair game, but inside, by unspoken agreement, life and possessions were sacrosanct.

The Beast of Rull had acknowledged this fact. He had made no attempt to impose his tyranny over these tiny independent outposts. To do so would have brought about their end, and consequently the virtual demise of the crucial, lucrative lifeline of international trade. Khimmur's rise had ironically promoted the flow of goods, for many of the brigands who usually made their living off the wagon trains that plied the trade routes had taken up service as mercenaries with the Khimmurian army.

Inside the caravanserai when we arrived was a single caravan: a train of forty wagons carrying salt, cloth and exotic items from Roscoaff and beyond. Over ale and a platter of meat, beans and bread, I struck up conversation with the driver. He was a hard-bitten old Solander, a veteran of many trails. I had hired him once or twice myself in the past, though we had never met.

He told us that he was bound for Khimmur and Sommaria. We learned that Grassheen, where we were heading, had been transformed into a garrison town and supply depot. I made vague allusions to other towns, wishing to gain information on Murdren further to the north, without giving away the fact that this was our alternative destination. It seemed that Murdren was well guarded, being used as a transfer station between Khimmur and Virland.

'And you are joining the West Road, into Khimmur?'

The driver nodded, perhaps anticipating my next question.

'Have you room for a couple of extra guards as far as Grassheen?'

He grinned cannily, spooning beans and bread into his mouth. He looked us up and down. 'No, but I can offer you transport for a modest fee.'

I smiled. 'Then let us settle terms.'

When the deal was done the driver added, 'You would

do well to join me further along the route. The *Marg'dhua* are here; the secret police. If you are seen to leave with me I will be stopped before I have covered ten miles. It's nothing to me, I have nothing to hide. But yourselves, I expect, would rather avoid such an interview. I shall be leaving here soon after dawn.'

'We will await you on the trail,' I said.

We replenished our rations, including a couple of good leather sacks of red wine, and left the caravanserai just after dusk, as the sentries were preparing to close the gate for the night. Yo, who had waited outside in the wild, rejoined us on the edge of the forest, and we made camp.

At first light we were up and moving west. The trail curved and weaved between low grassy hills. After an hour's walk we climbed to the summit of one of these. From there we could look back upon the caravanserai below us in the distance. Thus we saw the caravan snake slowly through the gate in a long train, and resume its journey west. Some minutes later we were able to witness five mounted figures depart the caravanserai and set off slowly in the wake of the wagons.

'*Marg'dhua*, almost certainly,' observed Inbuel acidly.

'With hired hoods,' I added. 'They will almost certainly follow the train and arrest us when we depart at Grassheen.'

'Then it's blisters and calluses yet again.'

'And if they are waiting for us at Grassheen, we will have to take the longer and more arduous route, to Murdren.'

We withdrew from the hilltop and set off once more, keeping wide of the trail and hugging the trees. After three more days we turned to the north-west.

So it was that another two days' foot-slogging saw

us well inside Khimmur's borders, close to the outskirts of Murdren.

The question now was, what next? I had no means
of contacting the Hierarchy, other than through bound
allies in the Realms, and the risk of summoning them
here was too great. We were expected, either here or
at Grassheen, so I assumed that some person awaited
us somewhere nearby. But who, and where? How could
we find out without giving ourselves away to the wrong
people?

We were half a mile from the outskirts of the township, looking down upon it from a copse above fields of
vines, corn and sunflowers, and lush woodland through
which a small river meandered. The place was well
garrisoned, with Khimmurian and some Kemahamek
troops. Wagons, carts, livestock and persons on foot
or horseback came and went. But all passed through
checkpoints on the roads leading in and out.

'They are searching everything pretty thoroughly,'
said Inbuel. 'Is it worth trying to enter?'

'Only if we have a really good reason, which we
don't.'

'Then what?'

I shook my head. 'We wait, and make our presence
known, but only to the right people.'

'I wish I had thought of that,' said Inbuel dryly. He
lay back and stretched out on the ground, chewing a
stalk of grass, his ankles crossed and his head cradled
in his hands.

'There is a way,' I said. 'I can cast a rapture which
will let the Hierarchy know that I am here. Though
others will witness it, it will be meaningless to them.'

'But will the casting not bring hostile troops down
upon our heads? There could well be *Zan-Chassin*
agents here.'

'Almost certainly there will be, and they will be

252

watching the Realms. But they can detect only summonings, or the entrance into the Realms of a discar-
nate spirit. A simple rapture has no effect in the
non-corporeal plane.'

'Then cast it, Sir Dinbig. The sooner we are gone
from here the better.'

'I will wait until dark. Let's hope that there is someone here who will recognize the sign for what it is.'

That night there appeared in the sky over Murdren
a strange and beautiful sight. A globe of pure, silvery
radiance, dazzlingly bright, which hovered high over
the roofs, and threw a ghostly, shimmering luminescence onto the buildings and streets below.

In Twalinieh, more than two years earlier, I had
created a similar apparition. To facilitate my escape
from the barracks in which I was trapped, along with
Shimeril and his paladins, I had conjured two radiant
silver circles in the night sky: a symbol sacred to the
Kemahamek people, representing the Unity of the
Twin Wona Souls that were their living gods.

I had intended a mere diversion, but the manifestation had had unpredictable effects. The people took
it as a portent, and had been thrown into bewilderment
and confusion. Appearing as they did, at the time of
the invasion of Twalinieh and the proclaimed 'assas-
sination' of the Wonasina, Seruhli, the twin circles
became the subject of varying interpretations.

And I recalled that when I dissolved the rapture, the
circles themselves had failed to disperse, to fade
quickly back into the invisible essence out of which
they had been formed. Instead they had moved apart.
One had faded, contracted, lost its brilliance and disintegrated as it fell to earth. But the other had maintained
its perfect form. As if with a volition of its own, it had
begun to rotate, pulsing and increasing in magnitude.
I had watched it then as it floated over the city until

it came to rest directly above the Palace of the Wona. There it hovered for some seconds, then suddenly shot away skywards. Leaving a blazing trail of light, it had risen higher and higher into the sky, until eventually it vanished, leaving only darkness.

In the light of events as I later came to understand them – and even more so now, with Count Inbuel's revelation of the corruption of the male Wona-line – the uncanny behaviour of that sorcerous manifestation seemed freighted with significance. I had no explanation, but as I cast a similar rapture in the sky over Murdren I was a little apprehensive, wondering whether its appearance might import something that I was wholly unconscious of. Magic is always a mystery, never wholly mastered. No practitioner can predict with total accuracy the results of raptures cast, and likewise none can claim an absolute understanding of the forces they manipulate.

However, this globe to my knowledge bore no specific symbolic meaning. It was a pulsing light in the sky. It would awe the many and pass a simple message of my arrival to a few. Beyond that there would be a certain amount of speculation; tales passed down over generations would take on a life and character of their own, bearing little or no relation to fact. But I could not envisage anything more.

Of course, the globe would be seen by *Zan-Chassin* collaborators within the town, but they would know nothing of its message. Whatever their interpretation, it should not place myself or my friends in any greater danger.

I held the silvery light over Murdren for about two minutes. I allowed it to move, floating slowly over the town. Its spectral radiance illuminated the streets, bringing people out of homes and inns to stare upwards in wonder. From time to time we heard distant voices, carried to us on the warm night air. When I was certain that nobody in the town could have missed it, I dissolved the rapture.

I watched with a certain trepidation. To my relief the globe simply faded and vanished.

'Most impressive,' commented Inbuel with a weighted voice beside me. He stared at me curiously. Evidently the similarity between what he had just witnessed and the 'vision' that had appeared over Twalinieh two years earlier was not lost on him. But he made no enquiry, simply saying, 'What now?'

I scratched my stump. 'We wait.'

IV

We waited through the remainder of the night and the following day. Looking down over the long ranks of vines and the great bowed heads of the sunflowers we observed the comings and goings at Murdren. Nothing out of the ordinary drew our attention. The day was long and hot. We grew restless; there was nowhere to go, nothing to do.

As dusk approached, a column of horsemen, about twenty strong, rode slowly out of the town. They made their way along the narrow road which wound below us along the riverbank. We watched them for a minute or so until they were lost from sight as the road took them beneath the deep green foliage of the woods.

I was aware of a growing apprehension. Something I could not place, a quivering of the psychic nerves, a sense of unspecified peril.

I looked around me with deep misgiving. An imminence gathering. My skin tingled, yet I could locate nothing.

Then a voice inside my head: *'Master, there is danger here!'*

'Gaskh! You endanger both yourself and me by coming here!'

'The danger is already present, Master. I know the risk, but I came to warn you.'

'What do you perceive?'

'An entity.'

'Where?'

'In the leaning pine tree, a little way behind you.'

I looked but could see nothing.

'What manner of thing is it?'

'A Spy, I think. It is difficult to say, for I have encountered nothing of its type before.'

'Can you banish it?'

'I have tried. The entity lacks offensive capabilities, yet when I approach it vanishes, only to reappear moments later elsewhere. I don't have the strength to do more on this corporeal plane.'

'How has it found us?'

'My assumption is that it has been painstakingly searching the area for some time – hours, perhaps days. Finally it came upon you.'

'And now it reports our presence.'

'If you leave, Master, I may be able to distract the entity to prevent it following you. You can perhaps win free of its surveillance and escape. One other thing – I bring you word from the Chariness: help comes!'

From beside me came a sharp cry. 'We are attacked!'

Inbuel, kneeling close by, was pointing down the hillside. The horse-troops that we had been watching had left the road and made their way in secret up through the woodland. Now they had broken out of the trees and were galloping between the vines, up the slope directly towards us.

There were too many to fight; our only hope was to

run. Behind us, on the other side of the copse, was a small meadow, at the bottom of which was a steep wooded slope. The slope would hamper the horsemen. We might just be able to lose them in the deeper woods.

'Gaskh, do what you can. We must flee!'

Inbuel was pulling at my arm, trying to drag me into the woods.

'This way!' I cried, a wild panic mounting in my brain.

I could hear the soft thump of hooves on the powdery soil, the clink of iron, the breathing of the hard-pressed mounts and the bellowed war-cries of their riders. Yo bounded at my side. We raced between the trees and broke out into the sunlit meadow. The first of the horsemen had crested the slope and were among the trees now, their horses' hooves pounding like thunder.

Across the flower-speckled meadow the lip of the slope was fifty yards away. We ran, leaping frantically over lichen-clad rocks that studded the earth. I glanced back. The horsemen were bearing down on us, but we might just make it.

Then came a great whoop from my left. Three mounted soldiers were galloping across the meadow, having come from open country around the side of the copse. Swords drawn, they were on a course to intercept us.

We veered to the right. Yo, with greater speed, was ahead. Inbuel ran beside me.

'To the bushes, there!' I gasped. 'Their horses will not be able to follow us.'

But it was too late. I heard the leaden roar of hooves and the jangle of harness immediately behind me. Instinctively I threw myself aside, clutching my hands around my head. A sword swished through the air, almost cleaving my scalp. The horse thundered by, kicking up dirt, the smell of its sweat filling my nostrils. I scrambled to my feet and ran on, stumbling, but now the enemy were on three sides. We could only run across the meadow, on a path parallel to the lip of the slope.

Inbuel ceased running. He turned to face back up the slope, drawing his sword and standing firm. His face was flushed and gleamed with sweat; his lips were drawn in a tight grimace.

'Stand back to back!' he yelled. 'If we must die, we will at least take some with us!'

I saw that further flight was futile. I unsheathed my blade and moved to him. Lungs burning, I faced down the slope to where the three on our flank hurtled towards us.

Yo ran back to join us. As he came he flicked a dart at the mount that had just rushed past me. The horse screamed, twisted, reared. Its rider was hurled from the saddle. Yo was upon him in an instant, sinking his sword into the man's chest.

Ten yards now separated us from the nearest horseman. He urged his mount on, leaning from the saddle, sword held high. His teeth were bared in a fierce grin of triumph, his eyes wild and flashing.

I tightened my grip on my sword-hilt. There was a soft sighing sound, passing quickly. Something hissed over my head. Then another, and another. The horseman toppled suddenly from his saddle, somersaulting across the grass and coming to rest inert at my feet. An arrow protruded from his cheek.

There were cries and yells from the riders as arrows planed through the air into their ranks. Another man fell, then another. The horses whinnied and ramped, their riders wheeled them around in confusion.

Now I heard shouts from another direction, off across the meadow. I looked around. From trees away to our right came men on foot and horse. A dozen knelt upon the grass with bows drawn, sending arrow after arrow into the Khimmurians. Others ran on forward, yelling, brandishing swords. Five on horseback charged head-long across the grass, light lances couched. The arrows ceased to fly. The horsemen ploughed into the Khimmurians, taking five lives in as many seconds, and the five hurtled on to swerve and reform for another charge.

As soon as the riders had passed, the archers resumed their fire. The Khimmurians milled in panic. A third of their number were down, and others were falling. The foot soldiers were among them now, and other riders, hacking and stabbing. The archers took aim with careful intent, picking off any who tried to break from the melee.

And now one of our mounted rescuers galloped down the meadow towards us. In his hand I recognized a singular weapon. He brought his horse to a halt in front of us. He wrenched off his helmet and shook free a head of sweat-soaked grey curls. Swinging a leg over his mount's withers, he slid from his saddle to the ground. His face split into a broad grin as he stood before me.

'Shimeril,' I said.

10

I

'We expected you at Grassheen,' Shimeril said as we made our way west through the wildlands of Su'um S'ol, deeper into Khimmur. 'That was where I waited for you. Then I received a message late last night, that you had shown yourself at Murdren. We came at best speed, without pausing.'

'And not a moment too soon!' I said. 'But I'm puzzled. I only revealed my presence last night. If you were at Grassheen, how could you possibly have learned of it?'

'Ha!' Shimeril tipped back his head and emitted a curt chuckle. He turned to me, grinning. 'I am one of you now, Dinbig. I have received initiation. I am *Zan-Chassin*!'

I stared at him, momentarily dumbstruck.

Shimeril laughed. 'You are not sure whether to believe me, but I assure you it is true. I was initiated by the Chariness. I now command a bound entity, named Jogada. She is a message-bearer between the Chariness and myself.'

'You are almost the last person . . .' I began.

'Formerly I would have said so myself. But though I balked and shied, I was persuaded that it was the only way. And I must say, Jogada has more than proven herself.'

'Does this mean that you are at your ease now with magic?'

'Never! Every time Jogada alerts me to her need to

communicate with me, my blood runs hot and cold and my hair stands on end. It's beyond my ken, Dinbig. I'm a warrior, born and bred. By choice I would have nothing more. Tampering with the strange stuff of the worlds beyond this one is to my mind reckless and irresponsible.'

His sentiment brought to mind what I had recently learned from Shadd. In Qotolr the Drear-hag, Mesmia, had revealed to him the true origin of the Vulpasmage. Gloatingly she had told how we of the *Zan-Chassin* had quite unwittingly encouraged and permitted the manifestation of the Vulpasmage in this world. When I'd heard it I had wanted to deny it, for it was a truth that was almost too much to bear. But it had a ring of terrible authenticity. I said, half to myself, 'I am inclined to agree.'

'But in a sense I had no choice; that is if I wished to play a meaningful part in this struggle,' continued Shimeril. 'Without Jogada, for instance, I could not have been on hand to see you home. For that reason, if no other, I am glad that I did what I did.'

'I too.'

We were riding side by side, beneath tall beech and elm trees through which the dappled, green-gold sunlight filtered down. Shimeril reached across and grabbed my hand and squeezed it. 'Welcome home, old friend. Welcome home.'

It was late afternoon; we had been on the move since early morning. After our rescue outside Murdren, Shimeril and his men had taken us north for a few miles, until darkness made further travel impracticable. We had talked long into the night. I told him my story, to which he listened with eyes continually widening with surprise, shaking his head on the edge of disbelief.

'I was hard put to believe the Chariness when she told me she'd been in communication with you,' he said. 'By my reckoning, and everyone else's, you were dead, and that was the harsh, inescapable fact of it. And when she said you'd been in communication with Shadd . . . My imagination was stretched, yet how could I disbelieve her?'

'Aye, it's the strangest tale.'

'And your companion, Yo,' said Shimeril, inclining his head towards the vhazz that trotted beside our horses. 'Do you know of an encounter I had with a vhazz? The Chariness implied that you might have an explanation. With all that has transpired, I'm now inclined to think she knows much more than she has disclosed.'

I smiled. 'The Chariness was right, though it is through inspired deduction rather than direct knowledge of events. But it was not Yo that you encountered that night in the Mystoph woods. It was me. I occupied the vhazz flesh that is now Yo's.'

And I proceeded to relate to him the extraordinary facts of my rebirth as a vhazz, and how it was that I had witnessed the raid upon Kuno's H'padir warriors, and subsequently been in a position to save the paladin, Sar B'hut, from certain death. When I had done, Shimeril could say nothing, so full was his mind with the strangeness of it all.

'And there is more to tell,' I said. 'We have learned significant and disturbing facts about the origins of the Vulpasmage. And Count Inbuel has furnished me with new information in regard to the fall of Kemahamek. But all this must wait for now. The proper time to reveal it is when we meet with the Hierarchy.'

When we'd broken camp in the morning, Shimeril gave no clue as to our destination. He said simply that we were bound for the place which the *Zan-Chassin* had made their secret headquarters. We plied a winding path through forest and hills, Shimeril's fighters taking measures to ensure that we were not followed or observed. It was evident that Shimeril knew this land well. Every hillock, field, brook, every tree, almost, was familiar to him. He had utilized his time as an outlaw to good effect.

Now we rode across heathland above the Barrier Fell, the great scarp which spans Mystoph from west to east. We had come by the most roundabout route to arrive here. I knew that not far ahead of us was The Murth, the road that nobody travels. I wondered again and again as to where we could be heading.

In due course we ascended out of a wooded vale and stepped out upon The Murth. It was little more than a faint track these days, overgrown with grass and ferns, wild flowers and brambles. North it made off across Mystoph as far as the township of Sigath. South, it threaded its way down the steep Fell, winding along the borders of the *dhoma*s of Cish and Pri'in. Beneath the Fell it petered out altogether. At one time it had continued further south, into and beyond the shadow of The Howling Hill, that mysterious, unnatural basalt upthrust that dominated the land hereabouts, which was held to be a place of power, a remote haunt of Enchanters and their minions.

Ahead of us in the distance were the misty, snow-covered peaks of the Byar-hagkh Mountains. I felt a poignant stab of emotion deep in the pit of my guts as I gazed upon them. My heart began to thump. For the first time I realized that I was truly home.

'Is it a good sight, old friend?' Shimeril asked.

I blinked back tears. 'Aye, yet it fills me with sorrow and longing.'

Beyond those peaks, just three days' ride away, was Hon-Hiaita. There was everything I had lost. And close by, in the village of Little Malme, was a rude farmstead where lived Rohse with her aged parents, and our little girl, Eroniss. How close we were, but yet I could not go to them. In a sense I was still a thousand miles away.

I expected Shimeril to cross The Murth and travel on west, or turn northwards towards Sigath. Instead he took us south, following The Murth itself towards the Barrier Fell and the lowlands beyond. I made no comment, but my face must have shown my disquiet. Shimeril, glancing across at me, smiled softly to himself, but offered no explanation.

The way ascended as we approached the high ridge of the Barrier Fell. In the years before The Great Deadlock the Fell had defined Khimmur's southeasternmost border. Then the Liberator, Manshallion, freeing Khimmur of Kemahamek occupation, led his forces south to claim the weald below the Fell, which gave on to the Ashakite Plains. By this means the *dhoma* of Pri'in had been greatly extended, and the new *dhoma* of Cish was born.

We arrived upon the ridge. The hot sun burned our skin, a mild breeze wafting up from the plains below, ruffling hair and clothing. A magnificent vista opened before us: the rolling hills and woodlands of the low weald, stretching away as far as the eye could see. The day was clear and bright, bringing far objects into sharp relief. Visible a few miles away, standing out as a sudden dark blot amidst the rich, shimmering greens and greys, was the humped black-brown mass of The Howling Hill.

We did not pause, for we were somewhat exposed here. We commenced the descent, zig-zagging via long traverses down the steep slopes of the Fell to the lowlands. I noticed that Shimeril's troops were no longer in evidence. Now there were just the four of us: Shimeril, Count Inbuel, Yo and myself.

We came eventually to dank woods at the foot of the

scarp. Here it was scarcely possible to make out the existence of a road, so overgrown had The Murth become. Yet I knew the route, for I had been here many years earlier, to the village of Underfell which lay a little way ahead. I cocked my head, listening. From far away came a faint, eerie sound, an unnatural dirge that was the song of The Howling Hill. Its cause was the confluence of winds that blew about the uneven heights of the Hill, commonly believed to be magically influenced.

Yo came up alongside me with a whine. 'Master, I am unsettled here.'

'I too, somewhat,' I replied.

Shimeril led us on, picking his way with purpose through the trees and undergrowth. I could contain my curiosity no longer. I spurred my mount forward until I was alongside the paladin.

'Shimeril, this is the way to Underfell, and The Howling Hill beyond.'

Shimeril looked sidelong at me with a wry twist of his lips. 'I am not a stranger to this land, old friend.'

'Is it wise to come here? You know of Underfell's fate, the massacre, the abduction of the children. I was there.'

'I recall.'

'It is a haunted place.'

'So it is said.'

'Nobody comes here, at least not by choice.'

He looked at me with sharp amusement in his hazel-green eyes. 'Quite so.'

'Then . . . ?' I cut myself short. Suddenly it was plain. I felt foolish for having failed to see it earlier.

Shimeril chose to enlighten me anyway.

'We are going to the headquarters of the *Zan-Chassin*.'

II

In retrospect the Hierarchy could hardly have chosen a more suitable place for a hideaway. Underfell was deserted; by dint of its sinister reputation it was avoided by all, as was the surrounding region. Surely not even the Beast of Rull would think of looking here for his enemies?

Later I learned that Khimmurian patrols had passed through here on two occasions. They had made cursory inspections, not even dismounting from their horses. They found nothing, and seemed glad to be gone from the place.

What would they have found had they searched properly? Probably little, for the magical defences were sufficient to divert or disconcert almost any mind showing too keen an interest in the place. But a *Zan-Chassin* adept, working for the Beast, would have been aware of the subtle influences present here. And from the Beast's point of view, there was much to be found.

We came silently through what had once been Underfell's central street. It was now a dense mass of brambles, ferns and strong young saplings. The cottages on either side were crumbling and decayed, half hidden in the greenery that had grown up around them. Built of stone and mortar, once white, their outer walls were now greatly stained and pocked with age. Turf roofs sagged beneath jungles of grass, wild flowers, shrubs, even small trees. Many had caved in under the weight.

Shimeril brought our little troop to a halt outside one of the buildings. With a feeling of unease I recognized it as being the ruins of the inn in which I had lodged twenty-five years earlier. An iron bracket from which had hung the inn's sign still clung to the rotten wall, warped and rusted, pulling gradually free.

The name of the inn was the Lost Unicorn, I recalled. Our presence here evoked the memory of that night. I was a young man then. I had gone into the darkened countryside, out of curiosity, to gaze at The Howling Hill and listen to its haunting song. Late in the night I had witnessed an eerie procession descending from somewhere close to the summit of the Hill, its passage marked by dozens of flickering lights. Now I seemed to hear again, as I had then, the distant chant of voices which I believed were not human.

I had fled in terror that night. In fact, I now remembered that I had left my belongings at this very inn. The chances were that they were still here, for no one had survived the terrible butchery that followed my departure, and to my knowledge none had been here since.

The mournful song of the winds still sounded faintly at our backs. Shimeril had slipped down from his horse. He turned around to offer me a hand. I glanced uneasily at Inbuel, and we dismounted.

I turned to Yo. 'Yo, conceal yourself nearby and await our return or my summoning.'

'Must I wait here alone, Master?'

I realized that the poor vhazz was thoroughly unsettled by the atmosphere of this place. Perhaps he had some awareness of what had happened here. I stroked his head and silently invoked a Calming rapture. 'You will come to no harm here. I will return soon.'

He slipped away, and we entered the inn through a dark opening which had once been a doorway. The door had long ago fallen in; its rotting planks lay in the dirt, tall weeds grown up between them. In the dank gloom of the common-room the benches and tables still stood as they had all those years ago. Only now they were bowed and mildewed, thick with cobwebs and grime, and overgrown with pale weeds, toadstools and tough, stunted bushes. Tankards and firkins, crocks and bottles stood on lichen-covered, sagging shelves behind the bar. Fungi clung to beams and rafters, and grew elsewhere in fabulous configurations. The smell was dank, vegetal, earthy; the pungent reek of decay.

Shimeril led us through to a back room which had once been the kitchen, and down through a rotten, rickety door to the cellar. Here huge tuns and barrels of wine and ale stood unbroached, probably still full and their contents quite potable. Our eyes adjusted gradually to the dark. I sensed powerful magic, and noticed a Monitor Eye concealed between the rafters.

Shimeril spoke in a resonant voice. 'I have brought Dinbig, and a trusted companion, Count Inbuel m' Anakastii of Kemahamek.'

In a corner of the cellar something began to manifest. A faint shimmering, a wisp that grew in size, taking on shape and substance, until it formed into an arch in the wall, large enough for a man to pass through.

'Enter,' spoke a voice.

I stared in amazement. This was wizardry! To my knowledge *Zan-Chassin* powers had never been sufficent to work such powerful magic on the corporeal plane. Inbuel looked uncertainly at the Portal that had appeared before us; Shimeril, I noticed, was unmoved. I smiled to myself; he was a changed man.

'Come,' I said for Inbuel's benefit. 'Let's enter.'

I stepped through. I was in a small rectangular chamber with walls of damp, flaking stone, similar to the cellar I had just left. A torch upon one wall cast a dim, flickering light, and illuminated a timber door in the wall on my left. I turned to check that Inbuel and Shimeril had followed me through the Portal. Behind them the wall appeared solid; there was nothing to indicate a way through.

The door opened and the Chariness entered the tiny chamber. Her face was pale and customarily tranquil, as I remembered it. But when her eyes fell on me they lit up and she broke spontaneously into a radiant smile. She came forward, arms extended, discarding formality. She took my head in her hands and kissed my cheeks warmly.

'Dinbig. We are so pleased that you have returned safely.'

'I too, Revered Sister! And I must thank you for your endeavours on my behalf, in particular for dispatching Shimeril to aid me. I have come a long way and survived many harrowing adventures, but without your timely intervention I would have died yesterday, here on the soil of my homeland.'

'You have come a long way, as we always knew you could,' said the Chariness, and I sensed that she did not refer purely to my physical journey. 'Now we hope to discover just how far. As for dying, it has to be asked, What now can death hold for Ronbas Dinbig?'

'Ask away as much as you wish, but I must turn down all requests for a demonstration! Dying is not an art I consider myself a master of. I have done it once, and have no stomach for a repeat performance. There are too many pains and uncertainties in the process.'

'But the experience was a valuable one?'

'That is one way of looking at it.'

'We look forward to a full account – at a more appropriate time.'

I tilted my head towards the blank wall behind me. 'You have grown stronger. This is powerful magic.'

'We have been diligent and unflagging in our efforts to develop ourselves. Necessity has forced our hand. We are moving towards an unavoidable contest. But all is not what it seems. The Portal is real; we did not create it, merely garbed it in rapturous stuff to give it

269

the semblance of magical effect. It is an ordinary door concealed behind a fake wall. Evidently this place was a smugglers' den in former days.'

I nodded; this would seem quite feasible. 'I am forgetting myself. Allow me to introduce Count Inbuel m' Anakastii, an old friend. He brings important information in regard to the plight of Kemahamek and the role of the Vulpasmage there. As a Kemahamek Marshal, he may well prove to be a vital link between ourselves and those of his people we would wish to contact.'

The Chariness bowed her head and extended a hand graciously. With a gallant flourish, Inbuel stepped forward, took the hand and bowed, his lips almost, but not quite, touching her fingers. 'I am honoured, Madam.'

'Come,' said the Chariness, 'there are others who wait to greet you.'

We passed through the second door into a larger chamber, lit by half a dozen flambeaux. Here sat the crone, Crananba, on cushions placed upon a modest chair.

Alongside her were Cliptiam and old Farlsast, the two ritual Sashbearers, powerful members of the Hierarchy. When I had last seen Cliptiam she had been preparing to assume the role of Chariness *pro tem*, while the Chariness journeyed with Crananba to the Further Realms to search out and identify the source of the Darkening power that was affecting us all. They had journeyed under the aegis of the Vulpasmage, not knowing that the Vulpasmage was the very enemy they sought. By a miracle they had survived, but it was since that day that the *Zan-Chassin* had been forced into hiding.

Also present was Chrysdhothe, wife of Lord Yzwul. Most notable were the absences. Many – I did not know how many – had perished battling the minions of the

Vulpasmage. Others were now foes, fighting on the side of the Beast of Rull.

I gave the ritual *Zan-Chassin* greeting, and bowed, then introduced Count Inbuel. 'He attends this secret conclave by special dispensation. I believe his contribution to our struggle could be invaluable.'

The Chariness had moved to take her place upon a chair beside Crananba. She indicated an area on the floor before her where four other chairs rested. 'Dinbig, my Lords, please be seated.'

I seated myself, noting the fourth chair. Shimeril and Inbuel took places on either side of me.

Crananba spoke. 'Welcome back, Dinbig. I cannot fully convey how pleased we all are at your safe return. We were sorely grieved to lose you at Twalinieh. We believed you gone forever, yet we were never without hope. We knew your potential, but not how close you were to realizing it.'

I took note of her words, which echoed the Chariness's sentiment moments ago. What did they imply? Had it been suspected that I might have the ability to conquer death? Surely that was not possible?

Crananba spoke on. 'We received your communication and learned of your return with tremendous joy. But you still faced many trials. These you have risen to and overcome. You have proven yourself over and over again. Your deeds have marked your progress, and by them you have declared yourself worthy and well advanced. I have no hesitation, then, in announcing your promotion within the *Zan-Chassin* Hierarchy. I am pleased to bestow upon you the title High Master and Adept of the Fourth Realm. Regrettably circumstances do not allow for the enactment of the full ceremony of Initiation attendant upon this title.

'The esoteric ritual, particularly, must be put in abeyance, for you cannot journey into the Realms. The exoteric may be conducted as soon as is appropriate, with the construction of a River Ghost, in full accordance with the laws and precepts of our Way.'

A River Ghost. I was being honoured indeed. The ritual involved the building of an effigy in a rough likeness of the celebrant being honoured. The effigy was symbolic of the former personality of the celebrant. That personality, with all its needs and desires, had in theory now been overcome. The celebrant was a new being, liberated from the mundane considerations that had plagued his or her former existence. To symbolize the departure of the old personality, the River Ghost was placed in a coracle and set to float away on a river. It was assailed with arrows, stones, and any other missile that came to hand, to ensure that the old personality did not make the mistake of believing itself missed, and thus try to return.

I bowed my head. 'I accept the honour with humility and gratitude. I pray that I may live to prove myself worthy of it.'

Crananba sat back with shining eyes and a gummy smile. Now the Chariness took up the address. 'There are matters of great moment to be discussed. One other person has still to join us to make this conclave complete.'

She nodded to Cliptiam, who rose and walked to a door set in the wall at the other end of the chamber. She opened it and passed through, then beckoned to a person we could not see. Cliptiam stepped aside, a shadow slid across the door, then a tall figure, stooping, stepped through into the chamber, and stood erect.

'Shadd!' I exclaimed, and forgetting all propriety leapt to my feet. I moved rapidly across the chamber to embrace him. 'Shimeril, why did you not tell me Shadd was here?'

'I did not know,' came Shimeril's voice from behind

me, choked with emotion. I released Shadd and turned. Shimeril stood with brimming eyes, a quivering smile upon his lips, staring at his ward.

Shadd stepped past me. The two warriors embraced, emotionally, kissing one another's cheeks, hugging each other hard. Shimeril, too overcome for words, drew back, holding Shadd's pale face between his hands, shaking his head, the tears tumbling freely down his cheeks. They clasped one another again, then at last stepped back.

'I arrived here two days ago,' said Shadd, speaking to us both, and then he turned to me. 'Do not reproach me, Dinbig. We did not give up in our search for you. We followed you as far as the camp of Dagril the Chol. Rin entered the camp and spoke with Dagril. From him we learned that you had departed into the Magoth four days earlier. We took up your trail, but we were losing time. You must understand that to trail a man in terrain such as that is a difficult process, even for Aphesuk. We came under attack from forest primitives, and were driven back. When we eventually found your trail again you were many days ahead of us.' He paused, and brought forth on its chain the brilliant twin-stone, the Soul Crystal of the Gwynad. He held it firmly in the palm of his hand, his long, slender fingers curled around it. 'I knew that you were alive and safe. The more I thought about you the more I became attuned to your life essence. This stone has remarkable properties. As you know, I discovered some of them in Qotolr. When I left that land I became aware of a change. Contrary to what we thought when in Qotolr, the powers this Crystal has given me were not increased. In the atmosphere of the "normal" world, as we know it, the Soul Crystal affects me in different ways. Its effects are subtle and hardly definable. I believe I have much still to discover. But suffice it to say that through the Crystal's agency I was able to know of you. It was evident, then, that you would reach Khimmur far ahead of us. There was nothing to be gained by continuing to ply your trail. So we decided to move on by the most direct route at our own best pace.'

I nodded solemnly, scratching my stump. 'Had you acted otherwise I would not have held you culpable. You know that the important thing was to bring to Khimmur the object that you carry.'

Shadd turned to face Count Inbuel, who stood across the chamber watching us. Shadd advanced to face him; the two surveyed each other with a certain wariness. Shadd bowed his head smartly and offered his hand. 'Count Inbuel.'

The air was charged. This was a tense moment, and one upon which so much rested. But Inbuel was neither callow nor foolish. He knew about the events at Twalinieh – I had convinced him at the time that Shadd was not a traitor, and in recent days I had filled in much more of the picture. He therefore did not hesitate, but returned the bow and pressed Shadd's hand.

'Duke Shadd. It is my pleasure.'

I sensed relief. By his response Inbuel had declared amity. As far as he was concerned there was no lack of trust between us of Khimmur who fought the Beast of Rull, and Kemahamek. It was a major step.

III

'You all know,' announced the Chariness, 'that Duke Shadd has returned from Enchantery bearing an article of rarity and immeasurable value. We have conducted intense tests on the pages of unusual parchment which he has given us. Our findings thus far are as follows:

the pages are, as far as can be determined, genuine. That is to say, they are pages from Yshcopthe's Pandect. I don't have to tell you what this means. The parchment is formed of or imbued with a substance unknown to us. Its constitution seems to render it indestructible by normal means. Its contents defy replication – which is an extraordinary fact. The magic employed to safeguard these pages is ancient and wonderful, and beyond our ken. We have applied numerous techniques in our endeavours to unwork it, all without avail. We will of course continue to try, but quite frankly we are not optimistic about our chances of success. Finally, we are forced to admit, with regret, that we are unable to decrypt the contents of the Fragment. The Old Language of Qotolr remains a mystery to us, as it has done to others before us.'

I tried not to let my face show my disappointment. Somehow, without quite being aware that I had done so, I'd let my hopes and expectations grow over the preceding weeks, until they had come to far exceed what my rational mind knew to be likely or even possible. I had allowed myself to become half persuaded that if we could just get the Fragment to Khimmur and the *Zan-Chassin*, we might yet have the means at our disposal to decipher it.

I avoided looking at Duke Shadd. He, I knew, now entertained the most bitter disillusionment; on a personal level he was wounded far more deeply than I by the Chariness's words. Inbuel, too, would quite certainly have laid great store in the hope of the Fragment being deciphered. For him it meant life, both for his beloved Wonasina, and for his people.

It was Inbuel who spoke now, with a voice that betrayed his emotion. 'Are you saying that no such means to decipher it exists?'

'Outside of Enchantery there is, to our knowledge,

only the Beast of Rull who would know how to read these pages.'

I took in this statement, and said, 'We would appear to stand between an abyss and a wall of fire. What do you propose?'

The Chariness fixed me with her level grey gaze. 'We will come to that in a moment. First, let us look at our situation as a whole. Perhaps we might profit from some analysis as to how it might have changed now that you and Duke Shadd are back with us – not forgetting, of course, the important part that Count Inbuel may well have to play.'

Plainly, Shadd had already recounted to the Hierarchy everything he had learned, and there was little that I could add to that. Inbuel's account, however, was something new. I observed the faces before me as he told of the conspiracy among the Simbissikim priesthood and the dire pact with the Beast, and the generations-long corruption of the male Wona-line.

When he had finished speaking the Chariness nodded gravely. 'This conforms with suspicions we have arrived at through our own researches. It answers many questions. Count Inbuel, if you will permit us we would like to interview you further regarding what you have just told us, in confidence after this meeting is done. Names, dates, and any other information that you can furnish us with could prove to be of immense value.'

Inbuel bowed his head. 'Of course, though you will understand that there are certain things of which I am not at liberty to speak.'

'We will respect your integrity and the responsibilities of your station at all times.'

Shadd, with a brooding, troubled look, put in, 'After so many generations, is there anything that can be done to restore the male line? The child is surely lost, and cannot ever be found.'

Inbuel made to respond, but Crananba spoke quickly. 'That is not for us to say, nor even to directly involve ourselves in, Duke Shadd. The restoration of the male Wona-line, if it can be achieved, is an internal, private affair, which can only be dealt with by Kemahamek herself. Our role is to aid in any way we can the process by which Kemahamek becomes capable again of taking full and proper charge of her own affairs.'

'But the key to that is the Wonasina, Seruhli, is it not?'

'That is so. If we find that we hold here the Formula for the Antidote to the Semblance of Death, then we are bound to do all in our power to deliver it to the Wonasina.'

With passion, Shadd turned and addressed Count Inbuel. 'Are you able to lead us to her?'

'It is not that simple,' said Inbuel. 'You must understand that to those who guard our Beloved Lady, no one is to be trusted. That includes myself, for remember, she was betrayed by one or more of those closest to her. Now, of those who guard her, none are under any illusions. They know that you, Duke Shadd, are innocent of all blame in regard to the Wonasina's fate. Still, there remains a certain distrust between the Intimates and Khimmur – even the Khimmur that you and the Hierarchy here assembled represent. In short, were I to return to Kemahamek I would be able to establish contact with certain important persons. Under the right conditions they might open up a chain of contacts that would eventually lead to the Blessed Intimates who guard the Wonasina. But I must emphasize that qualification: *the right conditions*. If these fail to materialize, then not even I would ever come close to her now.'

'But possession of the Formula would surely meet all conditions?' said Shadd.

Inbuel nodded. 'Quite certainly. But as yet we do not know for sure that you possess it. Much as I wish it could be otherwise, the fact is that, without decrypting, those pages are quite useless to us. More, they actually constitute a terrible threat.'

Shadd's brow was knitted, his face haggard, his lips pursed in intense concentration. 'I have discussed this matter with the Hierarchy prior to your arrival. We are faced with a desperate situation; we have no choice now but to resort to desperate measures to attempt to resolve it. If we hesitate we will be lost.'

I looked from Shadd to the faces of each of the Hierarchy members. 'You speak as though you have arrived at some decision.'

'The Chariness has already stated that outside of Qotolr there are none who possess the knowledge to read the Fragment – with the sole exception of the Beast of Rull,' Shadd said. 'But *in* Qotolr there are at least five Enchanters who can perform the task. Each of them would do anything to get their hands on what we hold.'

I gave a leaden nod. Knowing his mind, I had to some extent anticipated his words. I was far from enthused. 'You are saying that we must return to Enchantery and by some means persuade, induce, bribe, trick or coerce one of these beings into translating the contents for us? It's impossible, Shadd. It can't be done.'

Shadd's moonlike eyes seemed to glow. There was a shocking intensity about his expression. Not for the first time I feared for his state of mind. 'Dinbig, you've got it wrong. We don't return to the Enchanter's domain. That's where they are strong. Instead, we bring one to us.'

'From Enchantery?'

He nodded. 'From Enchantery.'

I tried to remain impassive, for my initial reaction was to reject the proposition outright as preposterous, and I did not want this to show in my mien. I said, 'Just how do you propose going about achieving this?'

'That is not the problem,' replied Shadd. 'The process is already in motion; the wheels have begun to turn. It is for us now to prepare ourselves. An Enchanter will come; we must be ready to meet him.'

'Or her,' I said.

IV

I sat in silence, my eyes on Shadd, then the others. The countenances of Crananba, the Chariness and the remaining Hierarchy members were inscrutable. Shimeril was pale and drawn. Inbuel gazed in silent contemplation at the floor.

Crananba said, 'We discussed this at great length with Duke Shadd. When he first put his proposition to us we too were sceptical. The risks are enormous. Yet we must have the formula – if that is what it is – translated. We remain almost powerless against the Beast, but if Seruhli can be revived it will be a triumph. Disruption in Kemahamek under her influence would prove a major distraction for our enemy.'

'But it is not enough to destroy him.'

'We do not know how to destroy him, Dinbig. To kill the man, Oshalan, is a most difficult task, with what we know of his powers and the guard that protects him. But even if we succeeded the monster would survive, and will return, again and again, in other bodies, other forms, growing ever stronger. We are researching without cease in an attempt to discover the means to destroy the Vulpasmage – who knows, perhaps there is something written here, on the pages of the Fragment, which will help us. But in the meantime we must do everything we can to combat the Beast's forces on the physical plane.'

'Lord Yzwul is presently in Hecra on a crucial mission in this regard,' added the Chariness. 'He risks everything in the hope of success. We can do nothing less.'

I pricked up my ears at this. Yzwul, in Hecra? What possible mission could take him there? I had been absent so long, I knew nothing. I said, 'Then what have you done?'

'It was Temminee who proposed the plan,' began Shadd. 'And indeed, it is she who has forced our hand.'

'Temminee? You told me that she intended to betray you.'

He gave a melancholy half-smile. 'In a manner of speaking, that is what she has done. Knowing the situation as she does, Temminee declared that there was but one recourse, the one that we now find ourselves committed to. I remonstrated, for I considered the risk too great, for herself as well as us. But she went over and over the details, and would hear nothing of my objections. She told me that we had no choice.'

'Then what has she done?'

'Temminee's plan was to return to Enchantery. There she intends to approach each Enchanter, one by one, with a tale concocted to arouse their covetous instincts. The basis of her story is that I have made off with the sacred Soul Crystal of the Gwynad. I also have in my possession the Fragment from Yshcopthe's Pandect. In return for an Enchanter's agreeing to aid her in regaining the Soul Crystal, Temminee will bring the Enchanter to me, in order that they might take possession of the Fragment.'

I shook my head. 'This is folly.'

'Temminee can be a forceful little creature,' said Shadd. 'When her mind is made up there is no swaying her. Furthermore, she has an unassailable belief in Destiny – it is perhaps a trait of her kind. In particular she seems intent upon my Destiny. Temminee insists that by my actions in Qotolr I in some way singled myself out. She declares that I am fated to meet this crisis. I did not share her conviction, but now it appears I have no choice. She is intent upon her course, and nothing I could say would dissuade her from it. Whatever we may feel, we have little choice but to go with the situation.'

'Then what is to happen?'

'An Enchanter will manifest here,' said the Chariness. 'Or more precisely, near here, at the place of power we call The Howling Hill. It is one of the few locations outside of Enchantery where Enchanters may still manifest something in the order of their full powers. Under Temminee's guidance, that is where the creature will come, in search of Duke Shadd and the Fragment.'

'But who will come?'

'We know that there are at least five Enchanters still residing in Enchantery. Of these we know the identities of three: the Drear-hag Mesmia, formerly known as Strymnia; Yxon, Lord of the Laughing Blue Knights, and Urch-Malmain, the Diabolist. The remaining two, and perhaps others, remain unknown to us. Of the three, Temminee will not approach Mesmia, who is aware of the existence of the Fragment but does not know where it is, and who has already demonstrated unequivocal hostility towards Temminee herself, and Duke Shadd. Temminee will go to Yxon and Urch-Malmain, and will endeavour to seek out the others. But as to which one will manifest here, we cannot say.'

'And if all five come?'

'Temminee plans measures to safeguard against that,' said Shadd. 'She will approach each with a story differing in certain respects, but made up of half-truths and partial disclosures. Gauging their responses, she will reveal her knowledge of the approximate whereabouts of the Fragment only to one – the one she deems the most sympathetic.'

'Sympathetic? That is not a word that I would ordinarily associate with Enchanters.'

'Remember, their antipathy is towards each other, not us,' said the Chariness. 'In their eyes we are almost irrelevant. The Enchanter's sole aim will be to gain the Fragment, not necessarily to destroy us in the process. And again, we are in a sense allies, for we share a common enemy.'

I shook my head incredulously. 'Forgive me, I have to gainsay you. These are mighty beings. They would destroy us as soon as tolerate our presence. Though we do indeed share a common enemy, they are unlikely to consider us worthwhile allies in their cause. Do we really know with what we are dealing here?'

'No!' said Crananba sharply. 'But we are irreversibly committed upon this course. Whatever comes, we must face it and overcome it, or die.'

I could see that, indeed, our hand had been forced. Resignedly I said, 'Then when the Enchanter comes, what next? He or she will not simply sit down with us at table and offer assistance over a tankard or two of ale.'

'We will bargain,' said Crananba. 'In return for decrypting the Fragment and giving us the Formula for the Antidote, we offer the Enchanter the remaining contents.'

Again, I could scarcely believe what I was hearing. 'I mean no disrespect, but do you know what you are saying? Do you know what it means if one of these creatures gains the power that that Fragment may hold?'

'We know, Dinbig. We are preparing ourselves as best we are able. A trap is to be baited and sprung. The creature will be lured to The Howling Hill, and then away. Once beyond the influence of the Hill, he or she will be greatly restricted in power. That is the point at which we may act. But this is not the time to explain everything. When this meeting is done we will relate to you in full the plan we have worked out.'

'Understand that it *is* the only way, Dinbig,' said the Chariness. 'If we fail to act on this one slim hope, then we fail in everything. We have here a potentially valuable weapon in our fight against the Beast of Rull. We cannot let the chance pass us by.'

Certainly that was so, I could not deny it. But the prospect of what we were now committed to face filled me with deepest foreboding.

'Do we have any way of knowing when the Enchanter will come?' I asked.

'We have Monitors placed upon The Howling Hill. They will report any unusual activity. There will almost certainly be an energy flux, a build-up of unusual force, which will signal the Enchanter's imminent approach.'

'What if Temminee, through misfortune or catastrophe, has failed?'

Shadd spoke. 'She has met with neither misfortune nor catastrophe, this I know. I am no longer able to see through Temminee's eyes, as I could in Qotolr. But I can sense her being, just as I sensed yours. With deep concentration I am able to pick up something of her state of mind. Thus far, her plan is working.'

'Our remaining time is precious,' said the Chariness, preparing to bring the conclave to a close. 'Incidentally, it may interest you to learn that during our presence here in Underfell we have had contact with some of its former inhabitants.'

'The villagers?' I said, amazed.

'Their ghosts. They haunt this place. They pay us no heed. It is possible that they are not aware of us. Indeed, they may not know that they are dead. We have conducted rituals of Transmigration, but they appear to have had no effect.'

'They are perhaps bound to this place.'

'It is possible. Before they can be released, we would have to know what binds them.'

She rose, as did the others, and announced the meeting done. I found my thoughts going once again to Rohse and Eroniss. I had hoped, upon my return to Khimmur, to find an early opportunity to travel to Little Malme to see them. Now events moved with such dispatch that this was impossible. Knowing what we were about to face, I could not help but wonder whether it would ever come to be.

11

I

Across Rull the shadow of the Beast was cast. The greatest single empire known in the recorded history of Firstworld had been born with startling rapidity and ease. But the Beast was far from done.

In the south, Tomia and Dyarchim still stood free. The Beast was impatient to have done there and return forthwith to Khimmur. The indications were that now, with the fall of Ghence, the two nations would accede to Khimmur's demands without further conflict. Khimmurian emissaries rode to the palaces of the kings of both nations. They brought missives expressing King Oshalan's hopes for immediate peaceful settlement, along with veiled threats of the consequences should they choose to resist. Lest there be any doubt in their minds, a mighty army was assembled on Tomia's border, a force far greater than anything Tomia might hope to put into the field.

Assured of Tomia's capitulation, and following it that of Dyarchim, the Beast of Rull gave charge of affairs in the south to his most trusted deputies. With White Blades, Gneth and an army three thousand strong, he departed Ghence.

Far away in Hecra, Lord Yzwul of Tiancz survived desperate adventures and fearful escapades. Bloodied and weary he searched on, as yet fruitlessly, for the all-important artifact, the Hecranese Cartouche. Elsewhere the faithful priests and priestesses of Kemah-amek maintained their ceaseless vigil over the wan and motionless form of their beloved Wonasina. And who knows what dream-thoughts and images came to her as she lay like a corpse, helpless in the unnatural state that was neither life nor death?

In Khimmur the *Zan-Chassin* occupied themselves in their researches and meditations, preparing for the fateful encounter that was possibly only hours away. None voiced their thoughts, but all were aware that their failure in this endeavour would mark the end of their struggle against the evil they had unwittingly unleashed upon the world.

The forest folk of Virland huddled deep in the sanctuary of the great Magoth. From there, so remote did all matters of the world seem, they were at times able almost to forget that tyranny ruled their land. Not so the other occupied nations: Pansur, Miragoff, Chol, Putc'pii and elsewhere, where the people were bound into slavery, suffering extremes of hardship and deprivation under their bloody oppressors.

The lonely fortress of Drurn March in the south-east of Chol still held out against its besieging foe. Within its walls the beleaguered Prince Regent, Fhir Oube, paced almost ceaselessly back and forth, wringing his hands in agonies of indecision.

Fhir Oube's men had gained heart from the successful repulsion of Lord Marsinenicon's attempted assault. Yet their situation remained hopeless. They were cut off without prospect of succour. Frequently Fhir Oube stood before an arrow-slit in Drurn March's keep. His gaze was upon the east, and his one possible avenue of escape.

Two things puzzled Fhir Oube. Firstly, why had Lord Marsinenicon chosen to launch such a mighty assault against the fortress? The decision had been rash, unnecessary, and doomed to failure from the outset. It had cost Marsinenicon many good men.* Secondly, why had Khimmur not blocked the way east, into the forbidden land of Enchantery? Marsinenicon's troops could by now have forged a path through the heights to secure that road. It was as though the way had been deliberately left open; as though Lord Marsinenicon was inviting, or perhaps challenging, the Prince Regent to choose that way out.

In Enchantery itself five mighty beings were moved to individual response by strange reports and unsettling tales of events beyond their borders. Each, as always, endeavoured to spy upon the other four. Each employed methods and means peculiar to himself. Each knew varying degrees of success.

Thus, four had been aware for some weeks of certain exertions made on the part of the Drear-hag, Mesmia. Her spies and informants had essayed to increase their intelligence-gathering activities; her minions had been seen far from her usual domain. Mesmia herself was known to be in a state of high excitement and emotional excess bordering on hysteria, but the cause of her

---

* The traitors, Odus and Dade, had survived that night of battle, despite the evidence left by Duke Shadd to point the finger of complicity at Drurn March's commander. By sheer fortune it had been Dade who first came upon Odus, trussed up as Shadd had left him. Dade released him and disposed of the incriminating notice. Between them they contrived a tale of Khimmurian special troops secretly scaling the wall in an attempt to unbar the door to the outer compound. By this account the pair were seen as heroes, who had saved Drurn March from enemy infiltration. None were the wiser as to the real events of that night. Odus was now obliged to loyalty to his Prince Regent, at least for the present time, for he knew that in the valley below Lord Marsinenicon gnashed his teeth and swore a hideous revenge against the Drurn March commander he believed had betrayed him.

condition was undetermined. Now, with the arrival of a winged messenger at the four remote strongholds of the Enchanters, telling a tale of quest and discovery, theft, flight and impending cataclysm, Mesmia's eccentricities were revealed in a clear and unambiguous light.

The Enchanter, Yxon, Lord of the Laughing Blue Knights, occupied a castle called Madgard Keep which clung to the face of a line of low Qotol crags which had never been named. From here his élite guard of battle-loving Blue Knights routinely sallied forth, inflicting summary justice upon the folk of Yxon's domain, and ejecting or eliminating by force any company unwise enough to have ventured uninvited into the region.

On this day Yxon occupied a first-level chamber in a high tower of Madgard Keep, from the glazed window of which a view of wide scope extended over the countryside. Watery sunlight filtered in through the thick glass, which had grown lavender with age. Yxon entertained a visitor, with whom he was deep in conversation.

Yxon struck a powerful figure, having taken the semblance of a man of perhaps thirty years of age. He was tall and striking, with strong limbs, broad shoulders and confident poise. He had affected to give his skin a purplish tinge. Dark eyes glared piercingly from beneath dark purplish brows. His face was handsome, fierce and proud, with an aspect of decadent barbarousness. Yxon was garbed in a billowing purple puff-sleeved chemise, open at the front to reveal a muscular chest. He wore baggy purple breeches stuffed into soft doeskin ankle-boots. Bracelets adorned his wrists; rings his fingers. Upon his head was a turban of rich purple cloth threaded with gold; a small dark beard adorned the tip of his chin.

'How much of what you have told me is known to Mesmia?' asked Yxon.

The Gwynad, Temminee, stood before him on a table-top of blue porphyry, her exquisite wings folded upon her back. 'She knows that Duke Shadd had the Fragment. Indeed, it was she who sent him to recover it. Then it was stolen. She suspects by one of you.'

'Aha!' Yxon straightened. 'Much is explained!' He stared down at her with a mannered smile. 'Mesmia's attentions of late have become more irksome than before, and less than subtle. Now I see why. I assume she has subjected the other three to similar treatment. And all the time the Fragment is elsewhere. Do you know where it rests now?'

'It is in, or close to, Khimmur,' said Temminee, choosing her words with care. 'Duke Shadd has taken it there for safekeeping, in the hope of learning its secrets.'

Yxon gave a disdainful snort. 'He is a human. He will never learn what is written there.'

'Nonetheless, he has the Fragment, and others who covet it have not.'

Yxon scowled. 'But you can lead me to it?'

'I am of the Gwynad; we are attuned to the essence of the Soul Crystal. Duke Shadd carries the Crystal as well as the Fragment. He holds each in almost equal esteem, which is to say he will not willingly part with either. I can lead you to the Crystal.'

'And then you require my assistance.'

'I cannot take back the Crystal without help.'

'And in return the Fragment will be mine?'

'I have no interest in the Fragment.'

Yxon strode away a few paces, musing to himself. He scratched his nose. From outside came the sounds of marching feet, bellowed commands, and laughter as the Laughing Blue Knights were put through their drill upon the parade-ground below. Yxon turned, fingering his beard. 'But the other Enchanters also know of this.'

'I have told them far less than I have told you, Lord Yxon.'

'Why?'

'I spoke first to Urch-Malmain, with words carefully chosen to whet his appetite. His response was one of wrath and vengefulness. Such heated emotion I judged an unreliable asset. Thus I did not disclose the whereabouts of the Fragment to him, nor the fact that it is in Duke Shadd's possession.'

'And he let you go?'

'He would have imprisoned me, to force my knowledge from me. But I convinced him that I had no knowledge then of the whereabouts of the Crystal, and hence the Fragment. I told him I must meet with another to secure that knowledge, and that I would return subsequently. Urch-Malmain had me followed, but I managed to elude his thugs without great difficulty.'

'And what of the other two?'

'Similarly they demonstrated attitudes that I deemed undesirable in the fulfilment of my own quest.'

An ironic light came to Yxon's eye. 'Whereas I . . . ?'

'Your powers, Lord Yxon, are as great if not greater than those of the other Enchanters. Yet you have responded with cool judgement and sober thought. I know each of you covets the Fragment; my feeling is that it would be less liable to misuse in your hands.'

Yxon massaged his jaw. 'Khimmur, you say?'

'That is where we must go.'

'Hmm, it is not impossible. But I am curious. Your race is extinct, or so I had believed. What purpose can be fulfilled by chasing your sacred stone now?'

'It is a relic of great antiquity and inexpressible importance to my kind. If all are dead – and that is not yet proven – then their souls will know torment until the Soul Crystal is returned to its proper resting-place.'

'How noble,' said Yxon with sarcasm. 'Or perhaps

sentimental. Whichever, it strikes me as pointless. I fail to understand the motivation.'

'You are perhaps above such things, Lord Yxon.'

'Yes, I believe I am. Emotional attachments are the stuff of lesser races. Such afflictions have been the downfall of many.'

'Yet you covet the Fragment.'

'It is a different thing. Recovery of the Fragment serves a utilitarian purpose. Your little Crystal will have no greater practical value here, in Khimmur, or lodged upon a far moon of Estabril. It is a pointless quest, embarked upon purely to salve your own conscience. Still, what is it to me? Yes, I will accompany you to Khimmur. We will confront the thief, Duke Shadd, and take back what is rightly our own.'

'Do I have your bond that you will not endeavour to trick me?'

Yxon smiled condescendingly. 'Little Gwynad, you fail to understand. You are not worth the effort it would take me to trick you. You and your Crystal are irrelevant to me. I will take it from Duke Shadd and give it to you. You may then do with it as you please. My word is my bond. Take it or leave it.'

Temminee gave a small shrug. 'Let it be so.'

'Good. Now, I must make certain preparations. You will remain here as my guest. Do not attempt to leave. You will be accorded every hospitality.'

II

Yxon departed the chamber, leaving Temminee alone with her thoughts. She unfolded her wings and rose from the table, flew across to the window.

'Do not attempt to leave!' commanded a strident voice.

Temminee darted back, startled. There was no one in sight. 'I was not leaving, merely looking through the window.'

There was no reply. She approached the window again.

'Do not attempt to leave!' commanded the same voice. 'You have been warned. Any further attempt will result in more definite confinement.'

Temminee sighed and returned to the centre of the chamber. A serving-wisp drifted in and enquired whether she desired refreshment.

'Perhaps a fruit cordial.'

'I lack drinking-vessels of an appropriate dimension,' said the wisp. 'Will a darning thimble suffice for your cordial?'

'That will be fine.'

'Something to eat?'

'No, nothing. How long am I to be kept here?'

'How would I know?'

The wisp floated away. Temminee resigned herself to waiting.

Lord Yxon strode with purpose through the passages of Madgard Keep, arriving in short order before the entrance to his workroom. He uttered a few words to disarm the defensive spells set about the Portal. Taking from a wallet at his waistband a key of black iron, he unlocked the door and stepped through. Inside, Yxon locked the door once more and re-established the defences.

Then he spoke. 'Have any entered or attempted to enter this chamber in my absence?'

A voice, soft and dull, replied, 'None.'

'Have any pried or spied, or otherwise attempted to gain information pertinent to myself or my affairs?'

Again the flat response, though this time it was less comforting. 'Certainly.'

'What is the identity of those who have sought to spy?'

'They are minions acting on behalf of your four low and reprehensible adversaries.'

'And what have they learned from their efforts?'

'Only that you reside here; that you are you; that this is your home; that you are potent; that you have . . .'

'Yes, yes. I do not require a full and unexpurgated list of my every attribute and quirk. Be succinct, please.'

'In short, then, they have learned nothing beyond what they already knew.'

Yxon looked about the chamber, which was replete with magical apparatus and adjuncts of sometimes bizarre and exotic construction. He crossed to one wall, in which were embedded, in a row, four plates of mirrored glass. Into the first of these he peered, disregarding the fact that it reflected no image. Yxon made a sign and issued a curt command, 'Window, open the way.'

The mirror grew distorted, as if a film of cloudy water passed across its surface. An image shifted in and out of focus. Presently the dark, brooding, malign figure of the diabolist, Urch-Malmain, was revealed hunched over a table. Upon the table were four objects which Urch-Malmain studied with interest. The objects were carved from pure grey chalcedony. They resembled small figurines which lacked limbs or features. They might have been pawns from a chess-set, but Yxon knew them to have another function.

Yxon smiled to himself: Urch-Malmain was engaged in precisely the same activity as he: observing the other four Enchanters. As Yxon watched, Urch-Malmain looked up sharply with an expression of extreme irritation. He spat a soundless word and gave a sudden gesture of the hand. There was a flash of brilliant green light in the Window through which Yxon gazed. Yxon stepped back, blinking, momentarily dazzled. The image in the Window vanished, leaving only blankness.

Yxon thought quickly to himself. Evidently Urch-Malmain had grown aware that he was observed. He would not have known which Enchanter spied upon him, however, unless by coincidence the figurine he happened to be studying at that moment had been the one that represented Yxon himself. If that were so, then Urch-Malmain would have observed Yxon observing him.

Yxon gave a low chuckle. He had used the Windows countless times; it had become something of a game. Now, however, the stakes had suddenly undergone a dramatic rise. Yxon's knowledge as to the activities of the other four Enchanters had taken on an importance unlike anything he had known for centuries.

He quickly conducted a similar exercise with the remaining three plates in the wall. Presently, satisfied as to the current status and whereabouts of Mesmia and the other two Enchanters, he withdrew to seat himself at a table to one side of his workroom. He focussed his thoughts on the business of preparing himself for his journey.

First he required a simulacrum. If he was to leave Madgard Keep, and Qotolr itself, his first priority was that the other Enchanters should know nothing of his absence. He toyed with a secondary idea: that of allowing Mesmia to believe that he did indeed have custody of the missing Fragment from Yshcopthe's Pandect. This would certainly deter her from searching elsewhere, and thus possibly interfering with Yxon's own designs in Khimmur.

A brief consideration of Mesmia's possible responses caused Yxon to discard that notion. Yes, Mesmia might be taken in. But should she choose to investigate while Yxon was absent, she might well succeed in overcoming the simulacrum, and even take control of Madgard Keep.

Yxon busied himself for several hours in his work-room. First he took an ancient book from a shelf, opened it upon his work-table, and studied certain texts inscribed upon its heavy parchment leaves. Then, he set about arranging various items of apparatus, placing them with meticulous care upon and around a bulky rectangular cabinet which stood in one corner of the chamber. From time to time he referred back to the ancient book on his work-table, to assure himself that he was following its instructions precisely.

At length, satisfied that all was as it should be, Yxon stood back. He raised his hands and began to recite a long series of incantations. Then he laid himself down upon a bench, again arranging certain articles about himself, and continued his magical recitations.

Presently he fell silent. He lay motionless, eyes closed. The apparatus hummed; a curious thing happened: a stream of vaporous stuff, pale-pinkish in colour, began to rise slowly from Yxon's still form, gather in a small cloud above him, then pour in another stream into the cabinet, entering through a small hole in its top.

An hour passed. In due course the pink faded. The apparatus became silent and still. Yxon awoke, sat up on the bench and planted his feet upon the floor. He looked weary, enervated; his skin had paled to a faint violet tint, and he hung his head between his shoulders as if it were a great weight. Shakily he rose. He stared for some moments at the cabinet, then approached and threw open the door on its facing side. Inside sat a still figure, a man, naked, his eyes closed, identical in all respects to Yxon.

'Rise,' commanded Yxon.

The figure opened its eyes. It rose and stepped from the cabinet. Its look was dull, its face blank.

'You are me, Yxon, Lord Enchanter of the Laughing Blue Knights,' said Yxon. 'You are created in my image, using my essence, which will be recognizable to others. You are to be me in my absence. You will remain here in this room, deep in study. You will permit no one to enter, nor will you leave, except to attend to matters of emergency. Upon my return you will relinquish all responsibilities. Do you understand?'

The simulacrum nodded. 'I am you, Yxon, Lord Enchanter of the Laughing Blue Knights. I am created in your image, using your essence, which will be recognizable to others. I am to be you in your absence . . .'

Yxon went to a cupboard and brought forth undergarments, black trousers, green tunic, and green, curl-toed slippers. 'Garb yourself,' he said.

Sluggishly, the simulacrum began to don the clothes. Yxon busied himself at a large wooden chest, examining articles within, choosing certain items of equipment he reasoned might be of use in his forthcoming venture. Done, he turned to inspect his simulacrum, which now stood fully clothed, staring emptily at its creator.

Yxon stroked his jaw, musing. 'A less than perfect substitute. Still, the synthesis is done. To all intents and purposes you will be me. You will be convincing from afar.' He addressed the simulacrum directly. 'Come along, now. You are slack-jawed and zestless. Lose that vacant expression, put vigour into your movements, bear yourself with confidence and pride. That's better. I will soon depart; remember my instructions and do not veer from them by so much as a shadow of a notion.'

The simulacrum spoke. 'I can but obey.'

Yxon strode to the door, nullified the defensive magics. He paused, cast his eyes once around the room, then departed.

During the Enchanter's absence, Temminee had found
ample opportunity for boredom and mounting apprehension. With no distractions other than to eat and
drink the refreshments provided by the disdainful
serving-wisp, she quickly became preoccupied, her
thoughts dwelling on the perils of the escapade she had
embroiled herself in. All seemed to be going to plan,
yet the plan itself was at base flimsy. So much was at
stake, and so much might yet go awry.

Time passed and Temminee tried to sleep. She chose
for a bed a soft cushion of plush blue velvet which
rested upon a divan. Sleep would not come. Again and
again she went over in her mind the events of the preceding days. Had she been thorough in her arrangements? Had she done all she had intended to do? Were
the Enchanters persuaded by the tale she had given to
each of them?

She was not convinced that this was so. The three
Enchanters that she had approached prior to Yxon had
evinced attitudes quite startling and disturbing to her
mind. She was reminded again that these were not
ordinary beings, stirred or motivated in the way that
normal folk were. By general reckonings they were
irrational and quite beyond understanding. Yxon
showed a more amenable face, but Temminee was
deeply wary of him, equally. He was, after all, one of
them. They were awesome creatures, jealous gods,
with aspirations and ambitions that could never be
properly measured in human terms. Her familiarity
with them – with the possible exception of Mesmia –
was rudimentary to say the least.

Rising like monsters from the deep came terrifying
visions of the manifold things that might go wrong.
With each one her body was racked with profound

shudders. Everything was uncertainties, founded on the most basic calculations and analyses of the anticipated responses of the five Enchanters. She had gone over the details of her plan many times with Shadd. They had allowed for wide variations. But if they had misjudged, if the Enchanters responded in a manner they had not calculated on, the consequences could be disastrous.

And if the Enchanters did respond as anticipated? Even then, there was so much that could go wrong. Temminee could not think about it, yet she could not stop herself. Over and over in her mind it went, unrelenting, ever-returning, until she thought she would burst asunder with the pressure of it all.

It was a relief when Yxon returned. He came slowly into the chamber, peering about him in an effort to locate the Gwynad. Temminee watched him for some moments. Then she rose from her cushion and hovered in the air before him, that he might see her.

'The preliminaries are complete,' said the Enchanter. 'Now it remains to establish the way to Khimmur. And of course, there is you. Am I correct in assuming that you lack experience in regard to instantaneous transport between locations?'

'That is so,' replied Temminee. She had noted Yxon's appearance. He was haggard, hollow-eyed, seemed drained, depleted. Was the strain of this endeavour telling even on him, or had something happened of which Temminee had no knowledge?

Yxon was also regarding her closely, his gaze travelling up and down her tiny form, and she saw a certain gleam come into his eyes.

'Little Gwynad, you are exquisite to behold.'

Temminee lowered her eyes. 'Thank you, Lord Yxon.'

'It has struck me that before we depart we might avail ourselves of an hour or so's pleasurable diversion.'

'Do you mean what I think you mean? That is surely an impractical suggestion.'

'You refer to the difference in size between us? That need not be an obstacle. With a word I can transform you to my own size, or alternatively reduce myself to yours.'

'Nonetheless, I feel we should occupy ourselves for the present solely with the matter in hand. Others might be moving even now to preempt us. Remember, they know something of what is afoot.'

Yxon considered this, pursing his pale purple lips, then heaved a resigned sigh. 'Ah, perhaps you are right. Later, then, when we return. You will wish to celebrate.'

'I trust I shall.'

'Good. Well then, we must take certain steps to ensure safe passage for you. Without such precautions you will be reduced upon an instant to your constituent energies, and dispersed randomly in a million particles to a million separate locations. It would be a pity, and would certainly mar our celebrations. Come, I will see you through the necessary procedures.'

He turned to leave the chamber, with Temminee following in his wake.

'When do we depart for Khimmur?' she asked.

'As soon as you are ready. A matter of perhaps two or three hours.'

They arrived at Yxon's workroom. 'I must also initiate certain processes which will establish our destination,' said Yxon as they entered. Closing the door, he left her to busy himself at a curious contraption, formed of small metallic globes and discs set on a network of slender threads and curving steel grooved troughs. Spread on a worktop beneath this apparatus was a large sheet of paper covered in intricate lines and configurations in a number of colours. Yxon worked to adjust the discs, globes, threads and troughs into a specific arrangement. He aligned them in some manner with the diagrams on the paper sheet. He muttered to himself as he worked, and seemed wholly absorbed, oblivious to all else.

Temminee took note of the simulacrum, who, when they'd entered, was standing before a bookshelf, inspecting the volumes arrayed there. It paid them no attention, but chose a large leather-bound tome from the shelf. This it took to a table, seated itself, and prepared to study its contents by the light of a fat candle, for the daylight was beginning to fade.

Temminee, apparently ignored for the present, fluttered around the room, taking in its features and unusual contents. The various pieces of apparatus were unfamiliar and quite alien to her, and the chamber exuded a strange ambience which she found unsettling.

She became interested in the simulacrum again, intrigued by its perfect likeness to the Enchanter. She flew to its shoulder and peered over at the book it was studying. The pages were covered in an alien script which she was unable to read. Now it became evident that the simulacrum was experiencing a similar difficulty. It looked up from the pages with a puzzled expression, scratched its nose, and muttered to itself, 'I am Yxon, created in Yxon's image, using the essence of Yxon. Thus Yxon's qualities and abilities are mine. I am commanded to absorb myself in study, yet I cannot read these words and glyphs.'

The simulacrum furrowed its brow, deep in thought. 'I am remiss in my grasp of things.'

A moment passed; the simulacrum looked up, brightening, and lifted a finger. 'Aha!'

The simulacrum drew open a drawer in the table. Within Temminee glimpsed a clutter of articles. Some were familiar and mundane, such as writing materials and instruments to aid in calculation and measurement. Others were perhaps ornamental, for they served no obvious function. Still others she could conceive no known use for.

From among these objects the simulacrum withdrew a small silver casket. This it placed upon the table, then closed the drawer.

It stared at the casket for some moments, again furrowing its brow. On the other side of the room Yxon uttered a curse as a globe slipped from its proper alignment and rumbled slowly along one of the troughs.

The simulacrum rose from its chair, smiling to itself. 'My memory is Yxon's. All things now come to me.'

It moved to small corner cabinet, opened one of its doors, reached in and took forth an object too small for Temminee to make out. Then it returned to its seat at the table.

Now Temminee saw that the simulacrum held in its hand a tiny silver key. This it inserted into the lock of the little casket. The lid of the casket flew open. Inside was something resembling a small feather, formed out of a light, golden metallic substance. With extreme care the simulacrum removed this from the casket and held it over the book. Using a particular motion it passed the feather four times over the page it had been attempting to study. Temminee watched closely, but descried no effect.

But the simulacrum seemed pleased. With a smile of satisfaction it put the feather aside and bent over the tome to resume its studies.

On the other side of the chamber Yxon at last stood back from his work. 'Good. The alignments are exact.' He peered around, seeking Temminee. She had descended to the table-top beside the simulacrum, but now moved swiftly to another position, placing herself in Yxon's line of vision.

'Ah, there you are,' said Yxon. 'Take care! Do not come too close. The apparatus is set. It creates a tunnel through which we may travel. Step into it too soon, however, and you will interfere with its creative process, rendering the tunnel untrue. You will also be killed.'

Temminee stared at the strange arrangement of globes, threads and troughs. The globes glowed and pulsed with a pale emerald light, as did the network of threads which linked them. The troughs seemed to fade in and out of vision. There was a sound of distant sighing, like a wind through a far mountain pass.

The air on the far side of the contraption shimmered and fluxed.

'Now, your turn,' said Yxon. 'The entrance to the tunnel will form outside, in the courtyard. By the time I have completed your preparation, it will be ready for us to make our journey.' He stroked his chin. 'Ideally I would wait a while longer. Synthesizing the simulacrum has taken much from me. But you are right, we must move quickly or others may preempt us.'

12

I

Our fear was that we had been manipulated for generations, that anything we did might yet be playing into the hands of the very monster we opposed.

Knowing what we now did of the origins of the Vulpasmage, and the manner in which it had worked unseen for so long, preparing for power, provoked within us all a sense of paralysing shock and profoundest misgiving. The Chariness and Crananba said little, but I could see in their faces just how gravely they viewed this. Our confidence had been totally sapped. The very core of the *Zan-Chassin*, that which we held most sacred, had been ripped open and laid bare, and revealed as rotten. Likewise the Simbissikim priesthood of Kemahamek. We'd believed ourselves wise, and in doing so had revealed our ignorance. Consequently we had been played upon and used by an evil far more powerful than us.

It was I who voiced the unspoken fear. We all beheld the spectre of Twalinieh. We had been fooled to the last by the Beast. We'd known of his coming, had searched high and low to uncover him. Yet all the time the trails that we followed had been laid intentionally to lead us astray. The Beast had been there in our midst all along. One of us. He had directed us and controlled us. He almost destroyed us, and we did not see him.

'We are forced by what is happening to look within, and question ourselves and the nature and purpose of our existence most deeply,' replied the Chariness.

'Perhaps in this the good may be found, through an understanding of how we have been previously led to permit this situation to come about.'

Crananba spoke. 'Remember, we are but human and fallible, insignificant particles in an infinite, callous, perplexing universe. We cannot hope to fathom the cosmic scheme of things. But we are pledged now to the good; where we see evil manifest we must challenge and if possible exterminate it.'

'But that is our dilemma,' Shadd remonstrated. 'That we may not recognize evil for what it is, and that despite our efforts and intentions, we may unwittingly be contributing to it.'

Crananba shook her head. 'We know within ourselves that we are without evil intent. We know that the Vulpasmage seeks the debasement and probable destruction of mankind. Therefore we oppose him, for we must, to the best of our abilities, trusting that what we do will advance the good. We can do nothing more.'

'Consider,' said the Chariness. 'Perhaps even the Vulpasmage, potent though he is, is yet acting within the scheme of another invisible, unfathomable power. Perhaps something directs him, even as it directs us; something unknown and unknowable.'

'Moban,' I said.

'Moban is a name, nothing more. In the context in which we speak it serves no purpose to use that name or any other, for we cannot really know anything of Moban. The Great Moving Spirit which created all things is the ultimate mystery. The universal purpose to which all things, animate and inanimate, aspire is beyond our scope to comprehend. We perceive ourselves to be in crisis, yet perhaps through this very crisis a creative process is accelerated. We do not know. But the strongest single motivating factor that is within us, any of us, is to *survive*, as individuals and as a race. This is what we direct our efforts towards.'

They were to prove to be fateful words.

The Monitors placed on and within The Howling Hill reported the first indications of unusual activity. An intense build-up of energy had occurred, modifications in the normal flux.

'It's as we had anticipated,' said the Chariness. 'The initial stages in the establishment of a Farplace Opening. Something is preparing to manifest.'

We of the *Zan-Chassin* left Underfell straightway. We made for The Howling Hill. Shimeril, who could play no part in this undertaking, returned to take command of his soldiers in the heart of Mystoph. With him went Count Inbuel, who also, lacking magical facility, was unqualified for the task of confronting an Enchanter. And if we perished in this endeavour, these two at least might live on to continue the struggle.

Shadd, with his companion Antinomy the Hylozote, took himself off to a prearranged location. Crananba remained with him. Shadd kept charge of the Fragment from Yshcopthe's Pandect, also the Soul Crystal.

We rode on horseback from Underfell, covering the few miles to the foot of The Howling Hill. As we approached, the vegetation thinned to scrub and stunted trees, then ceased altogether. The bare soil was powdery and black. The Hill reared before us like some dark, colossal chancre which had erupted out of the earth. Above us the weird winds moaned and sobbed.

The horses were uneasy, even with the aid of Calming raptures. We dismounted lest they become uncontrollable, and gave them into the care of a groom who led them back to the trees. On foot, we covered the remaining distance to the Hill. A dry, scorching, shrieking wind blew up suddenly. We were forced to bend our backs and huddle in our cloaks. The black dust rose in furious flurries, choking us, clogging our mouths and nostrils, stinging our skin. It blotted out the sun so that we struggled on in near-darkness. So powerful was the wind that we could scarcely make any progress, and at times were almost driven back.

It took long minutes to cover the few hundred paces to the base of The Howling Hill. At last we arrived. The wind died down a little, allowing the dust to settle. We paused to regain our breath, gazing up at the dark basalt mass that loomed over us. Nothing grew on its steep slopes; it was like a dead thing. Yet I could not rid myself of the feeling that something here lived, that the Hill itself possessed an unearthly, brooding sentience, that in some way it was aware of our presence.

A vague pathway could be made out, twisting up between harsh folds of basalt. This we followed. I glanced back as we ascended. The village of Underfell could not be seen, even from above, so fully had it merged into the wooded landscape. I had learned by now of Lord Yzwul's discovery at Kuno's stronghold in the north of Mystoph. I was saddened and disquieted by Yzwul's theory, and my thoughts went back again to that night in Underfell long ago. The village was haunted now by the ghosts of those who were slaughtered, probably never knowing by whom or what. Did they long for life? Did they pine for their lost children, who now, after a lifetime of brutal suffering, had been transformed into inhuman killers and the progenitors of more inhuman killers?

The path grew steeper as it approached the crest of the Hill. The eldritch dirge of the winds was deafening and fierce. The path levelled abruptly and we found ourselves upon a small plateau. The weald opened far below us, the Barrier Fell rising to the north, the Byar-hagkh Mountains further away to the west. Before us was a ragged opening in the rock.

The Chariness leaned close in order to shout into my ear. 'You and I will enter. The others will remain outside.'

Cliptiam, Farlsast, the Lady Chrysdhothe, and two Lesser Hierarchy members named Fonial and Belythe moved away to take up positions among the rocks around the entrance.

I stepped in first through the opening. Immediately the sound of the winds ceased. The sudden silence was for a moment disorienting, and hardly less unnerving. We were in a narrow passage which led down into the interior of the Hill. A soft, uneven, greyish glow illuminated the way, cast by fungus-like growths which clung in shapeless masses to the rock walls and roof.

I whispered over my shoulder to the Chariness. 'Do you think we are observed?'

The empty passage took up my words and passed them back and forth between the stones in an eerie sibilance. Over and over again the whispers sounded, losing all meaning. When at last their sound had faded the Chariness replied, in an even lower voice, 'It is not possible to say.'

Again the echoes, amplified above the volume of her original utterance. They chased and darted around our heads, as if on invisible wings. The words became disjointed, gibbering and dispossessed, like the whispers of madness echoing inside one's own brain. They filtered deep into The Howling Hill, and eventually were gone.

Without saying as much we resolved to speak no more. Even so, as we moved on, the slap and scrape of our footsteps on the rock floor set up a relentless percussion which accompanied us throughout our descent, giving warning of our approach to any who might have an interest.

At length the floor levelled out. The passage slowly widened, then abruptly opened into a cavernous chamber, illuminated like the passage by masses of the glowing fungal growth. In the centre of this chamber was a curious form, perfectly ovular, about the size of a shield, which hovered in the air a foot or so above the ground. The oval was not shaped by any frame or definite outline, but rather by a pale greenish mist which swirled and fluxed within it.

I stared, intrigued. The Chariness said, 'It is the Farplace Opening.'

Mercifully her words carried no echo here. I observed the swirling mist within the oval. It seemed both close, as though I might reach in and touch it, and infinitely far away. I made to approach it for a better look but the Chariness stayed me with a hand upon my arm.

'Not too close, Dinbig. We know too little of its properties.'

She spoke into the air. 'Has anything manifested here?'

The voice of a Monitor replied, soundlessly, inside my mind and, I knew, the Chariness's also. 'Nothing.'

'Has there been any other incident of note?'

'Simply that the energy has continued to build at a consistent rate. As it has done so the oval, which at first was barely discernible, has come into sharper focus.'

The Chariness nodded. She spoke to me, wonder tingeing her voice. 'A Farplace Opening . . . Long have we pondered upon the nature of such a phenomenon, and whether indeed it could exist. It is a magical fabrication which defies the limits of time, space and matter, a sorcerous aperture linking one location with another, providing instantaneous transport between the two, regardless of normal restraints.'

I stared for some moments more, then said, 'In essence there is surely a correspondence with the phenomenon which permits journeying within the Realms, or the ability to communicate thoughts between two or more minds over large distances?'

'These are non-material phenomena, unlimited by physical constraints,' replied the Chariness. 'The transference of physical objects, and indeed persons, is something else entirely. We have never succeeded in creating a Farplace Opening, though we have tried, utilizing every metaphysical resource at our command. We have never come close to understanding or mastering the laws of its manifestation. Dinbig, you and I are possibly the first human beings ever to gaze upon a Farplace Opening.'

II

The soft green mist swirled and billowed, held within the invisible membrane of its mysterious oval. New colours appeared: pale violet, then blue, pink, orange. The voice of the Monitor spoke once more in my mind: 'It is changing again!'

'Back!' said the Chariness.

We moved into the shadows of the chamber, close to the wall. As we watched, the mist within the oval intensified in brightness and colour, throwing a weird, shifting illumination into the cavern. Suddenly a bright plume of vapour gouted forth out of the centre of the oval. It formed into a dense column, then seemed to implode, gathering rapidly upon itself. It spread across an area of the floor before the oval, then dispersed. A figure was glimpsed, human maybe. It seemed to form out of nowhere, above the ground, in the mist. It was held for a moment, static, its arms and legs outspread. Then it tumbled to earth and sprawled headlong.

The mist was gone. The oval remained, its inner vapours returning to soft green. The figure on the floor moved, coming onto hands and knees. It was a man, well dressed in pale linen shirt, breeches and boots, with a light grey cloak which had fallen forward over his head. He climbed to his feet, muttering to himself, freeing his head of the cloak. He cast his gaze around the chamber, dusting himself off, seeming unsure of his whereabouts. His eyes fell upon the two of us.

'Ah, good-day, sir, madam! Forgive me, I am somewhat mystified. Would you do me the courtesy of telling me where I am?'

The fellow bent to pick up his hat, which lay upon the floor: a floppy, grey, wide-brimmed affair which matched his cloak, surmounted by a lavish blue ostrich-feather plume. He stepped towards us. I stared at him in some surprise. I knew him.

'You are lost?' enquired the Chariness.

'To say the least!'

'Then how do you come to be here?'

The fellow shrugged, lifting his eyebrows and spreading his hands. 'That is a question I was hoping you might be able to answer. Certainly, I am at a loss to do so. One moment I was relaxing in my home, the next – *poof!* – I'm here, sprawled without dignity upon the floor of this gloomy cavern!'

His eyes went from one to the other of us, quizzically. I had the impression he was searching for something. Then he turned and gazed at the glowing green oval. 'And what is this object, do you know?'

'Sleen,' said I – for he it was, who had accompanied Duke Shadd into Ciracar's Warren; who in battle had slain my vhazz companion, Yaoww; who had

310

subsequently been wounded by Yxon's Laughing Blue Knights, and had taken his leave of our small party while still in Qotolr. His appearance here in The Howling Hill put me ever more on my guard. 'Sleen, can it be pure coincidence that brings you here?'

Sleen swivelled to face me, his pale, thin face inquisitive. His small, dark eyes glittered brightly in the unnatural light. He smiled. 'You have the advantage of me, sir. I do not believe I know you.'

Only now did it come to me that in Qotolr I had occupied the body of the vhazz, Huwoorsk. I made a secret signal to the Chariness, to discourage her from intervening, and said quickly, 'Ah, perhaps you do not remember. It is true, our meeting was brief, and conducted in a somewhat hectic manner as we discussed with numerous other folk the merits of certain goods on sale in a remote Qotol market-place.'

'I see.' Sleen studied me shrewdly, plainly unconvinced. He seemed slightly troubled. His fingers, glittering with rings, stroked his immaculately trimmed goatee beard. He viewed me sidelong, then nodded to himself as if satisfied. Something in his look made me uneasy. I had the distinct feeling that he was now quite aware of who I was. 'Well, perhaps you might advise me as to where I am, and how I came to be here.'

'You are inside The Howling Hill, in Khimmur,' said the Chariness. 'As for how you came to arrive here, we can say only that you appeared through this aperture which is a doorway between remote locations, which we call a Farplace Opening.'

Sleen's eyes settled upon her. 'Thank you, my Lady. You are most gracious, and most beautiful. My name, as you have gathered, is Sleen.'

He doffed his hat and performed a deep, sweeping bow.

'Why have you come?' I asked, not wishing at present

to announce myself or have the Chariness reveal her identity.

'I have told you, I do not know. I had no hand in it.' Sleen gestured towards the Farplace Opening. 'I can only assume that this "thing" somehow brought me here, perhaps for reasons of its own, or at the behest of another. But what of you two? You surely have a purpose here, for this is hardly the place for a romantic liaison, and you do not look the kind to linger by habit in dingy caves. Or is it that you, like me, have simply discovered yourselves here, knowing neither the why nor the how of it?'

'We are awaiting someone,' said the Chariness. 'We do not know who.'

'I see. Most interesting. Well, I am confused. There is mystery here. Mystery indeed.'

Sleen strode away from us to stare, hands on hips, into the glowing oval aperture. Then he made off as if in inspection of the rock walls of the cavern. 'Aha! There is an entrance here!'

He disappeared into the passageway through which we had entered. The Chariness turned a questioning gaze to me.

'I am far from happy,' I said. Hurriedly, I revealed to her all I knew of our visitor. 'His arrival here is surely far from coincidence.'

'He seemed discountenanced when confronted by you, Dinbig.'

'It was as if he was expecting me to be here, and was then thrown by not recognizing me.'

'And he was scarcely taken in by your explanation.'

'My apprehension was that he saw through me, that he is now reassured as to my identity.'

'That was my feeling also.'

'He is perhaps attuned in some way to my essence, and therefore is able to know me for who I am. My

312

physical guise was a surprise, for he had not expected the change.'

Sleen had not reappeared. We heard the receding echo of his footsteps in the passage.

'We should not let him depart,' said the Chariness.

I went to the opening and called out, 'Sleen! Come back! We would talk with you!'

There was no reply, but after a moment the echoes ceased briefly, then resumed, though with a slightly altered timbre and rhythm, becoming more pronounced.

'He is returning,' I said, moving back to rejoin the Chariness.

She shook her head and pointed. 'He is not. Look.'

I turned.

In the passage entrance stood a child. Two small white hands rested upon the rock, a cascade of copper curls, lit by the strange light, tumbled around pale elfin features. She wore a blue smock-dress. Large, diffident eyes peered into the chamber.

I stepped forward. 'Eroniss!'

The Chariness was suddenly before me, barring my way. 'No! Dinbig, take care!'

The little girl looked up at me, then smiled. 'Daddy!' She took several steps into the chamber, holding out her arms for me to pick her up.

'It is not her, Dinbig! You know this. This is not your daughter!'

Tears stung my eyes. I knew it. It could not be my daughter. Yet, to look at her . . .

The child stopped, her arms still extended. 'Daddy. Daddy.' She stared up at me with incomprehension, then reproach, then fear. 'Daddy.' Her lower lip drooped and quivered. Her pretty face puckered, reddened. She sniffed, her eyes brimmed, and she began to bawl.

The Chariness, too, was moved. That much was

plain. But she remained resolute, perhaps more so than I could have done had I been alone. Without taking her eyes off the little girl she reached out and took my hand. 'Be strong.'

I felt her strength pour into me. It was hardly necessary now, for I had recovered from my initial shock, and had my emotions in check. I stared down at the child who was so perfect an imitation of my daughter. Still I felt torn, for she was a dear and pathetic sight. Yet I knew now that this could not be Eroniss, and my heart hardened.

Through her tears the child fixed her eye on me. Gradually, seeing that her ploy had not had the desired effect, her crying subsided. There was cold calculation in her gaze, then, childlike again, a resumption of the cries, little chubby arms extended imploringly. I stood stony-faced. The child ceased crying altogether. Just briefly, in her eyes and expression, there was a flicker of something demonic. I shuddered, recoiling, in no doubt now as to what we faced.

The bogus Eroniss turned upon her heels and wandered off across the chamber, towards the glowing oval that was the aperture to elsewhere. Passing behind it she was obscured from our sight. Suddenly there was something else in that cavernous chamber. A huge shape, a shadow at first, gaining substance. A roaring, billowing sound that filled our ears and made our teeth vibrate inside our skulls. The thing leapt howling towards us, clearing the Farplace Opening in a single bound.

In my mind was an invocation, ready to throw against the monster. Yet I held back, for we had agreed beforehand that we would use magic only in the most dire extremes. We could not afford to expend energies here, in this location, where we knew we had no real hope of besting our adversary.

The monster stopped. Now we could see it clearly. It resembled a colossal hound, perhaps eight feet in height, even on all fours. Its hide was thick and black, standing out in stiff, matted spikes. Triple rows of curved fangs were bared, spittle and foam drooling to the cavern floor. The ears were flattened, eyes wild, rolling white.

It towered over us, menacing with snarls. We, unconsciously, had drawn back to the wall.

'Hold!' whispered the Chariness with harsh urgency. 'Now I know. This is another device.'

Bravely she stepped forward until she stood within inches of the great hound. The thing towered over her, might easily have torn her limb from limb. Very slowly she raised her hand.

She spoke. 'Greetings! I do not know whom I address, but I acknowledge your power. We know why you have come, and we are here to work with you. And you will know that this monster holds no terror for me. I tamed it long ago. Come forward, then. Reveal yourself, that we may discuss what is to be.'

Slowly she moved backwards to place herself beside me again. The great hound eyed us, its gaze narrowing with unnerving intelligence. Then suddenly it turned and leapt, away, into the entrance of the passageway. As it flew through the air its form seemed to diminish, and it passed out of the chamber as a black blur.

We stood in silence for some moments. I listened to the sound of my thumping heart as it slowly resumed its regular beat. The Farplace Opening glowed softly; there was no sound from the passage. I said, presently, 'I am curious. Who did you address? And what did you mean when you said you had tamed the monster long ago?'

'I addressed the Enchanter, whomsoever it might be, who has created this trio of manifestations that we

315

have just witnessed. The appearance of that creature confirmed a suspicion I had as to what was happening here. We are dealing with an extraordinary power. It seems that our adversary has some ability to reach into our memories and bring forth whatever it finds there. First, Sleen, the image of whom it picked from your own memory. It slipped up, for it was not to know that you are not now as you were then. So it attempted something else, choosing a guise that it knew would affect you in a powerful emotional way. Quite what its intention was I can't say, though I would suggest a seduction, or the forming of an emotional bond. Then the hound appeared, and I knew for certain that we were dealing with memory-probing of some kind.'

'The hound is familiar to you?'

'As a child of perhaps three years I was attacked by a hound. Without knowing what I did I calmed the creature. By this means I both saved my life, and revealed to others my suitability for *Zan-Chassin* candidacy. What is interesting is that the hound appeared now as it did to me then. That is, it is huge, and fierce beyond reality. What we have just seen is quite literally a child's memory, of a beast far larger than her, fiercer and more grotesque than even a war-dog. It has been plucked, quite literally, from my forgotten memory of that event.'

'And had it the power to destroy you?' I mused.

'An interesting question. Certainly I was terrified, for a moment, until I understood. What cannot be doubted is the power of the Enchanter who has created these effects.'

'Effects? Could not each one of them have been the Enchanter in person?'

'A Formshifter, drawing on the content of the minds of others for its inspiration. It may well be so.'

We gazed around the chamber. There was no sound,

bar that of our own breathing. The passageway to the outside world was also silent.

'Dinbig, go to the entrance and ask the others whether they have witnessed anything. Then return and tell me what they say.'

This I did. Ascending cautiously through the passage to step out into the warm, bright light, where the wind howled in my ears, I called forth Chrysdhothe and the others from their hiding-places and questioned them. They had seen nothing out of the ordinary. I returned to the chamber of the Farplace Opening. The Chariness now sat cross-legged upon the rock floor on the far side of the oval, staring into its misty depths.

'And you came upon nothing in the passage?' she asked.

'Nothing.'

'We must assume, then, that something is still here, somewhere. Either that, or there will be another manifestation. In either case, we can only wait.'

III

We waited. The oval remained before us, unchanging. No new manifestation occurred. We did not communicate. I sensed that the Chariness was concentrating deeply.

Perhaps two hours passed and at last the Chariness spoke, startling me, so accustomed had I grown to the silence.

'We must go,' said she. She rose erect from the position she occupied. 'Come.'

'We are leaving the chamber unguarded?'

'The Monitors will keep us informed. The others can maintain a vigilance at the entrance. But I would speak with Duke Shadd, urgently. I sense there is a need to modify our plan.'

'In what manner?'

'That I cannot say until I have seen Shadd.'

'And if something happens in our absence?'

'Something has already happened, Dinbig. That is the point. It has happened and we have failed to understand or make appropriate response to it. Don't you see? An Enchanter came, then eluded us. Now he or she is among us, somewhere, and we don't know where.'

She strode without further explanation from the cavern chamber, and I followed, up through the echoing, winding passage to daylight. The others joined us, and reiterated their earlier report: nothing had been seen to leave or enter the passage during our sojourn within.

The Chariness stood, gazing back at the dark gash in the rock that was the entrance to the passageway. I sensed her tension, a nervousness that I had never known her display before. When she spoke it was in clipped tones, issuing quick orders, gesturing uncharacteristically with her hands. 'We have failed to see! Perhaps it is already lost! We must make haste!'

At her word Fonial, Farlsast and Belythe moved back to their places to remain on guard. Chrysdhothe and Cliptiam accompanied us as we made our way hurriedly back down the basalt slopes of The Howling Hill. The winds vented their maddening dirge; the black dust whipped up into sharp, driving spumes, hampering our passage. The winds had changed direction: as we reached the foot of the Hill they thrust us forward as if to eject us like unwanted intruders from its vicinity. We reached the woods, exhausted, and found our horses, then struck out without pause for Underfell, where Shadd – we hoped – waited still with Crananba.

At length we were back among the rotting cottages. The Chariness led us to the inn of the Lost Unicorn.

She stood before the entrance, gazing first inside, then upwards at the trees and sky. She seemed perplexed.

'Do you think Shadd has returned here?' I asked. 'Is he not more likely to have remained with Crananba at the old grainstore, as we arranged?'

The Chariness looked at me as if suddenly cognizant of some fact that had eluded her. 'You are right, Dinbig. It's just that I have a strange feeling about this place.'

Her eyes, ordinarily solemn and grey, were animated and shining with a hectic light. Quite obviously she was profoundly troubled by something she suspected or knew, but had not yet chosen to divulge. I waited expectantly, in the hope that she might now offer some word of elucidation. But she said nothing, taking her horse's tether and leading it quickly away in the direction of the grainstore.

The grainstore was situated at the top of the old village. At one time it had been a long, low-roofed barn, used for communal storage. Now there was little more than ruined stone walls in varying states of dilapidation, and a few rotten timbers, all overgrown. It had been chosen as Shadd's waiting-place for a number of reasons. From its site one could look down upon the remainder of Underfell's ruins, and The Howling Hill further away across the countryside, and thus be aware of anyone entering the village. At its rear was a steep cliff which fell some forty feet to a rugged stream-bed. To Shadd, the cliff was a possible route of escape in an emergency, while to most others it would prove a difficult obstacle. At the front of the grainstore land subsidence had created a marshy hollow, with a raised pathway to one side which was the only way by which the store might be easily approached.

As we walked along the path the figure of Crananba, leaning on her staff, hobbled from the ruin.

'Where is Shadd?' demanded the Chariness.

'He conceals himself close by.' The crone looked from one to the other of us, her wrinkled eyes searching our faces. 'I sensed something amiss. What has happened?'

'An Enchanter is here, somewhere. We were fooled and rendered ineffective. I must speak to Shadd.'

'I am here,' said Shadd. His tall figure appeared beneath a nearby elm. I raked the area close by with my eyes, hoping to spy the two Aphesuk, Kekhi and Rin, who I knew were not far away. But it was a foolish exercise, doomed to fail.

Shadd came forward, his pale brow furrowed. The Chariness beckoned. 'Quickly, into the ruin.'

'Do you have the Fragment?' demanded the Chariness when we were within the old walls.

Shadd nodded, patting his belt, and waved away a mosquito.

'I must see it.'

Shadd's frown deepened.

'I must,' urged the Chariness. 'We have encountered a foe more skilful and deadly than we anticipated. It has already eluded Dinbig and myself, and the other Hierarchy members placed in vigilance on The Howling Hill. There is a possibility that it has already come here and stolen the Fragment without your knowledge.'

'Impossible!' protested Shadd.

The Chariness shook her head. 'I would have said so until I became aware of what we were up against.' She held out her hand. 'Please, Duke Shadd, we must be sure.'

Shadd reached inside his tunic and pulled forth the engraved ivory tube which held the lost pages from Yshcopthe's Pandect. He placed it in the Chariness's open hand. Quickly she pulled free the plug and drew out the rolled leaves of strange parchment. These she unfurled, and passed her gaze feverishly across each. Finally she gave a sigh. 'These are they.'

She rolled the pages back up and slid them into the tube. 'For the time being I will keep custody of these.'

'Why so?' said Shadd with consternation.

I noticed small beads of perspiration on the Chariness's upper lip and brow. She looked around her into the woods, then at each one of us. 'Because the nature of our enemy is such that you might easily be led to commit an action you would later have cause to regret.'

'Do you believe me so easily fooled?'

'We all have within us that which makes us vulnerable.' Briefly the Chariness detailed the events that had occurred within the chamber of the Farplace Opening. 'This creature can delve into your mind without your knowledge, and realize memories that lie hidden there. I do not know its full capability, but conceivably it is possible for it to bring forth anything. Thus is revealed your vulnerability. During our vigil in the chamber of the Farplace Opening I have strengthened myself, created mental defences which I hope will prevent the creature gaining access to any aspect of my memory. This the rest of you must now do. Until it is achieved you are all vulnerable.'

'How do we accomplish this?' enquired Shadd.

'You must be shown.' The Chariness turned to me. 'You can instruct Duke Shadd?'

I nodded. 'But the process will take time.'

'I know it.'

It struck me that much time could have been saved had the Chariness alerted me to this situation earlier, whilst we waited within The Howling Hill. I could then have prepared myself, as she had done. That way there would have been two of us, instead of one, more able to meet this threat.

'The two Aphesuk,' said the Chariness. 'Call them here, Duke Shadd. It is vital that we are all together.'

Shadd hesitated, then spoke loudly. 'Kekhi, Rin. You have heard. Come forth now.'

Almost instantly they were there, standing right on the edge of our circle, so close that both Chrysdhothe and Cliptiam jumped in surprise. I chose the moment to draw the Chariness aside. 'From the measures that you are taking here, I feel there is something you have not yet revealed.'

She gave a curt nod, and her eyes travelled again from one to the other of us. In a voice pitched so that only I might hear it, she said, 'I am not yet positive, but the evidence I have seen so far would suggest that this creature can assume the guise of anything that is resident within the memory of any person whom it chooses as its subject. That encompasses just about everything you might think of. My greatest fear is that it may appear as one of us.'

IV

Half an hour had passed. We sat in a group in the middle of the ruined grainstore. I had begun teaching Shadd the techniques of memory defence which would hopefully provide him some protection from the guiles of the unknown Enchanter. The others sat close by in meditation, preparing their own minds.

Shadd was a receptive student, quick to grasp the principles, adept with his mind. The process would not ordinarily take long, but he was distracted, as was I. It was not easy to apply oneself totally, knowing the disposition of our enemy.

Furthermore, effectiveness of these techniques was not guaranteed. The methods we used were those that would prevent another *Zan-Chassin* from stealing the contents of memory. Whether they would prevent an Enchanter was another question.

The day was drawing to a close, the light mellowing as the sun sank towards mountains in a splendour of red. Shadd looked beyond me to the entrance of the grainstore, where the Chariness stood with her back to us, keeping watch.

'What is it that troubles you?' I asked.

'I'm not sure. An intuition. Something.'

'I share your misgivings, but am at a loss as to a specific cause. Our situation is tense and uncertain. It promotes suspicion and fear.'

A gust of breeze played through the ruin, rustling the bushes close by us. Shadd eyed the shifting leaves, consternation on his pale face. 'This creature that we face – it could be anything, anywhere?'

'We must proceed on that assumption.'

Shadd shook his head, gripping his inner cheek between his teeth. His gaze went back to the Chariness. 'What happened there, Dinbig? Inside The Howling Hill. What precisely happened?'

'It was as the Chariness said.'

'You saw Sleen?'

'What I believed was he.'

'Then your daughter? Then some hideous creature from the Chariness's childhood memories?'

I nodded.

'And this last apparition then disappeared into the passageway, but was not seen by the others to leave the Hill?'

'That is so.'

'Then it might still be in there.'

'That's possible. Yet we sat for a considerable time before the Farplace Opening. We saw nothing more. That was why the Chariness was so concerned. She

323

believes it had already left. She thought it might have claimed one of us – possibly you.'

'But the Enchanter would be safer within the Hill, where its power is greater.'

I nodded. 'But that is not where the Fragment lies.'

'Then it may hope to draw us there, with the Fragment.'

'Or take the risk of leaving its safe place to seek you out. That was the Chariness's concern. Its power may be reduced beyond the Hill, but it is still a redoubtable foe.'

'And it is me that it will attack, though I no longer have the Fragment.'

'Aye. Unless it is already aware of the transfer.' I looked about me, at the woods where the shadows deepened, the trees beginning to lose their individual outlines. Clouds of midges flitted nearby. A tremor of unease gripped my entrails. 'Did anything unusual occur, Shadd, before we returned?'

'Nothing. That is, nothing that I am aware of.'

'The Chariness was greatly afraid that the Enchanter was already among you, that it might already have assumed the guise of one of you.'

Shadd gave a nod. 'And now we must all watch each other. It is reminiscent of Twalinieh, Dinbig. Mistrust is sown between us all, dividing us. None of us can be above suspicion.'

'You especially must guard your back.'

'Yes, but equally we all know who now has the Fragment. We must guard the Chariness.'

I looked back over my shoulder, following Shadd's gaze. The Chariness still stood in the remains of the doorway, one hand resting upon a slab of mossy stone. As I looked she turned, and for a moment our eyes met.

There was a murmured gasp beside me. *'Moban!'*

I turned. Shadd was on his feet, leaping past me,

shortswords drawn. In an instant he had covered the distance between himself and the Chariness. She saw him coming, but was not fast enough to respond. His swords darted and stabbed, and she fell with a mournful sigh, her heart pierced.

'Great Bagemm!' I was on my feet, drawing my sword. Shadd was bent over the Chariness's body, ripping free the ivory tube from her bodice. There was movement beside me, a waft of air and a blur as something shot across the intervening space between myself and Shadd.

It was the two Aphesuk. Suddenly they were positioned before him, weapons drawn.

At this point I was too shocked to react, and hardly took in the way they had positioned themselves. Rin faced out, watching us, ready to give his life if necessary to protect Shadd should we move against him. Kekhi, however, stood behind Rin, and faced Shadd, menacing him with her light sword.

The Aphesuk were as confused as the rest of us by what they had just witnessed. But their reaction had been sure and swift. Kekhi's stance told of both her uncertainty and her conviction. She sought the truth, and was there to kill Shadd – or the apparition of Shadd – if necessity decreed that course.

I stared in horror at the limp corpse of the Chariness. Shadd stood over it, gripping the ivory tube in one hand. His eyes flashed, and lighted on Crananba. She had hobbled forward, leaning on her staff, one hand raised.

'No!' cried Shadd, for he understood now how we all perceived his action. 'You have it wrong. It's not I, but she. Look!'

He stepped back, pointing at the fallen body of the Chariness. Before our eyes it was withering, turning to nothing. There was no blood. A reddish mist was seeping out of the corpse as it shrank, forming into a cloud above it. The cloud gathered itself and sped away, to disappear into the trees.

'There is the Enchanter,' said Shadd. 'I perceived the fact of it just now, as I spoke with Dinbig.'

He turned to me. 'There were moments, within The Howling Hill, when the Chariness was left alone. Is that not so?'

'It is,' I said, as understanding dawned.

'During those moments the Enchanter overpowered the Chariness, then assumed its own semblance of her.'

I noted that Kekhi had turned around. She stood now alongside Rin, her back to Shadd.

'Put away your weapons,' said Crananba. 'All is now plain. We were fooled – and almost lost the precious Fragment.'

'That thing is still here somewhere,' I said.

'And we do not know how strong.'

'And the Chariness?' asked Cliptiam.

Crananba stared away into the distance. 'We will not know until we return to The Howling Hill.' Facing the woods into which the red cloud had fled, she called out, 'Enchanter – we do not know your name, but we know that you are there, watching us and listening. Listen well, then. Your ploy has failed; we still hold the Fragment which you so desire. Come forward now and speak with us. Let us settle this matter without violence or deceit.'

We waited. The only sound was the far-off moaning of the winds about The Howling Hill. I glimpsed a reddish blur. Something came from around the angle of a ruined wall to my left. It slipped between Kekhi and Rin – a fluid, shapeless cloud of red. Before any of us could respond it had enveloped Shadd. He fell back, struggling. Kekhi leapt, slashing with her swords. The redness formed a tentacle which thrust outwards,

326

lifting her and throwing her backwards through the air. She landed heavily upon her back and did not move.

Shadd thrashed and writhed upon the ground. The mist formed into a dense ball, which slipped rapidly along his arm, taking the ivory tube from his grasp. Then it was gone, zig-zagging along the ground, back into the woods.

It had all happened in an instant. Shadd sat up, dazed, shaking his head. I moved to him. 'Are you all right?'

He nodded. 'As far as I can tell, I am not harmed.' He looked up. 'It has the Fragment?'

'Yes.'

He climbed groggily to his feet. A few yards away Rin crouched beside Kekhi. Shadd threw him a questioning glance.

'She is alive. I don't think she is seriously hurt,' said Rin. Cliptiam joined him, to apply healing to the unconscious girl.

'The Enchanter will be making for The Howling Hill,' said Crananba. She beckoned to us all. 'Summon your allies! Every one of them!'

'To do so risks alerting the minions of the Beast,' I reminded her.

'And to fail to do so means losing the Fragment. We must act. Quickly. Send your allies to The Howling Hill, to bar the chamber of the Farplace Opening until we can get there. Do it now!'

V

Shadd and Rin ran without pause from the grainstore to the horses outside. Mounting, they galloped down through the ruined village of Underfell, into the woods and out again onto the barren plain of black dust that surrounded The Howling Hill. The moaning, weeping winds bore down upon them, whipping the dust into their faces, almost halting them in their tracks. The horses shied and whinnied, and they were forced to abandon them and proceed on foot. They pushed on, reaching the foot of the hill, and ascending the treacherous black basalt.

We of the *Zan-Chassin* entered trance as one, to summon our allies from the Realms and send them with greatest dispatch to do what they could to bar the progress of the Enchanter who now carried the precious Fragment. Our commands issued, we too took horses and made off in the wake of Shadd and Rin. Cliptiam remained behind to tend Kekhi, who was still unable to walk.

Near the summit of the Hill, at the entrance to the passage that led down to the chamber of the Farplace Opening, where the winds howled and lashed, Shadd and Rin came upon a terrible sight. Old Farlsast, the *Zan-Chassin* Ritual Sashbearer, lay dead upon the ground. His neck was broken, his head twisted at an impossible angle. His frail old body was horribly lacerated, and blackened as though with fire.

Nearby were the other two Hierarchy members, Fonial and Belythe. Belythe lay propped against a boulder. Her eyes were closed, her skin also blackened and blistered. But she breathed. Beside her sat Fonial, in similar state, one arm crushed and bloody, but conscious.

'What has happened here?' cried Shadd.

Fonial focussed her gaze with an effort, raised her voice against the howling wind. 'There was a battle. We did all we could to prevent the Enchanter from passing, but even with our allies to aid us it was stronger than us. We delayed it for some minutes, but could do no more.'

'Then it is within?'

Fonial gave a haggard nod. Without hesitation Shadd

leapt through the opening into the passage. He raced down the twisting steps, Rin behind him, the noise of their footsteps chattering and resounding in a chaotic rhythmless tattoo. Shadd burst into the chamber. Rin, more cautious, blended silently into the shadows. In the centre of the chamber stood a tall figure, staring into the oval of the Farplace Opening, which pulsed and coruscated with mists of shifting, changing hues, sending rippling shadows across the rock walls.

The figure turned. It was human in form, garbed in a long, dark red cape and cowl. The outline of a face, reddish-black, could be made out within the shadow of the cowl. Bony hands with long red fingers protruded from wide, loose sleeves. In one of these was held the ivory tube which contained the pages from Yshcopthe's Pandect.

Shadd came to a halt. The Enchanter spoke. 'You have meddled with the Farplace Opening.'

Shadd shook his head. 'No. I have not the knowledge to do so.'

The Enchanter turned back to the oval. 'The conditions of the tunnel have altered. I am unable to enter; I do not know where it will take me.'

'I say again, it is not our doing,' said Shadd.

The figure straightened. Burning red eyes stared from beneath its cowl. 'Then there can be but one answer. Another Enchanter comes.'

Even as it uttered these words there was a sudden burst of dense coloured vapour from the Farplace Opening. The Enchanter stepped back. The vapour formed into an opaque column, then dispersed. A new figure stood there, a man, tall and strong, purple-skinned and clad in gleaming blue armour.

'Yxon!' declared the first Enchanter.

Yxon turned, hands on hips. 'Bartacanes! You thought to preempt me?'

Unseen, a tiny figure flew from beside Yxon and alighted on Shadd's shoulder.

'What is happening here?' whispered Temminee.

'Two have come, instead of one. We have lost the Fragment.'

The two Enchanters warily appraised each other. Bartacanes had placed his hands behind his back, concealing the ivory tube from Yxon's eyes.

'What do you do here?' growled Bartacanes.

'The same as you, I would imagine.' Yxon faced Shadd. 'And here is the thief. How convenient.' He stretched out a hand. 'Come here.'

'*Remember the Soul Crystal, Duke Shadd!*' whispered Temminee. In the same instant Shadd found himself gripped as if by an invisible hand. Involuntarily he took a step towards the two Enchanters, then another.

'The Soul Crystal!' The thought resounded in his mind. With a mighty effort he reached inside himself, gathering his faculties. He focused upon the force that drew him forward, found its nature, returned it.

He ceased to walk forwards. Yxon lifted his brows in surprise. 'So, you are not defenceless. Perhaps then I must kill you. Tell me first . . .'

He glanced up, at the entrance to the passage, disturbed by the sound of approaching footsteps ricocheting off the walls. It was I who descended, along with Yo. Lady Chrysdhothe came a few steps behind, and Crananba, who had not been able to keep pace with us, was somewhere outside.

Now, in the chamber of the Farplace Opening, in that moment of tense distraction, Rin appeared, a darting shadow immediately behind Bartacanes. He moved like an arrow, snatching the ivory tube from the Enchanter's grasp.

Bartacanes whirled with a cry as Rin sped on for the

330

passage. Bartacanes raised a clawed hand and shot a bolt of bright fire which struck Rin as he threw himself into the passage.

Rin screamed. He plunged forward onto his face, arms thrown wide. The ivory tube dropped from his grasp. It bounced and rolled, clattering along the floor of the passage. It came to rest almost at my feet. Instinctively, knowing nothing of what had occurred, I bent, took it, and thrust it between Yo's jaws.

'Go, Yo! As swiftly as you can. Far from here!'

Yo spun around and was gone. Within the chamber there was turmoil. Yxon, who at first had not been aware of Rin, had mistaken Bartacanes' movement for an attack upon himself. Yxon reacted quickly, casting a powerful spell which negated the magic Bartacanes employed. Only then did he glimpse the fleeing Rin, and realize his mistake.

Bartacanes rounded on Yxon in fury. Yxon threw up a shimmering membrane to protect him from anything Bartacanes might project upon him. Shadd edged back towards the passage, hoping to take advantage of their preoccupation.

I stepped over poor Rin's charred, twisted body and entered the passage. I faced the two Enchanters who, together, moved now towards the passage in pursuit of the Fragment. I lifted my only hand and, with a boldness I did not feel, I addressed them.

'Stay! The Fragment is gone. You will not be able to recover it!'

The two halted. From within his cowl Bartacanes sneered, 'Puny human!'

I was lifted off my feet and thrown aside.

'Go that way and you are lost!' I shouted as I sprawled upon the hard rock. 'The Fragment has been taken away!'

331

In the entrance Bartacanes wheeled. 'Then I will take it back.'

Yxon said, 'It cannot have gone far. We will search, and find it.'

'You have no time. Already its bearer has taken it from The Howling Hill. You are weaker there.'

Bartacanes gave a scornful laugh. 'Weaker than here, yet still far greater than you.'

'It is not us that you will face. Another comes, he whom you fear most.'

The faces of both Enchanters darkened.

'Consider,' I said. 'Bartacanes, you have just fought with our allies summoned from the Realms. We called upon them as a desperate move, knowing that their intervention would alert the forces of the Vulpasmage. It is he who will come here now, being informed that you are here. Your greatest foe, an Enchanter undiminished by the effects of the Great Pooling. Or perhaps he has moved already, into Qotolr, to take advantage of your absence from your own domains.'

Yxon turned upon Bartacanes. 'Is this true?'

'That I fought with their spirit-allies? Yes.'

A look of fury crossed Yxon's face. He glared about him apprehensively, in indecision. Finally he began to back away, towards the Farplace Opening. 'Then I will not remain here.' He glowered at Shadd and me, and Chrysdhothe who now stood at my back. 'Humans, I am not beaten. I will be back for the Fragment.'

He crouched before the Opening, uttered a word. A plume of purple and yellow vapour poured out and enveloped him then retracted into the oval. Yxon was gone. Bartacanes stood alone, facing us. His features showed turmoil.

'You too must go,' I shouted. 'Yxon will dissolve the magic which holds the tunnel open. You will be stranded!'

Bartacanes' crimson lip curled, his nostrils flared. Clenching his fists before him he vented a great yell of wrath. He too leapt for the Opening, was enveloped in vapour, and vanished. His last words hung hollow in the air, reverberating around the cavern: 'I too will return. Make no mistake!'

We stood in stunned silence, staring at the Farplace Opening. Temminee came from Shadd's shoulder. 'Both Enchanters will find themselves in the courtyard of Madgard Keep. There will be an interesting exchange. Even more so if the Vulpasmage has gone there too.'

'We must go,' said Shadd. 'It is true, the Vulpasmage will be made aware. If he has not gone to Qotolr he will come here.'

'A moment.' The Farplace Opening was fading before our eyes. I quickly searched about the rocks and crevices of the cavern. In shadows behind a large boulder I discovered the body of the Chariness. I attempted quickly to revive her, but there was no stirring of life. With Chrysdhothe's help I lifted her, to take her from The Howling Hill.

In the passage Shadd knelt, cradling Rin's head upon his lap, tears in his eyes. He bent and kissed the pale forehead. 'Jhoso, brother. You are the spirit of Aphesuk.'

Gently he lifted Rin's body. With leaden steps, our hearts filled with sorrow, we began the ascent out of the chamber.

13

I

I do not know if the Vulpasmage came to The Howling Hill that night. We removed all traces of our presence, including the Monitors, feeling that this was the preferable course. To have left anything would have been to declare ourselves and risk a search of the area by the most powerful of the Vulpasmage's minions.

The fact that we had time to return to Underfell unmolested leads me to believe that if the Vulpasmage did come, it was not until later. Perhaps it did indeed go first to Qotolr, to attempt to cut off the two Enchanters' route back. If that was so, one is drawn to wonder where Lord Yxon and Bartacanes ended up after re-entering the Farplace Opening.

We reached Underfell in depressed spirits, weighed down by the tragedy of our losses. We were like soulless things, as yet too numbed by the consequences for proper emotion. What consolation that, through Rin's heroism, we had the Fragment from Yshcopthe's Pandect in our possession once more? We had in fact gained nothing. We were still unable to translate its contents.

Wearily, we gathered in silence in the chamber beneath the Lost Unicorn inn, which had once been a meeting-place of smugglers and a storehouse for contraband. The bodies of the Chariness, Farlsast and Rin were placed for the time being in a cold-room next door. Their funerary rites would be conducted at a more proper time.

Yo had met us as we entered the village, and had presented the ivory tube containing the Fragment to me. Now I placed it upon the table and stared at it disconsolately, rendered mute by my feelings.

For a long time nobody spoke. The chamber was musty and dim; words seemed inappropriate. Then Temminee, the Gwynad, flew down and alighted upon the table-top alongside the tube.

'In Madgard Keep I saw many things that made me wonder,' said she. 'One thing in particular caught my attention. In the hope that it might prove of use to us, I purloined a certain object belonging to Lord Yxon. This is it.'

She brought forth a small, delicately wrought object, no longer than a woman's thumb, though in comparison to Temminee herself it was of no little bulk. It resembled a small feather, intricately worked, of a fine, exquisite, golden metallic substance.

Crananba extended a trembling hand to take the object. 'What is this?'

'I observed a simulacrum of Lord Yxon endeavouring to understand a text written in a language it evidently did not understand,' said Temminee. 'The simulacrum produced this object and passed it in a certain manner over the text. Though nothing was apparent to my eyes, it seemed that the text became immediately comprehensible.'

Crananba gazed at the little metallic feather with interest, turning it between her fingers so that its lustre sparkled in the subdued light. 'It has a magical purpose, that much is certain.' She took the ivory tube and unplugged the stopper, then drew out the scrolled leaves of parchment. 'Let us see.'

Taking the topmost leaf of parchment, the crone held the metallic feather over it. 'How was it done?'

'As I recall it, the simulacrum passed the feather four

times over the script in such a manner, thus . . .'

Crananba did as she was shown. She observed the parchment, then shook her old head. 'It seems to have no effect.'

'Try again,' urged Temminee. 'Remember, I saw no effect, yet to the simulacrum who held the feather the desired result was achieved.'

Crananba repeated the motion with the feather, then again. With a sigh she leaned back in her seat, shaking her head. 'I discern nothing.'

'Then perhaps I was mistaken,' said Temminee, downcast. We fell back into silence once more, but Temminee was not yet discouraged. 'Duke Shadd, please try. Remember the Soul Crystal.'

Shadd stared at her as if in a dream, then he leaned forward and took the parchment and the tiny feather. Following Crananba's example, he passed the object four times over the parchment and regarded the cryptic text with intense concentration.

We watched, breathless.

'Yes!' Shadd half rose, his body tensing, bent over the parchment. 'Yes. Something impresses itself upon my imagination. I see changes. The original text seems to fall away. Beneath it another is revealed.'

'Can you read the other?' asked Crananba.

'No.' Shadd seemed despondent again. 'No, it is a language unknown to me.'

'Ah, but can you copy what you see?'

'I will try. Quickly, bring me a quill and something to write on.'

This was done. Almost feverishly Shadd began to write. The text that appeared from his hand was something new, scarcely resembling that which we viewed upon the parchment. And, unlike the original script, it was not defiant of replication. The words and symbols he wrote remained fixed upon the paper.

336

At length he had done. Crananba took up what he had written and stared at it. Her eyes lit up. 'A marvel! We have it.'

'Is it the Formula for the Antidote?' demanded Shadd.

'Too early to tell. This language is strange to my eyes also. But I see now what it means. This is the true text. That which we see upon the leaves of the Pandect can never be decrypted, for plainly it is not a language. It is little more than a complex array of symbols and runes, essentially meaningless, designed to confound, mislead and frustrate. Therein lies the reason for our failure to understand it. This which we now see is the real language. This is what we must work on.'

She turned to us all. 'It is quite ingenious. A perfect disguise. Temminee, you have done us an immeasurable service by bringing this object here. We have hope, once again. Now, Duke Shadd, apply yourself immediately to the remaining leaves of parchment. Lest something go awry, it is vital that you write down the full text, as you see it, tonight. When that is done we can begin the work of translation.'

Through the night Shadd worked, never straightening his neck until he had completed his task of revealing the true contents of the pages. As he finished each page he passed it to Crananba, or Chrysdhothe or Cliptiam. They, likewise, with the aid of books and charts and old, old manuscripts, worked diligently. At last Crananba looked up.

'It can be done! I have broken the code.'

Shadd was on his feet, eyes blazing. 'Is the Formula there?'

'That I still cannot say. I now have a basic understanding of the form the language takes. An actual translation will require some days of work. But if it is there, I believe now that it is only a matter of time before I will have it translated.'

That morning Rin was cremated. He was accorded full *Zan-Chassin* honours, while his funeral was conducted in the formal Aphesuk manner. Kekhi and Shadd performed chants and rites, and the brave warrior's ashes were scattered in the nearby woods.

Later I bade my friends a temporary farewell and set off for Little Malme, taking this opportunity to see Rohse and my daughter Eroniss. I could do little while the pages from the Pandect were undergoing translation, and my presence was not essential for any other duties. Crananba was happy for me to go, though with certain precautions. She summoned Shimeril by means of the messenger-entity Jogada, the former servant of the Chariness. He was with us within two hours, which indicated that his current hideout was not far away. Together, he and I rode out of Underfell, with Yo trotting alongside. Some time later, having ascended the lonely slopes of the Barrier Fell, we were met by a troop of five of Shimeril's men.

'These paladins are your guard,' said Shimeril. 'They will go ahead to scout your way, and secure your flank and rear. You will not see them, unless you need them, but they will be with you at all times. You are less conspicuous travelling alone.'

The men saluted. Shimeril returned the salute and I nodded and raised my hand, and they melted back into the trees.

'Keep off the main roads as far as possible,' cautioned Shimeril. 'And certainly avoid the main towns. I will leave you now, as I have other duties. Go well, old friend. I will look forward to greeting you again in a few days. Remember, you can spend but the one day with your loved ones. When morning comes you must be ready to return.'

Our journey took three days and was on the whole uneventful. Though we saw ample evidence of troops, we managed to skirt sentry-posts and population centres. Where feasible we avoided the roads altogether. From time to time one or more of Shimeril's fighters appeared, either with some specific advice as to the way ahead, or simply to reassure me of their presence.

Now we were at Little Malme. We waited in the fringe of the undergrowth beside the forest path which led to the little stone cottage with the thatched roof that was the home of Rohse and her aged parents and Eroniss. We had been here only a few minutes. I was about to step out from cover to greet the young woman and child whom I saw approaching along the path, carrying baskets filled with figs.

'Remain here, Yo,' I said.

Yo had picked up their scent and the sounds of their voices long before I saw them. Now my heart was in my mouth, pounding so hard it threatened to choke me as I rose erect and walked out onto the path.

Rohse saw me, but at first took little notice. There were still fifteen yards between us. She chatted gaily with Eroniss; they were playing some sort of game which made them both laugh. Eroniss wore a white smock-dress and sandals. The sunlight made a bright halo of her copper curls. Rohse was dressed in a light linen peasant's skirt and blouse. Her own hair, the same colour as our daughter's, was tied back with a red ribbon.

I took a few tentative steps towards them. Rohse looked up again. Her eyebrows lifted. She stared, her eyes going wide. She gave a gasp. One hand flew to her mouth.

I smiled, opening my arms. Rohse gave a shriek. She dropped her basket, which spilled its fruit across the path. Still disbelieving, she stood frozen, half terrified.

'Master Dinbig?' She shook her head, tearful. 'No, it can't be!'

Now there was real terror in her eyes. And brave thing that she was, her instinct was to protect our little girl. She pushed Eroniss behind her skirts, extending one hand towards me in a warding gesture.

'What do you want? Are you a ghost? We have nothing.'

'Rohse, dear Rohse, don't be afraid.' I stood where I was. 'I am no ghost. What you see is real. It is me, Ronbas Dinbig, your lover, the father of your child. I have returned.'

Rohse's voice was pitched high, trembling. 'Master Dinbig was killed. They all said it.'

'They all believed it, and most still do. But I did not die, Rohse. I am the proof of it. Believe me. I have come back from a long, long journey, that I might be with you and with our little girl.'

I approached a step. 'Believe me, Rohse. Believe me. It is me.'

Wariness remained in her pale face, but the stark terror had gone. Eroniss peered curiously from behind her mother's skirts. I smiled at her. Shyly, fleetingly, she smiled back. I could contain myself no longer. Tears brimmed and tumbled down my cheeks.

'Oh, Rohse,' I said, and could say no more.

Now Rohse approached a step. 'Master Dinbig. Oh, Master Dinbig, it is you. But you look so different. What has happened to you? And your poor arm. What has happened? Oh, Master Dinbig, don't cry. Oh, I don't know what to say.'

Suddenly we were in each other's arms, both weeping floods of tears, unable to find words. Then Rohse drew back and reached down to reassure Eroniss. I knelt before my little girl. She backed behind her mother's skirts.

'It will take time,' said Rohse.

I nodded. 'For us all.'

'Oh, Master Dinbig . . .' Her cheeks were red, her eyes swollen with tears.

'You need say nothing, Rohse. It will all come out in time. But remember, I am no longer your master and there is no need to address me as such.'

'You are in a state,' said Rohse, taking recourse in maternal concern. 'Your clothes are all dirty. Come on, come inside. Eroniss, come along!'

Suddenly she stiffened and gave a cry, her eyes fixed wide on something behind me. I turned. Yo had emerged from the woods and stood upon the path.

'That thing!' shrieked Rohse. 'It came once before. It tried to take Eroniss!'

With an angry gesture I shooed Yo away. He turned and bounded into the forest.

'Don't be afraid, Rohse, he means no harm. I can explain. Let us go inside.'

When Rohse brought me into the cottage, her mother fainted. With her father, Rohse gently revived her, and the old woman set about preparing a feast to celebrate my homecoming, using the best food their modest life-style could provide. We passed a joyful, tearful day and night, but our time together was all too short. Rohse fussed over me ceaselessly; little Eroniss, shy at first, soon warmed to me. Before long she was sitting on my lap, telling me stories in her sweet, halting voice, and listening enraptured as I told stories to her. It made me happy that I was not an unfamiliar figure. Rohse had kept my memory alive, telling our daughter much about me. Little by little Eroniss revealed that she had a detailed mental picture and fond thoughts of the father she had never seen. It was perhaps the most joyous day of my life.

That night Rohse's parents took charge of little Eroniss, and Rohse and I lay together in the partitioned area that served as her room. We lacked the privacy we would have preferred, and thus were denied the full complement of cavortings that I would otherwise have celebrated our reunion with. But we loved one another, and later talked long into the night. We talked of life prior to the coming of the Beast of Rull, of Rohse's life since my 'demise', and of my own adventures. In the latter case it was all a little hard for Rohse to grasp, and I economized somewhat on details to make it easier for her.

The following morning saw an emotional parting. In the dewy dawn light Rohse clung to me at the garden gate, reluctant to let me go.

'You will come back, Dinbig. You will, won't you?'

'Never fear, Rohse. I have fought my way across nations and survived death and worse to be here by your side. I will not let us be parted for long – and I will see to it now that you have protection, and that I receive regular reports of your welfare while I am gone. Alas, this business must be done. Afterwards we can be together in peace, as a family.'

I hugged her. I hugged and kissed little Eroniss. I turned and walked away, looking back frequently to wave. They stood at the little gate, mother and daughter, waving until I passed beyond sight and entered the forest.

III

'Was it necessary to show yourself like that, Yo?' I asked as I mounted my horse. 'You caused them considerable alarm.'

'I'm sorry, Master. I was curious.'

'Remember, the sight of a vhazz is sufficient to arouse fear and loathing in the mind of any human. Had I not been present you might have found yourself in a most difficult situation.'

'Had you not been present I would not have been present either,' replied Yo with searing logic.

'Hold your impudence, please,' I admonished him.

'I meant it only as a statement of fact, Master. And had I been present without you, I would never have permitted myself to be seen.'

We proceeded on a short way, then Yo said, 'May I ask a question, Master?'

'You may.'

'Do you love the woman Rohse?'

'Well, yes, I believe I do.'

'That is what I was curious about. But, Master, if you love Rohse, what of the other woman in Twalinieh, the beautiful Melenda?'

'Melenda?' I eyed him sidelong. 'Well, it is a difficult question to answer. I have always felt great affection for Melenda, and certainly I delighted in her company, and treasure fond memories of our time together.'

'Yet you do not feel towards her as you do towards Rohse?'

'Possibly not. It is not an easy matter to come to a full conclusion on. Matters of the heart are complex, and never easily defined. History brims with tales of baffled lovers, the torments, tragedies and ecstasies of their plight. I know of no man or woman who can honestly claim mastery over their passions. I, certainly, would make no such assertion.' I wondered what he was leading up to. Melenda had been my mistress in Twalinieh, a most enchanting young Kemahamek woman whom, though I was at a loss to explain quite why, I had found myself growing distant from. While

343

I was absent in the Realms one night, leaving Yo as usual with custody of my fleshly self, he had audaciously made love to Melenda. Believing him to be me, she had construed the act as a demonstration of my renewed affection for her. Yo and I had yet to fully resolve this issue. He had always avoided mention of it. I was surprised, therefore, that he brought Melenda into the conversation now. 'Why do you ask, Yo?'

'Because I love Melenda, Master.'

I almost choked. 'You *what*?'

'I love her.'

Apparently he was in earnest. I suppressed my first instinct, which I confess was to laugh and flay him with jibes. I am not a cruel man.

'Master, since I was with her in Twalinieh, I have thought of almost nothing but her. I live to see Melenda again.'

'But, Yo, Melenda believed you were me.'

'I know, Master.' Yo's voice was plaintive; the poor entity was on the verge of tears.

'Yo, you knew her but briefly, in the physical sense, just the once.'

'But it was a wonderful, most thrilling experience.'

I fought down a twinge of envy. 'No doubt.'

'I do love her, Master. I do. I cannot forget her.'

'You are in love with the experience, Yo, not the woman. True love takes time to grow. It is not uncommon to mistake physical pleasure and besotment for love.'

'I want to see her again. I have to.'

I heaved a sigh. 'Apart from all else, Yo, you are a vhazz! Melenda would be terrified at the very sight of you, as would any other woman.'

'I am so unhappy, Master. It's too cruel. All I want is for Melenda and me to be together.'

344

'Oh, Yo,' I said. 'What am I to do with you?'

'Master, I have given a deal of thought to this. Consider my plight, my existence. Once I was an entity, free and untouched by physical desires. I roamed the Realms and knew nothing of your world. Then you came and brought me here. You gave me the body of a Wide-Faced Bear. Later, for a while, I took your form, caring for it diligently while you were absent. Now I am a vhazz. But why can I not be a man again? Why can you not give me a human form, that I might approach Melenda under the terms and conditions that normally apply when two humans meet and fall in love?'

I rubbed my beard and shook my head. 'Were that it were so simple, Yo.'

'But is it not possible?'

I considered. 'To my knowledge it has never been done. I don't know, Yo. Entities from the Realms, once bound, have always taken an animal form.'

'I know it. But my greatest wish has always been to experience the wonder of existence from the human vantage.'

'It is not as you might think, Yo. The human vantage is not without its pitfalls. Far from it. Already you have experienced something of the difficulties of being a man. You became distressed and addle-headed. It is a wonder you survived as long as you did. You are not a human being, Yo. You would never be a successful man.'

'Then you will not help me.'

His tone was filled with disappointment and resentment. I sighed again. 'I will look into the matter, Yo, as soon as I am able. But I make no promises. Your request is unprecedented in my experience.'

'If I were human, Melenda would love me, would she not?'

'That is a huge presupposition. Love, as I have said,

is a most complex issue. Innumerable factors play a part, and I would never attempt to make a prediction. Ultimately, of course, it would be for Melenda to make her own decisions.'

'I do love her so,' said Yo. He grew silent, absorbed in hopes and daydreams. I rode on, my head abuzz.

IV

When I returned to Underfell one of my first sensations was of shock. We assembled – the remaining Hierarchy members and Shadd, Kekhi, Temminee, Shimeril and Count Inbuel – in the secret smugglers' chamber beneath the Lost Unicorn. My dismay came from seeing the Chariness seated at the back of the chamber upon a low wooden bench. She was alive, though her features were blank and somewhat uncomprehending. She was slumped uncharacteristically, her back against the stone wall. She gave no greeting as I entered, nor showed any sign of recognizing me.

'It is not her, Dinbig,' declared Crananba, seeing my face. 'Her Custodian occupies her form temporarily, as a safeguard against intrusion until we may conduct the proper procedures.'

'And Farlsast?'

'Farlsast's flesh and spirit did not hold the secrets that the Chariness does. We have thus proceeded with the Ceremony of Transmigration and the Transmutation by fire in Farlsast's case.'

We seated ourselves, for I was about to receive the report on the Hierarchy's attempts to translate the new pages of Yshcopthe's Pandect. Only now did my eyes fall upon the other person who had joined us. He was a youngish man, seated alongside Crananba, completely bald and clean-shaven. His skin was tanned and weathered, his limbs well muscled, with broad shoulders and chest. Steely blue eyes held a resolute, commanding gaze. He wore a loose grey flannel shirt and trousers, with a broadsword buckled at his waist. He had the look about him of a fighting-man, and a leader of fighting-men. A linen bandage strapped across his chest, and another around his bare arm, seemed to corroborate this. Though I did not know him, something in his gaze and demeanour seemed familiar.

Crananba addressed us. Her speech was directed for the most part at me, for the others were already informed as to her progress. 'You will be pleased, Dinbig. We have had some success in translating the new language that was revealed to Duke Shadd via the agency of the Soul Crystal. Your efforts have not been in vain. I am able to state quite positively that contained upon these pages from the Pandect is a Formula for the Antidote to the Semblance of Death.'

'This is marvellous news!' I declared. I looked around at my companions. 'Marvellous. Thank Moban!'

'Other formulas are also inscribed hereon,' added the crone. 'Mysterious and wonderful, though, from my assessment, largely beyond our ability to comprehend or utilize. Much work is still required, but at all costs we must ensure that these writings do not fall into the wrong hands. For the moment, I am concentrating all efforts on the Formula which we believe may save the Wonasina, Seruhli. The translation must be true and precise; we can afford no space for error. Thus I require more time. In the meantime, however, Count Inbuel has agreed to depart for Kemahamek today. There he will endeavour to establish contact with Seruhli's guardians, to convey this wonderful news. When the translation is complete we will take the necessary steps to deliver the transcript to him.'

I turned to Count Inbuel, then to Shadd. 'I congratulate you both. I know what this means to you, both of you, personally.'

My eyes happened to fall on Kekhi, who sat somewhat apart from the others. She was gazing at Shadd, and though her face showed a half-smile her look was wan and wistful. I recalled another occasion, not so long past, at night, sitting upon the cliff at Drurn March, overlooking Lord Marsinenicon's Khimmurian camp.

Shadd had spoken of his pledge to Seruhli, and his fated love for her. And Kekhi had taken her place behind him, watching, listening, saying nothing. I had sensed then the weight of unspoken feelings in Kekhi's heart; I sensed it even more now.

She became aware of my eyes upon her, looked up briefly, then averted her gaze.

Crananba spoke again. 'I come now to another matter of great and urgent concern.' She turned to the bald warrior beside her. 'Lord Yzwul, perhaps you would recount your tale?'

I jerked in astonishment. 'Yzwul! I did not recognize you! Good Bagemm, how you have changed!'

'You also, Dinbig,' said Yzwul, rising with a broad grin. He reached out and embraced me.

'I was told that you had entered Hecra, on a clandestine mission,' I said.

'Aye. I returned only yesterday, and I am not the bearer of good news. I will be brief. I was sent into Hecra to try to recover an ancient artifact which was used by King Moshrazman III to summon Gneth during the years of The Great Deadlock. The artifact was believed to be still within the Tower of Soaring Light, in Moshrazman's palace in the old capital.'

I nodded. 'Of course, the Beast seeks access to the Under-Realms in order to summon more Gneth.'

'That's so. I will avoid relating to you all of the

348

horrors I discovered in Hecra. It is an accursed land, crawling with Gneth, their human slaves and their vile, mutated offspring. Accompanied by good Putc'pii fighters I found my way to the old palace. We searched thoroughly – as did others, for we were not alone in our endeavour. At least one other search party was in Hecra, sent from Khimmur, presumably for the same purpose. We came away empty-handed.'

'The Khimmurians found it?'

Yzwul gestured vexedly with his hand. 'No, the Khimmurians now lie dead within the ruin. But the story is not yet done. Assured that the artifact was not within the palace we made to leave Hecra. I took the risk of a slight indiscretion – considering the importance of my mission, I deemed it justified now, under the circumstances. I disclosed to my Putc'pii companions what it was that I sought. I used veiled terms, and made no reference to the artifact's power. But these men were more familiar with this land than I. They knew its history, and I felt now that I should seek their aid. And well I did. They conferred among themselves, then their captain, one Hurkan Voslion, told me that he believed he could give me some useful information. At his behest we detoured, travelling due south to cross the White River into Vyshroma. We went deep into that land, until we came upon a nomadic tribe who have somehow succeeded in remaining free of the Khimmurian bond that holds their country. Hurkan Voslion spoke with the tribal chief. At length a tale was told to me which caused my spirits to plummet. The chief was a man named Rallion, descended from a noble Vyshromaii line. He it was who told me of the fate of the artifact I sought.'

Yzwul paused. Though he had plainly told this tale before, he was evidently not less moved in repeating it now. 'Recall, more than five, or is it six, years ago.

The fiftieth birthday of our king, Gastlan Fireheart, the bewitched tyrant.'

'It was a grand occasion,' said I, 'with a fateful outcome.'

'Aye. And do you remember the gifts that were presented to the King?'

I rubbed my stump and shrugged. 'There were many. One – that of Prince Oshalan – overshadowed the others.'

'On the face of it, yes. But think now, there was a gift presented to Gastlan Fireheart by the Ambassador of Vyshroma.'

I let my mind fly back, a sinking feeling in my heart. 'A Hecranese Cartouche,' I said at length. 'Stolen from Hecra some time after The Great Deadlock.'

'Much more recently than that,' said Yzwul. 'According to Rallion, the Vyshromaii chief. He claims it was taken only twenty years ago, by a party of adventurers intent on glory. The party was led by his younger brother, who has since perished fighting Khimmur. The adventurers did not know what they had. They believed it to be an ornament, and it was as such that it was presented to Gastlan Fireheart. Needless to say, I did not enlighten Rallion. He knows it is valuable, but does not know the true reason.'

I tried to remember the gift that was presented to our former king. 'A tablet of streaked black meteorite, carved into a rectangular block. It bears upon its surface the likeness of an open scroll, with the insignia of a lizard grasping a rod between its jaws. The rod is inlaid with mother-of-pearl, and its tip is a blood-red diamond. It is contained within a coffer of malachite and gold, and bears the achievement of Hecra's royal house.'

I looked at Crananba, then at Chrysdhothe, Cliptiam and Yzwul. Their faces told me the worst.

weighed upon her. She loved Shadd, there was no doubt, yet she too was pledged, to her Tribe. What did that mean? I did not know. But she was lover, bodyguard, sister, friend, assassin and more. Kekhi was an enigma to me, almost as great an enigma as Shadd himself.

I looked across at Shadd, leaning beside the door. 'I would like to see him happy.'

Kekhi smiled, a beautiful, wide, warm smile that lit up her features and made me realize, perhaps for the first time, what a strangely beautiful young woman she was. She reached out and squeezed my hand.

'I too,' she said.

We sat a few moments longer, not speaking. Presently I rose. 'I am returning indoors. Will you join me?'

'In due course.'

'Then I wish you pleasant thoughts.'

She smiled again. 'And I you.' She lifted a hand. '*Jhoso!* Dinbig.'

And so it was that two separate yet intertwined strands were to set the course of our struggle over the ensuing weeks and months: the revival, now that the Formula was in our hands, of the hope of Kemahamek, the Wonasina Seruhli; and the search for that most dire artifact, the Hecranese Cartouche, which even now, unbeknown to the Beast of Rull, lay within his very grasp, somewhere in the Royal Palace of Hon-Hiaita.